**Kasey Michaels** is a *New York Times* bestselling author of both historical and contemporary novels. She is also the winner of a number of prestigious awards.

*Available from Kasey Michaels and Mills & Boon® Super Historical*

# LORDS OF NOTORIETY

## Kasey Michaels

MILLS & BOON®
Pure reading pleasure™

First published in Great Britain 2009
by Harlequin Mills & Boon Limited,
Eton House, 18-24 Paradise Road, Richmond, Surrey TW9 1SR

LORDS OF NOTORIETY © Harlequin Books S.A. 2009

The publisher acknowledges the copyright holder of
the individual works as follows:

The Ruthless Lord Rule © Kathie Seidick 1987
The Toplofty Lord Thorpe © Kathie Seidick 1986

ISBN: 978 0 263 87406 8

037-0709

Printed and bound in Spain
by Litografia Rosés S.A., Barcelona

# CONTENTS

# THE RUTHLESS LORD RULE

To Page –
the Consummate Miss Cuddy –
who let me be me; with deep gratitude
and affection

# PROLOGUE

*March 1814*

*PEACE!*

All England is rejoicing. Napoleon, that scourge of the Continent, has at last been put in his cage. Paris has capitulated, with the trusted Marmont leading his unsuspecting men straight into the Austrian camp in surrender. Now an emperor in name only, with but a scant four-hundred-man army and living on the charity of the country he had led in triumph for nearly twenty years, Bonaparte barely escaped France with his life and is living in genteel poverty on the unpretentious island of Elba.

His Royal Highness, the Prince Regent, is delirious with joy; so overcome that he'd had to be bled of twenty-seven ounces of blood. Indeed, for nearly a month, he languished in his bed, hovering between life and death.

The rush to cross the Channel is already in full force, with even the Duke of Wellington, now British ambassador to France, characteristically ignoring the angry glances cast his way as he saunters down the streets of Paris, dines on good, plain English fare at the Café des Anglais, and accepts the grateful thanks of the repatriated French nobility.

London is in a whirl, eagerly anticipating the arrival of

Czar Alexander of Russia, King Frederick William of
Prussia, and, wonder of wonders, the much loved Field
Marshal von Blücher. Indeed, the Grand Duchess Catherine
of Oldenburg, the czar's "platter-faced" sister, has already
disembarked and is royally ensconced in Pulteney's Hotel,
busily setting up the Regent's back with her Whig antics.

That this endears her to the residents of London is no surprise, for the Regent has been out of favor with his subjects
for some time. The younger generation has no memory of
the glorious Florizel that was once the Prince of Wales and
cannot think of him as the genial Big Ben. They see him instead as Swellfoot, an obese, grotesque, thoroughly evil man.
They glory in the little ditty penned by Charles Lamb:

> By his bulk and by his size,
> By his oily qualities,
> This (or else my eyesight fails)
> This should be the Prince of *Whales*.

Not that Louix XVIII, who had been cheered through the
streets as he headed toward the Channel Ports and a return
to his homeland, fared much better once he reached Paris.
The King, whom Lord Byron has irreverently dubbed Louis
the Gouty, seems to have spent his entire exile in thrall with
his host country's cooking, and is so thoroughly corpulent
that the Regent, after investing the King with the Order of
the Garter, and buckling the Garter around a leg even thicker
than his own, remarked, "When I clasped his knee it was exactly as if I were fastening a sash around a young man's
waist."

One German account of the King's appearance commented on both the advanced age and accumulated fat of
Napoleon's replacement. Telling of the King's entrance into
the room, the report centered on the fact that Louis, clad in

soft black satin boots and supported on either side, was so disablingly obese that he "would stumble over a straw."

While Europe laughs at reports of Napoleon's frugal inventories of mattresses and his drawing up of lists of his personal clothing ("my underlinen is in a lamentable state"), and ridicules his official-sounding Council of State that he has set up to investigate improvements in the iron mines and salt pits of Elba while considering the possibility of importing silkworms, the banished Emperor is reading of the high jinks being perpetrated by his vanquishers.

"They are mad!" he said of the governments that had a hand in putting Louis on the throne. "The Bourbons in France; they would not be able to hold their position for a year! Nine-tenths of the nation cannot endure them; my soldiers will never serve under them."

But none of the leaders of the world, their minds filled with plans for pomp and ceremony and grand celebrations, hear the words of Napoleon Bonaparte, or, if they do hear them, heed them.

Only a few shake their heads at the merry-making and wonder—wonder, if this glorious peace is really to be believed. Sir Henry Ruffton, one of the War Office's most intelligent members, wonders.

Then word reaches Sir Henry of one of Bonaparte's final statements before leaving France. "Between ourselves," Napoleon has told a trusted aide who had feared his Emperor would commit suicide, "a living drummer is better than a dead emperor."

So, while London rings with cheers and hangs bunting from the façades, Sir Henry pens two messages. One missive goes to Sussex by private courier. The other is sent by packet to Calais, to his most trusted operative. Both messages are the same: "Come to me, now."

# CHAPTER ONE

*May 1814*

"HONESTLY, MARY, that new coachman of Sir Henry's drives as if he's riding to hounds." Gratefully subsiding into a chair in the rather spartanly furnished drawing room, Rachel Gladwin removed her straw bonnet and proceeded to use it as a fan to cool her flushed cheeks. "While I applaud your guardian's hiring of returned soldiers, I do believe he should temper his generosity with a bit of common sense. I doubt if even Wellington would have survived if all of our troop charges into battle were accomplished with the same reckless fervor our driver just demonstrated on Bond Street."

Pushing at the dark coppery curls that had been slightly crushed by her fetching, if a bit imprudent, choice of head-gear, Mary Lawrence smiled into the mirror that reflected Rachel's frowning face. "Coming it a bit too brown, aren't you, Aunt?" she asked, using the courtesy title that lady had insisted upon. "Considering it was you who applauded so enthusiastically when that same driver sent that ridiculous dandy scurrying up the lamppost in fear of his life?"

Rachel's features relaxed into a small smile. "I will admit to being a bit amused by the spectacle," she owned cheerfully enough, "but I would be shirking my duty as your resi-

dent bear-leader if I did not stress once again that putting
one's fingers in one's mouth and whistling encouragement
to servants is just *not done.* Wherever did you acquire such
a disgusting talent, Mary?"

"In Sussex," Mary Lawrence replied, leaving the mirror
to take up residence in the chair across from Rachel's. "You'd
be surprised at the accomplishments I have mastered through
the kind offices of my last keepers, may they live long and
prosper. And you are not bear-leading me, no one could. You
are my friend and companion while I'm forced to live in
London."

Rachel shook her head. "Still singing the same sad song,
Mary? I thought Sir Henry had succeeded in convincing you
that this is the best, the safest, place for you at the moment."

"Bah! All the world is in Paris. The papers are full of *on-
dits* about the English lords and ladies who are scampering
about France, aping the latest fashions and gambling away
their fortunes at the Palais-Royal—among other things," she
ended, winking broadly. "I fail to see why Sir Henry refuses
to let me cross the Channel. It's so dreadfully flat here; I was
better entertained in Sussex."

Looking at the very young, very beautiful girl dressed in
the height of fashion, a girl who in her few short weeks in
the metropolis had already been dubbed the latest
Incomparable, Rachel suppressed a chuckle and tried for a
commiserating tone. "La, you poor, oppressed creature.
Forced to spend your time dragging yourself from ballroom
to theater party, your unwilling body pressed into wearing
an endless array of flattering silks and satins, while saddled
with the unpalatable chore of breaking every young male
heart in London. I daresay I admire you for not dissolving
on your bed in a flood of tears, so onerous is your trial."

Mary screwed up her patrician nose and stuck out her
tongue. "Wretch! You know I'm loving every delicious min-

ute of it. It's just that I should love it even more if I were doing it in Paris. Besides—surely *he* wouldn't be so odious as to follow me there to make my life miserable."

"Ah, we're back to that, are we?" Rachel chuckled, shaking her head. "My nephew seems to have gotten under your skin."

"Like an annoying splinter," Mary admitted irritably. "How that insufferable man dogs my every step! If you're afraid of the way our coachman drives, *I* am fearful that your odious nephew is going to drive *me*—into strong hysterics. Are you quite sure he wasn't a soldier, perhaps suffering from some head injury that makes him behave so toward me?"

"Tristan was never a soldier, Mary," Rachel replied, crossing her fingers in her lap. "There have been rumors about his actions during the war, but I discount them. No, my nephew is just being his usual annoying self."

Mary looked closely at her companion. "You sound as if you don't like him. Not that I blame you, of course, for he does not wear easily."

Rachel smiled sadly. "Not like him? Why, Mary, I couldn't love him more. Tris is loyal, trustworthy, unflinchingly honest and the staunchest friend a person could ever have."

"I once had a terrier with the same attributes." Mary sniffed derisively. "Only he was better trained. All your nephew seems to have mastered is the ability to heel! Besides, if Lord Rule is such a paragon of virtue, why do you always give such a deep sigh when you see him? Seems rather unloving to me."

Now the older woman laughed aloud. "Because he's such a royal pain in the rump, Mary dearest, why else?"

Mary decided to change the subject, as their discussion of the Right Honorable Baron Rule was fast beginning to give her the headache. She rose and walked over to take the card rack down from the mantel, meaning to sort out the cards of invitation for the one she needed for that evening. "We're expected at Lady Salerton's for her daughter's come-out. Shall I wear my yellow tiffany?"

"Not unless you want Elsie Salerton to throw her not unimpressive bulk against the door to bar you from entering. Really, Mary, can you not let the poor girl have her evening without spoiling it by ensnaring every young buck her mother is bound to have cajoled, blackmailed or bludgeoned into appearing?"

Mary smiled, showing up the very fetching dimple in her left cheek, then batted her large, wide green eyes innocently. "Why, Aunt, whatever do you mean? I merely enjoy dancing and chatting with people my own age. Anyone would think you believe me to be a heartless flirt." Her smile fading, she added, "Besides, once your dear nephew, Lord Rule, comes on the scene—which I am sure he will do as he seems to have an uncanny knack for knowing exactly which entertainment I have chosen for the evening—all my intrepid dancing partners will depart posthaste for the hinterlands, their tails between their legs."

"Maybe he's developed a *tendre* for you, dear," Rachel offered without much hope of being taken seriously.

"Not surprising. Who *hasn't* fallen head over ears for my beautiful ward?"

"Uncle Henry!" Mary cried, running across the room to give her guardian an enthusiastic hug. "Aunt Rachel has told me you have gotten us vouchers for Almack's. However did you manage it?"

The gray-haired, rosy-cheeked cherub who stood smiling inanely while his adored ward embraced him was Sir Henry Ruffton, a wealthy bachelor on the shady side of forty with a reputation as a truly guileless, completely lovable soul.

That he had the total admiration of his ward was obvious, and he felt the years fall away from him as he basked in her affection. "Silly puss, who could afford to ignore such a diamond of the first water as you? Not Lady Jersey, that much is certain. Besides, I do have a smattering of friends who were not adverse to pulling a few strings in the right places."

Rachel watched the scene unfolding in front of her, a sad smile on her face. Mary could have been his daughter, could have been *their* daughter, if only… "Henry, I do believe you're blushing!" she teased, rising to ring for refreshments.

Seating himself in his favorite chair, allowing Mary to curl up on the floor at his feet, her head pressed against his knees, Sir Henry acknowledged Rachel's words unself-consciously. "I admit it, Rachel, my dear friend. I have not been so diverted in years. Having Mary join me in the city was truly an inspiration. And finding you after all this time to act as companion and chaperon, why there are times I believe myself to be the happiest of men."

"Don't forget that the war is over, Uncle," Mary pointed out. "That's another reason for you to be happy."

"Napoleon is within spitting distance of Europe, child," he answered, suddenly looking something less than cherubic. "I cannot help but agree with Talleyrand, who fought to have Bonaparte exiled in Corfu, or even St. Helena, where he could be more closely guarded."

"Piffle," Mary argued. "Fouché, I've heard, suggested Boney flee to America and start over. I wonder how the Americans would have taken to that notion. Besides, Talleyrand is no good authority. I have read that Napoleon once called him 'filth in silk stockings.'"

"Talleyrand is an amoral thief, Mary, but he hasn't survived in France this long without being a fairly good judge of men. If he says Bonaparte still presents a danger, I tend to believe him."

"But—"

"Enough, child. You make my head buzz with all your silly prattle. I have given you my reasons and you have agreed to abide by my decision. Once some time has passed, and the governments conclude their deliberations, perhaps then I shall set you off to France with my blessing. I may even accompany you. But for now—"

"But for now I am safer in London," Mary ended fatalistically. "But all this pretense, I vow I cannot like it. Even my name—"

*"Perkins!"* Rachel interrupted rather loudly, startling the butler into nearly oversetting the tray of tea and cakes. "How famished I am. If you would set the tray on this table I'm sure we shall be able to serve ourselves quite well unaided. Thank you, Perkins."

Mary watched the butler's departing back, a rueful smile on her lips. "I almost gave it away just then, didn't I, Aunt? Thank you for your timely intervention." Then, momentarily feeling mulish, she added, "Though I still think this whole deception is silly."

Rachel and Sir Henry exchanged knowing looks over Mary's head and pretended not to hear her last statement. Biting into a warm scone, Sir Henry questioned, "Which one of Mary's suitors were you discussing when I entered the room? It's getting to the point where I have to keep a list with me at all times so that I may check them off when I am forced to turn down their requests for her hand."

Mary thrust her full lower lip forward into a pout. "Lord Tristan Rule, Uncle Henry, and he is not a suitor. He's a nuisance!"

"Tristan?" Sir Henry repeated, puzzled. "I've never known him to be in the petticoat line. My congratulations, my dear, he's a fine young man."

Mary leaped to her feet and glared at her beloved guardian. "If you have any affection for that fine young man, you will steer him swiftly away from my direction before I skewer him with my parasol! I cannot stand the creature!"

And with that, Mary quit the room, stopping only to snatch up a few fragrant scones, leaving Rachel to explain Lord Rule's recent behavior to Sir Henry.

TRISTAN RULE REACHED DOWN a hand to assist his opponent to his feet. "Sorry, George. It seems my tiresome temper has gotten the better of me again."

"On the contrary," Lord Byron replied, gingerly rubbing his aching jaw, "it was my fault entirely. I should have known better than to cast aspersions on our esteemed War Office while sparring with Ruthless Rule. Besides, I thought I had a better chin than I seem to possess. Just remember, Tris, the pen is mightier than the sword. I'll simply have to scribble a canto or two someday about our esteemed military gentlemen." Stepping out between the ropes held apart by his friend, Byron called out ruefully, "Tom, my good man, you'd better look to your laurels now that Ruthless Rule is stepping into the ring. I do believe he would make even you a fair competitor. Now toss me that towel and help me totter over to find a glass of wine, if you please."

Dexter Rutherford, who had been holding a towel at the ready for his idol, Lord Tristan Rule, dashed to the side of the ring, a look of slavish adoration on his young face. "What a leveler you served him, Tris!" he exclaimed, rubbing his hero's bare shoulders with more enthusiasm than expertise. "The great man himself, dropped by a single blow. What science, what speed, what—"

"What loss of control," Tristan ended crossly, effectively wiping the grin from Dexter's face. "We were only sparring, you bloodthirsty infant. George wasn't expecting that bit of home-brewed I served up to him. Thank goodness he's a gentleman." Taking the towel from his shoulders, Rule rubbed it briskly across his face and neck. "It's this deuced inaction, I feel like a coiled wire ready to spring. I can see that this peace everyone is so delirious about is going to take a bit of getting used to."

Tom Cribb, the retired "Champion Boxer of all England," approached the pair, a nearly full glass of wine held in front of him. "With Lord Byron's compliments, my lord. And may I say it was an honor to watch you in there. If you ever have a mind to go a few rounds, I wouldn't say no to you. Your right hand reminds me a bit of Ikey Pigg's, and I considered him a very worthy opponent in his day."

"Ikey Pigg!" Dexter cried scoffingly. "Molyneaux, more like, and it took you thirty rounds or more to best him too. Ikey Pigg?" Dexter shook his head. "Damned insult if you ask me."

"Nobody did, sprig," came a voice from behind the young man. "I'd say my good-byes now, if I were you, before Tom here takes it into his head to squash you like a bug."

Dexter whirled to greet his cousin. "Julian! Did you see him? It was nothing next to marvelous, I tell you. One moment Lord Byron was standing there, his fives at the ready, and the next he was rump down on the mat, with Lord Rule standing above him, breathing fire."

"Sorry we missed it," Julian Rutherford, Earl of Thorpe, mourned falsely as he joined the group. "Yet somehow I feel that we shall all be able to relive the moment *ad nauseam* over dinner this evening if Dex here has anything to say in the matter." Julian turned to address Lord Rule as Tom Cribb drifted away to talk to some of his other patrons. "You haven't forgotten Lucy's invitation, have you? I'll have the devil to pay if I tell her I've seen you here without reminding you that your presence is required at table."

"Not to mention what Jennie will do to me," Kit Wilde, Earl

of Bourne, put in as he too joined the small group, barely concealing a smile as he thought of his wife. "Your cousins are both rare handfuls in their separate ways, Tris, as you must know."

"Will your aunt Rachel and her charge also be present?" Tris asked, slipping his arms into the shirt Dexter was holding up for him.

"Mary Lawrence?" Julian asked rhetorically, winking slyly at Kit, who was hiding a grin behind his hand. "So it's true, what Lucy and Jennie say? I warn you, they've as much as made a match of it between you."

Tris looked blank, as indeed he was at a loss to understand what Lord Thorpe was talking about. "Make a match of it? With Mary Lawrence? What in blazes put a fool notion like that into their maggoty heads?"

"Not just them, Tris," Dexter supplied with all the innocence his ignorance of the world provided him. "Saw it in the betting book at Boodle's. At least three wagers on when the announcement will make the *Morning Chronicle*."

Tris snorted. "The *Morning Chronicle*—as if anyone would believe anything James Perry has to say in that paper of his. Why, I read one of his 'stories' just the other day that told of Prinny being applauded as he passed through the streets. As if being hissed at and having your coach pelted with cabbages can be called acclamation. Give me the *Times,* thank you. At least John Walter could be trusted to keep the war news straight." Then, belatedly getting down off his high ropes, he gave a bit of thought to just what Dexter had said. "Betting on me at Boodle's, are they? Who, damn it? Give me names, boy, and I'll call the bastards out, damned if I won't!"

"That's it, Tris, keep a cool head, just like you're known to do," Lord Bourne jibed, placing an arm around the other man's shoulders. "Besides, you have no one to blame but yourself, the way you act whenever the chit enters a room. Can't remember being so dashed silly about Jennie, even when she was leading me around like a puppy longing for a pat on the head."

Rule retied his cravat with more intensity than flair, his dark eyes flashing in a way that made Dexter decidedly nervous. "I only stand up with the girl for a single dance in an evening. I don't see where that should serve to set the world to hearing wedding bells."

Now it was time for Kit to wink at Julian. "I see your point, Tris. How like society to jump headlong to the wrong conclusion. Just because you show up everywhere Miss Lawrence happens to be as regularly as the sun rises every morning and claim her for a dance before retiring to a pillar and staring a hole in her back for the remainder of the evening. Imagine Lucy and Jennie, for instance, being so rash as to put any credence in the silly coincidence that you always quit the room just as soon as Miss Lawrence retires, or the fact that more than one young buck has reportedly withdrawn from the lists of those seeking the lady's favors due to the belief that you would call them out if they so much as looked in her direction." Lord Bourne shook his head sadly. "How sorely our motives are misinterpreted. What, precisely, then *are* your motives, Tris, if you aren't smitten?"

Rule answered with some questions of his own. "Who exactly *is* Mary Lawrence? Where does she come from? Who are her parents? What is she doing in London? Why is she living with Sir Henry Ruffton? My Aunt Rachel may be the girl's chaperon but she's as close as an oyster whenever I try to get a few answers out of her. I know about her botched engagement with Sir Henry all those years ago, but could loyalty to an old beau cloud her judgment to the point where she'd allow herself to be involved in…never mind, George is getting ready to leave. I really must offer my apologies to him one more time. Excuse me, gentlemen, I'll see you later this evening."

Before either Julian or Kit could gainsay him, Tris was off, his long strides taking him swiftly across the room, the ever-present Dexter scampering to keep up with him.

"What the devil was all that in aid of?" Julian asked his cousin-in-law, who was looking no more enlightened than he. "Rachel told me he was a strange one, alluding to some secret association with the war effort, but I do believe the years of pressure have served to unhinge his mind. Did you ever hear such ridiculousness? Anyone would think he believes Sir Henry to be harboring a lady of ill repute, or a spy, or something. No, can't be a spy. After all the war's over, isn't it?"

Kit was still watching Lord Rule, taking in his naturally belligerent stance and remembering how well the fellow had looked stripped to the waist. No soft London dandy was Tristan Rule. He had the look of a fighting man, even a Peninsula man, unless Kit missed his guess. Yet, for all the rumors about the man, no one could actually say Rule had ever been within a hundred miles of a battle. Strange, moody fellow. But a man of strong convictions for all that. And now he has a bee in his bonnet about Mary Lawrence. Kit turned to look at Julian, a thoughtful twist on his lips. "The war over, you say, Julian? For some of us, maybe. But not for *him,* it would appear." He took one last look at the man they called Ruthless Rule as the tall, black-clad figure strode toward the door. "I tell you, Julian, I'd give my matched bays for a glimpse inside Tristan Rule's head."

# CHAPTER TWO

LUCY GLADWIN RUTHERFORD, Countess of Thorpe, had great hopes for this dinner party, hopes she was foolish enough to share with her beloved husband, Julian, who quickly tried to dash them.

Stopping in the midst of tying his cravat, Lord Thorpe looked in his wife's direction as she stood fiddling with the contents of his dressing table. "Miss Lawrence and your cousin Tris?" He would have shaken his head if the knot he was tying was not just then at a very critical stage. "You're fair and far out this time, my love. Kit and I broached the subject this afternoon at Cribb's Parlor with the man in question, and I'd say Tris's interest is anything but loverlike."

A twinkle entered Lucy's eyes. "Ah, then you noticed his partiality for her too. My cousin is *definitely* interested in Miss Lawrence. You just misread the signs. Tris is nearly always stupid when it comes to women—he probably said something totally negative, if I know him."

Giving his handiwork a last satisfied look in the mirror, Julian turned to plant a kiss on his wife's forehead—while deftly removing his favorite pearl studs from her investigating hands. "I wouldn't say the man was stupid. Actually, thinking back on the conversation, I believe Tris is more than casually interested in the girl. But no, it is most assuredly not with an eye to setting up his nursery."

Lucy interpreted her husband's words in exactly the wrong way. Her small face taking on a look of horror, she gasped. "Surely you don't think he intends to set her up as his light-o-love? I won't believe it!"

"Such a fertile mind you have, Lucy. I fear I must begin rationing your consumption of Minerva Press novels," Julian threatened kindly, and then his features sobered. "To be serious for a moment, love, I do believe your cousin has taken some wild idea into his head about your Mary Lawrence, something to do with her ancestry. Is Tris by chance a bigoted sort?"

"Never!" Lucy protested, flopping into a nearby chair with total disregard for the gown it had taken her maid two hours to press. "I can't understand any of this, Julian. Surely you must be mistaken."

"Kit too?" he nudged, selecting a plain gold signet ring for his finger. "But don't go into a decline, dearest. Surely you and Jennie can find another young couple to work your matchmaking wiles on before the Season is over. What about Dexter?"

"That nodcock?" Lucy exclaimed, momentarily diverted. "He may be your cousin, but he's still the silliest thing on two legs. The way he has attached himself to Tris, why a person could wonder just how much of his feeling is hero worship and how much is—"

"Lucy! You fill me with dismay! You're not supposed to know about such things, much less talk about them."

She smiled up at him impishly. "Not even with my beloved husband, Julian? Don't be so stuffy."

Julian reached down and pulled his wife to her feet and up against his chest. "I am never stuffy, madam, and I have had that reassurance from your own lips." He looked down into her upturned face and gave a bemused smile, glad he had not yet called his valet to help him into his formfitting evening coat. "Ah, yes, my dearest, those lovely, enticing lips."

Lucy was forced to don another gown, as her maid, once she caught sight of her mistress some half hour later, had dissolved into tears and retired to her cot, in no condition to wield a hot iron.

THEY WERE ALL ENSCONCED around the gleaming mahogany table; the Earl of Bourne and his Jennie, Rachel Gladwin alongside young Dexter Rutherford—there to make up the numbers when Sir Henry pleaded another commitment—Lord and Lady Thorpe at the head and foot of the table, and Tristan Rule and Mary Lawrence smack beside each other on one side, just as Lucy had cunningly engineered the thing earlier.

Jennie was still wearing a benevolent smile, as she hadn't as yet had either the benefit of her husband's opinion on her matchmaking scheme or been able to speak alone with Lucy, who was not looking quite so chipper. Indeed Lucy was looking almost solemn, and had been ever since Miss Lawrence, beautifully attired in pale green silk, had greeted the sight of Tristan Rule with an unenthusiastic "Oh, *you're* here."

For her part, Rachel, who had recently taken to plotting her first attempt at a novel of her own, had decided to view the barely veiled hostility her charge directed at her nephew as ink for her scribbling pen. How interesting it would be, she thought as she helped herself to a portion of stewed carp, to have a heroine who insists on ignoring her attraction for the hero. Perhaps, she mused idly, I shall have my heroine outrage her mercenary guardian by refusing to stand up with the hero at her come-out ball. Would Maria Edgeworth approve? Was it too farfetched? Rachel shrugged her shoulders and took another bite of carp.

If Mary had been privy to her companion's thoughts, she might have added her bit to the story, a little plot twist that had the heroine surreptitiously slipping a bit of poison into the hero's fricassee of tripe and then running off to the Continent to become the reigning toast of Paris. But then Mary's mind was at the moment too overcrowded with thoughts of the man sitting so intrudingly close to her right side to have much heart for solving anyone's problems but her own.

Look at him, she instructed herself as she ignored her filled plate. He even cuts his meat with a cool, meticulous care that makes my flesh crawl. And those hands—those hard, tanned hands with their long, straight fingers. Everything about him screams leashed power. *Ruthless.* How apt. Energy seems to flow from him like a never-ending stream. Rachel may think that he's interested in me. My suitors may think he's trying to cut them out for my hand. But I know better. I can feel the animosity that charges the air whenever he looks at me. Why does he dislike me so? Why is he making it his business to unnerve me with his unwanted, discomforting presence? And why, dear God, *why* must he be so maddeningly intriguing, so damnably handsome?

While Mary sat staring at her plate, precisely as if the fish that lay there had just winked in her direction, Tristan Rule was building himself into a temper—not a new experience, granted, but he could not in his memory recall another instance when a female of the species had been able to crawl so deeply under his skin. Maybe it was that bloody black velvet ribbon she had tied tightly around her neck, just like the ladies of a generation ago had worn red ribbons in sympathy with the French nobility that had lost their heads on Madame Guillotine.

Fashion, his saner self told him. Nothing of the kind, his

suspicious self contradicted. That ribbon is just one more nail in her coffin, one more revealing slip that another, less discerning man, might overlook. She was *mocking* those dead Frenchmen, no more, no less. But it would take more than a bit of ribbon and an inconclusive inquiry into Miss Lawrence's background to convince Sir Henry that he had been made the victim of a Bonapartist sympathizer. It was time he made a move, time he took a more positive step than merely to observe her as she pulled the wool over society's eyes with her portrayal of a young miss in her first Season. He was determined to unmask her for what she was. Why in the fiend's name, he snarled inwardly, did she have to be so beautiful?

"I had not known that you would be here this evening, sir."

Tristan's fork halted halfway to his mouth as Mary's softly spoken words startled him. As she had made such a point of ignoring him while they waited for dinner to be announced, he had resigned himself to having his ear bent all through the meal by Dexter, who sat across from him but wasn't about to let any silly dictate of good manners keep him from talking nineteen to the dozen across the table if he so chose. "You didn't?" was all he responded, eyeing her smiling face closely as he sought to understand her seeming friendliness.

"No," she answered, her voice still quite low. "I saw you striding through the drizzle the other day in the park and had figured you to have developed lung fever at the very least by now."

Tristan decided to take her words literally. "What would make you think a bit of spring drizzle could lay me up by the heels?"

Mary shrugged delicately, almost Gallically, in Tristan's biased opinion. "Oh, I don't know. I guess that it's just that you are of an age that I would have expected you to have served in the war if you weren't afflicted with a weak chest or some other such hidden *weakness*. Lord Bourne served on the Peninsula, you know, and Lord Thorpe was very involved with the war effort in Parliament. But you—why, if rumors are to be believed, you spent the last several years traipsing about the Continent like some sort of sightseer. In places far removed from the fighting, that is."

Tristan laid his fork carefully on the edge of his plate. Turning his head slowly in her direction once more, he smiled dangerously, his straight white teeth clenched. "If you were a man, I would call you out for that, you know," he said in his low, husky voice, a voice that went well with his chiseled features, dark eyes, and darker hair.

Another woman would have fainted. Lord, any sane woman wouldn't have taunted him so in the first place! But Mary Lawrence was made of sterner, if somewhat more fool-hardy, stuff. She kept her chin high and didn't so much as blink. "Name your seconds, sir," she dared recklessly, ignoring her rapidly beating heart. "Although you neatly circumvented serving in the war, I have no doubt you've stomach enough to shoot a woman."

Now Tristan's smile was downright evil. "Too messy by half, madam. I prefer to impale my opponents on my sword. Now, madam, if you're still game…?"

There was no pretending she didn't catch the double entendre hidden in his words, and no way she could slap his face at Lucy's table without creating a scene that would have Rachel wringing a peal over her head for a sennight. Her gaze locked with his for a few moments more, brazening it out before her eyes shifted nervously back to the fish on her plate.

She waited until Lord Rule had resumed his meal before speaking again. Just as he had deposited a medium-size bite of succulent fish in his mouth she shared a bit of unusual knowledge with the rest of the company. "Did you know that many tradesmen inflate their meat—and most especially their *fish* by having gin drinkers blow into the bodies? Indeed, and much of the seafood and meat that reaches our tables looking so thick and juicy has been made that way by having the poor animals heated or beaten while *still alive* in order to swell the meat. Isn't that interesting?"

The meal ended shortly after that, as the rest of the diners had somehow lost their appetites (indeed, Dexter, who had fled abruptly from the table, lost even more than that), which, while the thought of ruining Lucy's dinner party sat heavily on her mind, did at least serve one of the ends Mary had intended—getting herself shed of Tristan Rule's embarrassing presence before he drove her into strong hysterics.

Rachel had said he was a hot-tempered sort, prone to short, violent explosions of wrath. Putting all her eggs in one basket at the dinner table in hopes of having the man lose his composure, and therefore some of the esteem in which it seemed the rest of the company held him, had been the second reason for her outburst, but Rule had failed to perform according to his reputation, so that the affair had concluded with Mary being the one who now sat in the corner of the Ruffton carriage in disgrace.

"Really, Mary, that was very poor-spirited of you," Rachel Gladwin was saying, for at least the third time in as many minutes. It took a lot to discompose Rachel—considering she had served as Lucy's companion during that trying time when the girl was so obviously pursuing an obviously fleeing Lord Thorpe—but Mary's inelegant observations at the dinner party had done it.

"I know, Aunt," Mary agreed sadly. "I promise to apologize to Lucy and Julian again when we reach the ball. I'll even send round a written apology tomorrow. But I was sorely tried, I tell you. If you have any idea what that odious nephew of yours had the nerve to intimate to me—"

Rachel could see Mary's blush even in the dim light cast

by the flambeaux hung outside the carriage. "I'm listening," she nudged, remembering the smug look Tristan had been wearing as he and Dexter took their leave.

Mary gave a weak chuckle. "You may listen all you want, Aunt. His words were unrepeatable. I won't so demean myself as to quote the scoundrel."

Now it was Rachel's turn to smile. "Bested you, did he, little girl? I begin to scent a romance here myself. Won't Sir Henry be pleased?"

From the corner of the carriage came the unmistakable sound of fragile ivory fan sticks being snapped neatly in two.

MARY HAD JUST BEGUN TO RELAX when Tristan Rule and his ever-present shadow, Dexter, entered the Salerton ballroom and took up positions at the edge of the dance floor. He's playing me like a fish on a line, Mary fumed silently as she went down the dance with her latest partner. Ever since he first sank his hook into me he's been feeding me more and more line, making me believe I'm about to gain my freedom, and then, just when I'm feeling secure, yanking hard on the pole again.

As she whirled and dipped, flirting outrageously with the hapless young swain who had nearly tripped into a potted palm at the edge of the floor when Mary flashed him her brightest smile, she kept one eye firmly on the black-clad figure who looked as if he was about to spring on her even as he relaxed one well-defined shoulder against a marble pillar.

She never remembered what she said to her partner as he escorted her back to her aunt at the conclusion of the set, but if the youth's bemused expression was to be believed, her vague response to his parting question just might have gained Sir Henry yet another application for her hand on the morrow. Mary frowned, for she was not really heartless and had certainly not meant to lead Lord Hawlsey on, but then, as the musicians struck up the new, daring waltz, all thoughts of Lord Hawlsey fled as her spine automatically stiffened when she felt rather than heard Lord Rule's approach.

Bowing in front of Rachel for her permission—a curiously tunnel-sighted Rachel who seemed not to see her charge's frantic signal in the negative—Tristan availed himself of Mary's small hand and led her firmly onto the floor.

Lord Petersham always wore brown, Mary thought spitefully, and only succeeded in looking dashed dull. Then there was that silly man who wore nothing but green, like some sort of living plant. It stood to reason that Tristan Rule, who dressed only in funereal black, should look dull, or silly, or boringly unimaginative, or, at the very least, depressing. So why did he look none of these? Why did he look like his muscular torso had been carefully poured into his formfitting coat, his, in this instance, black satin breeches lovingly painted on? Why did his black-on-black embroidered waistcoat call such unladylike attention to his flat abdomen, his snowy cravat show to such advantage against his deeply tanned features, his equally white stockings delineate muscular calves that owed nothing to the sawdust stuffing so many men felt forced to use to supplement what nature and a sybaritic life had left lacking?

"I'm waiting, Miss Lawrence."

The sound of Lord Rule's low, husky voice jolted Mary from her musings and surprised her into looking directly into a pair of the deepest, darkest eyes she had ever seen. "W-waiting, my lord?" she stammered, irritated for allowing a tremor to slip into her voice. "Whatever for?"

Tristan cocked his dark head slightly to one side. "Why, for you to commence flirting with me, what else? You flirt with every man you dance with—every man save me, that is. After weeks of standing up with you only to have to propel you woodenly, and silently, round yet another endless ballroom, I have decided to take the initiative. Please, feel free to bat those outrageous eyelashes at me. I'm stronger than I look, I can take it."

Mary nearly tripped over her own feet as she stood stock-still for a moment, in mingled shock and outrage, while Tristan kept on dancing without missing a beat. "Me? *Talk* to you—the Great Sphinx? *Flirt* with you—the Great Stone Man? Why should I so lower myself as to try to converse with you when you've never so much as asked me if I thought the weather was tolerably fine? Besides, I'd rather flirt with portly old Prinny than waste even a moment's time searching my brain for anything civil I'd wish to say to you." Believing she had succeeded in making her position crystal clear, Mary lowered her head and went back to staring a hole in his cravat.

"You can't flirt with pudgy old Prinny, Miss Lawrence," Tristan returned conversationally, "unless, of course, you wish to incur the wrath of the pudgy old Marchioness of Hertford, who is our Royal Highness's current favorite. In any event, the Regent is otherwise engaged these days, with he and his brother, the Duke of York, indulging once more in their favorite pastime, drinking each other under the table. Pity, though," he ended facetiously, "as I do believe it would be a sight not to be missed."

Feeling the heat of his left hand through her gloved fingers while sensing the steel in the hand that held her waist so firmly, Mary fought the urge to break away from the man, knowing that he was just obstinate enough to refuse to let her go—causing a scene of no mean proportions right in the middle of the ball. "Why, my lord," she settled for saying, "I do believe your cousins to be entirely wrong about you. They have hinted on more than one occasion that you were a secret, valuable tool of England's war effort. Wouldn't they be crushed to learn that in reality you are nothing more than a spiteful, gossipy old woman?"

A slight tick appeared along one side of Lord Rule's finely chiseled square chin, but he refused to allow this infuriating chit to bait him into unleashing his legendary temper. Let her continue to believe he was harmless, it would be easier to learn what he had set himself to discover if she continued to underestimate him. "Ah, Miss Lawrence," he returned, smiling, "you have found me out. But then, what else is there to do now that peace is here but tear up our contemporaries behind their backs? It is a prerequisite of anyone claiming to be of the British upper class."

"Bah? You British—" Mary began, then just as quickly ended. "You British men are all alike. You make a vocation out of refusing to take anything seriously. Why, Sir Henry has even said that English lords go to war with much the same enthusiasm as they approach grouse hunting, except that they don't tend to regard war quite so seriously."

The waltz ended, and Tristan put a hand under Mary's elbow and steered her toward a door to the first-floor balcony without her ever realizing their destination. "Sir Henry is absolutely correct, Miss Lawrence," he supplied smoothly as he helped her over the raised threshold and out onto the flagstones. "I've heard it more than once that we English believe all foreigners to be deucedly poor shots. Yet, be that as it may, we vain, arrogant English *have* succeeded in winning the war."

"Have we?" Mary countered, seating herself on a low stone bench and watching as Tristan eased himself down beside her. "My uncle mutters that the only change thus far in Paris is that the newspapers and pats of butter are now imprinted with *fleur-de-lis*."

Tristan berated himself for noticing how intriguingly

Mary's clear complexion captured the moonlight and added, "But that is not the worst that is being said, Miss Lawrence. Although I cannot claim to know anything about it, I have heard that it was English money used to bribe Napoleon's generals that won us this war, just as it has done down through history, and that, in truth, Napoleon is very much Wellington's superior."

"As they have not faced each other across a battlefield, I believe that last to be a moot point, my lord," Mary replied, wondering why her answer had brought a thoughtful frown to Lord Rule's face.

"Then you have no preference between Napoleon and the duke? Surely you must have an opinion?" Tristan pressed.

"I must?" Mary shot back, suddenly realizing that she had somehow allowed herself to be isolated with a man she thoroughly detested. "Why? Surely a woman is not expected to have a head for war or politics. All that concerns me is that we are now free to visit Paris and investigate all the latest fashions."

"And yet you are still here in London," he pointed out, much to her chagrin. "I find it hard to believe you were not off to the Continent the minute Napoleon's abdication was declared."

This subject was close enough to Mary's heart to cloud her earlier suspicions. "And I would have been, if not for Sir Henry's summons," she blurted before getting a belated hold on her tongue. Why was she feeling like a butterfly pinned down to a table for examination? Why did this seemingly innocent conversation seem so contrived, so full of probing questions? Why was she sitting here in the moonlight with a man she thoroughly abhorred in the first place? Rising to her feet with more haste than grace, she told Tristan that she had been absent too long from the ballroom and must return.

Tristan rose with her, once more taking firm possession

of her elbow. "We wouldn't want the tongues to wag, now would we, Miss Lawrence?" he agreed, just as if she had voiced the notion that the two of them were becoming thought of as a couple. "Besides, I do believe I heard another waltz beginning. I should be pleased to partner you."

That stopped Mary in her tracks. Wheeling to face him, she gritted, "Are you mad? *Two* waltzes? Add that to our disappearance from the room and the whole world will have us betrothed."

Tristan, who had decided to intensify his campaign with Mary by sticking as close as a barnacle to her side until he made up his mind about her once and for all, only smiled—causing Mary's hand to itch to slap his handsome face. "Yes, they would, wouldn't they? Ah well, I daresay Sir Henry won't mind—he's always seemed to like me a bit. Do you wish a long engagement?"

# CHAPTER THREE

LISTENING TO TRISTAN'S WORDS, then whirling about to look into his disgustingly handsome, smiling face, caused Mary to spend the last coin of her self-control. "Marry you!" she shrieked, causing more than one interested head to turn in her direction. "Why, I'd rather be the sole woman on an island inhabited by shipwrecked sailors!"

Rule barely stifled an appreciative smile, which only served to incense Mary all the more, and bowed deeply from his waist. "And here I thought we were getting along so well," he said, making a poor attempt at looking crushed by her words. "I stand corrected, madam."

"Only until I knock you down, sirrah!" Mary retorted, trying to disengage her elbow, which he had maddeningly taken in his grasp. "Which I promise you I shall do shortly, if you do not release me."

Any lingering trace of humor left Lord Rule's face as he, by the simple means of closing his strong fingers around Mary's tender elbow, steered her over to a secluded corner of the balcony and lowered his head to within scant inches of hers. "What kind of woman are you?" he demanded harshly, giving her abused arm a shake. "I try to be civil to you, even flatter you by indulging in a bit of mild flirtation such as you females demand of us men, and you repay me time after time with cutting words, insults, and now threats of violence."

"Flirt with me! You call your outrageous suggestion *flirting?* And what do you mean by lumping me in with a bunch of chits with more hair than wit who giggle and simper as some ridiculous fop or other compares their crossed eyes to brightly shining stars?" Mary was so angry now that she either could not or would not take notice of his lordship's set jaw and narrowed eyes. Raising her chin just a bit more, she sniffed dismissingly. "If you are going to ape your betters, I suggest you choose your models with more care."

She was going to drive him straight out of his mind! His short-lived idea of insinuating himself into her good graces (all the better to keep a close watch on her) died an undignified death as his quick temper overrode his seldom-exercised discretion. Tristan stepped further back into the shadows, pulling Mary along with him willy-nilly, and took the back of her neck in his firm grip. "I am done playing games with you, Miss Lawrence. You tell me I am no gentleman, yet I have only your word for it that you are a lady."

Mary's heart began to pound as she belatedly realized that her sharp tongue had gotten her into yet another tight spot. "Apply to my uncle if you wish a tracing of my family tree." She brazened it out, her green eyes spitting fire in the darkness. "I am not about to justify my existence to you."

"I have talked with Sir Henry," Tristan informed her to her dismay, "and all he says is that you are the daughter of an old friend. You have the man so besotted he'll say anything to protect you, but I am not so hoodwinked by your beauty that I can overlook the fact that you have somehow established yourself in the house of one of the most important men in the war effort."

Even in the midst of her fright Mary took a small bit of satisfaction in the notion that Lord Rule thought her beautiful, but that admission did not serve to overshadow the fact that he was accusing her of—what *was* he accusing her of? "You think I'm Sir Henry's *mistress?*" she squeaked at last, feeling something akin to relief.

Tristan's fingers tightened on the soft, slim neck. "Mistress?" he repeated, brought up short. "No, Rachel wouldn't stand still for being a party to that, not even for an old friend…would she?" he questioned softly, as if debating with himself.

Mary reached up and tried to remove his hand, finger by tensed finger. "Look, my lord, either throttle me or let me go. Make up your mind." In the space of a moment she had decided that Tristan Rule was not ruthless—he was ridiculous! But if he was suffering from overexposure to battle or some such thing, he should take himself off to some spa for the waters, not run amok in London searching out nonexistent intrigues. Besides, she reminded herself as she attempted to lift his thumb from the pulse point at the base of her throat, it wasn't as if there was no intrigue about her presence in Sir Henry's household—even though her true identity was not all that earthshaking. The last thing her uncle would wish for was this man meddling in their affairs.

Lord Rule shook his head a time or two, bringing himself back to the matter at hand. And that matter was, to be obvious about the thing, that the matter at hand *was* his hand—for somehow it had found its way around Miss Lawrence's slender throat. God! The woman had the power to drive him distracted. And the thought that she could be Sir Henry's mistress did something evil to his insides that he was powerless to deny. Looking down into her angry face, Tristan cudgeled his brain for a way out of this latest coil into which the dratted chit had succeeded in goading him.

"Well, sir," Mary prompted, puzzled by the slightly dazed expression in Lord Rule's dark eyes. "Which is it to be—a quick snuffing or sweet freedom?"

What would Julian do in a situation like this? Or Kit? Tristan cursed under his breath as he realized neither of those esteemed gentlemen would have allowed themselves to be drawn into such a tangled mess in the first place. But then neither of those men had ever stood within a heartbeat of the beautiful, willful, mysterious Miss Mary Lawrence. Any man could be excused for losing his head in such circumstances, he assured himself, regaining a small bit of his consequence while fueling his flagging temper with yet another shovelful of Mary Lawrence's supposed sins against him.

The firm clasp turned abruptly into a rough sort of caress as Tristan Rule smiled evilly, and Mary found herself wishing he were still scowling. "Wh-what are you going to do?" she asked, already knowing the answer.

"What do you think I'm going to do?" Tristan returned in a soft growl. If he was already in trouble—and he knew he most assuredly would be the moment Sir Henry heard of this night's work—he'd already decided he may as well be hung for a sheep as a lamb. His dark features nearly blotting out the moonlight as they descended on her, Tristan ended huskily, "I'm going to throttle you, what else?"

"No!" Mary protested swiftly, but not nearly quickly enough to keep her denial from being smothered by Lord Rule's punishing mouth. Nor did her hands move rapidly enough to prevent his arms from capturing her slim body in his rock-hard embrace.

Mary had been kissed before, she was sure she had, but all of those kisses paled beneath the reality of Tristan's mouth as it curved, and slanted, and moved possessively upon hers. As his strong arms forced the very air from her lungs, he captured her breath in his mouth and breathed his own life back into her. It was so personal, so intimate an action, that she felt herself to have been actually violated. When the tip of his tongue slid along the edge of her teeth as his mouth opened more fully over hers, then brazenly penetrated, Mary instinctively fought back.

"*Ouch!* You hellion!" Tristan spat, jumping back to reach a finger inside his mouth to inspect his wounded tongue.

Her hands balled into fists at her sides, her firm chin outthrust in indignation, Mary warned coldly: "Touch me again, you miserable creature—even come within a mile of me—and I'll have you horsewhipped!"

Watching appreciatively as Mary's indignant figure stomped back into the ballroom, his hand held to the cheek she had slapped with some force in order to punctuate her parting warning, Tristan mused aloud, "She'd probably do it too. And at the moment, by God, it almost seems worth it."

RACHEL HAD OBSERVED Mary's departure with Rule, and had counted the minutes until her charge had returned alone to the ballroom, looking more than a little the worse for wear. But before Rachel could cross the floor to find out just what her infuriating nephew had done this time, Mary was claimed for a dance by some violet satin-clad exquisite and disappeared into the crowd of revelers.

That left Tristan, and Rachel was determined not to let the fellow get away without an explanation of what had transpired on the balcony. She found him lounging against the doorjamb, boring a hole in Mary's unsuspecting back like some hot-headed halfling. She looked from Tristan to Mary and then back again, hardly believing what her eyes were telling her. It couldn't be. It was utterly impossible. The Ruthless Lord Rule pricked by Cupid's dart? Tristan was just shy of his thirtieth birthday, and in all that time he had never once shown any signs of being the romantic sort. True, she owned to herself, he had been hopping about the Continent and God only knew where else these past seven years or more, but considering the multitude of rumors about his involvement with the military, it seemed impossible for him to have carried on any serious romantic interlude without all of London finding out about it one way or another.

Tilting her head to one side, she inspected Tristan's expression as he stood rock still, his whole body taut with suppressed—what? Fury? Passion? Lust? "Good heavens," she whispered, "this novel writing has made me into a hysteric. Soon I'll be reading Byron and swooning dead away." Still, she thought as she looked at her nephew again, more objectively this time, Rule does have a certain look about him— the same sort of look, if I recall it correctly, that he had at the age of twelve, when his father refused to allow him on that great big stallion. And when Rachel recalled that Tristan had eventually not only mounted that stallion, but broken him to saddle, her fears for her charge began anew.

"Tristan," she said, tugging on his sleeve to get his attention, "you look like a thundercloud. Kindly smile at me as if you didn't wish me at the farthest corners of the earth and stop casting a pall over this entire company. I swear three totally innocent gentlemen have already departed the ballroom, believing you had them in your sights."

Distracted, Rule ignored his aunt's sarcasm, if indeed he had understood it. After all, he wasn't deliberately striking a pose or any such thing. He was merely being himself—his intense, determined, passionate self. He might, in his more candid moments, admit to possessing a bit of a short fuse, but he consoled himself with the knowledge that he was never purposely mean. He leveled one long, last piercing look at the scrap of female that could just be the exception to his self-imposed rule of absolute chivalry where the weaker sex was concerned, and turned to address his aunt. "You wanted something, Aunt? A cooling glass of lemonade, perhaps?"

Rachel clenched her teeth in frustration. Tristan had al-

ways had this maddening ability to turn her up sweet just
when she was about to tear a wide strip off his hide. A glass
of lemonade, indeed! Better to have three fingers of whiskey if she was about to try to beat some sense into the idiot's
thick head! "No, thank you, dear," she somehow trilled, taking his arm. "But it is dreadfully close in the ballroom.
Perhaps you could bear me company for a stroll around the
balcony?"

Again Tristan looked to the dance floor, where Mary was
busily flirting with three gentlemen who were all vying for
her hand for the next set, and then back at his aunt. "A stroll,
you say? On the balcony? Couldn't you just stand here in the
doorway and take a few deep, bracing breaths?"

"Tristan Montgomery Rule!" Rachel snapped, longing to
do him an injury. "Come with me willingly or I'll pull you
along by the ear like I did when you were in short pants!" And
with that, she sailed off through the archway—her reluctant
nephew trailing along behind—and prepared to bribe, blus-
ter, threaten, or cajole the truth out of him. She owed it to
Henry!

"'ERE NOW, ARE YER GONNA EAT wit dem dabblers on?" Ben
questioned Mary, who had yet to relinquish her gloves into
the servant's waiting hands. "Yer be 'ere fer yafflin', ain't
yer? Montague's done up a treat, so's yer best be clammed."

Mary turned to her aunt. "What did he say?" she asked,
prudently giving over her gloves before the little fellow
stripped them from her hands. "And what's a Montague?"

Rachel nodded to the now deeply bowing Ben and pro-
pelled her charge up the stairs to the drawing room where
Jennie and Lucy waited. "Montague is Jennie's idea of a
French chef, and you'd better be hungry or there may be the
devil to pay. It's a long story," she conceded as Mary's mouth
opened on another question. "Suffice it to say Jennie has

these little *projects*. For the moment, my dear, just follow my lead." They stopped before the drawing-room door so that Ben could dash by and announce them, muttering something about earning his pantler's keys (butler's keys, to the uninformed, which Rachel, to her own regret, had not been ever since her chaperonage of Lucy). After allowing themselves to be trumpeted into the room like minor royalty, Rachel called the three young women quickly to order.

"I know it is my custom to retire to a corner and let you girls natter as you will, but I have requested this luncheon with a definite purpose in mind," she began, quickly taking Jennie and Lucy's interest away from Mary's fetching new walking dress and onto herself.

"What ho? Do I sense some deep intrigue?" Lucy asked happily, clapping her hands.

"You *always* sense some deep intrigue," Jennie commented to Lucy without rancor before turning back to her aunt. "Has someone unsuitable offered for Mary?" she asked, her thoughts, as usual, running along matrimonial lines.

"Has Uncle Henry at last agreed to send me to France?" Mary chimed in, immediately crossing her fingers for luck.

"Perhaps, no, and no, *definitely* not," Rachel replied, pointing to each of the trio of young hopefuls in turn. "This meeting concerns one Tristan Rule. Something has got to be done about the boy."

"Marry him off!" Lucy and Jennie declared in unison, while Mary's only reply was to pucker up her nose in an expression of distaste, saying, "And a more boring subject I cannot imagine."

Rachel sat down gingerly on the edge of the satin settee and addressed her next words directly to Mary. "You won't believe it boring when I have told you just what maggot my nephew has taken into his head about you. I don't remember him going off on such a wild tangent since that time he decided Lucy was really a boy in disguise and her father had put her into skirts so that he wouldn't have to spring for an education at Eton."

Jennie whirled on Lucy, who was laughing uproariously. "Lucy!" she exclaimed. "He never did! How old was Tristan when this happened?"

Lucy had to take refuge in her handkerchief as tears of mirth streamed from her eyes. "T-ten!" she chortled. "I was just a little past three myself. Oh dear, you would perish on the spot if I told you how Tristan was at last proved wrong. Thank goodness I have little but a hazy remembrance of his triumphant unveiling of my 'masculine' form in front of the vicar and his sister. I swear, Tristan couldn't sit down for a week after my father got through with him!"

Mary found herself laughing in spite of herself, and in spite of the deep animosity she felt for Tristan Rule—especially after the events of the previous evening. The fact that she knew she couldn't confide in either Rachel or Sir Henry without somewhat incriminating herself for her own less than ladylike behavior did not detract from the poor opinion of the man. Trying to keep her mind on the subject at hand, she put in, "I gather, Aunt, that your nephew's latest incorrect assumption is even worse?"

There was no way to dress the thing up in fine linen, and Rachel was not about to try. Taking a deep, steadying breath, she announced baldly: "Tristan believes Mary might be a spy in the pay of Napoleon."

Looking quite clearly puzzled, Jennie murmured, "But Napoleon is imprisoned on Elba. The war is *over*. Surely Kit would have told me if there was any danger. We plan to travel there next spring with Christopher and my father. And Montague was so looking forward to it too—he's French, you know."

Rachel shook her head. "*We* consider the war to be over,

pet, but even Sir Henry is uneasy about the laxity of Bonaparte's imprisonment. There has been more than one rumor about forces being at work to reinstate the man in Paris. He still carries the title of emperor, you know, even if he is in exile."

While Rachel was explaining all this to Jennie, Lucy was observing Mary shrewdly out of the corners of her eyes. The girl was sitting as stiff and still as a ramrod, looking as if steam would commence pouring from her ears at any moment. Obviously Mary did not share Rachel's apprehension, Jennie's confusion, or her own hilarity—no, Miss Mary Lawrence was, in a word, *incensed!*

"How dare he," Mary whispered nearly under her breath, and then more loudly. "How *dare* he!"

Immediately Jennie set out to placate her guest. "Now, Mary, don't be so out-of-reason cross. Tristan has simply made an error in judgment. Surely Aunt Rachel has already set him straight."

"It's not for myself that I'm angry, Jennie," Mary explained, rising to her feet to begin pacing up and down the length of the carpet. "It's the insult to Sir Henry that I cannot and will not abide! How *dare* that ridiculous man cast such aspersions on the intelligence and discretion of one of the nation's greatest patriots? For myself I care nothing, for Tristan Rule's opinion of me is not something I would lose any sleep over, I assure you, but if Sir Henry were to catch wind of this—why, I cannot imagine the consequences."

Rachel could. Rachel had. Which was why she was sitting here amid a group of painfully young ladies instead of pouring out her fears to the one man who she felt could settle the matter once and for all. Oh yes, she had thought of confiding in Julian or Kit, but since it was so pleasant to have her two nieces so happily married, she should hate having to start over from scratch finding replacements once that hot-

headed Tristan had made them both into widows. Especially
Lucy—dear Lord, getting that one bracketed had cost Rachel
more than a few gray hairs!

"I have, unlike you, had a full night to ponder our problem, so I have entertained a few ideas…" Rachel slid in before Mary could snatch up her reticule and go off searching
for Lord Rule in order to bash him soundly about the head
and shoulders. All three pairs of young eyes immediately
concentrated in her direction.

Agreeing with Mary that Sir Henry was best left ignorant
of Rule's assumption, Rachel admitted that the only concrete
idea she could come up with was that Tristan Rule needed
to be taught a lesson—a very strong lesson. She was now,
she told them sincerely, applying to three of the most agile,
devious, determined minds she knew for ways to render to
her nephew the trimming he so obviously deserved.

"We could have him impressed in His Majesty's service
on a ship bound for deepest Africa," Mary offered most
evilly.

Rachel declined that option, warning, "Mary, my dear, if
you would please try for a little more elegance of mind?
Besides, knowing Tristan, he would incite a mutiny within
three days of leaving port and return here with a full crew of
faithful sailors bound to help him expose your dastardly purpose. No, much as I wish it, we shall have to *deal* with
Tristan, not merely transport him."

Mary just shrugged, then suggested a second option—
something vaguely connected with boiling his lordship in oil.

"Oh, I do like this girl!" Lucy said, giggling. "No simpering miss, this."

Slowly it dawned on the company that Jennie had not spoken for some time. Lucy looked over at her cousin to find
the girl wiping away a tear, and promptly asked her what was
amiss. "I've been thinking about poor Mary, and how she

must feel to be supposed guilty of such a grievous crime," Jennie supplied before daintily blowing her nose. "It is horrid, simply horrid! I wonder how Tristan would feel to be placed in such a position. Perhaps if the slipper were on the other foot for a change, it might show him how unfair his assumptions can be."

Mary immediately stopped her pacing, an unholy grin lighting her beautiful face. Racing over to swoop the still-sniffling Jennie into her arms, she gave that girl a resounding kiss on the cheek. "Jennie, you dearest thing, you have hit upon it exactly. Lord Rule is long overdue for a lesson. For too long has he been allowed to make hare-witted assumptions about his fellow man and then set about proving how right he is, no matter what the cost to his victim. For Lucy's injured sensibilities as a child, for his insult to Sir Henry, and for all the other people he has persecuted with his single-minded, not to mention simpleminded determination—*we shall teach him a lesson!*"

Lucy tipped her head to one side. "I agree about the rest of it, but I don't know if you can truthfully say I was a victim," she corrected impishly. "After all, I have it from my old nurse that I quite enjoyed showing off for the vicar, and repeated the practice every time an adult came into range for the next few months—until Papa finally broke me of the habit."

"How did he do that?" Jennie was the only person interested enough to inquire.

"By the simple expedient of basting her drawers to her shift until she got the message," Rachel supplied, smiling a bit to herself. "It was my idea, actually. Hale wrote to me in desperation."

Ben entered the room and announced luncheon with all the pomp and ceremony Montague's creations deserved, and Jennie quickly ushered her guests into the dining room, where Mary once again commanded everyone's attention by unveiling the plan that had already grown to major proportions within her agile brain. If Tristan Rule had thought he could prove Mary to be a spy, she was going to be extremely helpful in convincing him of her guilt! In other words, if he wished her to act like a traitor, she would accommodate him—in spades.

"Oh, for a humdrum existence," Rachel said to no one in particular, envying every bored on-the-shelf spinster in all England.

Lucy was all for Mary's idea. Indeed, she even volunteered her every assistance, but she couldn't help but ask: "Just how is this going to provide Tris with his overdue lesson in minding his own business? I mean, skulking about leaving messages and acting suspicious sounds like whacking great fun, but surely it will only work to make Tristan more sure of his convictions."

"Not if I—with a little help from you, my dear friends— also behave, as if Tristan is the *real* French spy in our midst, and return his treatment of me twofold!" Mary told him confidently.

Lifting her glass in a salute to her new friend's genius, Lucy promised jovially, "And when it is all over, and Tristan has been suitably humbled, he will fall at your feet begging for your hand in marriage!"

Mary's smile faded as she remembered the events of the previous evening. "Then I will have him aboard that ship to Africa after all!" she vowed sincerely, not noticing Jennie's and Lucy's exchange of broad winks.

# CHAPTER FOUR

MARY FLUNG DOWN the magazine she had been reading, unable to sustain an interest in a gushing description of the latest fashions from Paris, and hopped up to pace back and forth impatiently across the drawing-room rug, her small hands clenched into unladylike fists. Oh, she was so angry! Drat that Tristan Rule anyway!

She halted in her tracks momentarily to stare malevolently at a Sevres figurine, seeing Rule's dark, well-made features rather than the smiling face of an innocent young country maid dressed in pink ruffles. Who does he think he is, she ranted to herself, to be judging me like the Lord on Doomsday? He's an obtuse, despicable, intolerable, opinionated... Mary turned on her heels and set about pacing once more, unable to continue her thoughts else she'd be forced to throw something.

And it wasn't bad enough that the man had all but convicted her of spying for the French, oh no—he had also shown her, by his actions of the previous week, that he was not about to do his accusing from the sidelines. Acting as if she had never warned him to approach her again, he had been up to his old tricks, standing up with her for the length of one infuriating dance and then retiring to a nearby pillar to glower at her like some angry ancient god for the remainder of the evening, just as if he expected her to give herself away some-how, proving his ludicrous theory to be correct.

Even worse, everyone was so all-fired afraid of the man. It was almost ridiculous to see all her former beaux defect-ing from the ranks one by one as they put their tails between their legs and ran from Rule's intense stares. How was she to have any fun at all if her main amusement—harmless flirting—was to be denied her? What it had come to, she re-alized as she brought herself up with a start, was that she had only two options open to her—either allowing Rule to court her openly so that she could at least go out in society with-out feeling like a pariah, or else retiring posthaste to a nun-nery!

*Crash!* It was no use—something had to satisfy Mary's outrage, and the china maiden had been elected. Staring at the porcelain shards scattered about in the cold fireplace, Mary was angered even more when she realized that she had broken a valuable piece of Sir Henry's property without the action easing her fury by so much as a jot. Oh, if only she could have Rule here in person; smashing *him* would be en-tire worlds more satisfying.

Almost as if she had conjured him up by sheer force of will, she whirled at the sound of the butler's announcement to see Tristan Rule striding big as life into the drawing room. "You!" she exclaimed, her eyes narrowing dangerously. "What do you want?"

Tristan quickly took in Mary's flushed cheeks and bellig-erent stance and impulsively decided to change his mission from that of seeing his aunt to the possibly more profitable one of trying to goad Mary Lawrence into betraying her guilt. *"Bonjour, mademoiselle,"* he pronounced in perfect ac-cents, making her an elegant leg.

"It was," Mary snapped peevishly, and then, sparked by an imp of perversity that she could no more deny than she could her need to breathe, she launched herself into a long, involved speech concerning the growing list of fêtes and receptions planned for the upcoming celebration of peace, all in faultless French. There! *If the man wants signs of guilt, I'll give him signs of guilt until he drowns himself in them!*

Tristan could not hide his triumphant smile. *The chit spoke French like a native of that country.* Even he, trained in several languages, could find nothing to fault in her accent or usage. "Your French tutor must have been an émigré, Miss Lawrence, to have taught you so well," he offered as bait.

Mary opened her mouth as if to speak, then lifted an anxious hand to her breast and stammered nervously. "Y-yes, yes *indeed*. How clever of you. That's *precisely* who it was. A poor émigré. The wretched creature so needed employment at the time that I ended up having a resident tutor for several years whilst I was in Sussex." *There,* she thought, hiding a grin. *That should serve to convince him I'm lying through my teeth. Ah, look at him, smiling one of his devilish secretive smiles, just like the cat who got into the cream. I'm surprised he hasn't already sent for the constable, so sure of himself is he.*

"Tristan! What brings you here today? And Mary, why didn't you have me summoned at once? You know you should not be entertaining a gentleman without a chaperon."

"Was I?" Mary commented under her breath as she looked apologetically at her companion.

Rachel's entrance into the room startled Rule into looking up blankly for a moment, and Rachel heaved a small sigh of relief when she realized that her nephew and Mary hadn't come to fisticuffs before she could place herself as a buffer between their two warlike personalities. "Have you come to see Sir Henry, nephew? He is out at present, but we expect him back directly."

"He is back," came Sir Henry's voice, shortly to be followed by that man's pudgy presence in the doorway. "Come courting, have you, boy? Since I saw you not an hour ago at the War Office, it can't be my face you were longing to see." Sir Henry nodded his head a time or two, a broad smile on his cherubic face. "Good, good. I rather like the idea of Tristan running tame in his house, Rachel. He's a hotheaded young puppy, but loyal as the day is long, and valuable. You couldn't make a better choice, Mary, my dear, not if you looked for a dozen Seasons. Right, Rachel?"

Rachel closed her eyes and shook her head, not knowing whether to box Sir Henry's ears or give him a smacking great kiss on the mouth. But one way or another—due to his foolish blustering—matters were about to come to a head, and Rachel couldn't be happier. All this scheming and plotting among Mary and her two nieces on the one side and Tristan, aided by his fertile imagination and stubborn tenacity, on the other was sure to lead her to an early grave— and with her novel just begun. At least now either Mary or Tristan, or both of them, would be forced to own to the truth before Sir Henry went posting the banns.

Tristan, however, was not about to look what he saw as a gift horse in the molars. Instead of denying that he was indeed love-bitten, or even running from the house and matrimony in full bachelor flight, he was saying something ridiculously silly about wishing to take the charming Miss Lawrence for a ride in the promenade in order to convince her that he was sincere in his regard for her.

Clearly, Tristan had twisted everything round to his own advantage and could care less what Sir Henry supposed as long as he could proceed unimpeded in his quest to have Mary to himself in order to ascertain once and for all whether or not she was a traitor.

That left Mary, and Rachel turned to look at her appealingly, hoping that the child had reconsidered her plans now that Sir Henry could end up the innocent victim in the affair. But if sane, rational thinking in the face of impending disaster was what Rachel had hoped for, she was due for a disappointment that would keep her up nights for a long time to come.

Mary, hiding her furiously clenched fists behind her back, was just then smiling sweetly and denying nothing. Indeed, she was looking up into Tristan's handsome features with a look so cloyingly sweet that Rachel knew she, for one, would be put off sugaring her tea for a sennight.

Tilting her head slightly to one side in a move meant to be coquettish, Mary blushed becomingly (a trick she had mastered in her cot) and simpered, "Oh, Sir Henry! Do you think I *should?* After the marked attentions Lord Rule has been so kind as to show me, I scarce wish the vulgar tattles to have more to prattle about." She then hesitated, overdoing things a little bit, Rachel thought, by putting her fingers to her mouth and giggling, before admitting, "But I would like to ride up beside Lord Rule above *all things!*"

"I'll have your maid bring your cloak and bonnet, Mary," Rachel volunteered from between clenched teeth, frantic to quit the room before she did either her overacting charge or her sleuthing nephew an injury.

Within ten minutes, a beaming, benevolent Sir Henry and a resigned, realistic Rachel were standing at the front door, waving the young couple on their way.

BY THE TIME THEY ARRIVED in the park, Mary's good humor had been much restored, thanks to the brilliant idea she'd had as she spied a rather down at the heels *frizeur,* hatbox in hand, crossing the street in front of them. Catching the Frenchman's attention by the simple expediency of a maidenly screech supposedly caused by the distressing sight of a rather large, slavering dog, Mary took great pains in gift-ing the hairdresser with a broad wink and a furtive-looking wave of the hand before hastily pretending an unnatural interest in one fingertip of her right glove.

It is superfluous to report that this supposedly covert sig-nal was witnessed by the ever-alert Tristan, just as any of that man's enemies would be quick to point out to the assumed-to-be-careless Miss Lawrence.

Filing away a mental picture of the Frenchman before urg-ing his team forward once more, Tristan determined to seek out Mary's "contact" and question him as soon as possible, a notion that Mary—just then snickering into her gloved hand—found distinctly amusing. Soon, with any luck at all, she'd have Tristan so busy chasing ridiculous false leads all over London that he wouldn't have a single moment left free to tease her with his unwanted attentions.

If she had any slight qualms about the course of action she had embarked upon since hearing of Tristan's assumptions about her, his earnest reaction to her pretended message-passing effectively banished the last of her more tender feel-ings.

But it would not do to have this thing all onesided. As Jennie had said, it was time Tristan learned just how it felt to be pursued like some helpless deer hunted in a fenced wood. Yes, it was time she started giving him a hint or two about her own, deliberately amateurish investigation of *his* loyalties.

She began the moment Rule's curricle was eased into line behind a dowager countess's rusty black barouche, ready to take their part in the late-afternoon promenade. "You under-stood my French quite well, my lord," she began innocently enough. "Perhaps you too have a French émigré as a tutor?"

This seemingly artlessly posed query brought surprising results. Not accustomed to being questioned on his personal life, Rule answered her question with one of his own. "Why do you ask?" he shot back quickly.

Mary took refuge in another girlish giggle. Goodness, the man was touchy! "Lud, my lord," she needled him, "anyone would think you had learned your French at Boney's knee, for all you're so ticklish about the subject. I told you about *my* tutor; surely *your* knowledge of the language was not gained through some nefarious means, was it?"

What the deuce was the girl up to? Tristan pretended to concentrate on his horses while he cudgeled his brain for an answer. She was only playacting at being a brainless ninny; he was not so obtuse as to not see through her pretense, but he was at a loss as to why.

Besides, it was he who had questions that needed answering not she. *She* was the one with no traceable background, just as if she had been hatched full-grown from an egg three months earlier. It was *she* who had installed herself snugly in Sir Henry's house, hoodwinking that poor, naïve man with her deadly charms; *she* who could be anyone from Sir Henry's by-blow to Bonaparte's first cousin. *She* was the one who had some serious explaining to do, and he was not about to allow her to turn the tables on him and try to make *him* England's fiercest patriot, into a person of questionable allegiance.

Turning in his seat, the better to see her reaction to his words, Tristan smiled broadly, saying, "Why, Miss Lawrence, what an odd imagination you have. *Nefarious* French lessons? You didn't strike me as one of those females who's addicted to those novels full of dark danger and imperiled innocents adrift in a cruel world."

Mary dug her fingernails into her palms until she could control her urge to do Lord Rule an injury. Then, returning his smile just as brilliantly, she trilled, "But Lord Rule, your own aunt is penning just such a novel. Surely you must hold her in disgust if your opinion of her chosen medium is so very low?"

"My aunt is merely filling her time until Sir Henry wakes up and realizes he cannot risk losing Rachel a second time and makes her his wife. I'll not begrudge her this little hobby if it makes her happy," he ended, just as if he had anything at all to say about the running of Rachel's life.

Looking around at the greening landscape and seeing everything through a red haze of anger, Mary found herself amazed yet again at the maddening way Lord Rule had of putting everything and everybody into neat little boxes, then labeling them as he saw fit. It was as if he had inherited some of Jennie's matchmaking tendencies—his cousin's burning desire to settle everyone happily into perfectly fitting niches—and some of his cousin Lucy's single-minded determination in following through on any project once undertaken, no matter what the odds, as well as more than his fair share of Lucy's tendency to meddle in whatever she considered to be her business.

What Mary had yet to fully understand was that Tristan—being the male of the species and therefore more prone to looking upon his less desirable traits as sterling qualities—had grown into manhood with his determination hardening into firm, unwavering resolve, while his wish to settle people changed into managing interference and his natural curiosity about his fellowman twisted into suspicion and mistrust of those he could not neatly categorize. And all of this had happened because no one had ever yet had sufficient courage to tell him he was fast becoming an opinionated, arrogant, fire-breathing Don Quixote—out to right the world's wrongs as he was so clearly, in his own mind, called upon to do.

Having been deeply involved with the defense of his country for the past seven years, his talents (or failings, depend-

ing on whom you applied to for a judgment) had been honed
and refined until he felt himself able to judge and mentally
file away a man within mere minutes of making his acquaintance. He did not give any credence to hearsay or rumor—
and paid only a little more attention to the official documents
he was frequently provided with to use as a guide—choosing instead to make up his own mind in his own way. In this
manner he had decided that, seeing that Lucy trusted Julian,
the man was obviously innocent of any involvement with the
death of a young woman who had claimed to be his discarded
mistress.

Yet, perversely, he had decided that Mary Lawrence—
vouched for by his trusted superior, Sir Henry—a girl of no
background who had popped up in the household of the
same so-important Sir Henry, was a very dangerous woman.
The unnerving way his skin tightened at the mere sight of
her; the tendency the hair at the back of his head had of bristling—tingling his scalp—at the sound of her unaffected
laugh; the unnatural talent she had for bewitching all who
came within her charmed circle; everything about Mary
Lawrence screamed out at him *danger—danger.*

Although he could not, if pressed, produce a single damning piece of evidence to support his theory, Rule stuck buckle
and thong to his initial conclusion—either in deference to his
seldom-off-target intuition or because of that inborn streak
of stubbornness, not even he was able to say. All he knew
was that in all his nine and twenty years of living, he had
never before experienced this sense of very real personal danger that he felt every time he stood up for the waltz with Mary
Lawrence.

His life had for many years depended on his ability to
judge people, and Mary, even though she was living under
Sir Henry's protection, even though she looked as innocent
as a newborn lamb, even though she was the most beautiful,

fascinating woman he had ever met, was a prime suspect in the newly discovered plot to free Bonaparte from Elba and return him to Paris as emperor. Hadn't he suspected her from the moment he had arrived back in London after Sir Henry's summons only to see the girl already entrenched in Sir Henry's own home? And now, having decided for himself that he was correct in his assumptions, he would not rest until he uncovered her entire scheme and unmasked her co-conspirators.

Tristan looked over at Mary again, pretending an interest in a showy stallion just then being edged along the path by his proud owner, and experienced yet again the unnerving tingle that her mere proximity to his person invariably provoked. Guilty as sin, he assured himself yet again, unanswering in his belief in his own intuition—and, unbeknownst to him, demonstrating yet again his total ignorance of the body's power to recognize what the mind refuses to accept.

THE SILENCE THAT HAD descended upon the pair ever since Tristan's casual dismissal of Rachel's motives for penning a novel had not bothered them as long as they were each locked in their own private thoughts.

While Rule's mind had traveled yet again down the same narrow road—the one that ended with proof of Mary's guilt being irrefutably laid at her doorstep—Mary had taken her mind down quite another path entirely, one strewn with roadblocks set up to catch the sleuthing Lord Rule unawares and send him spinning posthaste into a water-filled ditch.

The man was more than insufferable, she had decided, with those condescending remarks about his aunt just another example of his overweening arrogance—and he was fast becoming a menace.

Oh yes, she had seen the dashing young Hussar smile and begin to approach the curricle before realizing who she was sitting up beside and beating a hasty retreat lest he run the chance of getting on Ruthless Rule's wrong side. And she had fumed impotently when three other gentlemen, two on horseback and one out driving his purple-turbaned mama, had only waved to her furtively and then scurried away—the latter gentleman nearly toppling his mama from the squabs in his haste to be off.

Lepers have more human contact, Mary thought in disgust. What is it about this fellow that sends strong men racing for cover and makes young ladies feel faint and reach for their hartshorn? Yes, she owned reluctantly, he was handsome enough to cause any number of swoons, but so far she had not seen even one enterprising miss work up sufficient nerve to so much as flutter an eyelash in his direction.

Mary smiled to herself. I must be some sort of extraordinary being—not only am I able to sit up alongside this man without suffering a hint of the vapors, but I am totally unafraid of the man or his disgusting nickname. And that presents me with a puzzle: for either everyone else is overreacting to the man's reputation and ridiculous affectations of black clothing and blacker stares, or I am contemplating the greatest folly imaginable by plotting intrigues against the most dangerous man in all of England.

And so it was that, just as Tristan was covertly peeping at Mary to assure himself once more of her guilt, Mary was, in her turn, covertly peeping at him, guilt written all over her beautiful oval-shaped face. Tristan's normally severe expression hardened into a cold mask as Mary's creamy complexion heated to a fiery red, and the two broke eye contact self-consciously to concentrate on viewing the scenery with a thoroughness that would make anyone suppose they were considering redesigning the entire park.

Now the silence became noticeably uncomfortable for both parties. Tristan watched as Mary's gloved hands folded and unfolded nervously in her lap, and he experienced a rare feeling of compassion—which he quickly squelched. They were caught up in the heavy traffic of carriages and curricles, and would be for at least another half hour, and he was not about to let this golden opportunity escape him.

"Miss Lawrence," he began, surprised to hear a hint of tenderness in his voice, "have I told you that I have recently been across to Paris?"

"Have you?" Mary commented, pushing down the urge to tell him he should have stayed there and spared London and herself his obnoxious presence. "I hear it is very gay. Sir Henry says we may travel there next spring, but I am hoping to convince him it is quite safe enough now to visit. After all, *everyone* is there."

Continuing to direct his attention to his team, which was still at a standstill behind the rusty black barouche, Rule prodded, "You have a strong desire to set foot on French soil, Miss Lawrence?"

"I have a strong desire to set foot in a French dress shop, sir," she replied frankly. "And to visit Versailles, and see all the places I have only been told about, and to be invited to one of the exclusive salons, and to have my hand kissed by a dashing Frenchman." She sighed. "I desire only what every young woman in England desires, my lord. What did *you* find to amuse you whilst in Paris? Gambling houses? Beautiful women? Intrigue?"

He almost believed her, but her question, that seemed so innocent, set his defenses at attention once again. "I was there on orders from my government, Miss Lawrence. I found nothing to admire in a country that waged such a costly war against our people."

"Oh, my lord, how rigid you are!" Mary exclaimed, momentarily forgetting the part she had decided to play. "Surely you cannot condemn an entire country, an entire people, for the ambitions of a few? Surely it is Bonaparte's thirst for power and territory that must be condemned, and not the people he ruled. After all, they suffered too. Why, look at that disastrous retreat from Moscow. I understand thousands of poor soldiers perished in the snows."

"'From the sublime to the ridiculous is but a step,'" Rule quoted quietly.

"What?"

"Bonaparte made that remark just before he deserted his troops to run back to Paris and raise another army to replace the one he squandered so carelessly in Russia," Rule told her informatively.

"How would you know that?" Mary asked, much impressed in spite of herself. "Surely you would have had to have been there to—oh my, sir, I do believe I'm beginning to place a bit more credence in the rumors I have heard about your exploits as a master spy!"

Rule's dark eyes took on a shuttered look as he recalled his infiltration into the ranks of retreating soldiers, wearing a filthy, torn uniform, his bare feet wrapped in the bloody rags he had taken from a man who had no further need for them, and remembered again how Bonaparte, before stepping back inside his closed coach, had placed a reassuring hand on his shoulder and promised to see them all again in Paris. How he had hated that man for the way he had ridden off, leaving his army to grope along toward the border without his guidance or the inspiration of his leadership.

But Tristan had done his job, and had slipped back into the trees to where his horse was waiting to carry him to safety and the first of the many couriers who would pass on the valuable information he had gleaned during the weeks he had watched Bonaparte's invincible *grand armée* degenerate into the ragged band of disease-ridden unfortunates who could conquer everything but the wrath of the Russian winter.

"I'll say it again, my lord," Mary pressed as she could see that Rule had retreated into what seemed to be an unpleasant memory, "you must have been a very proficient spy, just as it has been hinted, to have gleaned such personal conversation. Now that we are at peace again, couldn't you please satisfy my curiosity by telling me exactly what it was that made you so valuable to Sir Henry?"

"I traveled," Rule said shortly. "And I reported on what I saw. Nothing more."

"You traveled a war-torn continent, my lord," Mary pointed out, knowing she was pushing the point. "You must have been in constant peril. Yet your reputation is for being ruthless, if I may be so bold as to point that out to you. Surely a mere informant would not earn such a title?"

Rule smiled at her, giving her credit for having the courage to put into words what other people—even his two audacious cousins and outspoken aunt—had not dared to ask. "People tend to draw romantic conclusions when they hear bits and pieces of events as told to them by some of the men I met in my travels. I assure you, I did not leave a trail of bloody bodies in my wake. I only did what was necessary to keep our government apprised of pertinent facts needed to plan strategies and judge the results of those strategies."

Mary shivered deliciously. "Imagine! One incident of incorrect reporting or incomplete information could have cost thousands of lives—maybe even lost the war. How modest you are, my lord, when it was you who single-handedly guided the direction of the entire war effort. No wonder my uncle speaks so highly of you. I vow I am impressed beyond measure!"

Tristan was taken aback by Mary's unaffected enthusiasm and high praise. He was also human enough to glory a bit in her display of esteem. Perhaps he had been overreacting— seeing guilt where there were only unanswered questions—

after all, this wasn't the first time he had felt a niggle of doubt about his judgment of Mary Lawrence. She surely didn't sound like a Bonaparte sympathizer. She sounded very much like a devout patriot.

"Well," Mary was saying, with some heat, "I think it is absolutely criminal the way the War Office hasn't given you a single word of commendation, or even a cash settlement or title for all you have done. I wouldn't be in the least surprised if you weren't thoroughly disillusioned with us all—if you decided that Bonaparte was the better man after all."

She swiveled on the seat to look at him piercingly. "You aren't happy, are you, my lord, now that the war is at long last over? You must miss the excitement—I vow I would. With all that you know, it would be a simple matter for you to contact just the right people to effect Bonaparte's rescue from that pitiful island and transport him back to Paris. I'm sure the Emperor knows how to reward the people who serve him—unlike England, that bundles you off when it has no further use for you."

"You think my allegiance can be bought, Miss Lawrence?" Tristan asked dangerously, rising to the bait.

Ah, if only Jennie could be here to see her cousin finally getting his comeuppance! "Everyone has a price, my lord, whether it be in gold or by way of appealing to something deep inside that craves to be recognized," Mary nudged recklessly, glorying in her ability to finally get under this infuriating man's skin.

Rule's eyes narrowed as he stared at her. "And are you buying or selling, Miss Lawrence?"

# CHAPTER FIVE

MARY KNEW SHE HAD GONE too far. In her attempt to make him look guilty, and at the same time present herself as equally capable of treason, she had become overly ambitious—and stupidly careless.

She had meant to tease, to confuse, and to set him chasing madly after his own tail, but she hadn't planned on exposing her own neck to such an alarming degree. Lord, he looked fit to strangle her for the heartless traitor he took her to be—the scheming Bonapartist who dared suggest his loyalty could be bought.

She forced a silly giggle past her numb lips. "Whatever do you mean, my lord?" she asked, trying her utmost to look unintelligent—and only succeeding in appearing guilty as sin—"I was only funning. Far be it from me to suggest that—"

"That there are certain people who would like nothing better than to see Napoleon Bonaparte back on the throne in France, waging war against England again," Rule ended for her neatly, and with heavy sarcasm. "I don't find your assumptions amusing when they are applied to me, madam, and I can only question your reasons for broaching the subject at all."

*You* don't like it, do you? Mary shouted inwardly. Well,

how do you think I feel each time you eye me like some butterfly on a pin? Aloud, she exclaimed, throwing up her hands in disgust, "*Sacrebleu!* You have caught me out, my lord. I confess! I'm a Bonapartist loyalist, sent to England to recruit volunteers to sail to Elba. Sir Henry was just an innocent pawn in my dastardly scheme; my reason for being here was to recruit you, England's grandest spy, over to our cause. I tried my utmost, but your loyalty to your mad king has proved too strong for my frail female wiles, which, heaven knows, I have used in excess in order to bring you to your knees at my feet. Alas, I must go to my fate, beaten but unbowed. *Vive la république!*" Her speech concluded, Mary folded her arms and awaited further developments, secretly wondering if association with this overzealous patriot had seriously unhinged her mind.

The silence that followed Mary's impassioned confession lasted until Rule had steered his curricle back out onto the street and relative privacy—and beyond. Once they had turned into the roadway fronting Sir Henry's residence, Rule commented, his voice sounding quite weary, "I have been playing the spy too long, Miss Lawrence, and have begun to see danger where none exists. Please accept my deepest apologies for ever having suspected you of any crime against England. It's obvious to me now that my aunt has told you of my conversation with her. I can understand now why you have gone out of your way to convince me of your guilt— waving so frantically at that poor hairdresser, for instance. It was meant to show just how ludicrous my assumptions were."

"Congratulations, my lord," Mary allowed, but not too graciously. "And here Rachel gave me the impression that you had to be hit on the head—repeatedly—with a heavy red brick before you could be convinced of anything other than your own judgments. But I own myself astonished. Do you seriously mean you no longer view me as a member of a group plotting to free Bonaparte? You actually see me as innocent?"

Rule's spine straightened slightly. "You're no spy, Miss Lawrence, but you're not quite an innocent either. There's some mystery about you, I'd swear to that, but whatever it is, it's no business of mine—at least it won't be once I've convinced myself that you present no harm to Sir Henry or Rachel, or my cousins, who have befriended you for some reason."

"Like a dog with a bone, aren't you?" Mary sniffed, alighting from the curricle before Tristan could make a move to help her. "If I'm not a spy, I must be something else equally distasteful. Well, you know what, Lord High and Mighty Rule, you can just take your silly suspicions and your nasty little assumptions—and *stuff them in your hat!*"

After emphatically nodding her head, as if to put a period to their discussion—and their relationship—Mary whirled away to ascend the steps to the house. But she turned at the top of the short flight to make one last statement—or threat: "And don't ever suppose I will stand up with you on the dance floor, for if you approach me I shall surely go into strong hysterics and kick you firmly in the shins!"

The heavy door slammed on the sight of her departing back as Tristan sat where he was, rubbing his chin in deep thought. She was a real termagant, this Miss Mary Lawrence, or whoever she really was.

Because of her, he found himself having to rethink his conclusions for the first time in a very long time—a prospect that cheered him far more than he expected. He wasn't exactly sure of just what the future held for the lady and himself, but one thing he knew for certain—she hadn't seen the last of him, not by a long chalk.

After all, there was still that tingle to consider…and now

this strange *itch*...an itch that had begun to tantalize him as he watched Mary's trimly rounded bottom jiggling provocatively as she flounced away from him and up the steps.

IT WAS THE SEVENTH HEAVEN of the fashionable world, Almack's in the late spring of 1814, but to Tristan Rule it was a punishment worse than being forced by his fond mama at the tender age of twelve to stand up during a country dance with his cousin Lucy and be *oohed* and *aahed* at by a host of smiling relatives. Already he could see Lady Jersey measuring him from between narrowed eyelids, wondering whether or not she could coerce, bully, or otherwise persuade him into partnering any of the limp wallflowers that seemed to consider Almack's their own private hothouse.

But there was nothing else for it—as it was Wednesday, and if he were to seek *her* out this evening, Almack's was the logical place to start. Not that he planned to single her out for anything as ridiculous as the Scottish reel now in progress, even if the celebrated violinist, Niel Gow, was the one sawing away on the strings. He winced involuntarily as Lord Worcester whirled by with Lady Harriett Butler, the two of them panting and sweating like dray horses after a long run.

The things I won't do for my country, Tristan thought to himself as he pushed his lean body away from the pillar he had been reclining against and began another seemingly leisurely stroll around the rooms, his dark eyes searching—ever searching—for a sight of Mary Lawrence.

It was nearing the hour of eleven when at last his vigilance was rewarded and he espied his Aunt Rachel entering the vestibule, her tardy charge in tow. Mary was in looks tonight as, he reminded himself with a snicker of self-derision, she was every night, drat the infuriating chit anyhow. After disposing of her shimmering taffeta cloak, now being lovingly carried away by one of the stewards, Mary turned to face the ballroom and gave the assembled guests their first glimpse of her ivory-colored gown (that complemented her gleaming ivory shoulders and half-exposed bosom perfectly, Tristan could not help but notice). The entire bodice of the gown, along with at least ten inches of the hem and demitrain, were lavishly sprinkled with diamante dewdrops that winked and glistened with every move she made, every breath she took.

Twinkling diamonds lent an extra sparkle to her dark curls and glittered in her ears—even her dainty slippers were adorned with brilliant diamante bows. On another woman the abundance of sparkle would have appeared overdone, even slightly vulgar, but Mary carried it off beautifully. All around him Tristan heard the indrawn breaths of jealous debutantes and the hissing whispers of their disgruntled mamas, while the comments of the gentlemen within earshot only served to start a fire in Lord Rule's blood that had little to do with his zealous interest in the welfare of his homeland.

He was drawn to Mary's side almost without realizing he had moved, and the dozen or so hopeful swains who harbored plans of their own concerning Miss Lawrence hastily stepped off in other directions, unwilling to challenge Ruthless Rule's claim to the Incomparable for the country dance just forming.

The sparkle of Mary's attire dimmed beside the hard glitter now in her huge green eyes. After the way they had parted only that afternoon—and most especially after she had issued her threat to physically assault him if he ever dared approach her again—she had wondered about this meeting, even fantasized about it a bit, picturing the arrogant Lord Rule hopping about some ballroom in his elegant black dress, looking for all the world like a huge crow flapping its wings as he favored his injured shin.

But now reality, in the form of that infuriating man himself, was staring her straight in the eye, daring her to make cakes out of both of them within the most hallowed, and most prestigious, walls of Almack's. Almack's—the holy grail of young English womanhood, ever longed for, prayed over, dreamed about, and once attained, cherished close to her bosom forevermore. Damn his devious soul! she cried inwardly—he knows I can't make a scene here. He knows it and is standing there smirking at me, laughing at me, because once again he has won and I have lost.

But then Mary remembered her plans for this evening, plans she had somehow been reluctant to cancel even after Rule's admission that afternoon that he no longer considered her to be a French spy. Why not? she thought as she swallowed down hard on her ride and smiled at her worst enemy, holding out one French kid-encased hand to accept his invitation to join the other young couples on the floor.

As Tristan smiled at her knowingly, being human enough to savor the moment of his triumph—and male enough to be so foolish as to show it—Mary's gloved fingertips bit hurtingly into his forearm, reminding him once more that this particular kitten, although she looked so outwardly soft and cuddly, was not averse to using her claws. He may have satisfied himself that she was not the person he had been told to seek—the English connection in a Continent-wide plot to free Napoleon—but she was still an unanswered question in his mind. And Tristan didn't like unanswered questions. For all he knew, she could be twice as dangerous as the conspirator he sought, both to his friend and mentor Sir Henry and his cousins Lucy and Jennie.

Yes, he told himself as they parted momentarily due to the movements of the dance, he mustn't allow Miss Lawrence's obvious beauty and charm to blind him to the very real fact that now he had not one, but *two* problems. He held out his hand to Mary, leading her into the next movement of the dance even as he assessed her yet again, looking for clues he was not certain he would recognize even if they were pushed into his face, and wished once more for the simplicity of war, where your enemies were so much easier to spot. "You are, as usual, in fine looks this evening, Miss Lawrence," he baited her as they rubbed shoulders lightly before moving on, "and that heightened color in your cheeks is most flattering."

I believe I just might murder that man, Mary mused satisfyingly as she whirled out of earshot for a moment. "I do confess to feeling a bit of excitement, sir," she owned sweetly as they faced each other yet again. "I had heard so much about Almack's, you know, but the reality far exceeds the dream. Did you ever see so many exalted personages in one place at one time? I vow I am impressed!"

"You impress easily, Miss Lawrence," Tristan responded, taking her elbow as the dance drew to its conclusion and guiding her to a pair of chairs at the side of the room.

Mary looked up at him, her head tilted prettily to one side. "Oh, I doubt that, my lord, else I would be in a constant swoon at being so openly pursued by the famous Lord Rule. As it is, I cannot be more unmoved by the prospect. Do you think I am unnatural, my lord?"

Tristan sat himself down beside her, looking off into the distance as he did, and sending shivers down the spine of no less than seven gentlemen who had rashly decided to ask Miss Lawrence for the next dance. "We have already established the fact that you don't like me above half, Miss Lawrence. Do you really find it necessary to belabor the point?"

"I do, since you refuse to take the hint and *go away!*" Mary was pushed to exclaim before carefully busying herself playing with the silken tassel at the end of her fan. "Aunt Rachel said you always were a bit *thick,* but even an absolute dolt would have cut rope by now. What do you want from me, what assurance of innocence will it take, before you realize that you are wasting your time dreaming up intrigues in which I play a part?"

Turning his dark head slowly in her direction, Tristan said in a low, steely voice: "Tell me your name."

The previously folded fan unfurled and began beating the air in front of Mary's flushed face. "You are being absurd, sir, yet again," she pointed out with what she hoped was amusement. "You know my name."

"I know the name you go by, the one Sir Henry chose for you when first he established you in Sussex ten years ago, but I seriously doubt that Mary Lawrence—that simple, unassuming appellation—comes within a dozen miles of being the one that appears on some parish records somewhere."

The fan was beginning to stir up a mighty breeze. "My, haven't you been the busy one," Mary remarked, all humor gone from her voice. "Hot-footed it down to Sussex, did you, to see what dirt you could dig up at my expense? And what else, pray tell, did you find?"

Tristan leaned back on the uncomfortable chair and recited informatively: "You were an apt pupil in penmanship and the use of maps, although you persisted in drawing Italy to look more like a riding boot than your governess thought permissible. You despised needlework although your sampler was more than passable in my opinion. As a horsewoman you have few equals, even if you earned the undying animosity of several of the local gentry by running your horse across the trail of the fox in a deliberate attempt to save the poor hunted creature."

Mary smiled a bit at the remembrance of that little bit of foolishness, but then her indignation returned. "And that is all, my lord? Surely you have left out the time I poured honey down Miss Penelope Blakestone's bodice at a picnic

because she was making sheep's eyes at young Jeremy Stone
when she knew full well that I was deep in love with him myself."

"You were thirteen at the time, so I disregarded it," Tristan
put in smoothly, making Mary wish she had a handy pitcher
of honey hidden in her reticule at that very moment.

Closing the fan with a definite snap, Mary rose to her feet,
causing Tristan to scramble a bit as he strove to unwind his
long legs and follow suit. "You are a rude, snooping, mis-
chief-making *monster!*" Mary cried, clearly unable to carry
on any pretense that she cared not a snap for his ridiculous
investigation of her past. "How *dare* you pry into my life that
way! What earthly reason could you have given all those people when you went about snooping into something that was
never your concern? How can I ever show my face in Sussex
again after what you have done?"

"Do you want to?" Rule asked tauntingly.

Mary's eyes narrowed dangerously as she looked up into
his unrevealing face. "No, damn you, I don't want to! But
that's beside the point. I should tell Sir Henry what you are
about, that's what I should do, and then we would see just
who would be laughing, you cad."

Tristan took her elbow in a firm grip and began guiding
her over to his Aunt Rachel, who was sitting with the dowagers and looking utterly bored with the whole spectacle of
Almack's. "You'll tell Sir Henry nothing, Miss Lawrence—
you haven't done so yet, or else I should have been called
into his office for a thorough dressing down long since. It
would seem he sees you as purity itself, and protects you like
you were his own."

"Well, then? If Sir Henry, who, you'll have to agree,
knows everything about me, is not concerned or fearful of
allowing me in polite society, why can't you just accept me
as I am?"

"Sir Henry's judgment may be clouded by something or someone out of the past. I am objective. Even if you are innocent of any wrongdoing, your mere existence may give someone power over Sir Henry, power that could even force that patriotic man into actions detrimental to England. The mere fact that your 'uncle' refuses to confide in me makes me suspect something very deep and dangerous." Tristan drew Mary to a halt and turned her to him one more time. "Now are you willing to tell me your name. For Sir Henry's sake?"

"Mary, Queen of Scots!" Mary Lawrence snapped before jerking her elbow loose and completing her journey over to Rachel on her own.

IT WAS VERY LATE, and the dance floor was crowded with couples eager to wedge one more dance into the evening, when Mary, still observed by Lord Rule, walked unescorted onto one of the wide balconies outside the main room.

The small raggedly dressed man who crept stealthily out of the shadows approached the girl on quiet feet and the two exchanged a few furiously whispered words before a much-folded paper changed hands, and the man, the paper now stuffed inside his shabby coat, slid back into the shadows.

Mary was just placing one slippered foot back into the main room when Tristan Rule vaulted nimbly over the balcony railing to land on the balls of his feet in the soft underbrush that edged the small garden. Hanging back discreetly out of sight, Rule watched as the small man reappeared under a dim gas lamp, then made off down the street in the direction of Piccadilly. Waiting until he could mentally reach the count of ten, Rule then started after the man, intent on following wherever he led.

While Lord Rule, using talents he developed during long years in His Majesty's service, ducked into doorways and hid behind drainpipes as he followed the small man deep into the bowels of Jack Ketch's warren, Mary Lawrence was taking her leave of Almack's Assembly Rooms, first taking care to thank Jennie Wilde for the loan of her man Ben for the evening.

# CHAPTER SIX

MARY WAS SITTING ALONE in the breakfast room the next morning, still savoring her first victory over Ruthless Rule. Jennie had sent around a note earlier, describing Ben's elation at having eluded his pursuer after leading him a merry dance until the wee hours of the morning.

This single success had naturally led the volatile Mary into considering other relatively harmless pranks aimed at keeping Lord Rule out of sight while she tried to make the best of what was left of the Season. Already she realized one flaw in last night's plan: she should have had Ben appear much earlier in the evening, then she could have avoided their confrontation on the dance floor altogether. Ah well, as a fledgling conspirator, she couldn't believe she had done that poorly overall.

Now that she knew exactly why Tristan was dogging her—believing her very existence to be a danger to Sir Henry and the national security—she knew she could proceed without fear of her adopted uncle's censure if he should ever discover what she was about. After all, if Sir Henry had wanted Tristan to know her history, he would have told him long since. Besides, she assured herself as she buttered a second muffin, it wasn't as if she were really a danger to Sir Henry—being French was no longer considered a sin in London.

Actually, she couldn't understand Sir Henry's insistence that she hide her heritage from the world.

The matter of the plot to rescue Napoleon from Elba, the plot Tristan had told her was his reason for suspecting her in the first place, was really none of her concern. Wiser heads than hers, notably Sir Henry's, would certainly scotch any such attempts before they could be born. Napoleon was defeated, soundly and forever. After all, wasn't all London gearing up for a gigantic round of celebrations even now? Surely all London couldn't be wrong—no matter what that ridiculous Lord Rule said to the contrary.

Having eased her conscience all around, Mary was just about to rise from the table and go in search of Rachel, who had been closeted in her rooms tussling over a minor snag in the tale of her hero and heroine, just then at each other's throats over a silly misunderstanding that was throwing up boulders in the path of True Love, when she was surprised to see Dexter Rutherford enter the room, a sheepish expression on his face.

"Dexter," Mary greeted him, "I see the operation was a success. You have actually succeeded in separating yourself from Lord Rule. My congratulations to your physician, and may I please have his directions as I too am in need of his services."

Dexter stopped dead in his tracks, examining his person as if looking for signs of recent surgery, before coloring brightly and chuckling weakly. "Oh, you're funning me, aren't you? I admit to admiring Tristan—he's a capital fellow, you know—but it ain't as if I'm living in his pocket."

"That's a relief, seeing as how the man seems to be trying to live in *mine*. Having you in there too just might make me list more than a little to one side, don't you think?" Mary teased the young man before waving him into a chair. "To what do I owe the honor of this visit, or am I mistaken and it is Aunt Rachel you have come to see?"

Dexter ran a nervous finger around his suddenly too-tight cravat (a glorious creation that flattered his valet no end). "*Ac-tu-ally*," he squeaked, "it was the two of you. It seems I find myself in need of some reputable females to act as companions for a young lady I'm seeing."

Mary shook her head. "Not that I'm doubting that you have a problem, Dex, but what about Lucy or Jennie? Surely they're reputable."

The young man became fairly agitated, twisting in his chair as if he had just discovered a nettle in his breeches. "Those two—good God, as if I need those busybodies poking into my life, matchmaking, and twitting me unmercifully! No, I'm not that stupid that I'd lay my head on that block! I thought about getting m'friend Bertie Sandover's sister to help, but she's known me forever and threatened to tell Kitty everything about me—can't have that, can I?"

"Kitty?" Mary prompted, barely suppressing a giggle at the thought of the turmoil Jennie and Lucy could cause once they scented a romance in the air. Poor Dexter, he'd have to be truly desperate to let either of those ladies in on his plans.

Now Dexter's complexion turned a deep, fiery red. "Kitty Toland," he gushed, lowering his head. "She's only seventeen and the most beautiful woman in England—in the entire world! Her brother, Jerome Toland, is not averse to my suit, you understand, but he says Kitty must only see me if she is accompanied by trustworthy companions. I thought and thought, and at last I came up with you and Rachel."

"Any port in a storm, eh, Dexter?" Mary could not help but tease, enjoying herself more than a little bit at the young man's expense.

Dexter's expression became pained as he realized he had really put his foot in it—again. Why was it that he had inherited none of the suave, debonair talents of his cousin Julian? "I know I'm saying this badly—it's a habit of mine, you know—but you know what it is, it's that I think I'm in love. Never thought it would happen—kind of damps you, actually, but there it is, and I confess I'm not really sure how to do anything anymore."

Mary rose and walked around the table to place a commiserating arm around the young man's shoulders. "Ah, poor Dexter. What a beast I am for teasing you when you're so obviously in torment. Of course Rachel and I will help you however we can. Why don't we adjourn to the morning room and you can tell me all about your Kitty Toland. Such a pretty name, Kitty."

"*Ac-tu-ally,* it's Catherine." Dexter informed her as they walked arm in arm down the corridor to the morning room. Once there he proceeded to tell her more—definitely more than Mary decided she *ac-tu-ally* cared to know—about this paragon of a female who had snared his bachelor heart.

Beside her youth, Kitty was the very worst sort of female for Dexter to have come across, for she was also a Total Innocent. The young Lothario was well and truly smitten, and had been from the moment his roving eye first encountered the shy, blond beauty from Cornwall.

"She doesn't know *anything,* Mary, nothing at all. It's like setting a baby loose in a stable full of stallions to see her surrounded by all the dandies and rakes who'd like nothing more than to ruin her. She has little fortune, you understand, and for some reason that seems to make her fair game for all the randy—er—well, never mind," he ended hurriedly.

"That's all right, Dex, I believe I understand," Mary said, easing his discomfiture. "Rachel, hinting broadly of my *vast* dowry—compliments of Sir Henry—scotched any such ideas by some of the more pressing of my admirers early in the Season. Now I am only beset by penniless fortune hunters, but then no one can have every little wrinkle smoothed out for them, can they?"

"Jerome is trying so very hard, too," Dexter pressed on, clearly thinking in one track and not even bothering to comment on Mary's problem. "He's her guardian, you know, the parents having died of some disease caught from putrid drains, or something. They're shockingly to let, which is why Jerome's run of luck at one of the private gaming hells was so fortuitous. Instead of then gambling or wenching—sorry, Mary—it all away, he hied himself straight to Cornwall to bring Kitty to town and launch her so that she could find herself a proper husband." He turned to look at Mary intently. "It would be a bleeding waste to give her to some bumpkin farmer, really it would. She's a jewel—a diamond of the first water—truly she is. I can only marvel that she likes me even a little bit."

"I must meet this paragon," Mary mused, almost to herself.

"Oh! How happy I am that you say so," Dexter fairly shouted, hopping to his feet. "I'll bring her round this afternoon so that the three of you can get acquainted. You'll love her," he promised, already sprinting toward the hallway, "you'll absolutely *adore* her!"

Mary laid her head against the back of the chair, smiling broadly. "*Absolutely*, you lovesick looby." She chuckled happily before rising to seek out Rachel and tell her of their expected visitor. "After all, why should Jennie and Lucy have all the fun?"

WHILE MARY AND RACHEL were giggling like schoolgirls over the thought of a smitten Dexter waxing poetic over a beautiful child from the wilds of Cornwall, Tristan Rule was just rising from the bed he had lain in only a few, frustrating hours. What a profitless evening his had been—chasing through the slimy gutters and over the sooty rooftops of the worst section of London in pursuit of some crafty jackanapes who had had the temerity to elude him in the end.

Had Mary been passing instructions to the man—or had the man been collecting payment in exchange for his silence? Was Mary a conspirator, or the victim of blackmail? Oh, his head ached from all the questions that were rattling around inside, none of them with easy answers. If only Sir Henry were willing to take him into his confidence. Already he had wasted precious time believing Mary to be a French spy, giving the true conspirator free rein to continue with his plans.

Now that he knew she was not involved with the plan to free Napoleon, Rule felt real relief, but discovering that Mary Lawrence didn't exist until ten years ago had opened up an entirely new, different, kettle of fish that didn't smell that much better than the last one. There was something particularly distasteful, even dangerous, about Mary's past, something so volatile that Sir Henry, who had never hidden anything from Tristan before, was insisting on playing all his cards very close to his chest.

If someone besides Tristan, someone with either blackmail or treason on his mind, discovered even the little bit that Tristan had unearthed on his quick journey into Sussex, there was no end to the amount of trouble Mary Lawrence's presence in Sir Henry's house could mean for England.

Throwing back the tangled covers, Rule leaped to his feet and stomped over to the washstand to pour a pitcher of cold water over his tousled black locks. Rising from his punishment sputtering and shivering, shaking his head like a dog coming out of an icy stream, he rang for his man and then grabbed up his robe, tying the silken sash around his waist with a vengeance. "Damn that green-eyed minx for not trusting me!" he swore to the room at large, flinging himself into a chair, his black stare serving to unnerve his valet more than a little bit as that man entered the room, a steaming cup of coffee balanced before him on a silver tray.

"Women!" Tristan sputtered, eyeing his man as if daring him to say something, anything, in that gender's defense.

"Indeed, m'lord." The servant gulped, already backing toward the door. "An' sure Oi am that we'd all be the better fer it if we could but live widout 'em."

"*I can,*" Tristan gritted before taking a large gulp of the too-hot coffee. "Damn it all anyway—I *will!*"

# CHAPTER SEVEN

ON THE THIRTIETH OF MAY the first Peace of Paris was signed in that city, giving yet another excuse to the celebration-mad populace of London to don their finery and make absolute cakes of themselves by eating, dancing and imbibing to the top of their bent and beyond.

One of the more sedate parties, a modest Venetian breakfast for no more than six hundred of the host and hostess's closest and dearest friends, was held near Richmond Park. That this breakfast did not commence until three in the afternoon, and was not expected to wind to a close much before the wee hours of the morning, meant little. The mood of the invited guests was jovial, even jubilant, the seemingly endless supply of strong drink notwithstanding.

Mary was in attendance, accompanied by Miss Kitty Toland, whom she and Rachel had agreed to chaperon, a circumstance that meant that Dexter Rutherford was also a member of their party. Indeed, as Mary had whispered to Rachel a few moments earlier in the carriage, it would have taken one of Congreve's rockets being strapped to his hindquarters and the fuse lit to blast Dexter away from his ladylove.

But then it was nice to have a gentleman in their party, since it was he who took charge of matters such as securing a comfortable, shady spot under a tree and then chasing after servants to secure some nourishment before they all wilted from hunger. Not that Mary would have had too much trouble convincing one of her flirts to play fetch and carry for her, but it had become so fatiguing to have to explain her association with the dangerous Tristan Rule to her apprehensive swains that she was just as glad not to have to go to the bother.

She had hoped that Rule's absence from her side for the past four days had scotched all those rumors she knew to be flying fast and furious about the *ton,* but she hadn't counted on the lack of starch her beaux had evinced when faced with the prospect of being thought to be poaching on Ruthless Rule's preserves. "It's like I have a sign hanging from my back that says 'Private Property—Trespassers Beware,'" Mary had complained to Rachel more times than that weary woman wished to remember, "and I don't know who angers me most—that dratted man or the silly fools who act as if he were some sort of furious Greek god who just might start hurling lightning bolts at them or something if they dare to cross him."

Even more infuriating, at least to Mary's mind, was the fact that she actually had found herself *looking* for the pesky man, and wondering just where he was that he had left off spending his time making her life as miserable as possible. Sir Henry had mentioned something or other that hinted of Rule being out and about the King's business, but no amount of prompting could nudge the older man into saying a thing more. "Probably out minding mice at crosswalks or some such important task," Mary had said, sniffing inelegantly, causing her guardian no end of amusement.

Whatever the reason for his absence, Mary was left to punish herself with the knowledge that it had left a large hole in her life—one that she would have sworn she craved more than a personal invitation to Carleton House to meet the Czar's sister, the Grand Duchess Catherine of Oldenburg. In fact, she thought, blushing yet again as she reclined in a studied pose beneath a leafy tree, she had been thinking altogether too much about Tristan Rule—about his dark good looks, his intense black eyes, the barely leashed power hidden beneath the stark black he chose to wear, his lips, cool and firm against hers for the length of a kiss stolen in the moonlight.

And that was the worst—that she couldn't help remembering that kiss, that deliberate insult that had seemed to amuse him as much as it still haunted her. How could she be attracted to a man who thought she was capable of destroying Sir Henry—indeed, all of England, if she truly believed his ridiculous claims! What perverse imp of nature had so constructed a woman that she could thoroughly loathe a man and at the same time search her horizons constantly just for the sight of his disdainful, condemning face?

Mary shook her head dismissingly and determinedly set out to change the flow of her thoughts, choosing to observe Kitty Toland and Dexter Rutherford as they sat yards apart on the blanket a servant had spread and stared at each other with blissfully vacant eyes. Try as she could, Mary could not see the attraction, either Kitty's for Dexter or his for her.

Not that Kitty wasn't a pretty girl, for she was; all pink and blond and still carrying a bit of nursery plumpness, with china-blue eyes that had a tendency to stare unwaveringly at nothing in particular in a way Mary couldn't force herself to believe reflected any great intelligence. Besides, the girl had a lamentable habit of saying, *"Oh, Gemini!"* before nearly every sentence she uttered, until Rachel had run posthaste to her rooms, inspiration for yet another character for her novel taking the form of a hare-witted debutante who spoke only in exclamations.

Dexter, for his part, wasn't exactly the sort from which storybook heroes were made. He was neither bold, nor dashing, and his conversation certainly couldn't rival anything written by the Bard, but when it came to portraying the sillier side of being struck with one of Cupid's tiny darts, Dex bore off the palm. Soulful sighs, yearning looks and garbled speech may not have been designed to set Mary's heart to pitter-pattering, but they seem to have turned the trick for Dexter when it came to winning the adoration of his Kitty. It was, Mary had informed Rachel the previous evening after the two of them had spent long, trying hours watching the two lovebirds coo at each other unintelligibly, as if some kind spirit had seen two halves of the same whole and quickly arranged for the two adorable nincompoops to find each other and become one great, amorous ninny, sure to populate the next generation with yet another set of incompetents in search of mates.

"Want an apple, Miss Toland?" Dex asked just then, if only to prove Mary's point.

"Oh, Gemini, I would like one above all things," Kitty simpered, her blushing cheeks looking like fine, ripe apples themselves. "But, oh, Gemini, how ever could I, when it is wearing that awful peel?"

Puffing out his thin chest just as if he had been asked to slay yon dragon to prove his love, Dex then fairly scrambled toward the large picnic hamper before the hovering servant could efficiently pare away the peel on a shiny apple he had already snatched up in preparation of being asked to perform just such a service, and wrestled both knife and apple from the poor young fellow. "It would be a pleasure, an *honor,* to remove this offensive covering so that you should not injure those fair lips and those delicate white teeth," Dexter vowed fervently as Mary and the dumbstruck servant desperately tried to look anywhere but at the young swain as he proceeded to mutilate the innocent fruit, putting his left thumb in imminent danger of being peeled as well.

"No accounting for tastes, is there?" Rachel offered, having approached the scene while Mary was otherwise occupied and was just then sitting herself down on the chair another servant had secured for her. "I had to discard my idea of patterning a character after the girl, though. After I had her say hello, I found she had precious little additional to add to the conversation. I didn't realize how difficult it is to find inconsequential things to say—do you think that means I'm a blue-stocking? Perhaps that's why I've been left so firmly on the shelf all these years."

"You're bright blue through and through, Aunt," Mary confirmed, then added, "but your mind is not what has kept you from the altar. It's your foolish pride that keeps you and Sir Henry from making a match of things. Isn't it time you forgave him for a young man's indiscretion?"

Rachel looked at her charge, her confusion easy to read in her face. "Henry's indiscretion? Whatever are you jabbering about? It wasn't Henry who destroyed our engagement. It was *my* indis—" Rachel's voice broke off suddenly as she realized what she had been about to say.

Perhaps the sun was too warm on her head, Mary thought as she reached to retrieve the bonnet she had discarded earlier. How could she have been so mistaken? From the few slips Sir Henry had made in her presence, she felt sure that he was the one responsible for the termination of the engagement just a week before the wedding. But now Rachel was saying Sir Henry was the injured party and she the one who had done something to cause the breach. "Forgive me for being so presumptuous, especially with a woman who is supposed to be my mentor of sorts," Mary apologized with a singular lack of contriteness, "but I do believe the time has come for you and my so-intelligent uncle to sit down together and go over the particulars of your estrangement in a bit more detail. Somebody seems to have scrambled the facts a bit, if I'm right."

"I don't care for a sad rehashing of long-ago sins, Mary," Rachel replied almost regally. "I have done my penance by donning my caps and playing the loving aunt to a series of nieces and nephews as they found their way into the world and beyond the need of my care. Why, seeing Lucy safely raised and launched was more than enough atonement for a dozen sins worse than my fleeting infatuation with Lord Hether—er—Mary! Isn't that Tristan over there, beside the buffet table?"

Rachel's impulsive confession was enough to keep Mary's attention riveted to her even if Mother Nature had at that moment decided to shower the assembled guests with hail the size of oranges, but nothing could keep her attentive once Tristan's name was mentioned. "Where?" she asked, already craning her neck in the direction Rachel had named. "Oh, drat, there he is, looking booted and spurred and ready to ride, as usual." Realizing she was looking more than a little interested in the man, she quickly busied herself retying her bonnet strings, asking Rachel in a whisper, "Is he looking this way? Does he see me? Don't wave to him, maybe he'll go away. How do I look? Drat this hot sun, I vow I look as wilted as yesterday's flowers."

Rachel could barely hide her smile as she watched Mary lost in uncharacteristic confusion, and silently congratulated herself at settling both her current charge and her troublesome nephew with so little fuss. Oh, Lucy and Jennie would doubtless take all the credit for the match, but that didn't bother Rachel. She only wished to have everyone neatly established so that she could leave London as soon as possible. Her plan to live quietly in the city had been foolish, she saw now, but who could have foreseen Henry coming to beg a favor of her after the way she had disgraced him all those years ago? She hadn't written a word of her novel since going to live in Henry's house—was only using the novel as the camouflage she would need once Mary was safely married and her past buried once and for all beneath her new husband's name—but Henry wasn't to know that. Just as he wasn't to know that she still loved him with every fiber of her being—for as much good that would do her when she was scribbling away in some cottage at the back of beyond.

What Rachel knew she definitely didn't need was to have Mary sticking her inquisitive little nose into affairs that were none of her business. If she had kept her past indiscretions a secret from Lucy and Jennie—and especially from Tristan—all these years, she was not about to allow Mary to stir up all that old heartache now! Thank heavens for Tristan, Rachel rejoiced silently, marveling as she did so that she would ever have reason to thank Tristan for anything, for he would keep Mary too busy for any dangerous snooping. So thinking, Rachel decided to give the struggling romance a bit of a nudge. "Does he see us, you ask?" she answered Mary just as that young woman was about to take another covert peek herself. "Why, yes, if that marvelous smile is any indication, I do believe he has. My goodness, do I mistake my man? I almost believe Tristan to actually have a certain *spring* to his step as he makes his way to us."

"He's probably just come from turning two hapless souls over to the high executioner for speaking French in a public place. Just the sort of thing to cheer him up, I do believe," Mary snapped, but her words held no real sting.

"Oh, Mary, you mustn't refine too long on Tristan's little follies," Rachel interposed, trying to calm the waters before this meeting between the two ended in yet another useless confrontation. "He has apologized for believing you part of that French plot—besides, Henry told me just this morning that they have captured three men who supposedly were working to raise funds for a ship to sail to Elba. Why, that may explain Tristan's absence these last days, don't you think?" But before Mary, whose head had come up with a jerk at Rachel's words, could answer, the older woman gave a very uncharacteristic shriek. "Oh, Lord, Tristan! *No!*"

Mary looked first to her companion and then, with some shock, toward the buffet table, where she had last seen Tristan, looking so dangerously handsome. But he wasn't there. He was running full tilt to place himself in front of the runaway curricle being dragged along behind a pair of wild-eyed stallions before it could cut a path of death and destruction through the throng of assembled guests.

TRISTAN HAD RIDDEN HARD most of the night in order to get back to London, the three conspirators he had run to ground in a hedgerow tavern near Maidstone having been handed over to the trustworthy agents Sir Henry had so fortuitously supplied.

His haste was hard to explain, even to himself, considering his oft-spoken distaste for silly affairs like this Venetian breakfast, but he knew Mary was to be in attendance and that thought served as the spur that had sent him galloping along the moonlit paths that led to the city. It was juvenile really, this burning desire to report the success of his mission to Mary in person, but he could not help but harbor the hope that the arrest he had made would put him back in Mary's good graces—if indeed he was ever there in the first place. At least she would be made to see that he had not entirely been hunting out mare's nests when he was investigating her background. After all, there *had* been a plot to free Napoleon, and the arrests proved it.

Of course, there was still that little matter of her true identity—and Rule's fear that she presented a danger to Sir Henry if there was even a trace of scandal in her past. Tristan wasn't about to turn a blind eye to that possibility, no matter how uncomfortable he felt about his earlier, erroneous assumption that Mary Lawrence could be in the pay of some French conspirators.

No, he remained adamant in his determination to uncover whatever secret Mary and Sir Henry were so steadfastly protecting, but he had used his hours on horseback the previous night to rethink his tactics. He would pretend he had given up the investigation and concentrate on courting Mary, winning his way into her good graces. He would do this to protect national security, he had told himself then, just as he tried to tell himself again at that moment—that electrifying moment when he had looked across the expanse of green lawn and felt his heart do a strange little leap in his chest as he caught sight of her sitting beneath the shade of an old tree, looking the picture of beauty, youth and innocence.

All his weariness had disappeared in an instant, and he had felt his usually expressionless features soften involuntarily into a wide, unaffected smile as his feet had immediately began propelling him along the straightest path to her side. He couldn't wait to tell Mary about his exploits of the previous evening—just like a small boy proudly showing off his first racing cup to his parents.

He had taken no more than a half dozen steps, and was just raising a hand to wave to his aunt, when he sensed rather than saw that something was wrong. Swinging to his right, he espied the driverless curricle careening down the lengthy incline, two heaving, foam-flecked horses galloping ahead of it in the shafts.

The peaceful scene was shattered within an instant. Where moments ago happy groups had either been strolling arm in arm over the closely clipped lawns or reclining at their ease at the base of shade-giving trees, there was now the sharp,

sickening smell of panic—the sight of fashionably clad ladies and top-o'-the-trees gentlemen scurrying like colorful
ants to and fro searching for cover, the sound of high-pitched
screams and baritone curses.

But Tristan saw none of this, heard none of this. Immediately his senses were concentrated on the horses and the
curricle that bounced behind it in imminent danger of over-
turning. His muscles tautened, preparing for action, and his
heart began to beat more rapidly, sending his heated blood
pulsing through his veins as he quickly calculated his options, weighed his alternatives.

Darting a quick glance behind him, he saw that the fleeing guests had somehow created an area of open ground that
led straight to the small, ornamental pond that lay at almost
a right angle to the course the horses were taking. His dark
eyes narrowing, Tristan's agile brain rapidly mapped a possible course of action to intercept the rampaging horses before they could get past him.

He ran swiftly, surely, to the spot he had chosen, sparing
only a second to glance in Mary's direction, silently praying
that she and his aunt had had the good sense to position
themselves behind a tree. They had—a white-faced Rachel
holding on fiercely to Mary, who seemed to be struggling to
be free, while Dexter stood staunchly in front of some blond
creature who was just then sobbing into his coat sleeve.

Then the thunder of galloping hooves and the loud clat-
ter of the rapidly disintegrating curricle commanded his full
attention, and Tristan spread his legs slightly for balance,
flexed his knees, and extended his arms in front of him, his
hands open, his fingers tensed, waiting…waiting…

He could smell the hot breath of the horse nearest him,
see clearly the white of one of its rolling eyes, feel the sharp
flick of its mane against his hands.

*Now!* his brain screamed. *Now!*

MARY BROKE FREE of Rachel's clinging hands and was just about to run toward Tristan when he reached out with both his strong, tanned hands—with those long, lean fingers she had told herself fitted his reputation for ruthlessness so perfectly—and grabbed two handfuls of mane, while at the same time leaping into the air, to end up landing himself neatly astride the horse's back.

"He's going to try for the leads!" Mary screamed to Rachel, who had hidden her head in her hands. "Oh, Tristan, be careful!"

Mary saw Tristan's head lying flush against the horse's neck as he reached across the space separating the two horses and made a grab for the other's halter. Then the curricle was past her, still traveling at a furious pace, but now being directed by Ruthless Rule, who had somehow gained control of the leads.

The horses changed direction, heading toward the pond that sat about two hundred yards away on the left. Mary ran along behind, her skirts lifted immodestly as she willingly sacrificed propriety for speed. It wasn't over yet, she knew, although she silently agreed with Rule that running the horses into the pond was the best chance he had of stopping them before any more damage was done.

Please let him be all right, the reckless fool! She begged any deities that may have been listening, then shook her head at the ridiculousness of her thoughts. Ruthless Rule—Reckless Fool—they even rhymed! Oh, whatever possessed the man, to have him taking such unthinking chances with his life? And what sort of brainless ninny am I to have even entertained the thought of going to his rescue before his masculine tendency to act the hero got him trampled into the dust? Anyone would think I'd cared one way or the other about the man!

Not that these unpleasant thoughts slowed Mary's pace—

she continued to race full tilt toward the pond, where she had seen a large splash just scant seconds earlier. By the time she reached the banks of the water the runaway horses were standing with their heads down in the shafts, their flanks still shuddering as they seemed to be trying to understand just what had happened to them.

Where was Rule? The curricle, which had once been a glorious equipage painted in scarlet with gold trim, lay on its side, half submerged in the pond, and Mary's fearful heart skipped a beat as she pictured Tristan pinned beneath the surface by one of the curricle's wheels.

She was just about to plunge her own body into the water when the surface of the pond was broken by Tristan's dark head and broad shoulders, as he rose to his feet to stand more than waist deep in the water, his attention fixed on releasing the exhausted horses from the shafts.

"Did you see that?" Dexter Rutherford fairly shouted in Mary's ear as he came up beside her, his awestruck gaze stuck fast to the sight of his hero. "What a first-rate sight that was! Puts those devil-dares at Astley's Circus to the blush, that's what it does. Isn't Tris a prime one, Miss Lawrence? Oh, I wouldn't have missed this for the world!"

By now Mary and Dexter were only a small part of a much larger audience. From all sides came the multitude of guests and scores of servants, all chattering, applauding, and generally acting as if Tristan Rule had single-handedly saved their lives—which he may very well have done. Several young bucks were sufficiently enthused as to plunge Hessians-first into the water, bent on helping the man of the hour lead the team of horses back to shore.

Mary watched Rule closely as his long strides cut waves through the water, bringing him closer to her with every step. His black hair was pasted to his head, showing off his handsome, chiseled features almost as advantageously as his clinging wet coat and pantaloons did his fine physique. Indeed, among the cheers and shouts of congratulations Mary heard more than one feminine gasp and giggle of appreciation.

For reasons Mary did not choose to investigate, this unconscious flaunting of his physical person served to touch off a spark of anger deep inside her that temporarily banished her earlier concern for his safety.

As Tristan mounted the bank to stand not three feet away from her, she tilted her determined chin toward the afternoon sun and remarked sarcastically, "Ah, if it isn't the knight errant. Good thing you left your suit of armor at home, sir, else you'd be rusted into a statue before you could enjoy all the hosannas of your many admirers."

What the deuce was the matter with the girl now? Tristan asked himself in righteous confusion. Anyone would think I stopped the curricle just to upset her. And to think I rode half the night just to open myself to more of her insults!

Bowing deeply from the waist, a move that caused one dark, wet lock of hair to fall into a roguishly becoming curl on his forehead, Tristan replied coolly, "On the contrary, Miss Lawrence. If I had worn my armor, I would not be here at all, but would still be trapped beneath the surface of the pond, the curricle riding on my back."

His dark eyes then raked her up and down as if he had weighed her up and found her sadly lacking. He took two steps before saying, "If you'll excuse me now, please? I think I shall be returning to my castle to have a tapestry commissioned commemorating my latest heraldic deed."

Then Mary was left quite alone, her mouth hanging open, as she watched Tristan being led away, Dexter's arm draped protectively about his shoulders while two dozen or more hangers-on trailed along behind.

"Never mind her, Tris," she heard Dexter say. "Women

don't understand these things like we men do. All they can think of is us getting our heads broken or something. She didn't really mean anything by it, I'm sure of it."

Mary couldn't quite hear Tristan's answer, but she certainly understood the tone. She had opened her silly mouth and put herself firmly back into Tristan Rule's black books. Now he would never see her as anything more than Sir Henry's ill-mannered ward—and as a possible threat to England's security.

He'd never see her as a woman. And that made Mary sad…it made her very sad indeed.

# CHAPTER EIGHT

"HE'S DOING THIS just to infuriate me, you know. Oh, don't shake your head, Jennie, for you know I'm right."

Jennie Wilde was hard-pressed to conceal her smile as she watched Mary flutter about the Bourne drawing room like a kite in a stiff breeze. "Inviting you to share a theater box with the Grand Duchess Catherine of Oldenburg infuriates you, Mary? And what, pray, would make you happy? Having him appear at the theater with some other young woman on his arm?"

"Yes—No! Oh, Jennie, you know what I mean. It's like that Lorenzo Dow fellow said: 'You will be damned if you do—And you will be damned if you don't.'"

"I believe the man was speaking about religion, Mary, not a festive night at Covent Garden," Jennie supplied, tongue-in-cheek. "But I cannot see how you can turn a simple invitation into something even remotely devious."

Mary flitted about a moment or two more, then came to roost on the settee across from where her friend was reclining at her ease. "The grand duchess is rewarding Tristan's courage in stopping that curricle last week—all the town knows it. Her theater box will be the cynosure of all eyes for the entire evening. And Tristan knows I would sooner shave my head and wear rags than miss such a spectacle."

"I understand what you are saying so far, Mary." Jennie nodded, picking up her knitting. "But where does the revenge come in?"

Mary rolled her eyes heavenward, unable to believe that Jennie—who was usually so awake on all suits—could be so dense. "For goodness sake, Jennie, Tristan *knows* if I appear as his companion for such a public display that everyone and his wife will have us as good as married!"

Jennie laid down her knitting to peer intently into Mary's worried green eyes. "And to think, my dear, the main presentation of the evening is to be an allegorical festival entitled 'The Grand Alliance.' My goodness, anyone would think the authors had you and Tristan in mind, rather than England and our allies." Shaking her head in mock dismay, she went on: "Perhaps you have been trotting too hard, Mary. Really, the ideas you get into your head amaze even me!"

Mary was not so self-involved that she could not see the humor in Jennie's words. Wrinkling up her pert little nose, she retorted, "Oh, pooh—I guess I am going a bit overboard, aren't I?" Then she became serious once again. "But, Jennie, I already told you how horridly I behaved to Tristan last week after he'd made his daring rescue. Surely he can't be *rewarding* me for such a terrible attack on his character? Have I told you that he has come to visit Aunt Rachel and Sir Henry nearly every day without so much as inquiring about me? Now, does that sound like the man is perishing for the sight of me—or that he would be desirous of my company? No," she answered for herself, "it does not. He knows full well how he has curtailed my social life, and he is purposely using this invitation to throw yet another damper on my fun."

"I think I'm beginning to get the headache," Jennie mused, lifting one hand to her temple.

"That's what Aunt Rachel says every time I bring up the

subject," Mary responded, shaking her head. "You all think I'm reading entirely too much into this invitation, don't you? Very well, I'll accept it. But remember this, Jennie, I do so only under duress."

"And because you wish to sit beside the grand duchess at the theater and queen it over all society for an evening," Jennie added facetiously, picking up her knitting once more. "Look at this, Mary. It's a sweater for Christopher—he looks so well in blue, you know, just like his father." Resting the half-done sweater once more in her lap, Jennie closed her eyes. "Lord, how I miss that little scrap of mischief. We're off to Bourne at the end of the week, thank goodness. I vow I don't believe I can wait to have Christopher dribbling down the front of my best gown again!"

Jennie had Mary's full attention now. "Leaving! But—but you can't! Tristan's still snooping about in my past like some Bow Street runner. I may yet need your Ben to help me throw a rub in his way."

"I've already discussed that with Kit and Lucy," Jennie told her soothingly. "Ben is to remain in London along with our grooms, Tiny and Goliath. Lucy has agreed to house them and keep them at your disposal if the need should arise."

"Tiny and Goliath?" Mary questioned. "I don't believe I've—er—had the pleasure."

Jennie grinned happily, always enjoying a conversation that had to do with the successful conclusion of one of her campaigns to find niches for every stray who crossed her path. She then gifted Mary with a full description of her valuable, if a bit outrageous grooms—a description that cheered Mary more than a little bit as she and her maid departed the Wilde town house and instructed the coachman to drive them to Bond Street and the modiste Mary knew to be capable of producing the most suitable gown for a gala evening at the theater.

To SAY THAT TRISTAN RULE WAS not enjoying his current status of hero would be reading far too much into his title of Ruthless, for Baron Rule was as human as the next man when it came to flattery.

Oh, he might have made a fine outward show of disdain and disinterest concerning the glowing reports of his bravery in the daily newspapers; he may have declined to purchase any of the flattering cartoons circulating about the city; he may even have tossed Dexter Rutherford out on his ear when that enraptured youth showed up on his doorstep dressed head to toe in black in emulation of his hero, but that did not mean he wished everyone would just forget the incident and let him get on with his life.

To be truthful, after long years spent laboring for his country in secrecy—never thinking of public reward—Tristan was finding the adulation of his peers to be comforting indeed. His reputation as Ruthless Rule added much to the stories now circulating throughout the metropolis, and Tristan found it a source of no little amusement to hear that he was personally responsible for military victories and governmental coups that would have necessarily placed him in three European capitals at the same time.

Not the least of the accolades accorded him was the personal invitation of the grand duchess to share her box at the Theatre Royal, Covent Garden on the evening of June 13. That the grand duchess was using him to draw some of the attention away from the Prince Regent, whom she cordially loathed, was not lost on Tristan, but as he also had little love for "Swellfoot," this did not dampen his enthusiasm.

The icing on the cake—although Rule would not have phrased it so—was the grand duchess's gracious inclusion of personal guests of Tristan's own choosing in the party. Even now, as he sauntered down Bond Street—out on the strut, as Dexter and his cronies would have so inelegantly put it—

Tristan could not help but smile at the look of confusion mixed with snippets of suspicion and ill-concealed delight in Mary's eyes when he first offered his invitation. Indeed, her consternation in the face of snipping off her own nose to spite her face went a long way toward Tristan's getting a little of his own back for Mary's insults the day of the Venetian breakfast.

And now, tucked securely in his waistcoat pocket, lay that same Miss Lawrence's hand-written acceptance of his invitation that had been delivered directly after luncheon. After a visit to his tailor—and a very much out-of-character interest in every aspect of the construction of a new suit of evening clothes—Tristan went on his way to a meeting with Lords Bourne and Thorpe, to ask their help in the investigation of Mary Lawrence's background.

"Here he is now, Julian," Kit called out, nudging his friend in the ribs, "the man all London has taken to its breast. How condescending of him to agree to be seen with us in public. It will do our combined consequence no little harm to be seen with the Redoubtable Rule, you know. Should we bow, do you think?"

Tristan could not help but overhear, which he was meant to do. "Redoubtable? That's one I haven't heard," he said as he fell into step with his two friends. "Julian?" he asked, turning his head to address Lord Thorpe. "Have you nothing to add—or has Kit poked enough fun at me to suffice?"

Julian Rutherford may have had more than his share of starch for a great deal of his life, but association with his madcap wife, Lucy, had made serious inroads on his hauteur. "My dear fellow," he drawled now, taking Tristan's elbow, "far be it from me to poke fun at your expense. By the by, is it true you will be performing your recent stunt twice nightly at Astley's, where the outlay of a trifling three shillings will allow all the ragtags and lowlifes to *ooh* and *aah* at your magnificence?"

By now they had walked as far as St. James's and were entering Boodle's, where they had planned to share a few bottles before the dinner hour. Tristan did not respond to Julian's teasing until they were all cozily ensconced around a table at the "dirty" end of the room, as Kit had gone riding earlier and was still clad in his buckskins. "Rumor, my friend, only rumor," he assured him. "I find myself content with putting Miss Mary Lawrence through her paces, actually. Lucy was right, Julian, inviting Miss Lawrence to make up my party for the theater has that lady jumping through the hoops quite in line with my directions."

Julian raised one finely etched eyebrow. "Lucy has been aiding and abetting again, has she? Kit, does that thought rankle with you as much as it does with me?"

Kit, who had given his permission for three of his servants to remain in town at Mary's disposal, moved uncomfortably in his seat for a moment. "Both our ladies seem to be putting their pretty noses into something that is not their business, don't they? Yet, Tris, I must tell you, I cannot be best pleased with that smirk you are wearing at the moment. Right now I believe Miss Lawrence to have been sadly betrayed—considering how she is laboring under the misapprehension that our wives are completely in her camp. Could it be that they have a plan of their own in the works?"

Julian took a sip from his wineglass. "Of course they do, my dear man. I've been hearing wedding bells ever since those two conniving females first set eyes on Tristan and Mary together on the dance floor."

Now Tristan spoke up. "No, no, Julian, you have it all wrong. Lucy is aiding me in my attempt to uncover the secrets of Miss Lawrence's past, that is all. In a way, you might say she is doing a service to her country."

Kit choked on his wine at Tristan's gullibility. "Did you hear that, Julian? Your wife's just doin' her duty. Perhaps she'll get a medal. God—to think two little slips like our wives could have succeeded in pulling the wool so firmly over our hero's eyes. Sickens a man, don't it?"

"Are you saying that Jennie and Lucy are still bent on marrying me off?" Tristan asked, a steely look coming into his eyes.

"Quick, ain't he?" Kit quipped, taking another drink.

Julian sat back against his chair, one hand to his chin as he considered the thing. On the one hand, Jennie and Lucy were helping Mary in her attempt to confuse and infuriate Tristan, while on the other hand, they were aiding and abetting Tristan in his search into Mary's past. Both ploys were only decoys—with the ladies taking dead-set aim on leading the two unsuspecting souls straight to the altar. "Kit," he said at last, kicking the legs of his chair front once more and placing his elbows firmly on the table, "I think we should do our utmost to aid Tristan in his determination to uncover Miss Lawrence's past. What do you say to allowing your servants Ben, Goliath and Tiny to remain behind with me in London after you return home to Bourne at the end of the week? That way they could be at Tristan's disposal if ever he should need them."

"But—" Kit began, knowing that he had already agreed to leave the three men behind to aid Mary. Then a slow smile played about his lips as he considered the havoc the three servants could cause if they served *both* Tristan and Mary without either of the plotters being the wiser. Oh, Julian, you're a deep one, Kit mused to himself—besides, why should the ladies have all the fun? "I agree totally, Julian," he said at last, keeping his tone as serious as he could make it. "Tristan may have need of their services in case things get sticky."

Tristan, believing things to be falling neatly into place, raised his glass in salute. "Thank you, gentlemen. I should have come to you at the first, and not relied on my scatter-witted cousins. It takes men to sort things out intelligently, doesn't it?"

Julian and Kit merely smiled and lifted their glasses.

# CHAPTER NINE

MARY WAS NOT THE FLUTTERING type, but she gave a grand imitation of that empty-headed sort of female in the days preceding the theater party. From spending three hours in front of her mirror arranging and rearranging her hair in different styles—to the frustration of her maid, who knew a hopeless case when she saw it, and Mary in a severe topknot was a hopeless sight indeed—to hounding Rachel about matters of protocol and the correct addressing of a grand duchess while seated behind her in a theater box, to badgering Sir Henry into trimming his beloved side whiskers in order to look more top-o'-the-trees, Mary was beginning to wear very thin on everyone's nerves.

Only Kitty was immune, even though she resided in the second guest chamber directly across the hall from all the hustle and bustle. For Kitty was in love, and all she needed or wanted—or, for that matter, acknowledged—in her world was one Dexter Rutherford.

It was, therefore, with great haste and breathless anticipation that she raced down the stairs and into the drawing room when Rachel told her—with an air of abstraction due to Mary's latest bout of hysterics over uneven hems—that she had a morning visitor.

Kitty skidded to a halt inside the doorway, her smile frozen on her lips, and whispered, "Oh, Gemini, it's you!"

"Not who you were expecting, am I, sis?" the puce-clad exquisite drawled as he minced across the room to take his sister's limp hand and raise it to his lips. "I hear you and that Rutherford dolt are about to make a match of it. Dare I remind you that your needs must gain my permission before launching yourself on the sea of marital bliss?"

"Oh, Gemini, Jerome, say you won't deny us!" Kitty pleaded, her large blue eyes already filling with tears. "After all, it was you who introduced Dex to me."

"And me who got you situated so cozily in this nice, deep gravy boat, if you'll recall," her brother added, taking out a scented handkerchief and lifting it to his nose. "And what I have been so magnanimous in giving I can just as easily take away—can't I, puss?"

"You—you wouldn't!" Kitty exclaimed, feeling her knees grow weak. She looked at her sibling, so alike in looks and yet so vastly different in temperament, and realized that, yes, he would. "What—what do you want, Jerome? Surely it won't be like that last time? Surely you won't ask me to *steal* for you again? Oh, Gemini, I think I'm going to faint."

Jerome pushed Kitty down into a chair and leaned over her, his hands pressed on either side of the cushions next to her head. "You're not going to faint, you silly chit, you're going to listen. I've taken care of you so far, haven't I? Now forget that little episode in Bath and concentrate on what I'm about to tell you."

Kitty listened, her hopes for a future with Dexter Rutherford by her side crumbling into dust at her feet as Jerome outlined his plans.

ACCORDING TO THE PROGRAM clutched in her nerveless fingers, the Monday evening production at Covent Garden was "in compliment to our illustrious visitors," which included Czar Alexander of Russia and King Frederick of Prussia, among others. To Mary, however, it felt as if the entire evening had been staged in order to try her endurance—not to mention her patience.

Her endurance had held up bravely under the strain, although it had made serious dents in Rachel's usually unflappable demeanor when it was discovered at the last possible minute that the flowers Rule had sent clashed badly with Mary's gown.

It was Mary's *patience* that was in sore need of reinforcement—and had been ever since Tristan showed up on the doorstep and Sir Henry announced that he and Rachel would travel together to the theater, leaving "the young couple to enjoy themselves without us old people around to throw a damper on things."

"Oh, Gemini, how romantic!" Kitty gushed, showing her first real animation in days, so that Mary could not find it in her heart to tell the silly girl that it was not romantic in the least—it was depressing.

Before her maid could settle her light shawl around her bare shoulders, for one fleeting moment Mary thought of sacrificing herself to lending comfort to Kitty, who had decided to remain at home that evening since Dexter was at the moment paying his twice-yearly duty call on his Great-Aunt Felicity in Brighton. But the feeling, never heartfelt, faded without regret when Mary caught sight of herself in the foyer mirror and realized that the stunning result of two weeks of dedication should not be left to molder away at home. It would be criminal to deprive the world of the sight of her new, soft-as-butter yellow silk gown because she objected to riding in the same coach with Tristan Rule.

But now, now as she sat in the grand duchess's theater box, awaiting that lady's arrival, Mary was having second thoughts. Besides being situated at the very rear of the box where none, save the servant handing around lemonade, could appreciate her splendor, Mary had already crossed swords with Tristan twice during the short drive—and lost to him both times.

It seemed that, while Mary had busied herself with gathering her ensemble for the evening, Tristan had been engaged in his favorite project—digging into Mary's supposedly illicit past.

They had not been in the coach above a minute before he had—by the simple means of declaring her to be five and twenty if she was a day—goaded her into telling him her correct age of eighteen. Within ten minutes he had the name of her first governess from her after twitting her that he had discovered information that led him to believe she had been left on some orphanage front doorstep with a note pinned to her nappy.

"Are you comfortable?" Tristan asked now as he seated himself beside her. "Once the grand duchess arrives, I'm sure we can secure chairs farther front, but I would not like to push myself forward now only to be asked to move to the rear."

Mary's head turned slowly, oh so slowly, in his direction, taking in his elegant dress and well-groomed appearance. "Move the hero of Richmond Park to the rear, my lord? Surely you jest! Why, I do believe there would be a riot in the pit if anyone dared do such a shabby thing."

Tristan had the good sense to drop the subject, for he knew himself not to be totally innocent of enjoying his new fame. Feigning an interest in the programme he held, he commented, "They're putting on a revival of *Richard Coeur de Lion,* with Mr. Barrymore as Blondel. Are you much impressed by historical romances of this type, Miss Lawrence, or are you looking forward to the farce *Dead Alive?*"

"I look forward to meeting the grand duchess, sir," Mary replied icily. "Nothing else could have induced me to spend even a moment in your company, as you well know." Drat it all anyway, she fumed inwardly, did he have to lean so close to her ear to speak to her? He was turning her insides to mush!

"And I would endure the grand duchess and all the crowned heads for a moment spent at *your* side," Tristan whispered into her ear, holding to his resolve to keep her confused by romancing her while persisting with his investigation of her past. The only thing that surprised him was that, although he considered his wooing to be a duty he owed his country, he was finding the project had personal rewards he had not considered, one of them being the opportunity to be close to the most beautiful creature in the theater that night. If only he could believe Mary had dressed with such care in order to impress him, he would have surprised himself by being the happiest of men—but his saner self told him otherwise.

The next few minutes passed in strained silence, Mary refusing to answer Tristan's latest sally, and as the grand duchess arrived only a moment before the musicians began tuning up their instruments, imperiously commanding Tristan and Mary to take seats on either side of her, there was no further opportunity for conversation.

Mary could now see from her clearer vantage point that the theater was full almost to overflowing, and she could barely make out Sir Henry and Aunt Rachel in a box near the stage. The royal box was full to bursting, the Prince Regent and his entourage, which included the Czar, bustling into their seats just as the curtain was drawn up to the singing of "God Save the King."

Tristan and Mary joined the chorus, as did Prinny and, to the patrons' pleasure, the czar. The sovereigns seated themselves once more and Mary was just about to follow suit when suddenly there broke out a round of shouting and applause, and the entire audience turned as one to look at the Princess of Wales's box, where Caroline, Prinny's estranged wife, was waving merrily to the crowd.

"Here we go," Tristan half whispered, and Mary saw that the grand duchess, far from being appalled, was laughing quite heartily at the Regent's dilemma.

Caroline was resplendent in diamonds and wearing a black wig—hardly flattering, but certainly eye-catching, which was most probably her intent. The czar—whom rumor said had taken to lecturing the Prince Regent on the advisability of reconciling with his wife—stood and bowed in Caroline's direction while everyone held their breath to see what would happen next.

Prinny pushed his not inconsiderable bulk to a standing position and gave a deep, graceful bow—as if acknowledging the cheering of the crowd that had lately taken to hissing him whenever he rode his closed carriage through the streets. Not once did he look in his wife's direction, and at last that woman had the good grace to sit down.

"Hummph!" The grand duchess sniffed. "We do not like him," she said quite audibly, leaving no one in confusion as to whom she meant.

Tristan, who privately thought the Regent to be a sorry sight indeed, found himself bristling at the insult. How dare the woman dislike the heir to the throne, no matter what his failings? He actually opened his mouth to defend the man, when Mary's slight negative shake of her head forestalled him.

She was right, of course. It wouldn't do to create an incident. Tristan subsided into his seat as King Richard, played by someone named Sinclair, took center stage. It was only as the presentation was drawing to a close that he realized he had deferred to Mary's judgment—something he had made it a rule never to do. Was he getting soft, losing his edge? Or, he mused ruefully, was Mary gaining some sort of power over him?

He sneaked a look in her direction as she sat forward in her chair, clearly caught up in the finale, and watched as the tip of her tongue darted out to moisten her slightly parted lips. Suddenly he wished the grand duchess, the czar, Prinny and his soiled princess, and all the rest of the world at the bottom of the deepest sea.

When the intermission was announced, he fairly catapulted himself out of his chair and over to Mary's side, requesting her company in the corridor. Without giving her a chance to decline, he prized her out of her seat by the elbow and pushed her in front of him until they had squeezed through the doorway and into the still fairly empty hallway.

"Really, sir," Mary protested, wresting her elbow out of his grasp, "you have the manners of a ruffian. You did not even tarry to inquire as to whether or not our hostess wished to accompany us."

"Hang the harridan," Tris was pushed to say, looking about quickly to locate a private bench where the two of them could talk without being overheard. "Here," he said, motioning his head toward a shallow alcove on the other side of the corridor, "come with me."

"Aren't you going to bring me some lemonade?" Mary asked once they had been seated as Tristan sat stiffly and as far away from her as the length of the bench would allow. "You're supposed to ask me if I wish some refreshments."

"Hang the refreshments!" Tristan nearly shouted, causing more than one interested head to turn in their direction. More softly, he added, "I mean, we already had some in the box, didn't we? Wasn't that enough? Besides, I want to talk to you."

"More questions, my lord?" Mary asked tightly. "Haven't you gouged enough information from me for one night?

When are you going to realize that you are chasing shadows that simply do not exist? I know my past; Sir Henry knows my past—and neither of us fears discovery will put England in danger. Really, sir, you refine too much on the ability of one frail female to—"

"And *hang* your dubious past!" Rule cut in ruthlessly. "I am more interested in your impact upon *me* at the moment!"

"My impact upon—" Mary began wonderingly, and then she raised her gloved hands slowly to her mouth as her feminine logic cut straight to the heart of the matter. "Oh, Tris, you are infatuated with me! This is famous!"

"I am not!" Tris denied hotly. "You are nothing more than yet another project I have undertaken in the best interests of my country."

Mary shook her head, her auburn curls dancing about delightfully. "Oh no, you are infatuated with me. Lucy and Jennie said you were, but I didn't believe them. Oh, those two—I must give them my congratulations, their intuitions were correct."

Tristan looked about him, hoping against hope they were not attracting a crowd. "Will you be quiet for a moment?" he nearly begged. "This is serious. I find myself doubting my own conclusions—even my motives—when it comes to you. I'm unaccustomed to doubt, as it has never plagued me before in my career. I've always been able to rely on my instincts to guide me. Now it—it's like I'm stumbling about in a dense fog, trying to feel my way." He took a deep breath and said heavily, "I'm thinking of withdrawing from public service, telling Sir Henry my services are not longer available."

Mary pressed a hand to her breast. "Because you find yourself infatuated with me?"

"Damn it, woman, I'm *not* infatuated with you!" he fairly hissed. "I must just be tired, and this last investigation has proved to be my undoing. What I need to know from you now is: if I agree to cease my investigation and retire to my estate and my badly neglected duties there, will you at least be honest with me so that I can be sure once and for all that your past presents no danger to Sir Henry?"

*Leave London? Retire to his estate?* Mary's heart did a little flip-flop in her breast at the thought. All she had to do to be rid of Tristan Rule was to tell him the truth—tell him her father had been French and that Sir Henry was worried her late father's old enemies might try to revenge themselves upon his daughter—and he would go out of her life forever.

A scant month ago this thought would have served to raise her into the boughs with delight. Now, she realized with quickening pulse, it was the very last thing she desired. He swore he wasn't infatuated with her—not that the man would know what infatuation was if it reared up and kicked him in the face—but she couldn't believe it, refused to believe it.

Look at him, she told herself, gazing tenderly into his confused, handsome face. He's so dear when he isn't scowling. For all his exploits, all his importance to the government, he is almost childlike in his experience in the real world—in *my* world. In just the same way he is learning that all is not black and white, that shades of gray exist everywhere. He is beginning to learn about the stirrings of the heart. And *I* am the first woman to have touched him romantically, for all his heart-breaking good looks and dashing reputation.

Mary began to feel the power women have always felt when they recognized the hold their frail fingers could place on a man's heart. Tell him everything now? Free him to go hide at his estate until his defenses were restored to their former iron-hard strength? She'd rather go back to Sussex and her rustic keepers!

"I repeat for the very last time, my lord," she said finally, "there is no great secret about me. I am Sir Henry's ward—no more, no less. If you wish to run away from a mere Ruthless Rule, it is not I who shall shed a tear as you ride off. But if you wish to stay, you shall have to do your own sleuthing. I shall not gift you with any clues."

So saying, she rose to return to the grand duchess's box for the farce. Just as she slipped into her chair, with Rule dutifully, if a bit belligerently, holding it steady for her, she whispered, "And you are too infatuated!"

# CHAPTER TEN

MARY WAS STILL IN a most jovial mood the morning following her visit to Covent Garden, and with good reason. The
sight of Tristan Rule in a temper, a frequent yet—as she
knew herself to be the reason for his chagrin—enjoyable
spectacle, had served to lift her spirits throughout the remainder of the theater party, and his grumbling and mumbling as
he fairly raced her home through the streets had placed the
perfect cap upon the evening.

She was flattered by his obvious infatuation with her, as
so correctly predicted by Jennie and Lucy, especially considering the fact that she had at last acknowledged her own
feelings in the matter. Tristan Rule, despite her initial protests concerning the way he had cut out all her other beaux
by his outrageous behavior, had become very dear to her.

Infuriating he might be, but he was also, as Rachel had
said, unfailingly loyal and completely sincere. Indeed,
Mary's retort to Rachel that she once had a puppy with the
same attributes came fairly close to the mark when it came
to Mary's interpretations of Rule's charms. She considered
him to be very puppylike beneath his bristly exterior, and had
decided he held the proverbial heart of gold hidden deep
within the stern, even aggressive man he showed the world.

That Mary found Tristan to be adorable—the exact word

she had used to describe him in her private journal—would have sent everyone who knew Rule into whoops of laughter. The world knew him only by the face he presented to them—a hotheaded though valuable man's man who was about as "cuddly" as a prickly pear.

Either Mary was blinded by infatuation herself, or she was far more intuitive than any woman had ever been when it came to solving the enigma of Tristan Rule—even she couldn't really be sure. She only knew that Tristan refused to acknowledge the one thing she knew to be fact: he was infatuated with her!

But infatuation was a far step from love, and Mary knew her own mind well enough to realize that it was his love that she wanted. She had been delighted by her ability to send him into a flutter with her teasing, but she knew that she'd soon catch cold if she persisted in pointing out his—as he must consider it to be—failing. And letting him see how she felt about him would be the best way to send him helter-skelter to the hinterlands and his precious estates in fear for his life.

No, the only way to keep Tristan in town long enough to convince him that he could not live without her was to continue heaping fuel on the fires of his suspicion. For that reason she had sent her maid to the Rutherford stables with a note directing Tiny and Goliath to be outside Sir Henry's kitchen door at midnight, ready to serve as her protectors while she set about laying yet another false trail for Tristan to follow.

Of course, setting false trails only worked if Tristan were aware that she was laying them, which is where Kitty came into the affair—Kitty and her devoted swain, Dexter.

Having asked a servant to tell Miss Toland that Miss Lawrence requested her company in the drawing room, Mary now sat awaiting that young lady's arrival, still trying without much luck to erase the happy smile that had been with her since Tristan's farewell at the front door the night before. He had been adorably flustered, Mary reflected now, as he stood there, so clearly torn between shaking her hand and crushing her against him in a tight embrace, that he had ended up by lifting her hand to his lips and nearly kissing his own fingers by mistake before backing down the steps to trip clumsily on the flagway as he forgot to watch where he was going. Ah, he was such a dear, she sighed, raising the back of her hand to her cheek, as if holding his kiss against herself.

"Mary? Mary! Oh, Gemini, I'm sorry! I do believe I startled you," Kitty apologized, hesitating in the doorway as if she were about to flee to her chamber in disgrace. "I'm such a bother, aren't I? My brother Jerome always says I tippity-toe on cat's feet, scaring him half out of his mind every time I come into a room."

Mary looked up to see Kitty standing in a puddle of sunshine, her pale golden hair making her resemble nothing so much as an innocent angel, and could not help but wonder to herself how the good Lord stood it, being surrounded by so much naïve sweetness. Not that she didn't like Kitty, for she did—very much—but Mary needed a bit more spice in her life, a bit more unpredictability. She smiled at her own thoughts—a bit more Tristan, she could have said.

"Nonsense, Kitty," she told the girl, patting the place beside her, encouraging Kitty to join her on the settee. "I was lost in a daydream, that's all."

Kitty nodded as if she understood, as she had been guilty of daydreaming herself, what with Dexter due back in town any moment. "It must have been above all things wonderful to be at the theater last night. Miss Gladwin told me all about it this morning over breakfast."

"Yes," Mary agreed, "it certainly was wonderful, though I still can't understand why she and Uncle Henry declined

Tristan's invitation at the last minute and chose to watch the performance from the box Uncle rented at the beginning of the Season."

Kitty blushed hotly and lowered her head. "Oh, Gemini, Mary, can't you guess? They wanted you and Tristan to be *alone*. Wasn't that sweet of them?"

Two things occurred to Mary then, the first being that she must make a point of being very nice to Sir Henry for the rest of the day. The second thought was much more selfish—as she realized she had certainly chosen her vehicle well—for Kitty Toland couldn't keep a secret if her life depended on it.

"Yes, well, Kitty," Mary said now, lowering her eyelashes a bit as she found it hard to lie directly into such an innocent, trusting face. "About Tristan—it seems I have this…er…*problem*."

Kitty leaned forward eagerly, glad to be considered worthy of Mary's confidences.

DEXTER, STILL CLAD in his travel dirt, ran Tristan to earth late that same afternoon just as the man was stepping out of Gentleman Jackson's Boxing Saloon, and rushed up to take his arm. "Tris, I have to talk to you!" Dexter imparted with uncharacteristic seriousness.

"My goodness, Dex, what nettle has gotten into your breeches?" Tristan teased, feeling much better now that he had bashed at least one of Jackson's underlings in his effort to work out the frustrations caused by yet another long, sleepless night. "Don't tell me you and your little Incomparable are having troubles—and don't think you are about to recommence being my shadow if you are no longer to be playing the lovebird. People were beginning to talk, you know, and I have enough on my plate right now without that!"

Dexter pokered up stiffly at this double insult. "Miss Toland and I are enjoying our customary felicitous relationship, sir," he intoned heavily, "and I would consider it a kindness if you would leave off poking fun at the woman I love."

Tristan stopped in his tracks. "Good God, did I do that?" he asked wonderingly. "And here I thought I was complimenting her good judgment—for casting such a looby as you aside could only be applauded as the action of a discerning female. There," he ended, clapping Dexter bracingly on the back, "have I succeeded in vindicating myself regarding the merits of your Miss Toland?"

"Yes, blister it, Tris, you have," Dexter countered, confusion written all over his face, "but now I do believe I'll have to call you out for your insult to me! Yet if I do that, I really would be guilty of being the stupidest person in nature."

Rule threw back his head and laughed aloud, feeling better and better as each moment passed. He really enjoyed Dexter's company, for the younger man's clear, if rather limited, outlook on life was a delight to witness.

The pair walked on until they espied a small tavern and Tristan suggested they step inside to share a bird and a bottle, which suited Dexter to a cow's thumb, as he had pressing business with Rule that he had momentarily forgotten—business that would surely serve to remove that genial smile from the man's lips.

Once they had been served, Dexter leaned forward in his chair, ready to impart his new-found knowledge, but then, realizing that he was in the most direct line of fire if Tristan decided to explode, he leaned back again and nervously cleared his throat a time or two before speaking. "Tristan… um…Tris, I happened to stop by Sir Henry's this afternoon to pay a call on Miss Toland and…um…*I say,* man, that's a devilish fine cravat! Do you think you could have your man instruct mine in the way of it?"

Tristan, who had tied the thing haphazardly himself after his stint in the boxing ring and knew himself to be looking casual, to put it politely, narrowed his dark eyes and measured the man sitting across from him. "Spit it out, Dex. There's something sticking in your craw and I'd say it's about to choke you."

Dexter was all admiration. "How'd you do that, Tris? Julian does it too—always did—reads me like an open book. It's a good thing I don't need to be devious, as I sure don't seem to have the head for it, do I?"

"Nor the face," Rule supplied with a grin. "Now out with it—are you in need of someone to bail you out of the River Tick? I thought you had given up gaming in those hells."

"Haven't touched the dice more than twice since I met Miss Toland," Dexter swore earnestly. "Besides, it doesn't have to do with me at all. It's Miss Lawrence."

Suddenly Tristan, who had been listening with only half an ear, was all attention. "Mar—Miss Lawrence? Is she all right? Was there an accident? You took your bloody sweet time telling me—" Rule was already out of his chair and heading for the door.

"She's fine!" Dexter called out, stopping Rule in his tracks. "At least she is now. It's later on tonight that worries me."

"Tonight?" Tristan repeated, numbly slipping back into his chair. "She's promised to Lady Jersey's this evening." At the sight of Dexter's raised eyebrows, he continued rather sheepishly: "Sir Henry keeps me informed of her whereabouts—in all innocence, I assure you."

"Of course he does. Of course it is," Dexter agreed, grinning widely. "Nothing at all out of the way about a thing like that."

"Julian should have strangled you in your cot," Tristan said, not pleased to have been found out. "Now tell me why

Miss Lawrence could be in trouble tonight before I do Julian's job for him. I assure you, I have experience enough to make the procedure relatively swift and painless."

Running a nervous finger inside the front of his cravat, as if to reassure himself his valet had left him adequate breathing space, Dexter made short work out of his explanation.

It seemed that Kitty had confided in him—in deepest confidence, Tristan was to understand—that Mary had a secret assignation shortly after midnight in Green Park. The only reason Mary had confided in Kitty was so that she would agree to accompany her home early from Lady Jersey's when Mary pleaded the headache. That way Mary would be able to sneak out of the house in time to meet "her tormentor" in the park.

"Her 'tormentor'?" Tristan questioned, his agile mind already deciding that Mary was indeed the victim of some sort of blackmail.

Dexter was nodding his head vigorously, happy to be done with his end of the mission, and grateful that Tristan hadn't taken it into his head to slay the messenger who had brought him the bad news. If Rule wished to believe that pack of nonsense, it wasn't up to him to convince him otherwise— even if Dexter did believe that Mary's appointment was in reality a romantic assignation. After all, what sort of deep intrigue could involve anyone like Mary Lawrence?

"You weren't to know," Dexter then volunteered, as he had never learned to leave well enough alone. "Kitty specifically told me that when she confided her fears in me. Not that I paid her any attention—after giving my solemn word that I'd breathe not a syllable about it to you—seeing as how you work for Sir Henry, sort of, don't you, and should be most concerned lest any scandal come to his ward over some fortune-hunting Romeo."

Dexter later told his friend, Bertie Sandover, that it was

then that he first swore he could see smoke rising out of Ruthless Rule's ears. "You think she's eloping with some other man?" Tristan had accused, his strong, lean fingers clutching the table edge in a death grip. "You think that's why Mary was so adamant that I above anyone else was not to know about her plans for the evening?"

"Kitty told me I had been chosen to waylay you in the card room or somewhere until Miss Lawrence could effect her departure from Lady Jersey's," Dexter squeaked in his own defense. "Plain as the nose on your face that she don't want you poking about in her business. Now, Tris—" he warned feebly as Rule gave a low growl.

"You're a few bricks shy of a load, Dex, do you know that?" Tristan gritted through clenched teeth, not knowing what had made him the angrier: Mary's assignation that evening or Dexter's assumption that she was meeting another man. "And stop sliding down in that chair; you'll soon be on the floor! Pull yourself together, man, or you'll be no help to me at all."

"You want me to help you?" Dexter asked, swallowing hard on a gulp. "I thought you wanted to *kill* me."

Tristan called out to the serving wench to bring another bottle to the table. "No, no," he assured the younger man, trying his best to remain calm and make his plans carefully. "After all, if I kill you now, you won't be able to corner me in the card room this evening, will you?"

MARY HAD BEEN CORRECT in her reading of Kitty's character. When it came to keeping other people's secrets, Kitty Toland showed a lamentable lack of dependability. This worked very much to Mary's advantage when it came to having Tristan informed of her plans for the evening.

It did not, however, work in quite the same way when it came to having Jerome Toland gifted with the same information.

"Did I do right to tell you, Jerry?" Kitty asked her brother fearfully as she watched him pace back and forth across Sir Henry's morning-room carpet. "You said I must keep my eyes and ears open and tell you anything that seemed the least important, although, oh, Gemini, I can't see how Mary's little indiscretion can serve to help you. Surely you don't plan to break into her rooms tonight while she is gone and steal her jewelry, like you did that time in—"

"I told you to blank that memory from your mind, you ridiculous chit!" Jerome interrupted, still gnawing on the side of his thumb as he turned the information he had just learned over in his mind. Actually, he had hoped to insinuate Kitty into some peer's household with just such thievery in mind, but once he learned of Sir Henry's important role in the government, he had revised his plans to include the selling of information to certain persons he knew who were still championing Napoleon's cause. Now he had this new kettle of fish handed to him.

"Will you promise now not to interfere with Dexter's and my plans?" Kitty, emboldened by the deathless love she bore her Dex, dared to ask. "You said if I helped you this one last time, you would agree to the match."

Jerome headed for the door, clearly preoccupied. "We'll see, puss, we'll see," he promised vaguely before quitting the room. "Just do your part tonight like the lady asked you, and remember—you're just as guilty as I am, so *keep your mouth shut about my past!*"

# CHAPTER ELEVEN

IT HAD ALL BEEN SO EASY—so ridiculously easy. She knew she was right to have counted on Kitty to spill the soup. Mary was convinced Kitty and Dexter had all but drawn Lord Rule a diagram of her plans for the evening. Dexter's maneuvering of Tristan into the card room had certainly lacked for subtlety, but then Tristan's transparent willingness to be led away from his customary pillar-bracing stance at the edge of the ballroom had caused Mary to wonder how he had ever gotten such a reputation for spying—an occupation that she assumed must take a certain talent for subterfuge.

But no matter. It was just striking midnight and she was going to be late if she didn't soon succeed in sticking her unruly mass of hair up inside the oversized toque Ben had supplied her with that afternoon. Really, she thought ruefully as she shrugged herself into the long, shapeless black coat he had told her was part of the customary dress of young apprentices in the city. Ben may have many talents, but an eye for fashion certainly isn't one of them.

After looking at herself one more time in the mirror—seeing a slim, out-at-the-elbows youth dressed in straight loose trousers that went halfway down to her ankles (now shapeless in thick woolen socks and heavy black shoes) and a loose, open-necked blouse whose limp ruffle somewhat hid her bosom—Mary headed for the servants' stairs, her bed-side candle held high to light the way.

Ben met her just outside the kitchen door, startling her as he appeared out of the darkness without a sound to whisper in her ear, "Git yer dew beaters travelin', missy, whilst Oi go tickle up yer shadows fer yer. Oi'll be 'ere waitin' on yer when yers git back, mindin' the store, like."

"Huh?" Mary asked inelegantly, still trying to figure out what "dew beaters" were.

Ben shook his head sadly, wondering just how he, once a first-rate kencracker, had been brought so low. "Please yer to start walkin now, Miss, whilst Oi goes to tell Tiny and Goliath yer're on her way."

Mary gifted him with a grateful smile. "Oh, of course. Thank you, Ben. I'll start moving my dew beaters on the in-stant."

"Bless yer, missy," Ben whispered gratefully before dis-appearing once more into the shadows, leaving Mary alone again in the foggy yellow moonlight.

She had already plotted out the shortest way to Green Park, carefully planning her route along the best illuminated streets, but that did not keep her from jumping half out of her skin when a noise from a nearby alleyway reached her just as she had finished congratulating herself for having completed half the journey without incident. "Mad as Bedlam," she told her-self aloud. "That's what you are, Mary Lawrence, traveling about the city with only a dwarf and a gentle giant as guar-dians."

She smiled then as she remembered her first sight of Jennie's two grooms that afternoon at Lucy's. Tiny, the be-nevolent giant, resembled nothing more than a huge, black mountain with muscular arms the size of cottage beams, while Goliath, clearly the senior partner in their friendship, stood only as high as her waist. In only a few moments Mary was convinced that, between Tiny's brawn and Goliath's brain, she had nothing to fear during her midnight foray in Green Park.

Besides, she told herself yet again, Tristan is bound to be out here somewhere, skulking behind trees and playing bo-peep in dark doorways, watching every move I make. The thought of Tristan seeing her dressed in such an outlandish costume caused Mary to pause a moment beneath a street-lamp to inspect her appearance in a nearby shop window.

NOW WHAT'S SHE DOING? Lord Rule asked himself as he flat-tened his body against the side of a building. Poking his head around the corner, he espied her adjusting her toque in a rather rakish tilt, "Plaguey queer time to be primping!" he muttered, wondering yet again (rather like Ben) how he had ever been brought to this pass.

Chancing a quick look behind him, he saw that Tiny and Goliath were still in sight. "Lord," he hissed, "that man is big!" Not that Rule didn't believe himself capable of han-dling any problems, but Kit had offered his services, and Rule had decided not to take any chances with Mary's wel-fare. Between the two of them, Tris and Tiny could hold off an army of cutthroats while Goliath led Mary to safety.

Safety. Tristan snorted, disbelief at Mary's naiveté mak-ing him shake his head sadly. You'd think she was out strolling the park with her maid at high noon, the way she's just walking along without once looking to see if she's about to be attacked from behind. Lord, if she were to turn around and see Tiny's hulking figure coming up on her out of the fog—*that* would serve to put a period to her shenanigans!

Rule waited until Mary had crossed the street and entered the park before darting across himself to run from tree to tree as she cut deeper into the park, his tall figure bent nearly in half. At last she stopped, looked around her a time or two—all without seeing either Rule or the two servants, who stood not twenty paces away from her in the shrubbery—before removing a folded sheet of paper and placing it carefully in a knothole of the largest tree in the area.

Rule motioned to the servants with a toss of his head, sending Tiny and Goliath back the way they had come as Mary turned for home, while he counted slowly to twenty before crossing to the tree and removing the message Mary had hidden there before he too quit the park.

Standing under the same streetlamp Mary had used to check on her appearance, Rule unfolded the note and held it up toward the light. "'Iz-js duy-typ-zfe jy—' What the bloody hell? It's in *code!*" He lifted his head just in time to see yet another dark-clad figure disappear into the fog. The man the message was intended for? He asked himself, even as he stuffed the paper into his coat and started off at a dead run to capture Mary's "tormentor."

"NEARLY TWO," Mary said aloud, listening for the chiming of the hall clock and wondering what on earth could be keeping Rule. She had returned home and run up the servants' stairs just as fast as her heavy black shoes could carry her, to stand in the window and wave her candle slowly back and forth across the window three times—signaling to Ben that she was safe in her room, but hoping Rule would take it as more proof of her clandestine activities.

She had then hastily ripped off her clothes and dived into her nightgown, expecting Sir Henry to be calling her downstairs at any moment for a confrontation with her accuser. She had even, as the moments dragged into minutes, sat herself down at her dressing table to arrange her hair becomingly and dab on just a hint of that lovely lip pomade Lucy had loaned her.

So where was Tristan? Mary had counted on him not waiting to decipher her note, had relied on his reputation for action before thought. It just wasn't like him to retire to his rooms and patiently work out the code.

"Oh why, oh why hasn't he come crashing through the front door bellowing like a bull?" she asked herself, pouting. "How like him to be so contrary as to spoil all my fun!"

"WHAT IN THUNDER ARE you about?" Sir Henry demanded, lowering the pistol he had aimed at the intruder's heart.

Lord Rule, one foot on the floor, the other still hovering on the sill, halted in his progress through Sir Henry's bed-chamber window. "I should have remembered, shouldn't I?" Tris answered, pulling himself entirely into the room. "Many's the tale I've heard about you in your younger days." Drawing himself up to his full height, he then bowed. "Sir, your most obedient—"

"Yes, yes, get on with it," Sir Henry prodded, "and spare me any recital of my foolish salad days in the field. I'm just on the sunny side of fifty now, even if my ears and instincts remain good. What brings you here in the middle of the night? More plots to free Napoleon?"

"If only it were, sir," Tristan said, lowering himself into a chair to rest a moment before—his hot blood denying him more than a momentary respite—he sprang to his feet once more. "I can deal with the mundane," he began in a rush, consigning an entire network of dangerous spies and conspirators to the everyday, "but I swear to you, this is beyond me!"

"Prinny?" Ruffton prodded. "A plot to kill him? It'd be the third this month."

Rule shook his head and reached into his pocket to pull out the incriminating paper and hand it to his mentor. "I found this stuck in a tree in Green Park. Your 'ward' put it there this evening, just after midnight."

Sir Henry looked at the paper for a moment like a man who had just been offered a snake, then snapped it from Rule's hand. "What in Hades was Mary doing in Green Park? And how do you know she was?"

"I followed her there," Tristan answered, running a hand through his hair before turning to stare out the window into the darkness.

"Plague take you, Rule, my ward is none of your business! I told you before that your suspicions of her are nothing but a great piece of nonsense. Shadowing her like some sneaking spy—you show a deplorable lack of confidence in me, Rule, and I vow I cannot like that," Sir Henry lectured, hunting the top of his dresser for his reading spectacles.

Tristan whirled to face the older man. "I begin to think we are talking at cross-purposes. Didn't you hear what I said?" he asked, not believing his ears. "Your 'ward'—your 'niece'—went to Green Park tonight to deliver a message to somebody. Whether it was spying or blackmail—aren't you the least concerned for her welfare?"

Sir Henry adjusted his spectacles—the nosepiece almost always pinched, which was why he usually tried to do without—and allowed a small chuckle to escape him. "If I know Mary, and I know her a great deal better than you do, my lad, she had a good reason for doing what she did. She's now down the hall, safely tucked in her bed, I presume?"

"She is," Rule said disgustedly. "Goli—er, my operative assured me of her safety. I could not see her back here myself, as I was too busy chasing down the man for whom she intended the message."

"Showed you a clean pair of heels, did he?" Sir Henry observed, looking up from his work of deciphering Mary's code. "What makes you think this man is involved? Could have been some innocent passerby you scared half out of his wits. Probably won't stop running until he hits John

O'Groats. Let's see here—I believe one letter just substitutes for another. Let's try *O* for *Y.*"

Rule, a mulish expression on his handsome face, looked at Sir Henry in astonishment. "I can't believe what I'm hearing! God give me patience! How does she do it? How does she constantly manage to pull the wool over everyone's eyes? Well, sir, I am not so easily duped. Either Miss Lawrence is the target of some nefarious scheme or you, sir, have nurtured a viper at your bosom!"

Sir Henry looked up at Rule over his spectacles. "Oh, stop being so damned officious, son. And before you start reading me one of your famous scolds, remember, I already told you that Mary has had a rather unorthodox upbringing. She means no harm, I assure you."

"Don't tell me yet again about how you left her in Sussex with none but rough-and-ready retired army men and half-witted chaperons to tend her," Tristan said indignantly. "Tell me instead *why* she was hidden away down in Sussex in the first place."

"*I* for *Z, T* for *J*—ah, yes, this is really quite elementary." Ruffton raised a hand to shush Rule as he scribbled quickly, crossing out letters and substituting others. "I am not yet in my dotage to be taken in by some green girl," he supplied off-handedly as he worked. "Whatever this message is, I'm sure it's nothing to do with either blackmail or the security of this great nation. You've been pesting her again, I'll wager, and now she's funning you to get some of her own back."

Tristan threw up his hands, not able to believe he had somehow found himself in Bedlam. "That's it? That's all you have to say on the matter? A young, defenseless—not to mention *witless*—girl goes sauntering about London after midnight and you tell me she's only pulling a prank. You *condone* this? You even, by your lighthearted treatment of her, *encourage* such—what is it? Have you broken the code? Sits it serious?"

Sir Henry, who furrowed his brow as the words began to fall into place, now sat back in his chair, his face entirely devoid of expression. "Sit down, son," he said now. "I don't believe I wish to involve Perkins in this if you swoon dead away and I have to get you boosted into my bed."

"I can't believe it," Tristan whispered. "I had all but assured myself of her innocence in any plots against the government. My only concern was that her past might somehow be discovered and used for private gain. But it isn't blackmail, is it? She wasn't in the park paying off some tormentor, was she?"

"Oh, I don't know," Ruffton opined, trying hard not to smile. "I begin to think she has paid him off quite as much as he deserved. Would you care to hear the contents of the message?"

Rule drew himself up to his full height. "Sir, I cannot, no matter what my personal feelings for either you or Miss Lawrence, shirk my duty to my country. If the contents of that message are vital to the government, you cannot make me hide what I know. Perhaps it would be better if you were to withhold the knowledge from me."

Now Sir Henry did let go with a small chuckle. "How very—er—*noble* of you, Tristan, to sacrifice England's safety for Mary."

"And for you, sir," Tris added, indeed feeling a bit noble.

"Of course, for me. It is a comfort to know I have someone willing to commit treason to shield me from the follies of my ward. But before you trot off to the country to fall on your sword in some wood, will you kindly oblige me by sitting down and listening to what the message has to say?"

Rule sat himself down, cleared his throat, and motioned for Sir Henry to proceed.

And proceed Sir Henry did. "It begins: 'With apologies to Little Jack Horner—

"My Lord Tristan Rule vows *he* is no fool;
At Deduction he's top of his *class*.
Swift judgments he makes, never fearing mistakes,
While quite closely resembling an *ass*.

"The Ruthless milord has accused Ruffton's ward
Of both spying and lying as *well*.
In her life he does pry, asking why-why-why *why?*
While the lady consigns him to *hell*.

"The ward's not confessin'; thinkin' Rule needs a lesson
That will greatly his confidence *rattle*.
So a ruse she plays out, meant to put him to rout,
And he hotfoots to Ruffton to *tattle*.

"Now Redoubtable Rule (obtuse but not cruel),
Too late recognizes her *gambit*.
He's been chasing his tail, for she's laid a false trail;
Rues he hotly: 'She's bested me, *dammit*.'"

Mary would have looked at Tristan and privately thought
he looked endearingly boyish in his embarrassment. It will
never be known what Sir Henry would have thought, for he
could not bring himself to look at the young man without fear
of breaking into his first fit of the giggles since his years at
Eton.

When at last Sir Henry assured himself that he could
speak without betraying his enjoyment of his ward's sense
of humor, he offered to do anything he could to ease Lord
Rule's mind further on the subject of Mary Lawrence.

"I would have you lock her in her chamber, but I doubt it
will answer the purpose," Tristan observed with unusual
geniality before, his temper at last getting the better of him,
he fairly shouted: "Damn it all, Sir Henry, tell me again what
a citadel of propriety she is when she swears like a trooper!"

Sir Henry merely shrugged his shoulders. "I told you
about her upbringing. Rachel says it is one of my great fail-

ings—using pensioned-off soldiers as house servants. But even if I had confined them all to the stables, I fear Mary would have sought them out. Was a bit of a tomboy when I first met her, you know."

But Tristan wasn't listening. He was pacing back and forth on the carpet in a flaming fury, his dark eyes flashing fire. "Why did she feel such a crushing need to stage this charade?—for it's as sure as I'm standing here that this entire evening has been enacted for my benefit. I thought she understood that I no longer believed her to be a spy."

"Ah, but was that enough for you?" Sir Henry asked, twisting the knife a little bit. "Or did you demand that she tell you all about herself—the same way you've been poking and prodding at me with that overly inquisitive nose of yours?"

Tristan slammed his closed fist into his palm. "You won't talk, either of you!"

Sir Henry looked owlishly at Tristan's balled fist. "Do you mean to beat it out of me, then?"

Tristan's anger deflated, just like a balloon when the air is let out, and he sank into a chair, his legs spread out in front of him. "She worries me, Sir Henry. If there's some scandal in her past, someone may try to hurt her with it—or you through her."

Sir Henry pulled up a chair to sit directly in front of the younger man. "Now why don't I believe that my safety—or even that of England's—is your first concern. Mary's past is her concern, you know. Hers and mine. But I'll tell you this much: her parents were old acquaintances of mine, people whose names still have the power to incite the need for revenge in some hearts. When Mary's mother died, I promised to take the child in and raise her under another name. And I will keep her secret until such time as no more danger exists. For instance, if she were to marry, well, then it would be up to her husband to take on the secret and protect her with his name. Am I getting through to you, son? Lift up your chin from your chest and show me I am not wrong in my estimation of your feelings."

# CHAPTER TWELVE

KITTY WAS IN the small, sunny morning room, engrossed in one of her favorite occupations—embroidering. Since joining the Ruffton household, she had decorated endless scarves, aprons, slippers, caps and stockings for all and sundry, much to the delight of the servants to whom she presented them as gifts, and to the dismay of the rest of the household, who were still trying to figure out how to dispose of the stuff without hurting the dear child's feelings.

At the moment she had just finished putting the final touches to a pair of garters meant for her beloved Dexter. She held one of the garters up to read once more the inscription she had fashioned with dainty stitches: "Pray keep me tight from morn till night." Smiling serenely, she then cradled the thing to her bosom, knowing Dexter would be overjoyed with her surprise.

"Daydreaming again, sister mine?" spoke a voice from the doorway, and Kitty whirled in her seat to see her brother Jerome lounging against the doorjamb, his hands in his pockets.

"Oh, Gemini, Jerry, you gave me such a fright! How did you get past Perkins?"

Jerome dismissed the thought of Ruffton's imposing butler with a toss of his blond head. "He knows I'm family. What did you think he'd do, bar the door?"

Kitty quickly lowered her eyes, remembering how she had heard Sir Henry grumble after Jerry's last visit. "Let that sort in once and he might take it upon himself to make a habit of it," he had told Rachel, winking broadly to Kitty to soften his words.

Sauntering over to a nearby chair, Toland dropped his lean body into it and demanded Kitty ring for refreshments. This so flustered the girl, who began saying something about being a guest in the house herself, that Jerome finally cut her off by the simple means of giving voice to a particularly vulgar expression.

Once he was sure he had her attention, he leaned forward in his seat and told her in a low voice filled with malice, "You ignorant chit! I've set you up so that you travel in the first circles, knee-deep in London swells, and what do you do? You persist in defacing innocent garments with your ridiculous stitchery and cowering like some half-wit scullery maid when asked to behave in line with your station. Even worse, instead of peacocking about in society like any sensible girl, you go and tumble into love with some penniless loose screw who doesn't know his hat from his hindquarters."

And Kitty *was* cowering, right up until the moment her brother had the nerve—the awful temerity—to insult her beloved Dexter. Then the little kitten reacted like a lioness whose cub was in peril. "You shameless creature!" she exclaimed in her high, childish voice. "You run through Papa's inheritance, let our estate go under the hammer, and then try to marry me off to some rich man who will pay for your reckless way of living. And if that isn't bad enough, you have set me up—as you call it—with no less than three families, just to gain entrance to their houses to rob them. Jerry," she intoned indignantly, "you are a horrid, ghastly man!"

Jerome hoisted himself slowly to his feet and rewarded his sister's outburst with a languid clapping of his hands. "I'd throttle you for that, sister mine, except that I've other fish to fry right now, thanks to your information about Miss Mary Lawrence's nocturnal habits. And this time I'll earn enough to keep me plump in the pocket for a long, long time to come. Resign yourself to the fact that I won't be carting you about any longer. If I don't see you again—good-bye, dearest Catherine. May you rot in hell!"

He had made it halfway to the door before Kitty could find her voice. "Does this mean you will give your permission for Dexter and me to marry? After all, what difference can it make to you?"

Jerome wheeled about slowly, a nasty smile on his face. "Oh, didn't I tell you? How remiss of me. Your swain dropped by this morning, brimful of April and May. I had to deny his request for your hand, seeing as how he refused to see the need to reimburse me for raising you. I could have left you to the workhouse when our dear Papa kicked off, couldn't I, though Rutherford didn't see it my way. It was something I most particularly regret, but I had no other choice than to decline his offer to remove you from my responsibility. I am your guardian until you reach your majority. Let's see—that's a little less than five years, isn't it? Surely not too long to wait for *true love*, is it?"

"Oh, Jerry, you're never going to destroy my happiness like this, are you?" Kitty pleaded, dropping out of her chair to fall to her knees, the pleading supplicant.

His answer was a blood-chilling laugh, and then silence. Somehow she dragged herself to her feet and made her way to her chamber before collapsing on the bed in a torrent of tears.

And in her despondency, she forgot all about Jerome's hints as to a plot concerning Mary.


SIR HENRY'S LIBRARY DOUBLED as his private office. It was not often that he allowed anyone save Perkins inside it, and the butler was only exempt because even such important surroundings did need occasional dusting to remain habitable.

But now Rachel was sitting poised for battle in one of the oversized leather wingback chairs, obviously very much agitated. She had dared to enter the library without permission, believing herself to be acting within the rights of a person who had been appointed as chaperon to a young, volatile girl. "I say to you again, Henry, I don't think I can continue bearleading your ward. I saw her tippy-toeing into her chambers last night past one o'clock, clad in the most outrageous costume it has ever been my misfortune to view. Lucy took the last of my fight from me. It's time I realized that I am past the age when I can be safely relied upon to keep a strong-willed young miss on a stout enough leash. Henry! Have you been listening to a single word I've been saying?"

Sir Henry, who had been sitting behind his desk, his fingertips steepled in front of his nose, lowered his hands to let his smile show. "Of course I've been listening. I've always listened to you."

"No, you haven't," came Rachel's sharp rejoinder, for she was feeling quite put upon this morning. "If you had, I never would have allowed Reggie Moore to—never mind. That's all ancient history anyway. What's more to the point—*what* are you going to do about Mary? Don't you think it's time you told her the truth before she does something that lands us all in the suds?"

Sir Henry rose to walk round the desk and lean a hip against one of its corners. "*Cant,* Rachel? Since when have you descended into slang? Perhaps you're right. All those years spent with the younger generation have corrupted you."

"Don't try to fob me off with that sad attempt at wit, Henry; I've known you too long for that. Now, since your lack of surprise tells me that you already know about Mary's actions of last night, perhaps you will allow me into the secret."

Smiling one of his most cherubic smiles, Ruffton announced: "My ward's in love with your nephew."

Rachel sat back in her chair and sniffed. "Tell me something I don't already know, if you please."

Sir Henry went on undaunted. "Your nephew is besotted to the point of idiocy with my ward."

Raising a hand to her lips, Rachel gave an exaggerated yawn. "And with this love he has also acquired an attic positively crawling with maggots. Yes, dear, I know. Again I have lapsed sadly into cant. But you begin to bore me, sir. Get on with it."

So goaded, Sir Henry went on to describe his late-night meeting with Rule, right down to the part where Tristan had refused Sir Henry's offer of an explanation of Mary's past, preferring first to win the heart of his fair lady and then hearing the full details of the story from her own lips.

"But she doesn't *know* the full story," Rachel was forced to point out. "Lord, I shudder to think of Tristan's reaction once he learns who Mary's father was!"

"Precisely, my dear," Sir Henry replied. "Which is exactly why I am allowing the boy to be noble about the thing. Once they've explored their love for each other a little bit, the truth should lose some of its sting. You know Tristan, Rachel. This isn't going to be easy for him."

Rachel shook her head. "You were always the master of understatement, Henry."

But Ruffton wasn't really listening anymore. Rachel's slip of the tongue about Reggie Moore, the twelfth Lord Hetherington, had sent his mind winging back into the past. What on earth did that oily womanizer have to do with anything? Mary had hinted to him that it was time he and Rachel had a talk about the breakup of their engagement—something about the two of them resolving an old misunderstanding—but for the life of him Henry couldn't remember Reggie being a part of it.

"Rachel," he said now, taking one of her hands in his, "tell me about Hetherington. You said I didn't listen to you when you wanted to talk about him. I'm listening now."

Rachel stiffened, trying in vain to draw back her hand. "Why should I tell you? It's more than you deserve, when you know as well as I you found me guilty at the time without even pretending you wished to hear my side of the story."

Ruffton gave her hand a squeeze. "I am an old man now, but my memories of that time have always seemed clear enough to me. Why can't I remember Moore figuring in them? Satisfy me in this, my dear. I think we might both learn something from the exercise."

He sounded so sincere, thought Rachel. But it was all so embarrassing. Look at him, sitting there so patiently, waiting. And there *was* Mary's odd suggestion—something about misunderstandings between them. Maybe…

Rachel gave a deep sigh, then capitulated. "You know how tiresomely volatile I was in my youth," she began hesitantly. "Perhaps that's why I have been able to deal so well with my various charges. Well, you were so busy doing something with the government that you paid less and less attention to me during those last weeks before our wedding was to take place."

"I know," Sir Henry broke in to confess. "I wanted to be sure no emergencies would crop up to keep us from our wedding trip. I had planned a leisurely tour of the Lake District. I thought you would have liked that."

Grimacing, Rachel quipped, "Well, thank you for that, Henry. You have surpassed my expectations and succeeded in making me feel even lower than ever about what I did. If I may continue?" she asked, tilting her head as she waited for his signal to go on.

"I promise not to interrupt again, my dear," he told her, lifting her hand to place a kiss on her wrist.

Flustered, Rachel cleared her throat and began again. "Anyway, Reggie was always hanging about my skirts, declaring his undying love, so I thought…maybe…maybe going into the garden with Reggie would shake you into showing me some attention. Well, how was I to know that busybody Harriet Whitstone would go running hotfoot to you with some harebrained story about my…my gown being undone? And who would have thought you'd send round that simply horrid, stiff note saying you would allow me to be the one to cry off…and then lope off like that to the country without even so much as talking to me again. Oh, drat it all anyway, Henry, what does it matter now? Give me your handkerchief, I'm blubbering like a schoolgirl."

"But—but," Henry stammered momentarily as he tried to marshal his thoughts. "I can't believe this! I never heard anything about you and Moore. It was Harriet who tricked *me* into being alone with her at Lord Malmsley's rout and then ran to tell her mother I had all but raped her behind the shrubbery," Henry said, confusion evident in his voice. "I *had* to cry off our engagement, seeing as how Harriet's father had a pistol—at least figuratively—to my head. It was either that or involve you in scandal."

He stopped speaking for a moment, as if considering what Rachel had said. "Reggie Moore, eh. Never did like that rum fellow above half. Lucky for him he's married to that Isobel creature now, else I'd have his liver and lights. Isobel's more than enough punishment, no matter how well to go her father was. Lord, has a face that would turn the cream, doesn't she?"

Rachel closed her eyes tightly and shook her head. Why was Henry prosing on about ugly Isobel? Didn't he realize what the two of them had just learned? It had all been a crazy mistake—each thinking himself the reason for their broken engagement. Why, if it weren't for Harriet Whitstone, she and Henry would have been wed twenty years ago. Kill Reggie? Hang Reggie! It was *Harriet's* blood Rachel wanted!

"Harriet died last year, did you know?" Henry was saying now. "She ran away with her dancing master before her father could get me to the altar, thank the Lord, and spent her last years in some benighted Irish village hiding from her husband's creditors."

The two onetime lovers remained silent for some minutes, Sir Henry still keeping hold of Rachel's hand, each deep in his own thoughts. In the background they could hear the low rumble of male voices and then Mary's rather overdone welcome of Lord Rule as a morning caller. From the sounds emanating from the hallway, it was easy to figure out that Tristan had called to ask Mary out for a drive and that Mary was agreeable to the plan. A few moments later the heavy front door closed and the house was quiet once more.

Henry allowed the silence to stretch nearly to the snapping point before saying softly, "We're a pretty pair of fools, d'you know that? We let it slip away from us, didn't we? Our love. Our youth. But it's not too late for a bit of connubial happiness, is it, my love?"

Rachel lifted her tear-drenched eyes to gaze at his dear, cherubic face. "Connubial happiness?" she repeated, giving him a watery smile. "Why, Henry, are you talking smutty?"

"More cant?" he observed, shaking his head and trying to hide the moistness in his own eyes. Slowly, he drew Rachel to her feet as he too stood. "Say whatever you like, my dearest. Us old fogies have the right to be as smutty or as syrupy as we please." He stopped speaking for a moment, then went on, his voice a bit husky, "There's never been anyone but you, Rachel. You know that, don't you?"

"Or for me, Henry," Rachel returned on a sigh. "We'll scandalize everyone, you know. Why, we've even been living under the same roof."

Henry was pulling her closer. "Ah, yes, but we have had Mary here as chaperon."

Rachel lifted her head from the resting place it had found against Henry's ample chest. "Mary as chaperon? *That* will certainly cause a royal tow-row!"

"And again cant?" Sir Henry observed, his head lowering toward hers. "I must make it my first duty to find a way to end this deplorable new habit of yours, my dear."

Lifting her face to meet him halfway, Rachel whispered, "You were ever a master at tactical maneuver, my dearest Henry," before allowing herself to be silenced by his warm mouth.

DEXTER AND KITTY WERE ALONE in the second drawing room, seeing that Mary was out driving with Tristan, and Rachel, whose job it was to act as chaperon at times like these, was still in the library, comporting herself in a most unchaperonlike way.

The two young people were holding hands and sighing deep sighs that were enough to melt the coldest heart.

"I approached your brother this morning to—"

Kitty sighed. "I know. 'Tis monstrous cruel of him—"

"He's been running shy of luck at the gaming houses of late. Probably hanging out for a suitor more plump in the pocket—"

"Jerry has always been horridly disobliging—"

"A cod."

"*Oh, Dexter!*"

"*Oh, Kitty!*"

There was more handholding and more sighing before Dexter spoke again. "He didn't even want to hear about

Great-Aunt Felicity. I'm her heir, you know, and she ain't well, not that I wish her below ground, you understand. We'd be well enough to go for now, but I couldn't spare any for your brother."

"He once took me to Bagnigge Wells and called it a holiday," Kitty mused aloud. "You're right, dearest. Jerry's a *cod.*"

"I just left then, like some crack-brained cringe in the boots. Julian would have popped him one, I know it. I guess I still held out some hope we could bring him round. But now you say he's told you no too." He gave out yet another deep sigh. "I should have popped him."

"Bagnigge Wells is frequented by only the lowest sort of tradesmen. And the sheets were damp. Why should I be loyal to someone who lets me catch my death on damp sheets?"

"I should have just stood my ground and *told* him we were going to be married. That's what I should have done. *No!* I should have just turned my back on him and his refusal and carried you off to Gretna."

"Gretna? Gretna Green?" Clearly some of Dexter's ramblings had gotten through.

Dexter could feel his knees beginning to knock together and he swallowed down hard on a gulp. "Yes, Gretna!" he repeated with some bravado. "I can see no other way, for I will not be forced to wait until you no longer need your guardian's permission. Are you game?"

As a proposal it lacked something in the way of romance, but Kitty didn't seem to notice. After blinking her wide blue eyes a time or two, she returned a rather incoherent answer that Dexter decided to take for a yes, then burst into tears.

"That's my girl!" the young Lothario exclaimed bracingly. "Oh, what a rare to-do this will cause. Come on, Kitty, buck up, do. Can't have you acting the watering pot all the way to Scotland. Damp enough there as it is."

Kitty did her best to quell the tumult in her heart, for tears had always sent her nose to running in a most unappealing way. "Oh, Gemini, Dex, do you really think—"

Dexter silenced her doubts with a kiss—a kiss that left them so spent that after it was over they both sighed yet again and fell back against the settee to look wonderingly up at the ceiling.

"Oh, Gemini," they breathed in unison.

# CHAPTER THIRTEEN

IT WASN'T EXACTLY the most beautiful day for a ride in the country, but Mary didn't notice. She was still quite full of herself over the success of her exploits of the previous evening, especially after her late-night vigil had been rewarded at last by the sight of one very-much-on-his-dignity Lord Tristan Rule stomping down the flagway, Sir Henry waving him on his way.

"My trick, sir, I fancy," she had whispered from her position hidden behind the window drapery. Although sleep had been a long time in coming—for she could not, now that the deed was done, figure out whether it pleased her or distressed her to have played Rule like some monkey on a string—she had decided in the end to simply rejoice in her success and await further developments.

That it had turned out to be a short wait only delighted her the more. Rule had shown himself at Sir Henry's at an almost indecently early hour, begging her to accompany him for a ride in his curricle. She had been so full of herself she had even dared to tease him as they passed by London Bridge that it was lucky for her it was no longer the custom to impale the heads of traitors on spikes at either end of the drawbridge gate—a tongue-in-cheek reference to his earlier suspicions of her that had Rule grumbling into his cravat for the next few miles.

It was this headiness with her success that led them to their first real conversation, as Tristan had been extremely close-mouthed ever since he had handed her up into the curricle. "Did you enjoy yourself last evening, my lord?" she teased.

"I bloody hell did not!" Tristan responded hotly, looking at her piercingly.

Struggling not to smile, Mary schooled her features into an expression of injured innocence. "Oh dear, forgive me for asking. I had the headache and had to retire early, but the gathering seemed to be lively enough. Perhaps you had a bad turn at the tables?"

Tristan's face darkened as he realized she had purposely drawn him into disclosing his reaction to her nocturnal excursion without ever revealing her guilt. "Now *that* ties it!" he exploded, pulling the horses off the road, driving them through a sparse wood and deep into a grassy field.

Without another word he sprang down from the seat and set the brake before going round to haul Mary down almost roughly. Taking her unwilling hand in his, he growled, "Let's walk."

"Why not?" Mary chirped sarcastically. "I never liked these slippers above half anyway. Don't you go worrying your head about the damp grass, sir, for I shall not let it weigh with me."

Tristan stopped abruptly and turned to look at her. A lingering glance from those dark eyes she wouldn't have minded, but this was an outright stare, raking her from head to toe. By the time he was done, she felt she had been stripped down to her shift and had to fight not to raise her hands and cover herself.

"I followed you last night," he said at last, in a voice that chilled her to her very marrow.

Mary could feel her knees beginning to turn to jelly, and this immediately made her angry. "So?" she asked, lifting her chin, trying to give him back whatever he was able to dish out—doubled! "I was only being agreeable." She shrugged her shoulders. "You wanted intrigue. I was only giving you what you desired."

A small tic began to work in Rule's cheek. "And I'm sure you enjoyed yourself quite royally at my expense," he admitted before roaring, "but did it ever occur to you that you could have gotten yourself killed—or worse—walking about London unescorted at that time of night?"

Mary reached up to untie the ribbons on her bonnet, baring her gleaming hair to the watery sun. "Don't be ridiculous. You were there, weren't you? You wouldn't have let anything happen to me."

"Don't bet on it," Rule returned coldly.

Letting her bonnet hang upside down from its ribbons, Mary began walking about, picking wildflowers and using her headgear as a basket. "I hedged my bets, as I've heard it said. I had Jennie's grooms, Tiny and Goliath, along as well. I was never in any real danger. I'm not a complete idiot."

"No! Only a partial idiot!" Rule shot back at her before the entirety of what she had said sunk into his hot head. He reached out a hand and grabbed hold of her elbow. "Tiny and Goliath? They were there at *my* instigation. Kit lent them to *me!*"

They stood there, staring at each other in disbelief for several moments, before the absurdity of the thing finally began to dawn on them. Jennie and Kit—and most probably Lucy and Julian as well—had been having themselves a fine old time at their expense. Why, they were probably laughing themselves sick at this very moment, thinking they had pulled off a major joke.

The dimple appeared in Mary's left cheek just as Rule's shoulders began to shake. "What a fine pair of fools we are!" Mary chortled, dropping to her knees on the grass. "Taken in like greenhorns by a foursome of matchmakers. Wait till I see Lucy. Oh, she'll be crowing about this for a fortnight!"

"Don't forget Julian," Rule said, falling down beside her to lean back on his elbows. "He must be full of himself after turning the tables on his wife. Whoever said he was stuffy? I wonder if it occurred to him that we might both require the servants on the same night?"

"Can you doubt it?" Mary asked, giggling. "I wondered why Tiny was so obliging when I asked for his services. He said, 'I be goin' there anyways,' when I asked him to accompany me to Green Park. I wondered about it at the time, but I just assumed I hadn't understood him correctly. Oh lordy, what do you suppose they think of us?"

"I'd rather not guess, thank you anyway," Tristan said, yet another laugh escaping him.

Now that Rule seemed to be in a better mood, Mary began to feel a bit guilty about the poem. After all, it must have been quite embarrassing to have Sir Henry read what she had written. Picking up a handful of the flowers she had gathered, she leaned forward and began dropping them one by one onto Tristan's chest. "You really aren't obtuse, you know. It just fit the poem."

Rule let his body recline fully on the ground so that he could use his hand to take hold of Mary's wrist. "And I suppose you only employed the word *ass* because it rhymed so well with *class?*"

Mary used her free hand to pick up a blossom and tickle Rule's nose with it. "W-e-l-l, *actually*—" she began before Rule, moving so quickly she was unable to defend herself, had grabbed hold of both her wrists and reversed their positions, with her now lying on the ground, staring up at him as he hovered menacingly over her body.

Time hung suspended for long moments as she admired his handsome face, from his squared chin to his chiseled brow. The laughter was gone from his dark eyes, but it wasn't anger that she saw in them now. Oh, she thought to herself inanely, if Rachel could see her nephew's eyes right now, she'd have me locked in my room for the remainder of the Season. What was she thinking? If Rachel could see them now, in this oh, so compromising position, she would have Sir Henry posting the banns before the sun set!

"Tris—Tristan?" she breathed at last. "I apologize for everything I've done. It was silly of me to do it; I can't imagine what maggot I'd let into my head to think to tease you in the first place. You really should let me up now. Tristan?"

"Not until you've told me why you felt it necessary to hoax me in the first place," he returned, freeing one of her wrists so that he could brush back a curl that had strayed across her cheek. "I had already admitted you were not the spy I first thought you. Why did you persist in setting yourself up as guilty? I hate to admit it, but you gave me a few bad turns when I thought you were up to some mischief."

Mary, used to being the object of schemes designed by some young gentleman to pique *her* interest, was loath to admit she had planned the entire project in order to keep Tristan interested in her—and away from his estates in the country. But that strange "something" she saw in his eyes, that look that was rapidly turning her insides to soft pudding, had her tossing her pride to the winds. "Having a secret seemed the only way to keep you in town," she admitted in a whisper, turning her face away from his gaze.

Oh Lord, she felt ready to sink. What if he laughed at her? What if he teased her now about *her* infatuation with him, as she had done him at the theater? What if he got to his feet and just walked away, having lost interest now that he knew there was no reason for him to be concerned about some dark secret in her past?

Just when Mary thought she was going to either faint or

explode, Tristan shifted his body slightly to lie belly down in the grass beside her, turning her face to his by placing a finger under her chin. "It worked, you know," he informed her gently. "You have succeeded in riveting my attention. And much as I hate to admit that Lucy and Jennie could ever be right in anything, I can only tell you that it doesn't matter a fig whether you've got a secret in your past or not—I am top over tail in love with you, Mary Lawrence."

"Oh, Tristan," Mary breathed, a tremulous smile on her lips, her green eyes bright with unshed tears. "Do you think there was ever such a muddled courting? I love you too!"

All thoughts of secrets, schemes or threats of blackmail scattered to the four winds as Tristan used his finger to guide Mary's chin even closer to him. Turning slightly so that their bodies lay together in the grass, he leaned forward and moved his lips against hers in a soft, exploratory kiss.

Their arms moved to twine around each other, causing their bodies to be pressed close from neck to hip, a movement that unleashed their volatile emotions until they were clinging to each other desperately, their mouths fused together passionately, melting and reforming in the heat of their desire.

For so many years Rule had taken his pleasures where he found them, more to assuage his physical needs rather than to satisfy anything within his soul. This was different, so wondrously different; holding Mary in his arms had set loose tender feelings he didn't believe he possessed. Along with the burning need he had to hold her, touch her, possess her, to claim her now and forever as his and his alone, there was an awareness of her fragility, her innocence, her blind trust in him never to hurt her. He could feel her trembling within his embrace, awakening to the needs of her body, and while frightened of her intense reaction, willing to place herself entirely in his power.

Slowly, and with patently obvious regret, Tristan eased Mary's arms from about his neck and, with a few nibbling kisses, ended their embrace. "Since you have said you do not believe me to be obtuse, my love, I will return the compliment by telling you that I believe you to be intelligent enough to know, as I do, that we are in danger of crossing a line that should remain uncrossed until after our wedding."

Mary ducked her head against his broad chest to hide her flaming cheeks. "Is—is it always like this?" she mumbled into his cravat, trying hard to control her breathing.

She could hear the rumble of his laughter through the cloth of his shirt. "No, my sweetings, it is even better— much better. But now that I have a secret from you, I believe it best if I withhold it until our wedding night." He leaned back a little to look down at the top of her head. "You will marry me, Miss Mary Lawrence, won't you?"

She rolled away from him and hopped gingerly to her feet, brushing a few twigs and leaves from her skirts. "I'd better say yes, Tris, now that I will be returning to my uncle and your so-astute aunt with grass stains on my back."

Mary pressed her fingers to her mouth, giggling as Rule produced an exaggerated look of shock on his face. "Oh dear, that sounded horribly *fast*, didn't it? But if we are to be wed, I believe it is time you learned that my real name is not Mary Lawrence. You were right about that at least, you nosy devil you."

Rule made a small ceremony out of rising to his feet and brushing down his clothes. He had been so caught up in their mutual passion, so relieved to finally understand his reason for being so intrigued with Mary from the moment he had first clapped eyes on her, so heady with the knowledge that Mary was at last his, that any secrets in her past were, quite frankly, the very last thing on his mind.

He reached over to draw a small twig slowly from Mary's

tangled curls. "Sir Henry told me your parents left you in his care when they died. He also told me that they had some enemies of some sort who might have taken it into their heads to revenge themselves on you if he were to let your true identity become common knowledge. He also said," Tristan went on, bending to retrieve her bonnet and taking her hand as they began their walk back to the curricle, "that he would tell me everything I wanted to know if I really wanted to hear it."

"And did you?" Mary asked, leaning into him as they walked along. "What am I saying? Of course you did. I can't imagine you turning down such a grand opportunity."

"I did not," he corrected, tweaking her nose. "I stopped him, telling him I would learn the rest of your secret from you. Not that I can for the life of me understand why it should matter a snap now, or why it *ever* seemed to matter."

"That's what I've been telling Sir Henry, until I'm blue in the face. He's had me buried deep in Sussex ever since I was eight, surrounding me with servants that I know full well were hired with my protection in mind. And all because my father was French! How silly—half the *ton* could claim French blood."

"Sir Henry was ever a cautious sort," Tristan told her as he made to help her up onto the curricle seat. "I'm sure he had his reasons at the time."

"If you say so, Tris," Mary relented, standing on tiptoe to kiss his cheek before moving to climb up into the curricle. "But I believe I would like to use my real name for the marriage ceremony, even if I have been known as Mary Lawrence for so long that I probably won't answer to it when someone calls to me. Marie Lisette Vivienne St. Laurent— it has a certain ring to it, don't you think? Tristan…Tristan? You're breaking my fingers! What's wrong?"

"St. Laurent?" he asked in a strangled voice. "*Jules* St. Laurent?"

"Yes, have you heard of him? Uncle Henry says he was quite well known. Tristan, whatever is the matter with you?" Mary had gained the seat by now, and she wheeled about to watch Rule as he walked around the curricle to the other side, his face as dark as a thundercloud. "My father escaped the Terror and fled to England, where he met my mother. Uncle Henry says the people who confiscated the family estates may have thought I presented a danger to them, especially now that the war is over. As if I wanted anything to do with some moldy acres in Grenoble."

Mary knew she was babbling, but Tristan was scaring her so, she didn't know what else to do. "Uncle Henry was telling me the truth, wasn't he?" she almost begged. "Tristan, for God's sake, *speak* to me! Say *something!*"

"I've kept you out too long," he said at last, his voice wooden. "My aunt will tear a strip off my hide if I don't return her chick to her soon."

"A pox on propriety!" Mary snapped, her fears overriding every other emotion save the love she had for this man who now seemed so distant, so unapproachable. "What do you know about my father that I don't?"

Rule turned to her slowly, all emotion drained from his eyes and voice. "You'd better let Sir Henry explain, as it's been his secret for so long. I only wish to God it still was."

"But—but—" Mary began, then lapsed into silence. If she knew nothing else, she knew that Rule wouldn't be budged from his position. She could only cudgel her own brain as they rode along in silence.

Was her happiness to be so short-lived? Would Tristan—now that he knew all there was to know about her, and, obviously, more than even *she* knew—retract his proposal?

She couldn't stand not knowing. Crossing all her fingers in her lap, she took a deep breath and asked desperately, "Does this mean you no longer wish us to be married?"

In that same dead voice she had quickly learned to dread, Rule replied, "I said I'd marry you, and I'm not known for going back on my word."

Stung, Mary retorted smartly, "Well, don't let that bother you, I'll not blab it about that the great Tristan Rule went back on his word."

*"I love you, damn it!"* Tristan shouted at her, making her jump. "You just have to give me some time. I just have to have some time alone—to think."

Mary bit down hard on her bottom lip and the taste of her own blood filled her mouth. "You do that, Tristan," she answered softly. "And so will I."

Just as the curricle was passing London Bridge, the skies opened up and it began to rain. Mary silently blessed the raindrops, for they hid her falling tears.

# CHAPTER FOURTEEN

THE DOOR TO THE LIBRARY slammed shut with enough force to rattle the candlesticks on the mantelpiece across the room. Sir Henry looked up from the dispatch he was reading just in time to see his ward turn the lock and then remove the key, stuffing it into the bodice of her gown.

The girl looked a sorry enough shrimp, her gown and pelisse darkened with rainwater, her straw bonnet limp and drooping down over her eyes. "Is nothing sacred anymore?" he asked with a smile, releasing the dispatch and leaning back comfortably in his oversized leather chair. "First Rachel, although the results were well worth the upheaval, and now you, Mary. I may be overreacting, but somehow I don't believe yours to be a social 'break in.' Perhaps it is time to have a talk with Perkins; I believe, that as a bodyguard at least, the man might at last be getting past it."

The only answer to his words was Mary's short, unlady-like exclamation as she struggled exasperatedly to untie the tangled wet ribbons of her bonnet and toss the offending headgear into a corner.

"In case you're wondering about the results of Rachel's visit to my sanctum," Sir Henry went on placidly, rising to walk around the desk and pour the two balloon glasses of brandy he privately felt to be in order, "I am happy to tell you that we have resolved all our mistaken conclusions of the past and are now betrothed once more. Rachel was quite a belle in her day, you know, and could still give many a run for their money. To have captured her affections, not once, but twice, has me standing before you feeling rather full of myself, I don't mind telling you."

"My felicitations, Uncle," Mary said sarcastically, flinging herself into the chair Rachel had occupied earlier. "As it seems to take you several decades to resolve personal problems, may I then look ahead to say, 1840, in the hope you will have by that time figured a way out of the 'mistaken conclusion' now destroying *my* life?"

"You and Tristan have had a misunderstanding?" Ruffton prompted, handing Mary one of the glasses.

"Need you ask?" Mary replied dampeningly before saluting her uncle and then taking a healthy sip of the brandy. The unaccustomed strong spirit hit the back of her throat like liquid fire, and it was only after several minutes spent thumping his ward between the shoulder blades as she coughed and choked that Sir Henry could hope to hear exactly what had transpired.

"Stop trying to cosset me!" Mary told him indignantly, jerking her body away from Sir Henry's ministering hand once she recovered her voice. "And don't try to hoax me either. It's time and more I find out exactly who I am, for I am certainly not who you say I am. Start with my father, if you please, for it would seem the name St. Laurent is at the heart of the problem."

Sir Henry returned to his chair behind the desk and stared at his ward over the steeple of his pressed-together fingertips. Obviously the child had told Rule her true name and the results had been even worse than he had feared. "Did Lord Rule cast aspersions on your father, my dear?"

"N-no," Mary admitted, searching in her reticule for her

handkerchief. "He…he… Oh, Uncle Henry," she imparted shakily, "he asked me to marry him!" She then proceeded to hiccup before bursting into loud sobs.

Sir Henry tilted his head and nodded once. "Marry you, eh? I did give him my blessings last night, so that doesn't surprise me overmuch, knowing Tristan's penchant for rushing his fences. But really, my pet, if you don't want him, all you have to do is say so. There's no need to resort to tears."

Mary scrubbed at her damp cheeks before looking at her guardian as if he had suddenly grown another nose. "Not want him? Oh, Uncle Henry, how could you possible be so obtuse? Of course I *want* him! I love him!"

Ruffton sat front on his chair, pointing a finger at Mary's outthrust chin. "It would take an absolute idiot not to see that you're overset, but I do believe I've taken enough sauce from you, child. I am not so obtuse as to be unable to connect your tears with your demand to know more about your father. You told Tristan your real name, didn't you? Furthermore, I believe I can take it from your histrionic outburst—breaking into my library and then hiding the key in your bodice like some character in a melodrama—that his reaction to your disclosure wasn't all you had hoped it would be. He didn't… er…*hurt* you in any way, did he?"

Mary bit her lip and shook her head in the negative. "Forgive me for being so rude, Uncle. I admit to being a bit hysterical. And no, Tris didn't hurt me. At least not so you can see," she responded shakily, slowly getting herself back under control. "Everything was perfectly lovely, actually, until I told him I wished to be married using my real name. And then…and then…"

"And then he began ranting and raving and slamming his fist into his hand and generally making a cake of himself?" Ruffton offered, knowing his man well.

Mary shook her head. "If only he had. That I would have

understood. He's so adorable when he's in one of his rages—like a small boy throwing a tantrum. I could have handled that. Instead, he just suddenly lost all the color in his face and refused to so much as peek in my direction all the way home.

"Oh, he did speak to me once, to tell me again that he loved me—he *shouted* it, actually—but I can't say as I was much comforted by his declaration." She looked at her uncle beseechingly. "He's not acting true to form, Uncle, that's what really worries me. Whatever he knows about my father, it must be serious indeed, to have him turning from lover into stranger within the blinking of an eye."

"You landed him a real settler this time, pet, that's for certain," Sir Henry agreed gloomily. "But give him time," he ended by way of sympathy. "He'll recover—if his love for you is as deep as both Rachel and I believe it to be."

"He's leaving late today for his estate in Surrey," Mary supplied dully. "To 'think.' He told me that as he escorted me to the door. Then he left me standing on the doorstep and sprang his horses away as if the hounds of Hell were after him."

Henry nodded several times, considering this development. "Good, good. Tris has an ugly temper; it's a good thing he took himself off. He has to work through this thing alone. I wish I could have spared you this, Mary, my dear, spared the both of you, but it is better to start your married life with no secrets between you."

"We have one now, Uncle," Mary quipped with a hint of her old spirit. "*He* knows who I am—and *I* don't. Perhaps you will at last deem it appropriate in your master plan to enlighten me so that I can at least understand why Tristan is so upset."

Sir Henry was barely attending, as he was lost deep in his own thoughts. "I should have never told you your real name.

You had forgotten it, along with everything else, after the shock of it all. But how was I to know you would go tumbling into love with a man like Tristan, a man so strict in his loyalties? Perhaps I shall call Rachel in here; she'll know how best to go on."

"Forgotten it all? What have I forgotten? And how? And what do Tristan's rigid loyalties have to do with it? Uncle!" Mary demanded loudly, breaking into Sir Henry's reverie. "What on earth are you talking about?"

Ruffton looked at his ward, seeing her as she was ten years earlier, her clothing burned and smoky from the fire, her auburn hair singed nearly to the roots on one side of her head, but her chin still held like the little aristocrat that she was.

He sighed deeply, giving up the memory of the child who had so tugged at his heart and looked intently at the young woman who sat before him now, damp, bedraggled, but still every inch the aristocrat. "You'd prefer the unvarnished truth, I imagine?" he asked resignedly.

"Infinitely," she agreed, raising her chin yet another degree.

THE HEAVY VELVET DRAPERIES were closed tight against the late-afternoon sun, throwing the large chamber into near darkness. Rachel tiptoed into the room until she could see the outline of Mary's huddled body as it lay atop the high tester bed, facing the wall.

All in all it's been quite a day for the poor infant, the older woman thought as she crossed the carpet silently to sit down on the edge of the bed, agreeable to waiting in silence until Mary chose to acknowledge her presence.

It didn't take long. "Go away," Mary mumbled into her pillow, making backward shooing motions with her left hand. "I'm not receiving at the moment. Come back later."

"When?" Rachel nudged, her heart going out to Mary.

"Late September—I just might be willing to talk then," came the answer before the pillow was lifted and repositioned directly over Mary's head. "Now go *away!*"

"You plan on going into a genteel decline, child? How crushingly ordinary. Really, I had come to expect better from you."

Rachel's last statement had Mary flinging the pillow away from her as she shot into a sitting position to glare at her chaperon and accuse: "You knew, didn't you? You knew all along! How could you let me go out in society when you knew? Why give me a taste of what could have been, when you realized perfectly well that society would shun me if they knew the truth? Oh lord, I may as well set on my caps now, for once the story gets out and the world is done with my good name, I'll be as welcome as the plague in the fashionable drawing rooms, and you know it."

"Oh, I see," Rachel said placidly. "And that's what matters to you, does it? What society will think?"

"No. I don't care a snap what society thinks, and well you know that too," Mary said softly, yet another bout of tears not far from the surface. "It's Tris. If he pilloried me before, when he had only his suspicions for fuel, he'll hate me now. You didn't see his face, Rachel. He could barely stand to look at me. And I don't blame him."

"I imagine you're refining too much on that 'sins of the father being visited on the children' thing. Tristan is shocked, of course he is, but it's you he's asked to marry, not your father." Rachel reached over to wipe Mary's tears with her own handkerchief. "Give him a little time, my dear, he'll come around. He'll go off to Surrey in one of his mad takings like a sulky little boy for a bit, but he loves you, and in the end he'll see that your father's actions have nothing to do with you. Trust me in this, for I know Tristan well."

Mary took possession of the handkerchief and blew her nose. "I still can't take it all in. I just thought no one had much memory of anything below the age of eight. It never occurred to me that I was any different."

"Sir Henry saw no reason to try to prod your memory, since it could only cause you pain," Rachel explained now. "It was your mother's dying wish that Henry take care of you and he did the best he knew how, installing you in Sussex with his trusted retired soldiers to keep you safe. Why, your memory was so thoroughly erased that you spoke both English and French interchangeably, not really knowing which was correct. Henry had you surrounded by only English-speaking servants until you were fourteen, to help you forget. It was only then that he employed your French tutor, who Henry tells me considered you to be quite a prodigy in languages, as you picked up his lessons so well."

"My mother was English?" Mary prompted, as she had not asked Sir Henry very much about her mother—the story of her father had consumed her too much for that.

Rachel nodded. "I never met her, although we were much of the same age and social station. She was the daughter of a second son, none too plump in the pocket, so she was never presented. But it is from her that you got your beauty, Sir Henry tells me, and your good heart."

"You don't have to tell me from whom I inherited my less desirable traits," Mary quipped halfheartedly. "No wonder I was so ready to indulge in intrigue with Tristan. It was bred in the bone."

Sir Henry had already told Mary the truth about her father, so there was no reason for Rachel to try to dress the thing up in fine linen now. "Your father, aristocratic French blood to the side, was a villain of the first water, Mary. His main interest in life was the acquisition of money, and he made it by selling secrets to both France and England at the same time. That dual betrayal of trust cost many lives on both sides, and in the end St. Laurent forfeited his own life for his crimes. It was very much in character for him to start his house on fire to try to cover his escape that last time, not caring a single bit that his wife and child stood to perish in the blaze."

Her chin resting on her chest, Mary said, "But he didn't escape, did he? Sir Henry put a bullet in his back just before my mother tossed me out the window into Uncle's arms, begging him to take care of me. He—he told me she backed away from the window then, not wanting anyone to be hurt trying to save her."

Rachel drew Mary into her motherly embrace. "That she did, child, and a few moments later the roof collapsed. She was a brave woman and she died with dignity, even if her husband's activities had caused her to live a life of horror."

"She *was* wonderful, wasn't she?" Mary said, smiling a little. "At least not all my blood is bad."

Pushing Mary away from her a bit in order to look her directly in the eyes, Rachel said firmly, "Now you listen to me, you foolish girl. Take all this business about 'bad blood' and wipe it from your mind. You are Mary Lawrence, beloved of Tristan Rule, and you have a glorious future in front of you. Don't waste time looking back—it serves no purpose."

"Tell that to Tristan, Rachel," Mary responded resignedly. "He must have cut his sleuthing teeth on stories of the evil Jules St. Laurent and the havoc he had wrought, the deaths he had caused. Even if Tris loves me, can he stand looking at me, knowing what he does about my father? Good Lord, Uncle Henry wouldn't even let me travel to France because of my father's reputation. Imagine the tumult if I went flitting about Paris, inquiring about my St. Laurent relatives?"

The bit firmly between her teeth now, she went on, speaking as soon as the thoughts hit her. "Not to mention, of course, the repercussions in the government if it were ever discovered that Sir Henry Ruffton, that trusted patriot, was harboring the daughter of one of His Majesty's greatest enemies. No wonder he changed my name and hid me away in Sussex!"

"I doubt that consequence ever occurred to him," Rachel replied firmly. "He told me all about you when he first asked my help in presenting you to the *ton*. Henry was always very open about things, you know. The love that shone from his eyes when he talked about you—why, he couldn't love you more if you were his own daughter."

"Instead of the daughter of his worst enemy," Mary interrupted, shaking her head in disbelief. "Well, let me tell you—today we have buried Marie Lisette Vivienne St. Laurent for all time. I don't care for myself, you must understand. All that talk about society doesn't mean a thing. I was only grumbling about that to keep from thinking about Tristan. But Sir Henry is too dear for me to allow even a breath of scandal to sully his good name."

"And Tristan, Mary?" Rachel asked. "How dear is he to you? Will you allow him the gift of a little time before condemning him for his reaction to your news?"

A single tear found its way down Mary's cheek. "I don't believe *my* forgiveness enters into it, Aunt Rachel. I love Tristan, and he says he loves me. I guess all that we can do now is to see just *how much* he loves me."

The two women sat in silence for some minutes, their arms wrapped comfortably about each other, until they could hear the dinner gong in the hallway. "I'll meet you later downstairs, child," Rachel said, rising stiffly from the bed. "I want to go down early to ease your poor guardian's worried mind. He was feeling so guilty when I left him."

Rachel's words caused Mary to remember Sir Henry's

good news of earlier that afternoon and she grabbed the older woman yet again to give her a warm kiss on the cheek. "My best wishes to you, Aunt, on your upcoming nuptials," she congratulated sincerely. "I knew if only you two would sit down and discuss things you would find your way to happiness. What was the misunderstanding anyway?"

Rachel smiled a secret smile. "We've decided to let Sir Henry take all the blame," she quipped, patting her hair. "He was feeling so downpin about you that I thought it would take his mind off at least some of his troubles if I gave him the forgiveness he was so eagerly seeking."

"And Lord Hether-something-or-other? What about him, Aunt?" Mary teased, remembering Rachel's slip of the tongue at the Venetian breakfast.

Rachel batted her eyelashes at Mary, the picture of innocent confusion. "Lord who, my dear? I vow I *don't* know what you're talking about." She then clapped her hands together briskly. "Hurry now, Mary, or you'll be late to dinner, and Sir Henry has promised to bring out his best champagne in honor of our engagement."

Mary refused to let her smile waver as she realized they could have been toasting a double engagement this evening if it weren't for Tristan's abrupt departure after hearing her news. "I'll dress now and then go hasten Kitty along," she promised, already ringing for her maid. "You know how long she takes when primping for her dearest Dexter. As if he'd even notice if she came into the room with a sack over her head, so besotted is the fellow."

Rachel stopped just as she opened the door to leave. "Perkins said Dexter was here earlier today while I was out and you were closeted with Sir Henry. I'd worry about the properties, except I doubt either of them would know what to do in the first place. Dexter, for all his man-of-the-world claims, seems to be thoroughly baffled when it comes to dealing with innocents like Kitty. Ah yes, and yet another dandy succumbs to Cupid's leveling dart."

Mary chuckled at the little joke until the door closed behind the departing Rachel. Then her features reassembled themselves into a solemn expression as she sent up a little prayer that Tristan wouldn't take too long to decide if his love for her was strong enough to outstrip his hatred for Jules St. Laurent.

SIR HENRY AND RACHEL WERE just moving away from each other after enjoying a pleasurable embrace when Mary dashed into the drawing room waving a scrap of paper and laughing delightedly. "Kitty and Dexter have eloped to Gretna!" she exclaimed, tossing the paper into the air. "And I thought Kitty had nary a trace of spunk in her beautiful, dim head. Oh, this is wonderful!"

Rachel, now a betrothed woman, but still a chaperon, wasn't quite as delighted. Picking up the paper, she read Kitty's hastily scrawled note, that spoke of undying love and mean brothers. "And something about damp sheets, I think," she told Sir Henry, moving the paper closer to the light in order to better decipher Kitty's childish hand. "Who would have thought Dexter could engineer such a scheme?"

Sir Henry picked up his glass and took a small sip before saying softly: "Engineer it, yes. But carry it through to completion? Oh, no. Not if I know my man."

# CHAPTER FIFTEEN

ALL PLANS FOR THE EVENING were quite naturally canceled after Kitty's note was discovered, and Sir Henry sent a servant around to the Thorpe town house requesting the Rutherfords's company as soon after the dinner hour as possible.

Although Dexter had reached his majority three years previously, it was common knowledge that Julian, who continued to provide his cousin with a generous allowance, was still unofficially in charge of the younger man. Added to that, Dexter was Julian's heir, at least for the moment, and Lord Thorpe would quite naturally be interested in Dexter's choice of mother to the next generation of Rutherfords.

Lucy and Julian arrived just as Sir Henry was rejoining the ladies after enjoying the solitary cigar he allowed himself each day. "What's wrong?" Lucy asked without preamble, dropping into a chair and settling the skirts of her ballgown around her—for she and Julian had been planning to attend Lady Cornwallis's annual ball that evening. "Your invitation was curiously lacking in detail. As I told Julian, it seemed more in the way of a summons. Pray tell me it isn't bad news. Have you heard from Jennie? Is little Christopher all right? Has there been an accident? I—"

"Hush, pet," Julian soothed, standing behind her chair, a

reassuring hand pressed to her shoulder. "How can we learn anything if you persist in cataloging the possibilities and giving no chance for anyone to answer yea or nay?"

Lucy looked up at her husband and pulled a face. "You were guessing too, sweetheart," she reminded him. "On the way over here in the carriage you had me half convinced Kit had taken a toss from his new hunter."

"I had a letter from Jennie just yesterday," Rachel put in before Julian could make his rebuttal, "and all the Wildes are as fine as nine-pence. In fact, Christopher's just cut another tooth. It's just that something happened today—"

"Lucy, your Aunt Rachel has condescended to make me the happiest of men by consenting to become my wife," Sir Henry broke in, deciding he was not about to let Dexter's dramatic gesture overshadow Rachel's own news.

"Oh, Aunt Rachel, how perfectly marvelous!" Lucy exclaimed, jumping up and running to hug her relative. "May Jennie and I have charge of your wedding—and Mary too, of course? You can be married from Bourne Manor. It has the loveliest chapel, you know. Oh, we must start making lists this instant. When is the ceremony to take place? You won't want a long engagement, surely?"

Rachel took a peek at Mary, sitting slightly away from the rest of the group and looking so wistfully sad. "We'll wait until after Mary and Tristan's wedding, I think, as Sir Henry will be giving the bride away and we have already planned an extensive wedding trip through the Lake District."

Mary's cheeks turned chalk white, then rosy red, as she realized what Rachel had just made public. Rising to stand stock-still inside Lucy's enthusiastic embrace, she accepted everyone's best wishes in a small, wooden voice.

How could Aunt Rachel have done it? Already Lucy was asking why Tristan wasn't present, and Sir Henry, who seemed to lie with great ease, she realized, was accepting full blame for having sent the newly engaged man off on a mission that would keep him out of the city for at least a fortnight.

What if Tris decides to cry off? Mary screamed in silent panic. He'll never forgive me for making our betrothal common knowledge, not while the situation stands as it does now. He'll feel he's been trapped into going through with the marriage no matter what his feelings, if only to salvage his honor.

"I'm afraid our lovebirds here are rushing their fences, Lucy," Mary said at last, scrambling for a way out. "In their happiness they wish the whole world married. Tris has made an offer, it's true, but I haven't as yet formally accepted it. We're hoping this small separation will help us to be more sure of our feelings for each other."

"Fiddlesticks!" Lucy countered, crossing her arms against Mary's disclaimer. "You two were made for each other, and haven't Jennie and I told you so a dozen times?"

Julian, seeing that Mary was close to tears, cut in smoothly, "Put your arrow back in your quiver, Cupid, and promise Mary you won't breathe a word of Tristan's proposal until she wishes it made public. And that," he finished, tapping his wife gently on the tip of her nose, "also means you aren't to spill the soup in a letter to Jennie, swearing her to secrecy."

Putting out her full bottom lip in a becoming pout, Lucy reluctantly nodded her head before brightening once again as she begged to at least be allowed to be the one to give Jennie the joyous news once Tristan was returned and the engagement made official. "You surely don't mean to turn him down, do you, Mary?" she asked candidly, earning herself an admonishing "tsk-tsk" from her husband.

"You'll be the first to know my answer, Lucy, I promise," Mary sidestepped neatly. "Besides, although you believe yourselves to have heard all the news, you have yet to hear about Kitty and Dexter. They're the real reason we sent the invitation."

"Oh, yes, they aren't here, are they?" Lucy observed, looking about the large drawing room as if searching out the pair in a dimly lit corner. "That's strange. I had begun to think Dexter had moved in, seeing as how he's been camped on your doorstep day and night since Kitty took up residence. For such a dedicated flirt as Dex to have fixed his interest on a green girl like Kitty Toland fairly boggles the mind. Why, only last year he was amusing himself by pinching upstairs maids and chasing opera dancers."

"I'm afraid your cousin has done more than 'fix his interest' with Miss Toland," put in Sir Henry before Lucy could be off again, relating an incident concerning Dexter, her personal maid, Deirdre, and a large billiard table. "He and the lady in question are on their way to Gretna Green, to marry over the anvil."

"Of all the paper-skulled idiot stunts!" Thorpe exploded angrily. "How can he profess to be in love with the girl, and then proceed to ruin her reputation that way? There's a proper way and an improper way to go about things, and m'cousin has always displayed a marked tendency for taking the incorrect turning. But this—this is beyond belief. It's more than incorrect, it's—it's—"

Now it was Lucy's turn to calm Julian. "Low-bred?" Lucy finished tongue-in-cheek before Julian, displaying all the starch and arrogance that had gained him the reputation of a high-nosed snob, realized that everyone around him seemed to be much amused, thoroughly enjoying his momentary lapse into stuffiness—a legacy of his privileged upbringing that marriage to the irrepressible Lucy had pretty much put to rout.

Julian smiled, as the ability to laugh at his own foibles was yet another gift from his understanding wife. "Now that I've given you *my esteemed mother's* opinion on Dexter's recent course of action," he went on, once again positioning himself behind Lucy's chair, "I believe *I* may have a few questions. To begin—does anyone know the reason behind this melodramatic flight?"

Mary produced the letter she had found but did not bother trying to read all of it—most of it being either unintelligible or embarrassingly unintelligent. "To sum up her note as best I can," she informed Julian, "Kitty's brother Jerome, her guardian, has refused consent for his sister's marriage to Dexter. Rather than waiting out the nearly five years until Kitty comes of age, Dexter elected to spirit her away to Gretna, just like the hero in some Theatre Royal comedy. I imagine they've been on the road since early this afternoon."

Rachel spoke up then, apologizing to everyone for her failure to adequately chaperon Kitty. "How I could have scraped through without a scratch with a termagant like Lucy, and then failed so abysmally to ride herd on a wet-be-hind-the-ears schoolgirl I'll never know," she mourned, shaking her head in disbelief.

"You had other things on your mind today, my dear," Sir Henry defended staunchly, lifting her hand to his lips as Rachel blushed beet red, looking much like a flustered schoolgirl herself.

Julian walked over to the collection of decanters residing on a side table and poured himself a drink. "Nobody's blaming anybody here," he said dismissingly. "If there's any blame to be placed, then I'd say we can safely lay it on Dexter's plate. What a devilish silly thing for him to do, no matter how pure his intentions. Has anyone thought to inform this Jerome person of his sister's flight? He may want to give chase, you know."

Mary spoke up then, telling Julian that an underfootman had been sent around to Toland's rooms but no one answered his knock. "We'll try again in the morning. I don't believe the two of them to be very close, however, even if Dexter was impressed with the way Mr. Toland used his gambling winnings to bring Kitty to town for a chance at a Season. I only met him myself by chance one day when he was here visiting his sister, but he impressed me as a man very much out for himself. He treats Kitty like a child, which she is of course, but he's not kind about it. She's always in the glooms following his visits." She shrugged. "I don't know. I have no siblings. Perhaps theirs is a commonplace enough relationship."

"You make him sound like a dog in a manger. After all, if he doesn't care for her, why would he turn down the chance to have her taken off his hands?" Lucy puzzled, turning to Julian for an answer.

"I'd be willing to wager a tidy sum that if Dex were more plump in the pocket, Toland would have handed his sister over to him on a silver platter—as long as he was handsomely rewarded for his trouble," he offered, earning for himself a snort of agreement from Sir Henry.

"Oh, that poor girl," Lucy murmured, her tender heart touched by Kitty's plight. "I never realized before how very lucky I have been, being surrounded all my life by people who truly love me."

"And I," Mary added solemnly, looking straight at Sir Henry and Rachel as she spoke. "Having people willing to sacrifice their life for you, people prepared to protect you no matter what the possible cost to themselves, people caring enough to risk losing your love in order to help you see things in their true perspective rather than to only concentrate selfishly on how they affect you—I can think of no greater blessing."

Sir Henry swallowed down hard on the sudden lump in his throat. Finding Rachel's hand, he gave it a quick squeeze, whispering huskily, "I told you she was special. From the first moment I saw her, I knew. If Rules dares to hurt her, I'll have him stripped to the bone—I swear it."

"Tristan's your protégé too, my dear," Rachel reminded him softly. "He's had a shock, realizing he's tumbled into love with the daughter of nothing less than one of England's premier enemies of modern times. If St. Laurent had spied only for the French, serving his native country, it wouldn't be quite so bad. After all, what was Tristan himself, if not a spy? But a double-dealing secrets merchant who feigned loyalty to both countries while lining his pockets at the expense of the troops his misinformation as good as sent out to be slaughtered…well, putting that behind him is going to take a bit of doing."

Lucy and Julian, who had been discussing the possibility of intercepting the runaways and "negotiating" Toland's approval so that Dex and Kitty could be married from Hillcrest, Thorpe's country estate, hadn't paid much attention to the older couple's withdrawal from the general conversation.

As for Mary, she had once again descended into a brown study, believing everyone else in the world to be lucky in their love, while hers had been beset on all sides by unfortunate timing, sad coincidence and outright bad luck ever since she and Tristan had first met.

Rachel and Sir Henry had seen their love triumph over time and misunderstandings. Lucy and Julian had faced down ugly rumor and a possible charge of murder to find a love that had enriched them both tenfold. Jennie and Kit had taken a forced alliance and turned it into a voluntary joy. Even Kitty and Dexter, as madcap and ill-advised as their elopement might be, had taken the first steps toward the happiness they were sure awaited them.

Only I, Mary mused ruefully, could have managed to be nearly seduced, proposed to, and then deserted, all in the space of a single afternoon. If Kitty and Dexter were playing out a Theatre Royal comedy, were she and Tristan resembling characters in a Haymarket melodrama?

Did they possess the patient love of Sir Henry and Rachel, the dogged determination of Lucy and Julian, the gift for giving displayed by Jennie and Kit or the blind faith and trusting hearts of Kitty and Dexter?

Would Tristan be able to separate the Mary he had fallen in love with from the man he rightfully despised, or would he be defeated by his lifelong belief that people were either black or white, allowing for no softening shadings of gray? Could he put a rein on his quick temper and tendency to judge long enough to see that Jules St. Laurent, whether dead or alive, had only the power to hurt that Tristan chose to allow him?

Would she be able to forgive Tristan for his condemning attitude when faced with her true identity; his instinctive withdrawal from a woman he had just professed to love, but whose capacity for loyalty he might now always question? Could she cast off the shame she felt at having to own to such a father and leave her past behind her where it belonged, or would it always be there, lurking just below the surface, ready to raise its ugly head whenever she and Tristan quarreled, which she knew they would?

A sudden commotion in the hallway brought all five of the occupants of the room back to attention as Perkins entered to say that there was a "person" without demanding two pounds six for the rental of his hack or he would fetch the constable.

"A hack?" Sir Henry repeated, rising to his feet so that he could better reach in his trouser pocket for his purse. "Who in thunder engaged a hack?"

"I did, as a matter of fact," came a voice from the hallway, before Dexter Rutherford poked his head around the corner wearing his most winning smile and waggling his fingers in greeting. "Julian, do the pretty, will you? This oaf says he'll confiscate Kitty's satchel else. Hurry, do—there's no need setting the fellow's back up any more than it is."

*"Dexter!"* all five voices sang out at once, three in relief and two (the baritone members of the company) in exasperation.

*"Kitty!"* the three women then chorused as a woebegone little creature crept timidly into the room, her wide blue eyes red-rimmed with fatigue.

"Come here and sit down, dear," Lucy urged kindly, taking the younger girl's hand in hers and tugging gently. "You look burnt to the socket. What did that dreadful boy Dexter do to you? I swear he hasn't the wits of a flea. A hack, indeed! That cockle-head is foolish beyond permission."

"You found Kitty's note, I expect. It's either that or you're having a party and failed to invite me," Dexter remarked buoyantly, coming fully into the room once Julian had paid off the hack driver and secured Kitty's satchel. "Don't apologize. Kitty and I had ourselves a high old time of our own there for a while, bowling along lickety-split toward the north."

"And then you had second thoughts?" Mary prompted, thinking she was fast becoming an expert on such things.

Dexter laughed as he sat himself down at his ease on a small pillow he had dropped to the floor beside Kitty's chair. "I was never mad for the notion, you understand, but there was nothing else for it, so we were off. Second thoughts, you ask? It was nothing like. What sort of frippery fellow do you take me for—whisking a lady off to Gretna and then turning tail before we're halfway to the place? I have more bottom than that, let me warn you, even if there's many who'd try to tell you different."

"Whoever your detractors be, they may have my vote as

well," Julian quipped nastily as he reentered the drawing room. "Did you really think to ride all the way to Scotland, a three-day journey at best, in a broken-down hackney coach? Best plug up your ears, cousin, I do believe the stuffing's coming out of your brain."

"Oh, Gemini!" Kitty spoke up in her high, childish voice. "This is so prodigious unpleasant! You're all angry, aren't you? I told Dexter you would be."

"She's quick, I'll give her that," Lucy quipped, her cheerful grin taking the sting out of her words.

"It's all Jerry's fault, you know," Kitty persisted, willing to take on wild lions and tigers—or even a roomful of frowning people—to protect her dearest Dexter. "He was just being perverse, refusing his consent to our marriage. He doesn't really care a fig about me one way or the other. So what else were we to do?" she ended, looking to Sir Henry beseechingly.

"You might have thought to come to me, coz," Julian put in helpfully. "From what I've heard, Toland could have been bought off very easily, and then there would have been no need for your dramatic run to the border."

Dexter pulled himself up to his full height, although it added little to his consequence as he was naturally rather short and slight. "You would have me *buy* his consent, Julian? That's so—so—"

"Low-bred?" Lucy suggested, winking at her husband, who had the sensitivity to wince. "Nonsense, Dex, it's done all the time, and in the *highest* circles. But why, if you haven't had a change of heart, have you returned with 'the deed' still undone?"

"It wasn't for lack of determination, if that's what you're thinking," Dexter vowed, earning himself a watery smile from Kitty. "We ran short of the ready, as a matter of fact. I forgot I had paid some ridiculous sum on account to my tailor yesterday. It's so seldom I do silly things like that—is it any wonder it slipped my mind?

"Noticed it fast enough when I went to lay down m'blunt for our dinner at some pokey wayside inn, I'll tell you," he added feelingly. "Took my last groat to pay the fare, and the ham was stringy! The world's inhabited by thieves, do you know that? But that's not important. What matters is that now we won't be able to elope until my next quarter's allowance. Unless you'd care to advance me a hundred pounds, coz, in which case we'll be on our way again at first light and cause you no more bother."

Rachel pressed a hand to her mouth to suppress her mirth, as Julian's incredulous expression after hearing Dexter's meandering explanation—and most especially his last words—bordered on the comical. Just as Thorpe opened his mouth to deliver, Rachel was sure, one of his famous set-downs, she spoke up, saying briskly, "We'll discuss all this again in the morning when our thoughts are less muddled. Poor Kitty here is all but asleep where she sits. Mary, help Kitty to her chamber. Dexter, go home, dear—and take a bath. You reek of the stable."

"That doubting Thomas hackney driver didn't believe I'd make good on the fare and had me tending his broken-in-the-wind nags for him at our last two stops. Said he'd be hanged for a Chinaman if he wasn't paid one way or the other," Dex explained happily enough, noticing a stray piece of hay sticking out from under his lapel and disposing of it in a nearby candy dish. "I'll go if you say so, Miss Gladwin, but I'll be back first thing in the morning to see Kitty."

"You will be in my study at precisely nine of the clock tomorrow morning," Julian contradicted heavily, "to discuss your plan to set Miss Toland's and your betrothal moving along more orthodox, acceptable avenues. Is that sufficiently clear, cousin, or shall I repeat it for you?"

Dexter winced as if in pain, knowing full well he was in for a verbal drubbing on the morrow that would doubtless leave him reeling. Nobody could rip you up quite like Julian, and he did it without ever once raising his voice. If he weren't so frequently the recipient of his cousin's blistering lectures, Dex might actually be able to enjoy them, for they were delivered with all the skill of a bonafide master of the art of insult.

"Can't we just pretend you've already pointed out the error of my ways and forgiven me after listening to my heartfelt apologies and instead concentrate our efforts on bribing Toland into seeing things our way, since I have your word for it that such seemingly shabby tactics are within the bounds of propriety?" Dexter proposed magnanimously, willing to grasp at any straw.

"*Dex*-ter," Lucy warned, realizing the limits of her husband's patience had been stretched nearly to the breaking point. Poking fun at the foibles of high society at Julian's expense would not be Dexter's best choice if he wished to take up a new hobby. She motioned her head toward the doorway, and Dexter was quick to take her hint. "Good night, dear. We'll look for you in the morning."

Dexter grinned. If Lucy were to stand his ally, perhaps the interview wouldn't be too painful. "You'll be there?" he asked, his voice hopeful.

"I will," Lucy answered at the same time Julian declared, "She will *not*." Dexter escaped while the two of them stared at each other, primed to do battle.

"Well," Mary observed lightly, having hurried back to the drawing room after delivering Kitty to her maid, unwilling to miss any more of the proceedings than she could help. "It would seem Dexter has found himself a champion, Julian. You can scarcely tear a strip off his hide with your wife standing there hovering over him like a broody hen with one chick."

Julian merely shook his head in the negative, winking at Mary. "Then I shall simply accuse my cousin of seeking petticoat protection. *He'll* then ask Lucy to leave, just to prove me wrong, and *then* I shall give that young fool a lesson or two that will serve to remove the spring from his step for a space. Eloping to Gretna with only a few shillings in his pockets. My God, the mind boggles!"

Mary laughed appreciatively as Lucy, knowing her ace had just been firmly trumped, stuck out her tongue at her smug husband. "I shall retire gracefully from the field this time, Julian, leaving you your small victory."

"You have to do that once in a while," she then told Mary blithely as she gathered up her shawl and evening purse. "It boosts a man's self-esteem. I try to make it a rule to let him win at least once in our every ten encounters." She grasped Thorpe's arm in both her hands and smiled up at him coquettishly. "Isn't that right, darling?"

Julian tipped up Lucy's chin with his index finger and dropped a light kiss on her mouth. "By the time you and Jennie are through tutoring Mary, poor Tristan is going to wish there was a nice, quiet war left somewhere for him to fight. Come on now, brat, we may as well go home. I'm no longer in the mood for dancing."

"Yes, my dearest, anything you say," Lucy agreed meekly before throwing kisses to Mary and her aunt and allowing her husband to lead her away.

"It bears repeating: how I ever survived the rearing of that imp of the devil is beyond me," Rachel said, sighing. "Come, Mary. We'd best go check on our returned prodigal. Henry?"

"I'll be here, Rachel. Waiting." Ruffton's voice was full of promise as he reluctantly released her hand.

There are a total of three newly betrothed females in the Ruffton household this night, Mary told herself as she slowly mounted the stairs. Kitty will most probably be already asleep and dreaming, confident her Dexter is equal to any problems that stand between them and their eventual marriage. Rachel, for her part, will doubtless soon be creeping back down the stairs to snuggle in the drawing room with her beloved Henry until Perkins coughs discreetly and sends her off to her dreams of wedded bliss.

And what of the third affianced bride? Mary thought self-pityingly. Oh yes, she will be left all alone in her bedchamber with her unhappy thoughts, doubtless the only newly betrothed female in all of England who will be crying herself to sleep this night.

# CHAPTER SIXTEEN

THE GLOWING TIP of his discarded cigarillo drew a brief red arc in midair before disappearing into one of the high, unkempt weedy patches in what Rule's head groundskeeper had dared to refer to as the "informal garden."

He had been away playing at master spy too long, he told himself yet again—while Rule's Roost, his late father's pride and joy, had been left to the care of others. Pushing his body away from the ivy-choked brick wall he had been leaning against, he stepped more fully into the small patch of pale moonlight that was the only illumination in the cloak of darkness that served as cover for either the garden's or Rule's shame.

He had been at the Roost for three days, putting off the visit to his largest estate until last. By the time he had finished inspecting his horse-breeding property in Sussex and his orchards near Linton, he had thought he'd been prepared for the conditions he might find in Surrey, but the estate was in poorer trim than he had envisioned even in his worst predictions.

Oh, the farms themselves were well enough, as were the mills and the forestry holdings that had been his father's pet projects. Even though his inheritance had been thrust on him when he was still quite young, Tristan had shown the good sense to keep all his father's personal choices in their same positions of authority on the estate—bright young men who spoke of the "science of agriculture"—and his steady income over the years had given him no indication of anything being amiss.

Not that he would have tossed away his responsibilities to Sir Henry and the government even if he'd known anything had been wrong, he told himself now, shrugging his shoulders as he recognized the truth.

But the houses! And the grounds! How could he have been so blind? He knew his father's household retainers were already getting past it before he left home—after all, they had all been contemporaries of his father, or even older. One by one Tristan's housekeepers and butlers and gardeners had withered silently away, leaving the Roost and his other two houses to the indifferent mercies of young, mostly untrained servants whose main functions seemed to be equally divided between keeping their bellies full and doing as little work as possible.

Yet the worst, the very worst of it was not the overgrown gardens or the dusty furniture or the stained marble flooring or even the soot-blackened portraits. It was the fact that everywhere he turned, every place he looked, he immediately thought, Mary could set this place to rights in the wink of an eye, and enjoy every moment of it into the bargain.

While he sat in the small dining room, picking at his solitary supper, he imagined Mary sitting at the opposite end of the table, laughing and teasing him, badgering him into eating all his vegetables.

As he mounted the first step of the wide, curving staircase that hugged the wall as it rose gracefully to the upper rooms he could see Mary descending slowly, taking care to lift the hem of her gown, coming to join him as they waited for the arrival of their dinner guests.

When he rode out across his lands, his heart filled with the pride of ownership, it was with the thought of Mary riding at his side, listening to his dreams for the future—dreams that included the enrichment of his properties, in order to provide a legacy worthy of the children that would someday ride these same fertile fields.

And when he opened the heavy oaken door to the master bedchamber he was careful not to let his gaze stray to the wide bed, where night after night he envisioned Mary lying against the plumped-up pillows, her auburn hair unbound and tumbling over her bare shoulders, her smooth white arms outstretched, a welcoming smile on her face.

Tristan covered his face with his hands, his eyes tightly closed, trying to blot out the scenes that appeared so clearly, even in this dark, shadowed garden. "A week," he muttered, anguish in his voice, "seven bloody-by-damn days! And it doesn't get better. *It gets worse!*"

"I MURDER HIM, I MURDER him not," Mary recited dully, stripping the petals one by one from the inoffensive bloom she held in her hand. "I murder him, I murder him not. I mur—"

"Oh dear," Lucy interrupted blithely as she peered around the partially opened door of the bedchamber and caught Mary in the act. "Aunt Rachel told me you had progressed from the doldrums to the heights, but I did not realize you were making plans to *do away* with poor Tris."

Mary tossed the denuded flower away from her and turned to smile at her friend. "You may rest easy. I shall murder him *not,* at least according to *that* posy's prediction. Not that the thought doesn't have some mild appeal."

Rachel, with Mary's permission, had already informed Lucy of exactly what was causing the breach between the lovers, and Mary had come to look forward to Lucy's daily

visits—even if Lucy did persist in being disgustingly opti-
mistic. "Well," Lucy said now, seating herself cozily on a
wide chair, her toes tucked up under the hem of her gown,
"at least you're not still glooming in your chambers, believing yourself to be some sort of Pandora and responsible for
every ill to hit this world since the flood. Who knows," she
added brightly, "given another day or two, you might just find
you can face the world again—with or without my Master
Grump cousin Tristan."

And it *had* been a difficult week for Mary. As Lucy had
said, she had taken to her chamber, hiding herself and her
shame away from the rest of the world. But it had been the
loss of Tristan—and quite possibly Tristan's love—that had
plunged her neck-deep into the dismals. Concern for her
charge had prompted Rachel to apply to Lucy for assistance,
for if there were ever a better person for looking on the bright
side of things, Rachel couldn't imagine who it would be.

Lucy had more than lived up to her aunt's hopes, beard-
ing Mary in her den—her bedchamber actually, but Rachel
was fast becoming enamored of her own creative talents—
and making the girl see that, although her late father was not
the sort one would wish to have immortalized in oils for the
family portrait gallery, it did not necessarily follow that Mary
should shoulder any blame for her father's sins.

From there it was but a short step to the real heart of the
problem: Tristan's reaction to the news. But that too was dismissed with a careless wave of Lucy's small hand. "It's all
a nine days' wonder," she had told Mary confidently. "Tris
was always marvelous at 'causes,' championing the down-
trodden and fighting evil wherever it existed—even if it was
only in his own firebrand mind. In his youth, Tristan viewed
your father much like Robin Hood saw the Sheriff of
Nottingham. Imagine poor Robin's reaction if his fair Maid
Marion had been discovered to be the sheriff's daughter!

Still, I am sure Friar Tuck would still have had a wedding ceremony to perform once Robin realized that, just like in all the stories, true love *does* conquer all."

Lucy's words had served to break the dam of Mary's emotions, and the two women had held each other while Mary laughed, then cried, then reached deep down inside herself and began to think clearly for the first time since that fateful day when Tristan had proposed marriage.

She had rediscovered her own worth, and had found reasons to be confident that Tristan's love for her—combined with hers for him—was enough to take them across the highest hurdle and gain them the happiness that waited on the other side.

But for Mary—who had not once in her memory been complimented for possessing a history of displaying ladylike patience—a week was time and enough for Tristan to have come to his senses and ridden back to town to claim her hand in form. While Rachel shook her head and voiced her misgivings to Sir Henry, Lucy looked on in amusement as Mary's feelings for Tristan ran the gamut from apprehension, to loverlike concern, to breathless anticipation, to impotent frustration, to—as the second week of Rule's absence began—downright anger.

"Stubborn baboon," Mary was saying now with a decidedly militant air as she gathered up the scattered flower petals and disposed of them. "Not only could I box his ears for haring off to who knows where to leave me here with the whole mess of explaining his absence in my dish, but he is taking his sweet time in realizing that he simply cannot live without me."

Lucy peered at her owlishly. "Could this be the same watering pot who clung to my skirts blubbering something about having lost Tristan's love forevermore? I have to point out, my dear, that when it comes to self-confidence, there is

little difference between you and my redoubtable cousin."
She shrugged her shoulders and pulled a face. "But what do
I know—as I have never been the shy and retiring sort my-
self."

"Wretch," Mary retorted amicably. "First you do your utmost to convince me that Tristan and I have a glorious future
awaiting us, and then you browbeat me for my impatience to
begin it. I was a fool to ever doubt that Tris would see that
the past has less than nothing to do with us. I admit it freely,
but please do not try to hoax me by delivering me a lecture
on how I should not be angry with the man for stretching my
sanity to the snapping point while he dithers about in the
country scratching up the nerve to return to London and meet
his fate."

"Bachelors never walk eyes open into the bridle, Mary,"
Lucy pointed out, speaking from her own personal experience as she pretended to inspect her nails, "but eventually
they do all break to the saddle." Then, unable to hold her
woman-of-the-world pose, she collapsed into girlish giggles, trying to imagine her dear Julian with a set of reins dan-
gling from his aristocratic neck.

"You may laugh, Lucy," Mary told her, the light of battle
in her eyes, "but Tristan is still heaven knows where and I
am still sitting here stewing, waiting for him to come to his
senses. I don't mind telling you that for every moment I
spend contemplating getting a little of my own back for the
misery he is causing me, I spend two fretting myself sick that
he will feel it his duty to spend the rest of his life doing penance alone atop some far-off mountain for the dastardly sin
of falling in love with the daughter of his most hated enemy."

"It is a maddening mull, isn't it?" Lucy commented sym-
pathetically. "Perhaps it is time I sent Julian to Tristan. A little man-to-man talk might be beneficial. Where is Tristan,
anyway? In Surrey?"

"He can be in Jericho for all I care." Mary sniffed, feeling her recently acquired firm resolve to put a cheerful face on things beginning to crumble a bit at the foundation.

"Really?" Lucy asked doubtfully.

*"No!"* Mary rallied, hopping to her feet to cross the room briskly in answer to the knock that had just come at the door. "I asked Aunt Rachel that I not be disturbed unless it was something about Tristan. Do you think he might have at last settled all his demons and is even now waiting for me downstairs? Do I look all right? Oh, Lucy, I *don't* want to murder him, really I don't!"

She flung open the door to see one of the under-footmen standing in the hallway, a folded letter in his outstretched hand. Grabbing it with more haste than grace, she fairly slammed the door on the poor fellow's nose before skipping back to the bed, ripping open the plain, wax seal as she wiggled her bottom into a comfortable spot in the middle of the satin bedspread.

"It's from Tristan, I just know it is!" Lucy declared delightedly, scrambling onto the bed to peer over Mary's shoulder as her friend read the contents of what was sure to be a most intriguing communication. "His handwriting was always as atrocious as my spelling," she said by way of excusing her nosiness. "You may need me to interpret for you."

But before Lucy could catch so much as a glimpse of the letter, Mary had hastily crumpled it and pressed the paper against her breast. "What's the matter?" Lucy coaxed gently, seeing that Mary had suddenly turned very pale. "It *is* from Tristan, isn't it?" Her eyes narrowing dangerously, she continued, her voice deepening to keep pace with her darkening emotions: "If that lamebrained, looby has gone and done something stupid like setting sail to India to think things out, I will personally travel to Surrey to pull off his nose and stuff it in his ear! Of all the mad starts that idealistic moron has perpetrated, this one beats them all hollow! Why, I—"

"You can't pull off his nose, Lucy, if he is already aboard ship," Mary pointed out quietly, turning to look her friend in the eye. "Besides, this letter isn't from Tristan at all. The servant must have just assumed it was."

Lucy let out a deep sigh of relief before realizing that, whether the communication was from Tristan or not, it certainly contained *something* that had greatly upset her friend. She made a grab for the paper, but Mary quickly held it up out of her way."

"Lucy," Mary said earnestly, "your Aunt Rachel has told me what a scapegrace you are. If you will swear yourself to the deepest secrecy—promise not to breathe a word of this, even to Julian—can I count on you to help me?"

Lucy lifted her chin, willing herself to look competent and worthy of Mary's confidence. "Need you ask?" she pronounced dramatically. "But what about Tristan? If you need help, surely he is the one to whom you should apply. Besides, it would certainly serve to send him hying back here to London posthaste, if he believed his fair damsel to be in peril from some dragon."

Mary shook her head, dismissing the idea, much as it appealed to her. "Don't make me think about Tristan right now, Lucy, as it will only serve to make me even more angry than before, seeing that it is his fault that I am in this coil at all."

"How?" Clearly Lucy was confused. "Will you please stop holding that letter above your head like some sort of dark cloud and tell me what is going on? *What* is Tristan's fault?"

Mary lowered her arm and handed the letter to her friend. "Someone must have seen me that night in Green Park while I was playing the spy for Tristan's benefit. I'm to buy this person's silence about my scandalous behavior by stealing some papers from Sir Henry's desk. I don't believe it, Lucy, it's almost as if Tristan wished this catastrophe on me! *I'm being blackmailed!*"

JULIAN RUTHERFORD HAD ALWAYS had a rather high opinion of himself, and even if Lucy's advent into his life had brought with it the realization that he was merely human after all, he was not about to believe that he had become so insignificant as to appear to be transparent.

Yet that was how he must have looked to his wife later that same night as he entered their town-house bedchamber with romantic dalliance in mind. Walking up behind Lucy as she sat before her dressing table absently drawing her brush through her dark locks, he leaned down to nibble delicately on her left earlobe, a location he had long ago discovered to be one of his favorite nuzzling spots. Needless to say, her response of, "Julian, please, I have no time for that now," was not exactly the soft purr of pleasure he had been expecting.

He retreated a moment, then attacked from another angle, running his fingertips in soft, lazy circles slowly up and down her bare back, which lay exposed above the low neckline of her dressing gown. Lucy twitched her shoulders as if to shoo him away and complained, "Stop that, it tickles!"

Julian straightened, looking into the mirror at his wife's reflection. Uh-oh, he thought, remembering that particular expression on her face all too well. Loosely encircling her slim neck with both his hands, he asked in his most off-handed way, "Whose demise are you planning, dearest? Dexter has promised to abide by my decision to approach Toland with an offer I believe the man will find hard to resist, so you can't be plotting my maggoty cousin's next attempt at elopement. That leaves Tristan and Miss Lawrence, I believe. To be truthful, pet, I'd rather you refrain from poking your pretty little nose into Rule's affairs. I fear he might just take exception to your well-meant interference and break *mine* by way of retaliation."

"Tristan wouldn't do any such thing," Lucy argued, leaning her cheek against Rutherford's hand. "He likes you too much. At least," she added almost as if she were talking to herself, "he won't if he understands that you didn't know anything anyway, and therefore *couldn't* have told him, which you wouldn't because you're a man of your word, and I would make you give me your word before I told you— which I won't—so the whole question is silly, isn't it?"

"Dear me," Julian drawled after a moment of stunned silence, applying just enough pressure to Lucy's shoulders to have her rising from her seat so that he could turn her to face him, "I do believe I shall have to ask you to explain that last muddled statement. The only thing I have found to be worse than one of your harum-scarum ideas, my love, is to find out about it after the fact." Lowering his eyebrows menacingly, he prodded. "Lucy...out with it...*now*. I'm your husband, and wives should have no secrets from their husbands, should they?"

Lucy dropped her chin onto her chest, admitting defeat. "All right, Julian, I'll tell you," she said, sighing. Her voice was muffled against the front of her dressing gown as she added, "But you aren't going to like it above half."

He pulled her comfortingly against his broad chest, suppressing a manly smirk of satisfaction that would have had her ripping a good-sized strip off his hide if he had been foolish enough to allow her to see it. This marriage business wasn't so bad, he had discovered in the past year, just as long as he made sure to remind his wife occasionally just who was in charge.

Perhaps it was this preoccupation with his own brilliance in bringing his adorable widget of a wife to heel that blinded the Earl of Thorpe to the fact that his wife, now snuggling kittenishly beside him in the middle of their wide comfortable bed, was smiling in a way that would have warned him that she was telling him only what she wanted him to hear.

# CHAPTER SEVENTEEN

TRISTAN WAS IN HIS BEDCHAMBER packing his belongings with a fervor only marginally concerned with neatness. For the first time since he had ridden his curricle neck or nothing out of London behind his blacks nearly two weeks earlier, he lamented his decision to leave his valet behind, preferring to sacrifice his comfort for speed.

But now, now that his hard-won decision had at last been made, he could only wish for Bates to be with him, so that the necessary packing—and a more useless, time-consuming exercise he could not imagine—could be taken out of his hands.

Wedging his new black brocade waistcoat down inside a satchel to rest cheek by jowl with one of a pair of muddy riding boots, he cursed himself yet again for being a blind, stubborn fool. How could he have—even for one moment, yet alone the better part of a fortnight—ever thought Mary's parentage meant anything? What sort of blistering idiot was he to toss away his only chance at happiness because Jules St. Laurent, dead and buried these last ten years, just happened to be the father of the woman he loved?

He had reacted, that's what he had done. What he had not done, he reminded himself with yet another swift mental kick, was *think!* Damn him for the hotheaded fool everyone who loved him swore him to be. He had behaved like some lily-pure candidate for sainthood who had nary a mar or blemish on his own record.

Well, nearly two weeks of searching his own conscience had revealed to him that not all of his actions during the past war would hold up very well under scrutiny. He may not have played both ends against the middle, he may not have acted only on his own behalf, and damn the lives lost by his treachery, but the news he so carefully ferreted out and sent back to Sir Henry had more than once resulted in someone's death. Indeed, there were several men now below ground that Tristan had personally sent to meet their Maker. Yet he had never stopped to ask himself if Mary could learn to live with the blood that was on *his* hands.

Jules St. Laurent had been a villain of the first water, there was no doubt about it. That he had succeeded in siring such a splendid, loving creature as Mary went against all the rules of nature, not to mention Tristan's long-held notions of right and wrong, black and white, truth and falsehood. But Mary did exist, and Tristan knew he could not love her more if her father had been the exemplary Sir Henry Ruffton himself.

If only it wasn't already too late. If only Mary could find it in her heart to forgive him for the damned presumptuous ass he had been that fateful day when he had learned of her parentage. "Oh, God, what a dolt I was!" he exclaimed now as he remembered how she had strode away from him that day, her chin held high, as he had bid her a stiffly polite farewell. "Pluck to the backbone," he said out loud as he threw his closed satchel at the servant who had just entered the room unannounced, thinking that any woman who could withstand the shabby treatment he had served up to her that day and not crumble was a jewel he could hardly believe he was worthy to possess.

"Move it, man, I want to be on my way before the sun rises another inch in the sky or know the reason why," he said to the servant, who had caught the satchel in self-defense and was standing there holding the thing as if he was still wondering how he had come to have it in his hands.

"But—but, milord," the man squeaked timidly (for all of Rule's servants, recipients of a rare dressing-down once the master had finished inspecting Rule's Roost, were more than a little in awe of their employer), "George jist come in wit some post, an' seein' as 'ow ever one's fer yer, Oi—"

Tristan suppressed an impatient oath and held out his hand for the mail pouch. He'd give its contents a quick read as he gulped down some breakfast and then be on his way. Loping down the wide stairs two at a time, he quickly scanned the letters, five in all, and felt a small shiver of apprehension skitter down his spine.

They were all from London. "And none of them," he muttered darkly under his breath, "is an invitation to tea."

Once seated in the breakfast room, he tore them open one after the other and read the signatures. Julian. Lucy. Rachel. Sir Henry. Dexter. *Dexter?* Good Lord, that scatterwit was so averse to writing that Tristan had once seen him ask the dealer in some gaming hell to scribble his vowels for him and he would then add his initials at the bottom. Something very serious must be going on if Dexter felt it necessary to take up a pen.

He threw down all the letters, then picked up the first that came to hand, which proved to be a mistake. Lucy's florid handwriting, overpopulated with swirls and curlicues, was nearly impossible to decipher, and her sentences, hinting of dire happenings, seemed to run on forever without saying anything at all.

His Aunt Rachel's missive was no better, which set his inner alarm bells to ringing all the more, for Rachel could always be counted upon to keep a cool head in a crisis, and Sir Henry's note, probably because he had long since perfected the art of concealing information, did no more than comment on the crowds descending on London for the coming fetes and request Rule's own presence for the festivities.

His appetite for the plateful of ham and eggs sitting before him having fled as he examined the first three communications, Tristan gathered up Julian's note in his one hand and stuck Dexter's missive in his pocket before heading toward the front door at a near run. He'd read the letters during his first stop for fresh horses, he told himself as he vaulted onto the seat of the curricle and snatched up the reins from the waiting groom.

But right now his years spent developing a sixth sense that warned him of impending danger served only to heighten his fears as he knew, deep in his rapidly beating heart, that Mary needed him—now!

DEXTER WAS PACING BACK and forth across the Rutherfords' drawing-room carpet as his cousin watched in amusement. "I tell you, Julian, I had to do it. Ever since Kitty told me about her brother's past schemes—using her so shabbily to get himself inside the best houses and rob the inhabitants blind—I've been hard-pressed to keep silent. For he *is* her only relative, after all, and Kitty might take exception if I were to do something that would have the curst fellow clapped up in irons or something. But when she broke down and told me what Toland had said about Miss Lawrence—"

"It's all right, Dexter," Julian said soothingly, very much liking this new show of maturity his cousin was evincing, even if he didn't quite believe Dex completely comprehended the real facts in the matter.

"All right? All right!" Dexter exploded, throwing his slim body dramatically into a nearby chair. "If that don't beat the

Dutch! How can you say so? I introduce Kitty into Sir Henry's household and the next thing you know her rum-touch brother is loping off with the family silver! But even the shame of such a thing pales into insignificance when you think the rotter may be trying to run some rig on Miss Lawrence. Lord! Tris will have my guts for garters, and no mistake!" Dexter prophesied grimly, dropping his chin onto his chest.

"So you felt it incumbent upon yourself then to write to Tristan directly and apprise him of a—um—*situation* that might require his presence in London?"

"You may tick me off for it, coz, but I really had no choice but to write to him, considering how I thought I'd like to keep my head where it is—attached to my neck," Dexter confessed, not caring that it was obvious that self-preservation had accounted for a good bit of his concern for Mary. "Besides, the ladies at Sir Henry's have all been acting as queer as Dick's hatband for the last week, always sneaking away together to whisper in corners, so it's Carleton House to a Charley's shelter that *something* havey-cavey is going on."

"Miss Gladwin included?" Julian pressed, finding it hard to believe anything too untoward could be occurring with that down-to-earth female around to keep Mary and Lucy from doing anything too outlandish.

Dexter sniffed, dismissing Rachel as having anything to do with the subject. "Miss Gladwin and Sir Henry are full of April and May, coz, and I swear, it would take more than a roof falling on their heads for them to notice that anything was amiss. Not that Kitty knows anything to the point either—the poor, innocent angel. I've just taken two and two and made four of it, that's all."

Julian allowed a small smile to escape his lips. "And they say there is nothing new under the sun. My goodness, you see me standing before you, amazed," he drawled, lighting his cheroot with a spill from the candelabra. "As to your compulsion to write to Rule and tell *all,* my dear boy, I must applaud you for your decisive action, and would give a great deal to see Tristan's face when he reads what I am sure must be quite an eloquent letter, considering your infrequent communications to me whilst you were up at school. However, as I too have felt the need to inform Tristan of the goings-on concerning his Miss Lawrence, I have no fears that we won't be seeing the fellow's dear, scowling face anytime soon."

That got Dexter's full attention! He jumped to his feet to confront his cousin. "Julian, you plague a fellow out of his mind, do you know that! You've let me ramble on and on ever since I got here, confessing my dearest Kitty's deepest secrets when there was not the slightest need for me to betray her confidence, when all the time you already knew something queer was going on. Remind me to do something especially nice for Lucy next I see her," he said acidly, "for how she has the fortitude to put up with the likes of you I'll never understand."

Thorpe poured his cousin a drink and then slipped a soothing arm around the younger man's shoulders. "Heavens, I do believe you are somewhat incensed, bantling," he remarked cordially enough. "But before you go calling me out, let me tell you that although I am aware of what you call a *situation,* your information linking your false friend to it comes as quite a surprise. I only knew of a blackmailer. You, dear cousin, have given me a name. I commend you."

"Throw roses at his feet some other time, Julian," Tristan Rule advised tersely as he stormed into the room, still clad in his travel dirt. "Right now I want the bastard's name, so I can call him by it before I tear him into little pieces."

Dexter seemed to fold in on himself as he shrank inside Julian's comforting half embrace. "You can tell him without finding it necessary to jog his memory as to just who introduced Toland to Miss Lawrence, can't you?" he whispered pleadingly before ducking out from beneath Julian's arm and doing his best to blend in with the furnishings.

"Tris!" Julian covered neatly, crossing to Rule and holding out his hand in welcome. "You made good time, considering the state of the mails. I imagine you didn't spare the horses. No matter, Tiny and Goliath will see to them, I'm sure. I vow I shall miss those two when it comes time to return them to Kit. Come sit down and I'll ring for some refreshments. I'm sorry Lucy isn't here to greet you, but she's been living in Mary's pocket this last week, you know."

All through this prolonged greeting Tristan had been mumbling and grumbling, darting piercing looks in Dexter's direction that had the young man shaking in his shoes. "Did you ever try to make head or tail of anything that fellow has ever written?" he asked Julian as he accepted a glass holding a good three fingers of whiskey. "I've yet to decipher a word of it, or of Lucy's message for that matter, and Rachel and Sir Henry make a good pair, considering that between the two of them they managed to say nothing at all. Thank God for your note, Julian, else I might have been out of my mind with worry by now."

Julian acknowledged this faint praise with a nod of his head. "I can't tell you much more than I already have, I'm afraid. Lucy thought she could keep the blackmail scheme a secret from me, but I saw right through her, of course. She's promised to keep a close eye on Mary for me until you could return, but the blackmailer has yet to write again setting up a time and place for the information to change hands."

Tristan, remembering Lucy from their youth, narrowed his eyes and asked: "Are you sure she's holding nothing back from you? It's not like Lucy to be quite so helpful. It would be more in character if she were to combine forces with

Mary and have the two of them plotting to capture this black-mailer themselves just to prove that they could do it."

Julian tipped his head to one side and thought about it for a moment, then shook his head. "Not Lucy," he said firmly. "She's a wife now, and past such nonsense."

"Rutherford!" Rule called, stopping the young man with the stern tone of his voice as Dexter was about to slink out of the room. "Two questions, if you please. One—considering your cousin's last statement, have you ever seen a pig fly?"

"Are you questioning my assessment of my wife's character?" Thorpe began heatedly. "Let me tell you something, Rule—"

"And two," Tristan went on unheeding, "give me the blackmailer's name, since you seem to have discovered it. In return I promise to try not to break your foolish neck!"

"TRISTAN'S BACK!"

Mary, who had been standing beside the window looking out onto the street at the ragged urchin who was running off after delivering a second missive from the blackmailer, whirled about quickly, allowing the drapery to fall back into place.

"When? How?" she questioned, suddenly breathless.

Lucy dropped into a chair, fanning herself furiously with the glove she had just removed from her right hand. "I was just coming into the square when I saw his curricle pulled up in front of the house. It was a near-run thing, as Julian's coachman didn't take kindly to my order to have him return me to you so I could collect the glove I left behind—especially considering the fact that I had two gloves, already upon my hands—but I knew you'd want to be warned at once."

"Warned, Lucy?" Mary questioned, tilting her head as if

to better understand. "You were the one who swore to me that once Tristan came to his senses, he would rush to me and all but fall on my neck begging forgiveness. Why do I suddenly require a warning?"

Lucy lowered her eyes, trying to figure out a way of saying what had to be said without unduly upsetting Mary. "I wrote to Tristan, Mary," she began, only to be cut off by Mary's exasperated exclamation of disbelief. "I had to!" she insisted, flinging out her hands helplessly. "After telling Julian, it seemed the only safe thing to do. Think about it for a moment, Mary," she pleaded. "If Tris ever found out that Julian knew about the blackmailer and hadn't told him, and if you and I, perish the very thought, are discovered trying to capture this horrid blackmailer of yours—well, Tristan just won't like it if he finds out we all knew and didn't bother telling him, that's all."

"He'd punch your Julian square in his aristocratic nose, wouldn't he?" Mary agreed ungraciously, for Lucy's disclosure to Julian was still a sore subject between the two of them. "You realize, of course, that if you hadn't told Julian about the blackmailer, we wouldn't be in this coil now. I can only marvel that a mind so devious as to have the man believing you have told him the entire truth could have been so lamentably unable to keep the *entire* matter a secret."

"I was hoping Julian would take it upon himself to write to Tristan," Lucy said in a small voice. "Men—you can never count on them to do what you want them to do. I checked the mailbag every morning for the letter, but in the end I had to take it upon myself to write Tristan. After all, if you said it once this week, you said it a thousand times—you can't wait to see the look on Tristan's face when he realizes that you've captured a blackmailer." Lucy spread her hands as if she had just made everything quite clear. "Well, you can't very well gloat over him if he's buried deep in Surrey, can you?"

Shaking her head in amused disbelief, Mary asked, "Are you quite sure there is no blood relation between you and Dexter? Your minds seem to work in the same illogical, hare-brained way, you know."

Lucy snuggled more deeply into her chair and pretended to pout. "We can sit here all afternoon arguing, but what's done is done, and now Tristan is in London, and will doubtless be here within the hour, once Julian has told him everything he knows. As Julian believes me to be a spy myself, reporting all your actions to him, I am sure he will be able to defuse my cousin at least a little bit before he comes storming in here to tear you apart for not contacting him as soon as you learned of the blackmailer's existence. It's a pity we'll have nothing more to show him than that single letter."

"But that isn't all," Mary teased, waving the second letter in front of Lucy's face. "You know how you promised to help me, Lucy? Well, here's your chance. By the time Tristan runs me to earth I shall have taken care of the blackmailer myself—and saved Tristan from the gallows for having done the man in. Then I shall be more than happy to allow him to beg my forgiveness for having caused me all this trouble in the first place."

"And he will have realized once and for all that it can be very dangerous to jump to conclusions," Lucy added, reading the letter that called for an assignation later that same day for the purpose of exchanging Sir Henry's papers for the blackmailer's silence.

"It is nice to have everything coming together so neatly, isn't it?" Mary mused, wondering if it would be good form to wear her new blue walking dress to meet a blackmailer.

# CHAPTER EIGHTEEN

CONSIDERING THAT IT WAS BORN of necessity and formulated in haste, Mary's plan was, in Lucy's words, "none too shabby." Within an hour of Lucy's arrival with the information that Tristan was back in town, the two ladies were climbing into Sir Henry's closed town carriage, off to meet the blackmailer in a house just off Bow Street.

But alas, their departure did not go unnoticed. For just as the carriage was about to round the corner Lord Rule, with Lord Thorpe up beside him, came by tooling his curricle in the opposite direction. There was no doubt that the ladies had been seen and identified, a fact that was quickly substantiated by Mary, who looked out the back flap of the carriage to see Tristan wheeling his horses in a sharp turn, obviously set on following wherever the ladies led.

"We left it too late!" Lucy groaned, sinking back against the squabs in an attitude of defeat.

"Nonsense," Mary countered, already unbuttoning the top of her dress. "They are only following us because they know of nothing better to do with themselves. Why, we could be heading for the park for all they know."

"In a closed carriage?"

Mary wrinkled her nose at this reasonable question and quickly pulled the cords that lowered the privacy shades on either side of the carriage. "Don't quibble, Lucy, I'm nervous enough as it is. Now quickly, change clothing with me."

"What? Have you run entirely mad?"

"If we change clothes before we alight from the carriage, Julian will recognize your outfit and think I am you, that way I can meet up with Ben at the Bazaar as we have planned and you can lead your husband and Tristan off in another direction." Mary's bodice was completely undone by this time, and she was wiggling inelegantly as she tried to slip her dress down past her hips.

Lucy had chosen to pull her gown off over her head, so that her protest was faintly muffled. "But I'm supposed to go with you! How do you know the servants will be enough?"

Stopping what she was doing for the moment, Mary delivered Lucy a leveling stare. "*Tiny* will not be enough? Come now, dear, even you know that with Tiny and Goliath and Ben, you were only coming along for the thrill of the thing. Now hurry, I believe we're almost there."

"These bonnets are a godsend," Lucy said breathlessly, still huffing and puffing a bit after the exertion of completely changing her outfit within the confines of the carriage. "I vow I've never before seen such a profusion of ostrich plumes. No one will be able to recognize either of us from any distance."

Mary nodded, tying the ribbons of her own bonnet under her chin and arranging the plumes in concealing fashion around the left side of her face. "I thought much the same thing when I saw them on Bond Street the other day. Poor Aunt Rachel, she couldn't understand my sudden ecstasy for drooping bird feathers, telling me youth has no reason to hide behind such frippery stuff."

The carriage slowed to a stop, and within moments the door was opened and the steps were let down for the ladies to descend to the flagway directly in front of the bazaar. Mary poked her head out first and immediately espied Ben standing off to one side, a resigned look on his face. "Hurry, Lucy," Mary then instructed, chancing a quick peek down the street to see Tristan furiously berating the driver of a wagon-load of wooden casks who was blocking the way.

Immediately after entering the bazaar, Mary thought, So far, so good, as Lucy went off in one direction and she and Ben in another. It may have been bad form to have gone into public without the protection of a maid or footman, but Mary didn't wish to involve anyone else in her conspiracy. Besides, as she was meeting Ben at the not quite so *tonnish* bazaar anyway, rather than at Sir Henry's house, there didn't seem to be too much danger involved.

Now that Lucy was to be set loose alone, however, Mary did take the time to experience a slight qualm about her friend's safety, but the thought that Julian and Tristan would soon catch up with her alleviated some of her guilt. All that mattered now was to get to the house near Bow Street, confront her blackmailer, and have Tiny hoist the man on his shoulders and carry him off to the constable.

She'd show Tristan that she was loyal to England, by God, and that she didn't need a constant watchdog to take care of her either! If she and Tris were to ever have a chance at happiness, they would have to begin as equals.

"Ben?" she asked, after following the bandy-legged servant onto a side street and entering the hack he had waiting for them there. "How far is it to Bow Street? Are Tiny and Goliath already in position? You are armed, aren't you?"

Ben answered her last question by patting the bulge that showed through his clothing. "Be there a'fore the cat ken lick 'er ear," he assured her as they bumped along the road. "We'll be met."

"DEVIL A BIT OF IT, where are they?" Rule asked, exasperated.

Julian looked around again, trying in vain to pick out either his wife or Mary among the throng of shoppers, clerks and pickpockets that jammed the narrow aisles of the large building. "Wait a moment, I think I see Lucy over there," he said, pointing off to the left.

"No," Tristan disagreed, narrowing his eyes for a better look. "But it's good enough, for it's Mary you've found. I think I recognize that gown. God, Julian, but that's a deucedly ugly hat. Why do women persist on wearing such things?"

As Tris spoke they were moving steadily in the direction of the weaving ostrich plumes, closing in on the object of their search. "Mary's gown or nay, that's my Lucy," Thorpe persisted. "I may have overshot myself a bit thinking my wife above hoodwinking me, but I'll not have anyone tell me I don't know Lucy's body better than any man alive."

Rule might have dared a lot of things, but he wasn't going to touch Julian's last statement with a barge pole! In the end, it was academic anyway, for just as they came into three feet of their destination, Lucy turned about to face them, fear and relief showing on her face.

"Oh, dear, I'm in the suds this time, aren't I?" she asked, wincing a bit as she saw the scowl that had begun to furrow Julian's brow. "I'll beg forgiveness later, really I will, and I am prodigiously sorry, for it does begin to seem that this was a harebrained idea, doesn't it, though if you had made the smallest push, Julian, I would have confided in you, even if Mary were not already in full flight with her scheme, but for now I must tell you that I am quite concerned about Mary. I—I think she might require some assistance."

Julian shot a quick look at Tristan, who was becoming alarmingly red of face, and grabbed his wife by the arm to lead her back out onto the flag-way. "You've had a second communication from Jerome, haven't you? You promised to tell me if there were any further developments. I'm exceedingly put out with you, Lucille."

"Oh, Julian, don't go all stuffy on me." Lucy pouted, thrusting out her chin. "Just say you're mad as fire with me and have done with it. I—what did you say? *Jerome?* You *know* who the blackmailer is? Jerome *who?*"

"Jerome Toland, Kitty's brother," Tristan ground out, whirling his cousin around to face him. "The man's desperate for money. This isn't a game any longer, Lucy. Mary could be in grave danger." Lucy's determined chin began to crumple as a prelude to tears and he relented a bit, urging softly, "An address, pet, just give us some direction."

Wiping roughly at her tear-wet cheeks, Lucy, who would not have been so squeamish if it were she herself who were in danger, but whose tender heart was now filled with dread for her friend's safety, said in a rush, "Jennie's three servants are with her, Tris. You know even Mary and I would not think to capture the blackmailer on our own. It seemed so simple, you know. We would just hang back and wait for the man to show himself, and then Tiny would crack his skull or some such thing and the deed would be done. It was to be a bit of a lark, you see, and then you would have to apologize for causing the whole mess by being such a gloom-and-doom merchant in the first place. We—"

"An address, Lucille, or I'll turn you over my knee myself!" Rule threatened, having run out of patience."

"Julian!" she cried, appealing to her husband. "How can you let him talk to me like that?"

The Earl of Thorpe looked at his distraught friend, smiled slightly, and said, "I am afraid I must disappoint you, Tris. It is *I* who shall have that pleasure." Turning back to Lucy, he ordered sternly: "An address, madam, if you please. *Now!*"

NOTHING WAS GOING as she had planned. In the first place, Lucy was not with her, which cut down on her enjoyment by nearly half. Having caught a glimpse of Tristan as his curricle had shot by, and seeing his dear, intense face again just before entering the bazaar, had succeeded in destroying the remainder of her spirits, although she took great pains not to look downpin around Ben, who she could see was ready to grasp at any straw in order to cancel the scheme entirely.

The house the blackmailer had designated for their meeting was a depressing sight as well, and a far cry from anything Mary had imagined when she had dreamed of capturing the fellow. For one thing, it was situated on a particularly nasty-looking narrow street, crowded with other tumbledown houses and more than a few low gin shops whose drunken, slovenly patrons spilled out into the gutters to either sprawl there unconscious or become sick in the puddles.

Mary had thought she could remain outside and let Tiny and the others take care of the actual apprehension of the blackmailer, but she could now see that there was no way to avoid entering the house herself if the man were ever to show himself.

She and Ben had just completed a battle of wills, all fought in whispers, that had resulted in Mary's decision to cross the street and enter the house alone while the three servants found their way into the building through the back door or a convenient window. Once inside—and after, she was sure, being observed entering by the blackmailer—she would stand there until she counted to twenty and then return to the street, out of harm's way until Ben signaled her that everything was all right. The deed would be done, according to Ben "afore yer ken say Jack Robinson."

Mary, her back stiff and straight, her ridiculous ostrich plumes bobbing in the slight breeze, walked swiftly across the street to enter number sixteen without knocking, stopped just inside the door, closed her eyes tightly, and began counting aloud in a brave, if rather shaky voice: "One, one thousand, two, one thousand, three—"

The hand that snaked around her waist from behind squeezed tightly, robbing her of air, while the second had clamped down tight over her mouth before she could give voice to the scream that had already formed in her mind.

Obviously, she thought wildly as she felt herself being lifted off her feet and half dragged up the stairs, the blackmailer has plans of his own. Her eyes popped wide open in curiosity partly to see her surroundings, awful as they might be, and partly in the vain hope that she could see her attacker, who still held her from behind.

Thankfully for her battered heels that had banged sharply against every riser as they mounted the stairs, the man did not climb to the very top of the tall, narrow house, but stopped at the first floor, kicking open a door and roughly pushing Mary inside the room ahead of him. Catching herself against the side of a rickety table, she took a moment to catch her breath, and then turned.

*"You!"* she exclaimed unbelievingly as Jerome Toland closed and locked the door behind them.

Toland busied himself adjusting his lace shirt cuffs, which had been disarranged by his recent activities, and then made his captive a mocking bow. "One must make a living, Miss Lawrence," he said, shrugging. "Especially if one's idiot sister persists in falling in love with penniless men. You must understand I didn't set out to use you, but you played so easily into my hands that I found I couldn't resist. I apologize for causing you any trouble, and I'm sorry if you have suffered any upset."

"Oh, aren't you just!" Mary sniffed, remembering that she had never been very much enamored of this man, whose own sister did not seem overfond of him. "May I say, sir, that your concern leaves me totally unmoved."

Toland indicated the single chair in the room and suggested Mary sit down, but she shook her head and stood her ground. "I forgive you for those harsh words, Miss Lawrence, as I know this must be very unpleasant for you, but I believe we can conclude our business in short order. Have you brought the papers?"

The papers? Mary had to think for a moment before she remembered that she was to have brought some of Sir Henry's papers with her. Stupid! She berated herself silently. So sure had she been of the success of her plan that she had not even considered bringing along a false set of papers. She had nothing with her save her small reticule.

Tilting up her chin, she improvised quickly: "What sort of clothhead do you take me for, Mr. Toland? Of course I did not bring any papers. After all, what assurance do I have that once the papers are in your possession, you will make good your promise not to make public my—er—indiscreet behavior on a certain occasion?"

"You stupid chit!" Toland exclaimed, slamming a fist down on the table, shaking the oil lamp he had placed there, and making Mary back up three paces and sit in the chair she had shunned earlier. "What the devil do I care what you do or who you do it with? You could ride stark naked down Bond Street for all I'd care! I need those papers! I already promised them to—"

Toland cut off his tirade as he saw Mary looking hopefully toward the closed door as if she believed it would come tumbling in on them at any moment. "You didn't come here alone, did you?" he asked in a low, hard voice. Crossing over to where Mary sat huddled in the chair, he grabbed her arm and gave it a mighty shake. "Who did you bring with you? Rule's not in London. I checked. Who is it?"

He shook her again, and she thought she could hear her teeth rattle in her head. "No-nobody! I *swear* it," she cried, beginning to feel real fear creeping down her spine. Where were Tiny and Goliath? And Ben, where was he? He had promised her! She could have counted to a thousand by now! "Your note said to come alone."

Just as if the fates had set out to make a liar of her, there came the sound of running feet approaching outside in the hallway. *"Bitch!"* Toland cursed, and still holding tight to her arm, he swept a backhanded slap across her face, knocking her to the floor just as the door crashed open and Tristan burst into the room.

One look at Tristan Rule's face was enough to have Jerome Toland raising his hands in surrender, but Rule wasn't about to settle for turning the man over to the authorities. Toland had dared to touch Mary! He had hit her, *hurt* her.

Only one thing stood out clearly in Tristan's mind: Jerome Toland had to die. Tristan's hands bunched tightly into fists that ached to turn Jerome's handsome face into mush. "Defend yourself, you bastard!" he fairly growled.

Mary didn't know how Tristan had found her, and at the moment she didn't much care. All she could do was remain sprawled on the floor, staring in amazement as his beloved face turned into a dark mask of hate. So this is the man they call Ruthless Rule, she thought, at last understanding that Tristan's reputation was no trifling thing. When enraged, Tristan Rule would give pause to the devil himself.

Toland backed toward the wall, his head shaking slowly back and forth in the negative, until he was stopped by the edge of the table as it came up against the back of his legs. Reaching behind himself wildly for any weapon he could find, he grabbed up the oil lamp and sent it winging straight at Rule.

"Tristan, *look out!*" Mary screamed helplessly, scrambling to her feet as Rule ducked, and the lamp crashed against the wall. Immediately the straw pallet that lay against the wall was turned into a blazing pyre.

The old house was nothing more than tinder, and the fire, once begun, fed on it greedily. In mere moments one side of the room was transformed into a raging inferno. Tristan knew it wouldn't be long before the fire reached the doorway, effectively cutting off their only means of escape.

Toland must have realized it as well, for he made a mad dash for the safety of the hallway, slamming the door shut behind him as he went. Tristan only spared a moment to hope that Julian and Kit's three servants, whom he had browbeaten into staying outside, would not let the man escape before turning his full attention on Mary.

If Mary had been shaken at the sight of Rule in a rage, it was nothing to the fear that raced through *his* veins as he looked at her now. For Mary was backed against the far wall, cowering in abject panic, staring unblinkingly at the rapidly spreading flames. She was more than frightened. She was terrified, frozen with horror.

"Mary!" Tristan shouted above the roar of the fire. "Come to me, sweetings! We have to get out of here!" As Tristan spoke, he tried to open the door, which had jammed shut.

She didn't move, except to slip down closer to the floor. Whimpering, she covered her head with her arms.

Again and again Tristan pulled on the door, but it was no use. "Damn it!" he cursed, giving the door a kick before turning back to Mary. Smoke was rapidly filling the room and he had trouble finding her in the dim light. Pulling off his jacket, he held it about his head and upper body as a shield as he made his way to her, then draped it around her hunched body. "Mary," he crooned, sensing now the full depth of her terror even if he couldn't fully comprehend the real reason for it, "you'll be all right. I promise. Let me help you."

But Mary had retreated from the room—from the fire. Feeling Tristan's arms wrapping around her, she began to rock rapidly back and forth on her heels, like an animal in pain—or a child in its mother's protective embrace.

Tristan lifted her unresistingly into his arms and stood up, moving toward the single window in the room. Kicking out with his booted foot, he splintered the last of the panes that remained in the already-broken window and looked down into the street. He closed his eyes a moment in silent relief as he saw Julian and Tiny standing below him looking up at the window. Jerome Toland lay on the ground beside them, Goliath perched on his back, as Ben stood over the captive, a nasty-looking club in his hands.

Putting Mary down for just a moment, he wrapped his jacket around his arm and hit out the spindly strips of wood that clung to the window frame. The heat coming from behind him was nearly unbearable, and the smoke rushing toward the open window caused him to choke and cough, as stinging tears threatened to blind him.

Mary was once again cowering on the floor, holding on to his leg like a terrified child. He had to use considerable force to pry her loose from her tight hold on him in order to haul her to her feet. Putting a hand under her chin, he raised her face to his, trying to make out her features through the smoke that swirled all around them. "Mary? *Mary!* Listen to me! I've got to lower you down outside the building, and then drop you. Tiny is waiting down there—Julian too. They'll catch you, darling, I swear they will."

She looked at him then, her eyes wide and unblinking, even in the dense smoke. *"Maman?"* she breathed, tentatively reaching out a hand to touch Tristan's cheek. She shook her head in the negative. No. This was not her mother. Who was this strange man? Where was her mother? She wanted her mother!

Mary felt herself being lifted, her body being moved toward the open window. The man was going to drop her out the window. *No!* She didn't want to fall; she *knew* the feeling of falling, that awful sense of hurtling helplessly through space. She wrapped her arms tightly around the man's shoulders, holding on to him for dear life, refusing to let go. *"Non, maman! Non!"* she pleaded over and over again as she burrowed her face against the man's neck.

Tristan felt his blood run cold. He didn't know what was happening, what had turned Mary into the little girl now clinging to his neck sobbing for her mother. All he knew was that they were both going to die in this burning hell of a room unless he could break through to Mary somehow, make her understand that they had to get out of here—now.

Instinct guided him, instinct and love. "Marie," he crooned softly, into her ear. *"Mon pauvre enfant, je t'aime. Allons!"*

*"Maman?"* Mary asked, tilting her head to one side, her arms relaxing a bit, allowing Rule to breathe more freely. She looked into Tristan's face for a long moment, clearly fighting to understand, and then suddenly, her face crumpled in sorrow. *"Maman* is dead. Oh, Tris, my mother is dead!" she cried, as her memory, and complete realization of what had happened finally hit her. And then she fainted.

Tristan clasped Mary to him tightly, thanking every deity he could think of for the joy of hearing his name once more on her lips. Tears streamed down his soot-darkened face as he rained small kisses against Mary's cheeks and neck, until the loud crash of a ceiling beam breaking away and hitting the floor behind him brought him back to his senses.

He gave Mary one last kiss, then holding her limp, unconscious body by the wrists, he lowered her out the window as far as possible before dropping her to the street below, where Tiny stood waiting. The gentle giant caught her neatly as she fell and quickly handed her over to Julian before turning his attention once more to the first-floor window.

"I be waitin', milord," he shouted in his big voice. *"Jump!"*

## EPILOGUE

*July 1815*

"CRISTOPHER WILDE, you come back here at once!" Jennie's only acknowledgment from her offspring came in the form of a childish giggle, before the boy was off again, running as fast as his chubby legs could carry him, his nursemaids, Tizzie and Lizzie, huffing and puffing along behind in hot pursuit.

"Let him go, dearest," Kit said lazily, not moving from his lounging position up against the base of a comfortable shade tree.

"Only a man would say such a thing," Jennie retorted. "He'll get grass stains all over his new outfit—and he looked so adorable in church too." Turning to her cousin Lucy, now carrying her first child and more likely to be sympathetic to Jennie's motherly pride, she said, "He made the perfect ring bearer, didn't he?"

Julian Rutherford, who had been busying himself arranging a pillow at his wife's back as she sat in a soft, upholstered chair he had ordered carried out onto the lawn for just such a purpose, replied tongue-in-cheek, "He certainly did, Jennie. I especially liked it when he refused to turn over the ring to the vicar."

Kit chuckled deep in his throat as he lay with his hat tipped front over his eyes, earning himself a playful jab in the ribs from his wife's slippered foot. "Hey!" he protested, raising the brim of his hat an inch to smile up at Jennie.

Lucy patted her protruding abdomen and said soothingly, "Don't worry, sweetings, your aunt and uncle are only funning." Pretending to be stern, she warned her cousin and her husband that they were setting their as yet unborn relative a bad example.

"They don't have to, Lucy, with you as the poor child's mother," Rachel quipped lightly, just then walking up to the group arm in arm with her brand-new husband. "Why do you think I married Henry in such a rush after Waterloo? The mere thought of having to bear-lead your sure-to-be harum-scarum offspring had me begging the poor man to give me the protection of his name."

Sir Henry Ruffton, his cherubic face beaming with pride as he gazed at his bride, refused to be insulted and merely pulled her more fully into his embrace and kissed her on the cheek. "We could have been wed months ago if it weren't for that devil Bonaparte breaking loose from Elba just after Mary and Tristan returned from their wedding trip."

The group was silent for a few moments, each reliving the horror of those awful "hundred days," when Bonaparte roamed Europe again and it seemed that another long, hurtful war had begun. The three women exchanged looks, each remembering the long months when their men, along with Tristan, were gone from their sides, off defending their country.

But Bonaparte was well and truly defeated this time, and plans were already in train to have him banished to St. Helena, where many had said he should have been imprisoned in the first place. The men had all been home for nearly a month and Rachel and Sir Henry had at last been married from Rule's

Roost, with Mary and Tristan acting as hosts to the bride and groom.

"Where are Tris and Mary?" Lucy asked now as her thoughts led her to notice their hosts' absence. "Surely Kitty and Dex are long since gone on their way."

"Mary must have had something to do in the house after waving our other lovebirds good-bye," Jennie guessed, shaking her head as she remembered Dexter's barely suppressed eagerness to be on his way, anxious to have his bride of one week to himself once again.

Julian leaned down to whisper to Kit under his breath. "Bet they don't make it any farther than the nearest inn."

"As long as it doesn't have damp sheets," Kit quipped, and the two men laughed at the shared joke as their wives shook their heads at such nonsense.

Upstairs in Rule's Roost, far from the festivities taking place on the sunlit lawns below, Mary and Tristan Rule stood locked together in a quiet embrace, relishing the momentary respite from their duties to their houseguests.

"Aunt Rachel looked beautiful, didn't she?" Mary murmured into Tristan's shoulder, rubbing her cheek against the fine satin of his jacket. "So many delays, so many years wasted. Thank goodness she and Uncle Henry are together at last."

Tristan's arms tightened fractionally around Mary's slim body as he thought about the time he had wasted fighting his love for her, and how his realization of that love had nearly come too late for both of them. "She insisted on waiting until you had recovered your strength, and she could organize our wedding," he recalled, placing a kiss on Mary's hair. "I never truly appreciated my aunt's worth until I witnessed her care of you after the fire. She was magnificent."

Mary closed her eyes, remembering the long weeks it had taken her to come to grips with the memories the fire in the house off Bow Street had released in her mind. "She didn't do it alone, you know," she teased, looking up at her husband with love shining bright in her green eyes. "I seem to recall a rather handsome gentleman who came to call daily, bringing me flowers and pretty trinkets."

Tristan smiled down on her, his harsh features softening. "And do you remember a certain small cottage near Linton where that same 'handsome' gentleman spent six wonderful weeks trying to show you how very much he loved you, how very much he will always love you?"

Pulling her brows together as if trying very hard to recall such an incident, Mary asked, "Would that be the same man who then deserted me this past March to spend the entire spring transporting messages back and forth across the channel from Brussels? I do believe I remember him faintly."

"I've been home for over a fortnight!" Tristan objected in mock anger, sweeping her up into his arms to hold her high against his chest. "You know we've scarce had a chance to breathe, let alone be alone above a few minutes at a time. Can I help it if the place has been thick with relatives and servants scurrying everywhere preparing for the wedding?"

Mary tilted her chin down and looked up at her husband through her lowered lashes. "We're alone now, Tristan," she purred invitingly, enjoying the color that her words brought running into his lean cheeks.

"But our guests—" he began, his eyes darkening as he remembered the collection of relatives waiting for them.

"What about our guests?" Mary taunted, reaching up to nibble on a corner of his lips with her small, white teeth. "Be ruthless, Tris. Let them fend for themselves for a while."

Tristan spared only a moment to look out the window at the people relaxing beneath the shade tree before turning on his heels and carrying Mary over to the wide bed that lay waiting in the master chamber.

"My Lord Tristan Rule vows *he* is no fool!" he quoted softly as he lowered his wife onto the counterpane and the people waiting on the lawn, the memories of the past, and, indeed, all the rest of the world faded joyfully away.

# THE TOPLOFTY
# LORD THORPE

For Maryanne Colas,
who has been there for the laughter…
and the tears.

# PROLOGUE

My dearest Jennie, and Kit too, of course, It seems an age since last we saw each other, and had a long, comfortable coze, which of course it is not, considering that I stood as godmother to your darling Christopher not two months past. I am back in London now as you can see from the postmark, although Papa is not with me (as usual) and Aunt Rachel has been once more set to bear-lead me (again, as usual).

You know, dearest Jennie, that this will be my fourth Season since I first made my curtsy at St. James's. Papa says any chit with a whit of sense would have long since given it up and donned her caps, but he has agreed to finance one more foray, hoping against hope I shall at least catch myself a rich cit; but as I told Papa, what with Lady Cynthia's mama passing away so shortly into the Season last year, and with Lord Thorpe having so inconveniently retired to his estates as soon as was decent after the funeral, *my* latest Hunting Season was rendered unusually short.

Lady C. is at last out of black gloves (so far this marriage of hers has been delayed by no less than three expiring relatives), and she and Lord Thorpe are once more in town, with the wedding date again set. I know you both believe me to be some sort of Don Quixote, forever tilting at windmills, but I do believe it is Fate, not Lady Cynthia's wilting relatives, that have delayed the nuptials until such time as I can convince Lord Thorpe he would be making a Dreadful Mistake.

I am the better woman for him, I know I am, so you—and especially you, Kit—may draw comfort from the knowledge that my intentions, if not my actions, are only of the purest. Lady Cynthia may bleed undiluted blue when she is pinked, but she is not only rude beyond conceiving, but a dead bore into the bargain. Julian—that is to say, Lord Thorpe—must be Saved from Her at All Costs. Of course, my loves, the fact that I am Absolutely Mad for the man barely enters into this At All.

But now that the couple in question is back in town, with poor Lord Thorpe lugging that sad, bland creature hither and thither, my opportunities shall again present themselves. Oh, Lord Thorpe may have already been situated in the city for a fortnight or so before his fiancée returned, but he spent his time at his various clubs, barely coming into society. It is strange, is it not, how men seem to enjoy such places, especially since one of my young gentlemen friends (nobody you'd know, Kit, as he didn't serve in the army) told me that the atmosphere in all these clubs is so dreadfully fusty—rather like being in some duke's residence, with the duke lying dead in his chambers upstairs.

Please forgive me if I ramble on—Aunt Rachel says it is my only forte—but you can see, can't you, how this is my last chance to make Julian aware of me? It is time I took the bull by the horns, as it were, for after all, I cannot continue to rely on Lady C.'s relatives to so obligingly keep cocking up their toes before each scheduled wedding date, now can I?

Kiss little Christopher hello—he is such a darling—and cross your fingers for me, just for luck you understand, for I am sure that this time I Cannot Fail to make Julian love me.

> Your most affectionate cousin,
> Lucy

Kit Wilde, Earl of Bourne, put down the missive after reading it aloud to his wife as she cradled their sleeping son. "She cannot fail, she says," he repeated, shaking his head rather sadly. "I can only wonder at her optimism, kitten, seeing as how the poor girl has made such a sad hash of things so far."

"Oh, I don't know, Kit," Jennie replied, absently stroking her son's soft blond curls. "You'd be surprised to know to what lengths a woman might be willing to travel in the name of love. For what it's worth," she proclaimed, grinning saucily at her doubting husband, "*my* blunt's on Cousin Lucy!"

# CHAPTER ONE

IT WAS A TRULY LOVELY early-spring day, unseasonably fair and fine, especially when one considered the depressingly lengthy stretch of damp and drizzle that had so far this month curtailed outings in the park for all but the most dedicated or desperate promenaders, the former intent on exercising their horseflesh and the latter committed to the pursuit of elusive eligible bachelors, bits of juicy gossip, and cards of invitation to the most select social gatherings on offer.

Quite naturally this bright, sunshiny day found anybody and everybody converging on the park with a vengeance; the resultant crush of curricles, high-perch phaetons, ancient landaus, barouches, skittish, prancing saddle horses, and hopeful pedestrians quickly spilling over from the gravel paths to cut deep ruts into the soft turf and carelessly trample down the shrubberies.

Julian Rutherford, Earl of Thorpe, and his fiancée of long standing, Lady Cynthia Buxley, had been in the park upwards of an hour, having arrived with the notion that a lively canter for the length of the park and back atop their overly fresh mounts would make an enjoyable change from the inactivity the weather had enforced upon them.

To their combined chagrin, however, the only exertion either had thus far expended was by way of a constant tug-of-war with their high-spirited horses, who demonstrated their disappointment at the snail's pace necessarily set by their masters by alternately snorting, prancing, and tossing their heads in their eagerness to be off.

"This is perfectly beastly, Julian," Lady Cynthia complained in dreadful accents for perhaps the hundredth time. "How I abhor Sundays in the park, what with every upstart cit and ragged peasant given free access just as if they had a right to be here. I tell you, Julian, if we are not careful we will suffer the same dread fate as our fellow aristocrats in France. Stop it, Egyptian Dawn," she commanded firmly, breaking off her complaining to bring her mount back under control.

"Go easy on her mouth, Cynthia," Lord Thorpe cautioned as the woman hauled down sharply on the reins. "We'll be nearing a gate shortly, upon which time I suggest we disengage ourselves from this ridiculous parade and I escort you home. If it weren't for the multitude of acquaintances demanding our attention, holding our progress to an infuriating crawl, we should have been gone long since. It is only our popularity you have to blame, my dear, for our virtual imprisonment within this crush of humanity. Your friends have been too long without you, and feel the need of a few moments to renew their friendship."

"And to reiterate their sympathy concerning my sad loss," Lady Cynthia added, smoothing down the skirt of her dove-gray riding dress. "I do hope no one thought me fast to have come out of my blacks so soon after Mama's passing."

"A year is quite proper, Cynthia," her fiancé assured her matter-of-factly, neglecting to add that she looked most becoming in her half-mourning, just as he had neglected to show so much as a moment's concern over the possibility of Egyptian Dawn bolting in her agitation, and the resultant threat to life and limb this would present to his beloved.

They progressed along the path slowly but steadily, deigning only to bow or wave to the many who would have them stop beside their conveyances for a chat, and were almost to the gate when Egyptian Dawn, momentarily given her head as Lady Cynthia called a greeting to a turbaned dowager frantically trying to gain her attention, rolled her eyes wildly and reared, nearly unseating her rider.

Thorpe reacted quickly, grabbing for the mare's halter before the horse could gather her legs back under her and break into a dangerous gallop, and while nearby spectators alternately shrieked and swooned, he expertly brought Egyptian Dawn back under control.

"Whatever happened to spook her so?" Lady Cynthia asked, looking around her to see that Egyptian Dawn was not the only horse so disturbed. All around them tigers were running to calm their masters' frightened teams, while pedestrians prudently sprinted from out of the way of slashing hooves.

And then Lord Thorpe caught a movement off to his left and swung around in the saddle to get a better look at the flash of ruby red that was speeding down a nearby slope, heading directly for them. His light gray eyes narrowed as he sought to identify what looked to be some female person who was, unbelievably, perched precariously between a larger pair of rapidly advancing narrow-spoked wheels. "What the devil?" he was startled into saying, reaching wildly for his quizzing glass.

Attracted by her companion's rare descent into exclamation, Lady Cynthia looked at him askance, and then followed his lead and cast her gaze onto the nearby slope. "Oh, no," she muttered in an extremely unladylike style. "It is that dratted Gladwin girl again. Whatever can she be about this time?"

By now all in the vicinity had spied out the cause of their

animals' unrest and a minor uproar was in progress, with lords and ladies shaken from their usual sangfroid into garbled speech and a few members of the lower orders, in the park on their off day, cheering and yelling and generally encouraging the rider of what looked to be one of "dem newfangled hobbyhorses, like," to "give 'er all she's got, girlie!"

The rider, so cheered by her encouraging audience, lifted one gloved hand from the wooden cross-balance board to acknowledge them with a wave, a maneuver that nearly brought her to grief when the front wheel struck a small rock and for a short time her vehicle listed dangerously to one side. But that she was no novice to this mode of transportation was soon to be seen, for she made short work of leaning her forearm more heavily on the far side of the cross-balance board and redirecting the hobbyhorse onto more level ground.

As she dragged her jean-covered toes in the soft grass alongside the path, however, she soon realized that the advertisement lauding the hobbyhorse as being designed to allow her "drapery to flow loosely and elegantly to the ground" to be sadly inaccurate, as she felt the spring breeze ballooning her skirts and cooling her, at the moment, indecently exposed ankles, to the delight of all and sundry.

"It *is* Lucy Gladwin, Julian, just as I said," Lady Cynthia informed her companion unnecessarily, as anyone with two eyes in his head could not help but recognize that flamboyant young lady who had been setting the *ton* on its collective head for the past three Seasons. And, as if her face and figure were not sufficiently familiar, the young hussar standing nearby had confirmed the fact just moments before by shouting, "It's Old Hale and Hearty's girl, Lucy. What a great gun! Pluck to the backbone!"

"Old Hale and Heart indeed," the earl spat contemptuously. "Sir Hale Gladwin has much to answer for in his outrageous daughter. You'd think he'd marry her off to some backwater squire who'd keep her from making a fool of herself in town."

"Indeed yes," his fiancée agreed, preening her hair complacently, secure in the knowledge that *she,* the daughter of an earl and cognizant of both the responsibility and privilege of rank, would never allow herself to become such a spectacle. "Sir Hale, who is ramshackle past reclaim himself, probably due to some sad underbreeding of his ancestors, should be made to contain his daughter's mad starts or else remove her from polite society altogether. Such a vulgar, shameless creature."

The vulgar, shameless creature, she of the unattending father, had at last dragged her vehicle to a stop just where she had planned—directly in front of the Earl of Thorpe. "Good day to you, my lord," she chirped merrily as, unthinking of her windblown appearance, she gave him the full benefit of her dazzling smile.

Lord Thorpe, from his vantage point high above her, looked at her through his quizzing glass, intent on wiping that inane grin from her face. Lucy, small and dark-haired, was in full looks when dressed in red, and her sparkling eyes, ruby lips, and flushed cheeks gave her an all-over look of fresh, untrammeled beauty that caused the earl to shudder. It wasn't decent, nor was it fitting, for a female to look quite so...so abandoned. It was enough to stir a man's blood in a highly uncomfortable way, as he silently acknowledged by shifting slightly in the saddle.

"Miss Gladwin," he said now, condescending to favor her with a slight, very slight, bow. "I would deem it a kindness if you were to remove your, er, machine from the immediate vicinity. Its presence has greatly agitated Lady Cynthia's mount, and your continued presence brings the possibility of injury to both of you."

"What? My hobbyhorse?" Lucy questioned, shaking her

head. "What a silly animal to be frightened by such a thing. Why, in my opinion a hobbyhorse is—"

"I do not remember requesting your opinion, Miss Gladwin," Lord Thorpe cut in sharply, finally succeeding in wiping the smile from that young female's face. "I cannot, in fact, remember ever requiring anything from you other than your absence. Do I make myself clear, Miss Gladwin?"

As far as set-downs go, this one was definitely first-rate, and Lucy, sadly crushed by his harsh words, was foolish enough to lift her face to Lady Cynthia in mute appeal. If she had hoped for any tenderness from that quarter, however, she had sadly mistaken her woman. Looking down her rather long, aristocratic nose, Lady Cynthia added repressively, "Indeed, Miss Gladwin. Not only have you yet again made a complete fool of yourself, but you have become, at least to us, more than a little boring. For three Seasons now you have been dogging our every step, so it seems, until I vow myself to be quite out of patience with you. It would be a kindness, to us as well as to yourself, if you would simply *go away.*"

For one brief moment Lucy's dimpled chin betrayed a lamentable tendency to quiver, bringing forth an involuntary flutter of sympathy from the earl while prompting the production of a most self-satisfied smirk upon Lady Cynthia's thin face. While Lucy may have briefly entertained the thought of playing on Lord Thorpe's tender feelings (feelings which, there were legions who would willingly swear, did not exist), the sight of her rival's smug expression kept her from summoning up a tear in favor of taking that infuriating female down a peg or two.

"Why, Lady Cynthia, whatever do you mean?" Lucy asked innocently, assuming an air of genuine anxiety. "Do you often have this feeling of being followed? My Great-Uncle Herbert was just so afflicted, you know." She turned to look up at Lord Thorpe, who was rapidly adjusting his opinion of Miss Gladwin as being a brainless widgeon in need of rescue. "In Great-Uncle Herbert's case it was much the same; always telling us how people were staring at him, plotting against him." She shook her head. "They had to put him in Ringmoor, poor man. Nasty business it was, too, what with the chains and all."

"Oh! You *horrid* creature!" Lady Cynthia exclaimed shrilly, momentarily abandoning her role of earl's daughter for that of a highly indignant female. "Julian! She has insulted me. *Do something!*"

"What do you suggest, my dear?" Lord Thorpe replied in his usual unemotional tone. "Pistols at dawn?"

Lady Cynthia was saved from further indiscretion (and Lord Thorpe from having to remind his betrothed that she was in danger of making a cake of herself in front of half the *ton*) by the arrival of Lucy's Aunt Rachel, the older woman alighting from an open carriage that had just then pulled up alongside them.

"Here you are, Lucy," that harassed-looking lady said without preamble. "You promised to stay beside the carriage, dear. It took us forever to work our way around once you took off over that rise. Come away now, Lucy. It's time for tea."

"You are Miss Gladwin's keep…um…that is to say, are you in charge of this young lady?" Lord Thorpe asked, causing Aunt Rachel's thin shoulders to rise up protectively around her ears. If she had hoped, once she was close enough to see that her charge had once again landed in the brambles, that they just might be able to escape the scene with their skins intact, Lord Thorpe's deliberately rude question put a firm period to her hopes. Swallowing down hard on the lump of apprehension that had risen in her throat, the lady could do no more than turn and face her questioner, replying, "I am Rachel Gladwin, my lord, Miss Gladwin's aunt."

"You have my sympathy, Mrs. Gladwin," he responded,

favoring her with a slight bow as he looked down at her from his lofty height.

"*Miss* Gladwin, my lord," Aunt Rachel corrected. "I am Sir Hale's younger sister."

"Then I repeat my condolences twofold, ma'am, and hope you forgive me for requiring you to own up to the blood relationship in public. Therefore, since I feel it incumbent upon us to discuss what I believe to be a common problem, I will call upon you at your residence in the morning. Good day to you, ma'am," he concluded in a tone that made it clear he had dismissed her.

"And good day to you too, my lord," Lucy called after the two riders who had already begun edging their mounts on down the path, just as if she didn't know that they had cut her deliberately.

"Have Walter lift that horrid machine up behind the carriage, Lucy, and join me inside," her aunt instructed, already turning to be handed up onto the squabs. "We must hurry home so that I might indulge in a fit of the vapors. I do believe I have earned it."

"Oh, pooh, Aunt Rachel—" Lucy twinkled irrepressibly "—you never would be so missish."

"Knowing that your insufferable Lord Thorpe is coming to Portman Square tomorrow to ring a peal over my head about my delinquent niece may just be the nudge I needed to cultivate a tendency to find solace in nervous spasms. Oh yes," that lady went on imperturbably as her niece began to protest that Lord Thorpe was not about to do any such thing. "Or did you think he was coming to tell me he has fallen madly in love with you and has jilted Lady Cynthia so that the two of you can live happily ever after?"

Lucy squirmed comfortably against the squabs, a satisfied smile lighting her eyes. "The thought had occurred to me, my dear aunt. The thought had occurred."

## CHAPTER TWO

LUCY AWOKE the following morning with a feeling of warm anticipation that was totally unmixed with any touches of anxiety. Lord Thorpe was coming to Portman Square in a few short hours. Lord Thorpe, the man she had first clapped eyes on over three years ago, instantly losing her heart to the tall blond gentleman who had, by his magnificent physical appearance, filled every one of her girlish requirements for a perfect mate.

The fact that this gentleman had not been similarly emotionally poleaxed by the mere sight of a young dark-haired miss in virginal white muslin did not serve to lessen her enthusiasm a whit. Neither did the information that the gentleman of her dreams was already engaged to be married.

Against the pleadings of her aunt, who told her to give up her childish fantasies and concentrate on hooking herself a more landable fish, Lucy set out to ensnare the earl with her feminine charms. Alas, he seemed immune to discreet flirting overtop her fan or coy eyelash batting directed at him from across the room.

Deciding that stronger measures were in order, she had then taken steps to call herself to his lordship's notice. As those steps involved, for the most part, impetuous mad starts, harmless escapades, and one or two nearly risqué exploits, it was not too much longer before Lord Thorpe (not to mention the rest of fashionable London) was aware of Lucy Gladwin.

Society, always on the lookout for titillation, welcomed Lucy with open arms, and she was soon surrounded by a group of the more lively members of the *ton,* who thought her to be "a great gun."

Lord Thorpe, however, was not similarly impressed. Too late, Lucy discovered that her beloved was more than a little bit high in the instep and looked down upon people who, in his way of thinking, disgraced their lineage by their common behavior.

Anyone would be excused for believing that Lucy, once she discovered the arrogance that lay behind her intended's handsome face, would have washed her hands of the man and set out to discover a more suitable gentleman who would appreciate a woman like herself. But those foolish enough to consider such a possibility would likewise have been wise to refrain from laying odds on their supposition, for anyone choosing to put down his blunt on such an eventuality would soon be the poorer for his optimism, as Lucy was made of sterner stuff.

Positive she could not have been mistaken in her judgment of Lord Thorpe, Lucy had, over the years, got it into her head that the man was merely a victim of his birth and upbringing. There was a good, sweet, caring man beneath that pompous, straitlaced exterior, and she wasn't going to rest until the world at large (and Lord Thorpe in particular) was forced to acknowledge that fact.

For over three years Lord Thorpe, armed with his indifferences, had avoided publicly owning to his awareness of Lucy's none-too-subtle pursuit of his person. With his fiancée on his arm, he had chosen to pretend Lucy Gladwin did not really exist. His strategy had worked very well.

Onlookers who at first snickered at Lucy's antics were quickly silenced by Lord Thorpe's chilling looks and sarcastic put-downs, and soon Lucy was regarded as nothing more than a darling, rather madcap eccentric, and Lord Thorpe's name was no longer linked with hers.

But her antics of the day before, warning him of yet another Season to be spent warding off her ridiculous bids for attention and overlooking her preposterous follies, had forced him to take action. Not for a moment (well, maybe for just a sublime second or two in time) did Lucy believe the earl was calling in Portman Square for any reason but to warn her off in that blood-chilling tone he employed to such advantage.

Lucy, just now snuggling back down under her covers, an inane smile on her face, would not have been blamed for being frightened out of her wits at the prospect of Lord Thorpe's bound-to-be-scathing diatribe. Indeed, most *men*, if faced with the fact that Lord Thorpe would be arriving at their domicile to verbally tear a strip off their hides, would have suddenly found pressing business in far-off Cumbria that required their immediate attention.

But Lucy was not dreading the confrontation one little bit. As a matter of fact, now that she had decided on a course of action, she was looking forward to the meeting with every indication of eagerness.

As LORD THORPE TOOLED his matched grays through the early-morning traffic in Mayfair, he rehearsed the speech he would soon be delivering to Miss Rachel Gladwin. Mentally adding a word here or erasing a too-severe phrase there, he wished yet again that Sir Hale Gladwin was in residence in Portman Square. After all, this was a conversation best handled between gentlemen—not that Sir Hale, that red-faced, hard-drinking, blustering fool, could be counted on to realize the gravity of the situation.

Sir Hale embraced a mode of behavior that was the complete antithesis of every value Julian Rutherford felt a gentleman should display. There were times, thought his lordship as he edged his curricle past a delivery wagon that had no business still being about at this hour, that he wished that wealth and good lineage were not the sole prerequisites for admission to polite society. There should be some kind of test, he mused reflectively, some sort of examination, as it were, for young peers, that would exclude all but the more intelligent, the better mannered, from their ranks.

That he, Lord Thorpe, would score at or near the top in such a test was a foregone conclusion. He was intelligent, erudite, possessed only the highest instincts, was worthy of the loftiest regard, and, in general, exemplified all that was desired in an English nobleman. Anyone who didn't believe it could apply to his mother—who had devoted her life to making her son aware of his perfection—and she would be happy to supply a full listing of his attributes.

That he was in addition—alas, also thanks to his proud mama—arrogant, autocratic, pompous, blindly biased in his opinions, and insufferably straitlaced never occurred to him (and who, pray tell was there brave enough or foolhardy enough to bring such failings to his attention?).

Once fully grown, and already self-satisfied to the point of smugness, Lord Thorpe had advanced to the age of three-and-thirty years, still warmed by the knowledge that his fellowmen had yet to do anything to undermine his fine opinion of himself—or his bad opinion of them.

So why had he, a man who held himself above the plebeian antics of the underbred, allowed this silly Gladwin chit to get so annoyingly under his skin—and worse yet, remain there for over three long, uncomfortable years? Surely he should have been able to continue his pretense of ignoring both her and her atrocious behavior? But that was just it—his indifference *was* a pretense. He had never really succeeded in banishing her from his conscious mind.

Not that he was intrigued by her vibrant, volatile personality, or attracted to her petite but still somewhat earthy charms. On the contrary, he was repelled by them, and angry at himself for allowing any hint of base physical attraction to the chit to disturb the even tenor of his days.

Physical desire was for the lower orders and young peers out on a romp. It was *not* for distinguished scions of ancient houses. Every time he was forced to acknowledge Lucy Gladwin's existence, it was like being served a slap in the face, a disturbing reminder that he was, after all, only human, and therefore susceptible to common carnal lust.

Well, he reminded himself as he thought fleetingly of the way Lucy had looked the day before in the park, there is no place in *my* life for such animal weakness. A gentleman does not desire women of his own social level in that way—such base cravings were reserved for liaisons with opera dancers and other low women, whose lesser intellect and poor breeding opened them to all sorts of licentious behavior. Imagine Cynthia abandoning her cool air of self-possession beneath him as they writhed about in bed—preposterous! He would lose all respect for her—the woman whom he had chosen to bear the next proud generation of Rutherfords.

Lady Cynthia. She was another reason behind this morning's visit to Portman Square. It was his duty to protect her from further upset. The earl had studied long and hard before condescending to offer his hand to this exemplary female—she of the impressive lineage, elevated social standing, high standards, and impeccable manners (and straight white teeth, for such things must be considered). Cynthia knew full well the responsibility placed upon her by her rank, and was comfortingly cognizant of both the honor and the duties that came along with his proposal of marriage.

That all her fine blue blood and careful upbringing did not keep her from bellowing at him like some common Billingsgate fishwife once they were clear of the park the day before, Lord Thorpe chose to charge to a justifiable bout of nerves caused by Lucy Gladwin's sad exhibition of hoydenism—although deep down he believed that Lucy's supposedly artless, wide-eyed set-down hinting of an imbalance in Lady Cynthia's mind had more than a little bit to do with the matter.

Raving that Miss Gladwin was, in her words, "an insupportable person," Cynthia had gone on at length about the trials she had endured thanks to that "silly chit dogging our every step and throwing herself at your head every chance she gets." That this tirade did not serve to turn his lordship's head, seeing as how he could not help but assume that he was both the target of Miss Gladwin's slavish adoration and the man who had inspired Lady Cynthia's unseemly display of jealousy, was only due to the fact that he already had a very high opinion of himself and saw nothing unusual in either of the ladies' reactions.

He had, by the time they had reached Lady Cynthia's residence in Grosvenor Square, succeeded in convincing his betrothed that all would be settled before another day was out, finally penetrating her near-hysteria over the thought of her fiancé actually volunteering to place himself under the same roof as that vulgar girl. "I seriously doubt I will even be forced to so much as lay eyes on Miss Gladwin, my dear," he had told her as the acrid smell of the burnt feathers Lady Cynthia's maid had lately been waving beneath her mistress' nostrils found him seeking recourse to his scented handkerchief. "I am tempted to believe the aunt is reasonably intelligent. Surely a few words meant to point her in the right direction will be all that is needed to put an end to this infantile charade once and for all. I'm only sorry I didn't act sooner."

Now, turning his pair into Portman Square, the earl was still of the same mind as when he gave his assurances to Lady Cynthia. He should have done this years ago and saved himself a great deal of trouble. So thinking, he threw the reins to his tiger as that slim young fellow ran to the horses' heads, and leapt lightly onto the flagway, determined to complete his interview with the elder Miss Gladwin in time to keep an appointment with his tailor before noon.

THE EARL WAS JUST IN the process of spreading his coattails in preparation of seating himself in the bright, sunlit drawing room (choosing a wide, straight-backed armchair that he felt would cast him more in the role of host than guest, thereby gaining yet another subtle advantage on the sure-to-be-apprehensive Miss Rachel Gladwin) when a flurry of movement near the open double doors brought him back to a standing position.

The woman who had entered the room had her back to him for the moment, as she was fully occupied in bustling the reluctant butler away from the doorway. Once the elderly servant, just then whispering fiercely under his breath, was repositioned in the hallway so close to the entrance that his straining body looked as if it was imprisoned behind an invisible barrier of glass, the doors were firmly shut in his face—with or without inflicting a nasty pinch to the man's rather prominent proboscis, the earl was not to know.

"Now, then, my lord," Lucy Gladwin began, wiping her hands together as if in anticipation, "shall we get to it? To what do we owe the pleasure of your company?"

Lord Thorpe didn't answer at once, as he was caught between a silent inventory of Lucy's person, becomingly if not correctly (as it still lacked an hour till noon) attired in a formal gown of deep rose silk, and the dawning realization that the two of them were, most improperly too, alone together in a room whose doors he had just heard lock shut.

The twinkle he saw in Lucy's bright eyes was all the warning he needed (even if he were dense enough to overlook the distraught butler, the low-cut gown, and the bolted doors) to alert him to the fact that he had to do a good bit more than select the proper seat if he was going to convince Lucy—or himself—that *he* was in control of this interview.

Drawing himself up to his full, not unimposing height, he said coolly, "Tell me, Miss Gladwin, when you say 'we,' are you employing the kingly 'we'—or has your aunt mastered the art of invisibility?"

Lucy laughed and waved one small hand at him as if to say his little joke was amusing but not really worthy of a reply. Moving gracefully across the carpeting to stand in front of the settee, she inclined her head and bade her guest sit down and make himself comfortable.

"I shan't be staying," the earl informed her, already striding regally toward the door. "It isn't proper for you to receive male visitors without your chaperon present."

"Oh, pooh!" Lucy exclaimed airily, plunking herself down on the settee. "After all, who's to know if we don't tell?"

Thorpe pivoted neatly on his heels to face her and returned stonily, "*I* shall know, Miss Gladwin."

A wide smile rearranged Lucy's upturned face into a startling resemblance to the enchanting pixie princess featured in a favored storybook the earl had read during his days in the nursery and believed long since forgotten. "And will you *tell,* my lord?" she teased. "I didn't think earls tattled."

"That's enough, Miss Gladwin!" Thorpe decreed repressively, his palm itching to administer a few satisfying smacks to the chit's upturned derriere. "I bid you good day."

"No, you don't," Lucy answered serenely, arranging her skirts more becomingly as she eased back against the cushions of the green-and-white striped satin settee. "The doors are locked and *I've* got the key right here."

The earl, who was just about to grasp one of the door handles, turned his head just in time to see Lucy patting the neckline of her gown just at her bosom. Leaning his back against the door, he folded his arms and negligently crossed one foot in front of the other. "I always contended you were nothing more than a mischievous child. Now I see I was correct. What did you do with your aunt, you pernicious brat, lock her in the linen cupboard?"

Lucy had the good grace to blush. "Aunt Rachel has been called to her good friend's bedside in Half Moon Street on a mission of mercy. It seems poor Mrs. Halstead has taken a nasty fall and broken her leg."

"Now, why do I doubt that? Or did you attack that poor lady just to avoid telling an untruth after all your other crimes?" the earl questioned suavely.

Tilting her head to one side, Lucy brazened it out, although she was not best pleased at the way things were going. Nothing was happening as she had thought it would when first she had hatched this scheme. "No, it is all a hum, a great bag of moonshine I invented to draw Aunt Rachel away at the crucial moment. I sent the note myself," she ended quite unnecessarily.

Her little face suddenly quite solemn, she sat upright and held her hands tightly clasped in her lap. "It was wicked of me, I know, but I had to see you—I just had to!"

His lordship knew himself to be in a ticklish situation. He was forced to remain where he was unless he wished to so demean himself as to bellow for help like some calf struck in the briers, yet he could feel it in his bones that whatever Lucy Gladwin was about to say next, it boded no good for him—no good at all.

"Very well, missy," he countered with all the sangfroid he could muster, "you have gained your objective. Perceive me standing here. Now," he ended, straightening once again and directing his eyes meaningfully toward the door, "if that is all you required…" His voice trailed off suggestively.

"Oh, how insufferably priggish you can be!" Lucy exclaimed in amused frustration, fairly hopping to her feet. "I don't know why I even bother trying to talk to you. Aunt Rachel says I must have windmills in my head to—"

"Ah, then I was correct in my assessment of that estimable lady. It is a pity you don't strive to emulate her—your brain could do with an infusion of common sense."

Lucy's eyes narrowed to glittering blue slits as she continued recklessly, "You didn't let me finish, my lord. What Aunt Rachel said was that anyone who could see anything more in you other than an overweening conceit and a total contempt for your fellowman should hand himself over to the leeches for a thorough examination. I begin to see the wisdom of her words!"

Thorpe extracted his snuffbox and delicately took a pinch before, dusting his fingertips on his handkerchief, he drawled languidly, "I assume that charming little outburst brings our…er…*discussion* to a close? One can only hope it likewise heralds the death of your ridiculous puppy love and the cessation of your so fatiguing public displays of affection. A word to the wise, child—gentlemen prefer to do the chasing, not the other way about."

"Oh, *why* do I bother?" Lucy asked the room in general, now genuinely distressed. "You've been so blinded by your rank and position that you refuse to listen to the commands of your own heart. You're not so cold as you try to make people believe, I just know it. But if you don't stop worryi about your *outside* and start listening to your *inside,* yo never be really happy."

"I'm listening to my *inside* right now, you impe creature," he cut in heartlessly, deliberately looking into Lucy's tear-drenched eyes, "and it's telling m its luncheon. Now, are you going to open this door or must I be forced to endure more of these childish histrionics? By God, you are the most bold, ill-mannered girl I have ever met. Even as I stand here, I cannot believe we are having this entire conversation."

"You'll be sorry, my lord," Lucy sniffed, reaching into her bodice and extracting a small brass key. "If you marry for duty, with no thought to what will make you happy, you'll soon turn into the very man my aunt says you are. Please, consider what I'm saying. I know I'm being horribly forward and probably have disgraced myself in your eyes forevermore, but I see goodness in you. I have always seen it. If I can make you listen, all will not have been lost."

"Now she casts herself in the dual role of martyr and savior of my soon-to-be-damned soul. Please, after all I have been forced to endure from you over the years, can you not find it in yourself to spare me from your attempts at salvation!" Thorpe quipped meanly, more angry than he could remember being since… He hesitated, finally realizing that he couldn't remember *ever* having been this angry.

Quaking ever so slightly in her slippers as she flinched from the dark look that had settled over the earl's handsome face, Lucy knew she had made a complete shambles of this, their only real conversation in the three years she had known him. And after all her high hopes!

She walked slowly toward the earl, not knowing how appealing she looked wrapped in the cloak of her hurt and innocence, and placed the key in his waiting hand. "I beg your forgiveness for having behaved so badly, my lord. I have been guilty of many small indiscretions in the past, but I have really passed beyond the pale with this last scheme.

"It was only that I was so desperate, you know, although that certainly is no excuse. I thought I was trying to help you, t I see now that my motives were entirely self-serving. I duped myself, pursuing a dream that had no basis in reality. You are not the man I thought you were, for even if you could not find it in your heart to…to like me, the man I believed you to be could never have been so consciously cruel. Good day, my lord. You shall not be forced to endure my attentions in the future."

Looking up into his closed expression, she summoned a small brave smile. "See, my lord. The purpose of your visit has been accomplished after all—and before the hall clock could chime the half-hour. Congratulations."

Unlocking the door, Thorpe held out the key, but when Lucy just shook her head, her entire being concentrating on not bursting into tears and thus losing the last of her self-respect, he stepped past her to lay it on a nearby table. He didn't feel particularly proud of himself for this day's work; bludgeoning a mere slip of a girl with his tongue could not be looked upon as the gentlemanly thing to do. But if he had at last destroyed her ridiculous worship of him, convinced her to stop throwing herself in his way and disrupting his peace, he could not help but view his actions as necessary, in the interests of self-preservation at the very least.

"Good day to you, Miss Gladwin. Rest assured this conversation will remain solely between the two of us. There is no need for further hostilities, either privately or in public. A common nod when we meet will be sufficient to keep the tongues from wagging, I believe, and should not cause either of us any undue hardship."

Then, when she made no move to answer him, he did something he later told himself was no more than an impetuous act containing no real meaning: he lifted her hand to his lips, placed a slight kiss on her cool flesh, and then took his leave without a backward glance—leaving Lucy to cradle her hand protectively against her breast as she watched him walk out of her life.

# CHAPTER THREE

"DID YOU HEAR?"

"It's all over the city!"

"I heard that letters were sent to all the newspapers—it has to be true!"

"Such a scandal! Who would have thought it of him? And what about his poor fiancée? Has anybody seen her? Is he with her, do you think?"

"I cannot believe he'd dare to show his face! Not after what he's done! It's horrid, simply horrid!"

What a to-do! Ever since she and her aunt had set foot inside the ballroom there had been no denying that something was afoot—that some wickedly delicious bit of gossip was being passed around the flower-bedecked room, thoroughly taking the shine out of Miss Araminta Selbridge's debut at her painstakingly planned come-out ball.

The very air crackled with tension as the invited guests forsook the sanded dance floor in favor of standing about in tight little clumps, talking nineteen to the dozen while they gleefully shredded some unfortunate soul's reputation into tiny bits.

After depositing Aunt Rachel with the dowagers, her relative being nearly dragged into a chair beside the turbaned dragon who immediately began wetly whispering into the poor lady's ear, Lucy wandered off aimlessly, forgetting that she had promised to immediately join some young female acquaintances that were standing nearby, deep in frenzied conversation.

More than a week had passed since her disastrous meeting with Lord Thorpe, and although her aunt refused to do as her niece asked and allow them both to quit the city at once, Lucy's heart had not been in any of the parties, fêtes, or routs she had dutifully allowed herself to be dragged off to night after endless night.

She had seen Thorpe twice in that time, and he had made a point of acknowledging her presence even though Lucy had barely responded to his greetings before, shame burning in her hot cheeks as she remembered every scathing word he had said to her, she melted hastily into any nearby group of people or handy quiet anteroom.

Embarrassment played a part in her actions, but not a large one. She had, as she had acknowledged ruefully to her aunt when she confessed her crime, put her foot in it badly this time, but it was her bruised heart that was suffering, and not her pride. She had believed herself truly in love with Julian Rutherford, and even now her illusions about the man, having been struck down most unmercifully by his cruelty and indifference, were not really ready to die.

Waving languidly to several acquaintances who tried to draw her into their conversation, Lucy now contented herself with making a lazy circle of the large room, only idly wondering why no one was dancing. Whatever juicy bit of new gossip had taken their attention, it was still difficult to believe that it could keep the younger members of the party away from the floor when the musicians were playing such a lively tune.

Out of the corners of her eyes Lucy could see her aunt beckoning to her, very determinedly gesturing for her niece to join her at the side of the ballroom. Thinking that perhaps Aunt Rachel could enlighten her as to what was going forward, and not really interested enough to have to winnow out the facts from the extraneous exposition that excited gabble-mongers would generously sprinkle into their version of the scandal, she made for the woman's side and made herself comfortable on one of the fan-backed chairs.

"My goodness, Aunt, have you ever seen anything to match it? Anyone would think Prinny had just announced he was giving up his title to marry a scullery maid. Tell me, what is it you have gleaned?"

Now that she had her niece back at her side, Rachel Gladwin was torn as to exactly what she should do. While part of her wanted to whisk Lucy away before she got wind of what was about and made a cake out of herself in public, another, more realistic part of her knew that the time and place would make little difference to the news she had to impart. It would only be delaying the inevitable.

"It's about Lord Thorpe, dearest," she said at last, uneasily avoiding Lucy's suddenly widened eyes.

"Lord Thorpe ran off with a scullery maid?" Lucy joked, suddenly not wanting to hear the truth.

"If it were only that simple," her aunt sighed, reaching over to hold her niece's kid-encased hand. "I don't know the whole of it yet, so I don't want you screeching out loud or anything when I tell you, do you understand?"

"He…he's not…*dead?*" Lucy pleaded in a husky whisper.

"It's worse than that, my precious. They say he's… Oh dear, how do I say this to an innocent like you? He's gotten a girl in his home county into a…um…delicate condition, and left her to do away with herself in despair."

*"What!"* Lucy exploded, causing several of the nearby dowagers to cast curious glances in her direction. "What

nonsense!" she hissed, heeding the warning pressure of her aunt's hand. "Only a ninny would believe such a ridiculous thing."

"Be that as it may, Lucy, the facts speak for themselves. I understand there was a note telling all."

"A suicide note?" Lucy asked, still trying to reconcile her image of the man with the thought of Lord Thorpe rolling about in the hay with some village lass. "How has word of such a note gotten all the way from Derbyshire to London?"

While Lucy sat rigidly in her chair, her eyes staring blankly at the people who were busily destroying Lord Thorpe's reputation with their pointed tongues, her aunt outlined what she had heard.

It seemed that there had lived, in a village near Thorpe's estate, a young woman of quality whose family had fallen on hard times. Enter Lord Thorpe, promising marriage and a rescue from penury, and the plot began to thicken. As the story went—and the story had gone very nicely so far, seeing as how the young lady had written it down in all its sordid detail and then posted a copy to each of the London dailies—Lord Thorpe seduced this poor innocent, one Susan Anscom, on the promise of marriage, and then coldly discarded her when she revealed herself to be with child. After pouring out her grief to the gossip rags, the distraught girl had then chosen the only route open to her—she had drowned herself in the village pond.

"Ridiculous!" was all Lucy could respond once her aunt was finished speaking. "Who could ever believe such a bag of moonshine? Lord Thorpe would never sink to such a thing—he's too much the gentleman, for one thing. Besides," she added matter-of-factly, "he'd never stoop to consorting with any woman ranked lower than someone like Lady Cynthia." Raising her eyes to scan the room, she wondered aloud, "Where *is* Lady Cynthia? I thought I saw her father going into one of the card rooms earlier. Could it be she is circulating about the room defending her betrothed against such evil lies?"

Rachel looked about the ballroom, locating Lady Cynthia as she stood talking to a group of people who seemed to be hanging on her every word. "There she is, Lucy," she said as she pointed discreetly in that general direction, "standing beside Lord Seabrook. My goodness, she seems to be laughing. How can she be so unaffected by all of this?"

Lucy paused a moment in her worry over Lord Thorpe to give herself a mental kick for being so unkind to Lady Cynthia in the past. Obviously the woman was putting a brave face on this, acting as if nothing had happened, and circulating throughout the room explaining away any questions anyone might have.

"But where is Lord Thorpe?" her aunt went on to question when Lucy said nothing. "Surely he has accompanied her here this evening? They never go anywhere except together." Rachel blushed a bit, adding, "I'm sorry, pet, but over the past three years you have made me quite an authority on his lordship and his movements."

There was a sudden commotion at the doorway, releasing Lucy from giving some sort of answer to her aunt, and all heads turned in time to see Lord Thorpe enter the ballroom. He looked, as was his custom, magnificent. From his finely arranged blond locks to the tips of his shiny evening slippers, he was every inch the complete gentleman. Lucy's heart, always fickle when she counted on it for steadiness, did a little flip-flop in her breast as she drank in his handsomeness and the flagrantly arrogant stare he took up as he stopped to survey the room through his quizzing glass.

Spotting his fiancée at the far end of the floor, he began a leisurely progress down the room, and it wasn't until he was three-quarters of the way to his destination that he realized all conversation had stopped and he was the object of every eye in the place. Even the musicians had ceased their frantic fiddling meant to entice somebody out on the floor before Araminta Selbridge's papa refused to pay them for their night's work.

Turning slowly on his heels, Lord Thorpe looked back to see that all those he had already passed by were now standing with their backs turned against him. His spine stiffening perceptibly, he turned forward once again and, glancing neither right nor left, resumed his journey to his fiancée's side. As he walked on, one by one the guests he passed lifted their noses and pointedly turned their backs on him, until, when he reached the group he sought and prepared to bow, Lady Cynthia slipped a gloved hand into the crook of Lord Seabrook's arm and led her friends in a short procession that left them facing a potted plant in a corner of the room.

"They're cutting him!" Lucy burst out indignantly. "The bloody fools are cutting him dead! And to think I had for a moment believed that mean cat was human after all! *How dare she!*"

"Lucy," her aunt pleaded in an undertone, "please keep your voice down. Lord Thorpe will withdraw shortly and then we may quit this den of fools, but for the moment I can only implore you not to do anything you may regret. His lordship wouldn't thank you for it, you know."

Tears of mingled pity and frustration glittering in her eyes, Lucy could not tear her gaze away from the confused man who now stood looking about him dazedly, his broad shoulders slumped in defeat. He, a man who prided himself on his fine reputation, he, the leader of the small, select circle that he had for so many years ruled by means of his impeccable taste, exalted lineage, and impressive appearance, had just cruelly learned the true nature of his contemporaries. He was, to say the thing plainly, shocked spitless.

The nervous musicians, not knowing what else to do, struck up a waltz, thinking to fill the great void of silence with some soothing music. No one moved. Like statues carved from cold marble, the lords and ladies of the *ton* were waiting for the untouchable who had lately been their leader to take his offending self off so that they might not be exposed to his presence. Mud sticks, his former friends were well aware, and they were making sure to cut a wide berth around the man lest some of his dirt leap onto their spotless reputations.

Lucy took it for as long as she could (approximately ten seconds, eight of them spent disengaging her aunt's clinging hands) before rising to scamper hurriedly down the long room to tug at his lordship's sleeve. "Lord Thorpe!" she declared loudly. "I was so worried you had forgotten, but I can see you are a man of your word. Here you are, just as the dance you had me reserve for you is about to begin. I'm sorry you couldn't find me at once; I was bearing my aunt company with the dowagaers while waiting for you." Sliding her gloved hand around his sleeve, she smiled up at him, hiding the fact that her slim fingers were crushing his arm in silent warning. "Shall we, my lord?" she asked, steel in her voice, and the shattered, confused man at last responded, leading her out onto the floor.

They were, of course, the only dancers on the floor, and all eyes were on the couple that now waltzed around the room that suddenly seemed as wide and as dangerous as a battlefield. "Don't look now, my lord," Lucy told him, still maintaining her bright smile, "but Lady Fairweather, known to you formerly as Lady Cynthia, is making a great show of laughing at something that vile Lord Seabrook has whispered in her traitorous ear."

As her partner's only response was to grip her hand tighter, she went on, "Dance me over to the doorway, my lord, and we shall waltz our way out of this gathering of traitors. Only hold on a while longer, please, and we shall get you out of this yet with a whole skin."

Julian looked down on her imploring face with eyes that seemed curiously dead. His feet continued to move in the familiar waltz steps; his heart, he noticed randomly, continued to beat on in his numb body, so how could it be that he felt he had just lost all control over his own destiny? One moment he had been Julian Rutherford, Earl of Thorpe, and he thought without conceit, master of all he surveyed; and the next, he had been struck from his position of majesty, owing the fact that he even remained upright to the small girl he now clung to with the remaining vestiges of his strength.

Out of the corners of her eyes Lucy could see her Aunt Rachel standing just inside the main doorway, a footman bearing their evening cloaks hovering at her side. Good old Rachel, she rejoiced silently, I knew I could count on her to keep her head. Aloud, she soothed, "It's nearly over, my lord, you're holding up just fine. Only whirl me about a time or two, as sort of a farewell flourish—just to let these low-lifes know we don't give a fig for what they think."

Julian, who had for three-and-thirty years subscribed to Fielding's definition of the word "nobody" as meaning "all the people in Great Britain except about twelve hundred," and the word "world" as being "your own acquaintance," could not as easily dismiss the evident condemnation of his peers. His whole life had been crumbling around his feet ever since he'd first realized that no one, not even his fiancée, was going to stand behind him in his time of trouble, and his only ally was to be a young slip of a girl. The same girl he had cut from his life so ruthlessly not a fortnight before.

"Why are you doing this?" he asked now in a strangled voice.

Lucy's bright smile blazed up at him before she replied confidently, "Because I'm a bloody fool, my lord. Why else?"

LUCY AND RACHEL were up at the crack of dawn the next morning, setting the kitchen staff at sixes and sevens with their requests for an early breakfast, while the third under-footman was not best pleased to be ordered out into the streets to procure copies of every newspaper in the city.

Two of the papers had declined to run the story sent to them by one Susan Anscom, but a third, less scrupulous pub-lication (or perhaps less indebted monetarily to Lord Thorpe) printed the entire letter on the first inside page.

It was a thoroughly damning epitaph, set forth with a thoroughness not usually looked for in hysterical females. The missive detailed her seduction at the hands of Lord T—, her inevitable pregnancy, and that same man's callous indifference to her plight. It recounted how she planned, pre-sumably after posting her condemnation, to fling herself into the small pond behind her home in Alsop-en-le-Dale, a scant four miles from Lord T—'s country home, an action she did in fact take, according to the newspaper report. The story ended with the intelligence that Miss Anscom's suicide had "put a period to her young life and set loose the biggest scan-dal in many a year."

As if the article by itself were not enough, the footman also produced a few assorted caricatures from local print shops, where patrons could buy ludicrous drawings depicting Lord T— either standing with his heel crushing the head of some helpless infant, departing on horseback while an obviously increasing damsel stares distractedly into a becoming pool of water, or one particularly repulsive colored print (which cost all of a guinea, but with the ladies footing the bill, it seemed a small expenditure) that showed Lord T— actually stuffing

Miss A— into a sack in preparation for tossing her into the water. This last print Rachel wisely kept from Lucy's sight.

"How dare they lampoon him like this!" Lucy protested, ripping one of the cartoons into small pieces.

"If Prinny himself is not safe from such attack, my dear, I doubt Lord Thorpe can be considered above it," Rachel answered, shaking her head. "I can only wonder how Lord Thorpe is taking it. The story must have been fairly well spread last night for society to have already mounted a snub of such proportions. But now, now that every man on the street has been made aware of it, there's no telling what will happen next. Poor man," she ended, taking a sip of chocolate. "Poor, proud man."

Lucy sat back against her chair, her blue eyes clouded by the memory of Lord Thorpe as she had last seen him outside the Selbridge mansion. Standing ramrod straight, his wide mouth set in a thin line, he had thanked his rescuer with formal politeness before stepping into his waiting coach and driving away without a backward glance. The fact that he had neglected to see that the Gladwin carriage had been called for or wait until such time as it had arrived fairly screamed out his distraction.

"I should think he would like nothing more than to sit in some dark room and cry his eyes out," Lucy said now, wiping away a tear of her own. "He has been totally devastated by this thing. It is terrible to watch the mighty fall. Lord Thorpe has no experience of failure, you know. He has lived his life within a charmed circle. But now he knows how false his life has been and he cannot cope."

"Oh, Lucy, I think you might be overstating the case," her aunt contradicted weakly. "Surely not all the *ton* have turned their backs on the man. Why, I wager that by this morning he has found that many friends have rallied around him. Surely it is all a nine days' wonder, and the whole matter will be forgotten by next week."

"Really, Aunt? And they say I am an optimist!" Lucy stood up in preparation for leaving the sun-drenched dining room. "Well, one thing is for certain. *I* shall not leave him to face this morning's news alone. Aunt? Are you coming with me, or are you afraid to be seen entering his lordship's place of residence for fear of being tarred with the same brush?"

Laying down her fork, giving one long, wistful look at the curried eggs Cook had concocted just for her, Rachel rose and followed her niece out of the room. "I should have said yes to Lord Manton," she remarked to no one in particular. "Marriage to that wet-palmed man would have been tedious, but at least it would have been peaceful."

IF LUCY GLADWIN THOUGHT that Julian Rutherford was spending his morning sobbing into his porridge, she was fair and far out in her judgment of the man. Oh yes, he had been more than a little overset at the Selbridges' when he found himself on the receiving end of an *en masse* cut direct, but he had no intention of slitting his wrists over the affair. There had to have been some mistake, that was all. A few hot-heads, a few eager gossip-mongers, had succeeded in stirring up a tempest in a teapot. It would soon blow over, once his friends realized that he, Lord Thorpe, was not only too gentlemanly ever to lie to a woman, but too fastidious to bestow his favors randomly upon females not schooled in preventing what would otherwise be the inevitable outcome of such activities.

Why, at any minute his butler would enter the room to announce the arrival of friends come to support him in his hour of need. Hadn't he dressed and made himself available to callers on the basis of just this assumption? It was of no real consequence that Lord Royston, Lord Storm, the Earl of Lockport, the Duke of Avonall, and several other of his cronies were at the moment deep in Sussex at a house party—

there were others he knew he could count on to rally to his side. Ah, ha! There went the door knocker just now! Patting down his already perfect cravat, Lord Thorpe rose to receive the first caller come to declare himself an ally.

"Miss Rachel Gladwin and Miss Lucille Gladwin, my lord," the butler intoned solemnly before bowing the two ladies into the drawing room and withdrawing to finish the letter he had been penning to his cousin, majordomo to a duke, requesting his aid in obtaining a position for him in a less-tainted domicile.

"How can we help?" Lucy said baldly, not wasting precious time with formalities.

"I don't think you can," Lord Thorpe replied tonelessly, rather deflated by the thought that so far the only troops that had rallied to his cause were wearing petticoats.

"Oh, come now, my lord," Lucy admonished as she sat herself down on a nearby chair. "All is not so black as you may think. Have you no touch of spunk?"

"If you mean, have I yet ordered a length of rope sufficient for hanging myself from the chandelier in the foyer, no, I have not sunk that far," he returned, his upper lip curling just a little bit.

Lucy turned to her aunt, just now sinking into a chair set away from the center of the room, hoping to fade into the background. "See, Aunt Rachel, it's just as I told you. The man lives on his pride. Just like Mr. Darcy in Miss Austen's *Pride and Prejudice*. Of course," she added, looking back at her unwilling host, "he isn't quite the right coloring, is he? But no matter. It is much the same thing in the end. Mr. Darcy learned that pride has its price and overcame *his* failings."

When it looked as if Lucy was about to gift him with a synopsis of the plot of the novel that had just lately been published in the metropolis, he cut in, saying, "In my heart of hearts I'm *sure* there is a reason for this visit, ladies, or at least I devoutly hope so. I regret that I shambled off so abruptly last evening, but you must understand that I was pre-occupied with a personal matter. If I did not thank you sufficiently for your assistance at the time, I will try to remedy that lapse now."

"Oh, cut line, my lord," Lucy interrupted, wrinkling her nose at his fustiness. "We all can read, you know, and I doubt calling Susan Anscom's suicide a personal matter will wrest her story from the lips of every muckraking busybody in town. No, what we must do is defang the vipers."

"We?" his lordship repeated heavily. "I was not of the opinion that I had requested you or anyone else to become a martyr in my cause. Besides, what makes you think I would want your help?"

"Indeed," Aunt Rachel piped up from her corner of the room. "Seeing as how the place is already littered thick with those wishing to spring to your defence." Her small bit said, she closed her mouth and sat back to see if her little stab had pricked his lordship's arrogant demeanor.

The silence in the room following Rachel's blunt declaration was almost as ominous as the dark expression that had descended on the earl's fair features. Lucy could feel a slight prickle of nervousness creeping up her spine, and she wasn't even the target of his piercing gaze. But when Rachel kept her eyes averted, calmly running her gloves through her fingers, he realized that, facetious though her remark might have been, there was a germ of truth in what she said.

He walked over to the bell-pull and summoned a servant, requesting refreshments be brought immediately, and then sat himself down in a seat across from the one Lucy had taken up when she came into the room. "All right, ladies," he conceded in rare good humor, "you have made your point. However, I still fail to see why you are here. Especially," he added more softly, "considering the shabby treatment you have lately suffered at my hands."

Smiling broadly at his lordship's admission that his handling of their recent confrontation had been shabby in the extreme, Lucy decided once again that her reading of her beloved's character had not been in error. "Why, we are here to tell you that we don't believe a word of this nonsense about you and Miss Anscom," she told him fiercely. "And to offer our services, of course."

"Your services for what?" Lord Thorpe was moved to ask, still trying to shake the feeling that he was lost in the middle of a nightmare and showing no signs of waking up in the near future.

Lucy leaned forward conspiratorially and said grimly, "I have given this a good deal of thought since last night. I feel this whole thing is a plot to rob you of your good name and drive you distracted into an early grave."

"Oh, I seriously doubt that," Julian replied, biting back a laugh at the sight of Lucy's intense expression.

"No, really," she assured him, shifting so that she sat perched right on the edge of her chair. "Only think how thorough this Miss Anscom was—writing to all the papers."

"Hmm," he mused back at her, "and then drowning herself in the village pond just to lend credence to her story. I must agree, the woman certainly *was* thorough."

Now Lucy supplied the coup de grace. "My Lord Thorpe, how deep is the village pond?"

"I haven't the faintest idea. It is certainly not a big body of water."

"Exactly! The pond near our home is no more than three or four feet deep, even in the center. I imagine Miss Anscom's pond to be about the same depth. If she did indeed drown, as the newspaper says it has confirmed, I find it mindboggling to understand how she could have had such perseverance—holding her own head beneath the surface for the length of time required."

Lord Thorpe jumped to his feet, two high spots of color in his cheeks. "This is how you're going to help me? By spreading about the insinuation that I've *murdered* this Miss Anscom? A little more 'help' from you, madam, and I shan't have to go to the trouble of purchasing my own rope!"

# CHAPTER FOUR

IT DID PRECIOUS LITTLE to relieve Lord Thorpe's uneasy mind that Lucy Gladwin had been the only visitor ushered into his drawing room in the two interminable days following his embarrassment at the Selbridge ball. He was so alone in his misery, in fact, that he had almost begun to regret the fact that he had, at the time of that visit, come within ames ace of tossing that same Lucy Gladwin out onto the flagway on her dainty little ear.

"I *am* getting desperate," he told himself ruefully as he slouched inelegantly in a chair in his private sanctum, his book-lined study at the rear of the Thorpe mansion. "Anyone who would feel the least pang at the absence of that outrageous little baggage has got to be desperate. Or else," he muttered, looking owlishly into the near-empty brandy snifter he held in his hand, "well and truly corned, which I do believe I am."

Poor, poor Lord Thorpe. He was truly a man alone, with his only company the half-dozen decanters of fine old brandy he had been consuming steadily ever since bolting himself inside his study the previous morning. His fine clothing, donned the day before in anticipation of putting on a brave front for his supporters as they rallied around him, was now sadly crushed and dotted with brandy stains—and perhaps a tear stain or two?

That he had dealt so cavalierly with the one supporter who had braved society to comfort him he reconciled to the fact that the dratted chit had, while supposedly lending him solace, damn near come out and accused him of murder!

"Perhaps it is better I am alone," he told a bust of Nelson that sat in a niche across the room. "Many more like her and I'll find myself in Old Bailey fighting for my life." The admiral only stared off into the distance with his one good eye, refusing, so it seemed, to acknowledge his lordship's scandal-tainted presence.

His lordship's servants had been cutting a wide berth around him, but had delivered to him the small box that had arrived earlier by messenger, a box containing the Rutherford ancestral betrothal ring and nothing else. After Lady Cynthia's behavior when last he saw her, Julian had not been too surprised, although her action had not measurably enhanced his opinion of women, which had never had much reason to be more than it should be.

Tossing off the remainder of his drink, he thought fleetingly of his mama, the grande dame who had been the first to impress on him the honor and duty attached to being born a Rutherford. That she was for the moment in the far reaches of Scotland, dutifully burying a distant relative (and sniffing about for any bit of inheritance that might come her way), could only be considered a gift from the gods, for the old lady would have murdered him for allowing his good name to be dragged in the mire in this tacky way.

"Here's to you, Mama," the earl quipped, holding out his empty snifter and then dashing it to the hearth. "You taught me everything I needed to know about being a titled gentleman. 'Tis a great, bleeding pity you didn't teach me how fickle it all can be."

He stood and walked to the fireplace to inspect the damage he had wrought and found it to be depressingly insufficient. Turning back to face his desk, he swept the pile of tradesmen's bills from the surface with one angry swipe of his arm. "The meanest cut of all," he observed feelingly as he watched the papers flutter about the room before settling on the floor. That the common man had felt the need to call in their bills showed just how far his disgrace had plunged his good name.

But if he had thought he was already as low as a man could go, the note his butler brought him a few minutes later showed him that he had no idea of the thoroughness of his fall from grace. Clutching the note in his fist, he called for a servant to send word to have his closed carriage brought round immediately.

And as he gave his coachman Lucy Gladwin's direction, he took the first step into becoming the man Lucy had thought him to be all along.

"I DESPAIR OF EVER making him understand," Lucy said gloomily as she sat in the morning room, her embroidery lying forgotten in her lap. "When I think of how...*overset*...Lord Thorpe was when I mentioned that bit about the pond, I cannot help but despair of his *ever* listening to reason while there is still time to help him."

Lucy's audience of one—her long-suffering Aunt Rachel (who had been hearing this sad refrain for the past four-and-twenty hours)—now replied evenly, "A bit more 'despair,' pet, and I shall begin to believe it is *you* who are going into a sad decline, and not Lord Thorpe. Really, my dear, I think you refine too much on this murder theory of yours. This is just another garden-variety *ton* scandal, and will blow over by next week."

"I think not, Aunt!" Lucy returned earnestly. "A scandal of these proportions does not blow away like a puff of smoke.

Oh no! Mark my words—I smell a deep intrigue here, I'm sure of it."

"You scent a chance to endear yourself to Lord Thorpe while that man is vulnerable to an assault on his tender feelings, you mean," her aunt contradicted without rancor. "You may hoodwink others with that wide-eyed look of innocence, missy, but you're wasting your efforts in trying to convince *this* particular audience of your selflessness."

"Oh, pooh!" Lucy tossed out lightheartedly. "I never said I didn't hope to take advantage of this chance to alert Julian to my finer qualities. But I do mean it when I say I think he is in real danger. Someone went to a lot of trouble to launch this scandal, and I can't make myself believe simple mischief was the motivation."

"The Earl of Thorpe, ma'am," the butler intoned in a suitably awed voice from the doorway, then stood aside as his lordship lurched past him into the room.

Lucy could not help the involuntary gasp of incredulity that escaped her lips at the sight of the disheveled earl. He looked, so she thought, as if he had just come off the loser in a heated battle, and she could only stare at his unshaven face and red-rimmed eyes.

"My lord," Rachel said calmly, indicating a nearby chair, which Julian dropped into gratefully. "Biggs," she said in an aside to the gape-mouthed butler, "I do believe we should like a pot of coffee as soon as possible. A rather *large* pot, actually."

"Oh, I knew it! *I just knew it would come to this!*" Lucy exclaimed, rushing to shut the door on Biggs's departing back. "They're after you, aren't they?"

"Who's after me?" the earl questioned, staring at Lucy owlishly as that female threw her back against the closed doors as if to ward off an imminent invasion.

"The constable! The Bow Street Runners! The *law!*"

"It pains me to disappoint you, brat," the earl said, regaining a bit of his dignity, and with it his sarcastic wit. "I am not, alas, in imminent danger of being clapped into irons and hauled off to jail. However, if you wish me to send one of the servants round to Bethlehem Hospital, I'm sure you'd find sufficient drama in having your own private piece of Bedlam to call your own. Really, Miss Gladwin, you must learn to control these wild flights of imagination. I do believe such transports may be injurious to your spleen or something."

Rachel choked delicately into her handkerchief as Lucy, her expression suitably chastened, returned slowly to her seat, at last ready to listen to what his lordship had to say. "Pardon me, my lord," she begged, her lower lip trembling appealingly. "I let my fears run away with me for a moment there, didn't I? But you look so…that is to say, you are not looking yourself…not that you don't look fine as ninepence, you understand…but…but…"

"I apologize for burdening you both with my outlandish appearance, for there is no need to dress it up in fine linen— I look like a common ruffian and I know it. I don't know exactly why I am here, to tell the God's truth, except that I could not think of any other door in all of London that would be open to me."

His little bit of humble pie swallowed, Lord Thorpe leaned heavily against the back of his chair and stared at the crumpled piece of paper he still held tight in his hand. "They've asked me to resign from my club," he muttered half under his breath. "Six generations of Rutherfords have been members. My disgrace is now total."

While some females may not have understood the gravity of this last snub delivered to Lord Thorpe by his contemporaries, Lucy Gladwin, who had been raised by a worldly-wise father, immediately recognized that the worst, the absolute *worst* had happened. "Oh, you *poor thing!*" she exclaimed, dropping to her knees at his feet.

Biggs interrupted the proceedings at that moment, bringing in the coffee tray—which might have been a good thing, for Lord Thorpe, at Lucy's show of sympathy, was perilously near to unmanning himself in the company of females, a truly unpardonable breach of gentlemanly behavior. Rising to walk over to a nearby window, pretending to look out over the rear garden until he could regain control of his emotions, he waited until the door had closed behind the butler before turning to face the women. "I...I'm sorry, ladies. It seems such a piddling thing, doesn't it, when compared to the rest? But somehow... somehow—"

"Mr. Dexter Rutherford," Biggs proclaimed, excitement evident in his voice as a dazzling young Tulip of Fashion brushed past him to stand in the middle of the morning room, quizzing glass stuck to his eye.

"I say, Julian, your man was right," the young exquisite remarked after bowing to the ladies. "Strange sort of bolt hole, I thought at the time, right here smack in the center of Mayfair, but then I said to myself, where else could Cousin Julian go? Surely not to Piccadilly!"

The earl looked at his cousin, his expression more pained than angry. "I trust you will explain that remark, Dexter."

Crossing his legs carefully after making much ado about the spreading of his coattails before sitting himself down in the most comfortable chair in the room, Mr. Rutherford expanded graciously, "I was on the hunt for you this morning, of course. I had to listen to a load of drivel from your butler—the man has handed in his notice, by the by, seeing as how he cannot allow his name to be linked with yours now that you are fallen so low—who told me you had hightailed it over here like some madman, without even lingering long enough to change your linen. I see the man was correct," he ended, looking his cousin up and down and shaking his head in sorrow. "God man, can anything be that bad, that you would run about in your dirt for all the world and his wife to see you?"

"They've asked him to resign from his club," Rachel put in softly, content to sit back and watch events as they unfolded, only tossing in a word or two at appropriate times to keep the thing lively.

"Oh, that's too bad of them!" Dexter commiserated feelingly. "Though I imagine they'd do much the same to me, except that in the clubs I frequent, such notoriety would probably get me a free round of drinks!"

Lucy, who had been in deep thought ever since Dexter's name had been announced, finally spoke. "They're after you too, aren't they, Dex? And it's that, and not cousinly concern, that has you flying over here this morning."

Dexter flashed his cousin an insouciant smile. "Sharp as a tack, ain't she, coz? Like Lucy excessively, you know, always have. But she's right, of course. You know, when I first heard of your plight I thought, couldn't happen to a nicer, more deserving bloke. The whole thing, actually, would have been ever so amusing except that now the world has got the needle into *me*—seeing as how I'm living on m'expectations. Only stands to reason—if you go down, your heir goes right along with you. I should think you would have considered me a little bit before tumbling the chit. Poor sporting of you, Julian, it really was."

A sound much resembling a low animal growl issued from his lordship's throat as he made to throttle the handsome blond, slim, younger version of himself as that gentleman stepped swiftly to stand behind Lucy's chair seeking petticoat protection in hopes it would save him from a bloody nose.

"Now, now, my lord," Lucy intervened, rising to her feet

and putting out her hands in warning (and barely hiding the smile that lurked at the corners of her mouth). "You can't blame poor Dex for feeling sadly used. Just think—all his props have just been cut out from under him, and when he runs to his beloved cousin for guidance, he finds you wallowing so deeply in your own self-pity that it is no wonder his tact has gone a begging."

"His *wits* have gone a-begging," the earl contradicted meanly. "I never thought my own flesh and blood would believe these calumnies broadcast against me."

"Oh, he doesn't really believe them," Lucy explained. "It's just that he's upset."

"I don't? I am?" Mr. Rutherford ventured confusedly. "That is to say, of course I don't! How could I believe such a thing of Julian? After all he's an arrogant bas—that is to say, a high stickler, he's a good old fellow for all that. Towed me out of River Tick more than once, as a mater of fact. I was merely overcome for a moment, wasn't I, Lucy?"

"Exactly." Lucy nodded emphatically, changing a look out of the corners of her eyes to see that his lordship, only slightly mollified but still very weary, had subsided once more into his chair.

"If I were an enterprising sort of female," Rachel remarked to no one in particular, "I should be out in the square selling tickets to this circus. Lucy," she prompted, deciding to stir the pot a bit more, "why don't you tell Mr Rutherford your theory about this whole thing being a conspiracy to have Lord Thorpe sent to the gallows."

Lucy's eyelids narrowed as she assessed the young man. She had been looking about for a likely suspect behind the plot, and Dexter Rutherford, next in line to the peerage, seemed as good a place as any to start. "I don't think it wise to discuss strategy with our prime suspect, Aunt Rachel," she intoned heavily.

Dexter looked about the room, realizing that he had suddenly become the center of some decidedly hostile attention. "Plot? What plot? Who's a suspect? *Me?* I didn't do anything. I haven't the brains, for one thing." He turned and spread his arms imploringly in his cousin's direction. "Tell her, Julian. Tell her what a slow-top I am. You know I couldn't be guilty. *Tell her!*"

Julian rubbed a hand across his burning eyes. "He's right, Miss Gladwin," he sighed, shaking his head. "At least he's smart enough to know he's stupid, if that can be any solace to his mama, for it surely is not to me. Relax, Dex, I'm not about to call you out."

"Or cut off my allowance?" the semi-relieved young man pursued.

"Or cut off your allowance," the earl agreed, silently wondering as to the future of the Rutherford line if Dexter *were* to become the next Earl of Thorpe. The resulting mental picture lent new resolve to his flagging spirits. "But I think I can no longer brush off Miss Gladwin's theory. Someone has gone to a lot of trouble to discredit me. The next logical step would be to prove me criminally as well as morally corrupt."

"I say, Julian, that's coming on a bit strong, isn't it? I mean, all you did was disappoint some country female. How was you to know she'd be such a gudgeon as to go jumping in the pond like some penny-press looby? It's not that you wouldn't have provided for the child. You *were* planning to, weren't you?"

"You idiot!" the earl exploded, causing his cousin once more to take refuge behind Lucy. "Try to get this through your thick skull—*I did not get Miss Anscom pregnant!* I didn't even *know* the lady!" After taking a deep, steadying breath, he continued: "The entire scandal has been made up out of whole cloth to discredit me. Try, if you can, Dexter, to see me as innocent. I assure you that I am."

"All right, cousin," Mr. Rutherford owned after indulging in a few moments' deep thought—a feat that brought a pain to his temples and made him wish he'd gone to Gentleman Jackson's like he'd planned instead of coming to Portman Square to confront his erring relative. "But the fact remains that Miss Anscom, whether you say you knew her or not— by the by, was that in the ordinary or the biblical sense?" As Lord Thorpe's left eyebrow was developing a warning twitch, he ended that line of thought and pressed on: "This Miss Anscom, lying though she may have been, is *dead,* Julian. If she didn't drown herself over you—whom did she do it over, or because of, or…oh, you know what I mean."

"Or did she drown herself at all?" Lucy added, crossing her arms over her bosom and making quite a business out of assembling her features in a judgelike expression of solemn inquiry. "Perhaps the lady had help?"

*"Murder?"* Dexter hissed audibly. "You mean the woman was murdered?"

"Exactly!" Lucy said authoritatively.

Dexter gnawed on his knuckle for a full minute while the others in the room awaited his opinion. At last he raised his head, a slow smile spreading on his vacantly handsome face. "If they hang you, coz, can I still be earl?"

RACHEL GLADWIN HADN'T been so diverted in years, and living with a madcap like her niece Lucy—that was taking into consideration a *lot* of diverting circumstances! After pulling the usually unflappable Lord Thorpe off his cowering cousin before any lasting damage could be inflicted, Rachel had taken charge, sending Mr. Rutherford off with a maid to have his bruised nose attended to, Lord Thorpe was off to his mansion to refresh himself before joining them again in an hour, and Lucy off to her room to do whatever it was Lucy was clearly set to do.

By the time the small party had reassembled in the drawing room, Lucy's intentions were clear. She took center stage immediately, only bowing to Lord Thorpe as that belatedly composed man sat glaring at her, clearly wondering how he had chanced to land amidst this gathering of fools. Dexter, seated at a comforting distance from his cousin, and dabbing quite obviously at his oozing left nostril with his lace handkerchief, was all ears as he waited for Lucy to speak, while Rachel, again seated a little away from the rest, took up her tatting and appeared unconcerned.

"Now that we have all had time to compose ourselves," Lucy began, shooting warning glances at both the Rutherfords, "I think we should review what we know and set about formulating a plan of action."

That was as far as Lord Thorpe let Lucy go before breaking in with a word or two of his own. Rising to his full height, his dignity as well as his toilette apparently repaired, he began, "I apologize for bursting in on you ladies this morning. My only excuse is a combination of too little sleep and too many bottles of brandy. I despise myself for my weakness and am here to offer my abject apologies."

Lucy could only smile as she looked at the earl. Even when he groveled, he looked and acted like a king. "Please do not apologize, my lord," she interrupted when it looked as if he were about to launch into a lengthy recitation of his sins. "We are flattered that you trusted us enough to come to us."

The earl bowed slightly, then resumed his rigid stance. "Does not the fact that I had nowhere else to turn dampen your enthusiasm even slightly?"

"I say, coz," Dexter ventured, seeing the sadness flicker in Lucy's eyes, "can't you unbend enough to thank the girl properly? God knows I'm not sure I would have let you across *my* threshold."

The earl had the good grace to look ashamed of himself, a thing Rachel found to be as disconcerting as it was out of character. It would be a pity if Lord Thorpe was drawn to Lucy like a waif seeking comfort—for what would happen to her poor niece once the man no longer needed her? "We are only doing the Christian thing," she pointed out quickly. "Lucy also has a penchant for stray dogs."

Rachel's words served to put his lordship back on his mettle. "I am no stray dog, madam," he informed Rachel coldly. "I was merely trying to explain my vulnerability, which, upon reflection, was highly exaggerated by my shock at being turned on so decisively by my peers. Your niece, in my confusion, seemed like the safest port in my personal storm. However, now that I have my wits about me once again, I have returned to Portman Square only to apologize and to collect my cousin. Dexter?" he ended, gesturing to the comfortably reclining youth to stand and follow him out the door.

"Rather not be seen with you at the moment, cousin," Dexter drawled, raising his index finger to tenderly stroke his abused nose. "Much as this hurts, you seemed almost human when you were knocking me down. Now you're back to being an insufferable prig, I don't believe I care so much for you. Besides, have you forgotten Lucy's theory? Seems to me we'd better put our heads together before you're carted off to jail."

"Are you insinuating that I cannot straighten out this misunderstanding on my own?" the earl questioned, now definitely up on his high ropes. "Moreover, are you really of the opinion that, if I should require assistance, although I do not believe I have alluded to any such eventuality, I would be desperate enough to enlist a young female and a disloyal idiot into my plans?"

Dexter grinned brightly. "Yes, and yes again, coz. You

need us, you know, much as the thought must bring you pain."

"Exactly!" Lucy applauded, running over to give Dexter a quick hug. "I have been giving this thing a great deal of thought ever since you left, my lord, and I have decided that the only thing we can do is to adjourn to your home and investigate the business where it first began. Now that Dexter has volunteered—" she eyed the young exquisite owlishly "—you did volunteer, didn't you—I think we shouldn't waste any more time before setting off."

"There is not the smallest need—" Thorpe began before Lucy cut him off by means of a very unladylike snort of disbelief.

"There is *every* need, my lord," she countered, raising her hands to begin ticking off her reasons on her fingers. "One, you cannot just go round bullying the villagers into talking to you about this Miss Anscom. Two, you need a reason to be leaving town in the first place, unless you wish it bandied about that you have been disgraced, jilted, and forced to flee with your tail between your legs. For that reason we will appear to be your guests at a house party that has been planned this age or more. Three, since you are the supposed guilty party, you must be seen to have the support of two London ladies of quality as well as that of your heir. Four, although you are a highly intelligent man, you don't possess the deviousness required to obtain information from unwilling witnesses, or the approachable appearance that is needed to have people confide in you. Five—"

"Enough!" the earl allowed, holding up his hand to stop her. "I'll admit to requiring a bit of assistance. I'll accept Dexter's offer with thanks. But I draw the line at dragging you two ladies into the matter. What sort of gentleman would open two innocent females up to conjecture and censure— being seen with a man so sunk in disgrace."

"A desperate gentleman?" Dexter offered, giving voice to the obvious.

The argument went on at some length—and with some heat—while Rachel sat in her chair and tatted, looking up only sporadically to make sure no one was about to resort to physical violence. For Lord Thorpe had lost his temper as only a very controlled, usually coldly common-sensical person can do, and it would not have surprised the lady if he were soon to begin throwing things.

"You poor abused man, don't you see you need help?" Lucy cried at one point.

"I am not your 'poor man,' madam," he shot back. "And I'm not likely to become an abused anything!"

"Oh, give over, Julian," Dexter needled. "You know less about sleuthing than you do about fuzzing cards. Come down from that tower you live in and face facts—all your money and title and grand old name will get you is cleaner straw in your cell."

On and on it went, well into the afternoon, until finally, possibly only to gain for himself a moment's peace, the earl at last agreed to the plan. They would depart for Thorpe two days hence, taking Parker Rutherford, his distant cousin and personal secretary, along as well.

"I don't see why we need that cawker," Dexter snapped irritably, not knowing well enough to quit while he was ahead. "Talk about your prunes and prisms."

"Parker is also a Rutherford, and it's his good name as well that is being dragged through the mud," Thorpe pointed out. Turning to Lucy, he said, in order to make himself completely clear, "Remember, if you please, that I've only agreed to any of this to clear my family name. None of this is for myself."

"Of course it isn't," his cousin gibed meanly. "You always wanted a longer neck. All the better for tying a neat cravat, what?"

"Will you be putting a notice in the papers—about the house party, I mean," Lucy asked quickly, as a deep red flush crept up his lordship's neck. "I saw the announcement that Lady Cynthia's father inserted this morning of your engagement coming to an end."

Bringing up that particular betrayal dampened Thorpe's rage and sent him plummeting forthwith back into melancholy. His heart was not broken—he couldn't and wouldn't deceive himself on that head—but his pride had taken a mighty blow with Lady Cynthia's defection. A notice of a house party with Miss Lucy Gladwin as his female guest would go a long way in getting some of his own back—considering his former fiancée's outrage at the mere mention of Lucy's name. "I'll see to it that Parker sends it off at once," he told her, his small smile going unnoticed by everyone except Rachel, who missed little.

Once Lord Thorpe had taken his leave and Lucy and Dexter had gone off to put their heads together planning strategy like two generals about to take to the battlefield—or two nursery brats consulting over their toy soldiers—Rachel retired to her room to pen a letter to her brother. Sir Hale may have put her in charge of his volatile daughter, but she wasn't about to bear the brunt of this one on her own. Oh no, brother Hale was to be ordered to send in reinforcements on this one. If he couldn't be trusted to keep Lucy from the briers, at least Rachel wasn't going to be the only one to take the blame. After all, the wisest general knew it paid to cover her flanks!

# CHAPTER FIVE

THE MORNING DAWNED bright and clear, a perfect day for traveling. By nine of the clock four carriages were well on their way north of London, loaded top, back, and sides with strapped-on luggage. Postilions rode their leaders proudly while outriders accompanied the main coach. One many-caped exquisite, controlling his showy steed with some difficulty, rode ahead of the others, unwilling to pass the time riding inside the crowded conveyance.

"I do so admire your carriage, my lord," Lucy, looking quite ravishing in her peacock-blue ermine-trimmed cloak, told her host—who was just then sulking in his corner of the seat opposite. "It is ever so much more comfortable than the public coach."

"You speak from experience?" the earl asked, already knowing the answer—for was there anything this Gladwin chit had not done on a dare or for a lark?

Lucy grinned in remembrance. "Indeed, yes. I was outrunning my governess at the time, you see. Papa had utterly deserted me for Newmarket and I was determined to follow."

"Indeed," Thorpe repeated repressively. "And did you, I sincerely hope, learn anything from the experience?"

Her blue eyes fairly dancing in her head, Lucy answered

promptly, "Oh yes, my lord. I learned never, *never* to sit beside a fat person!"

"That isn't funny," the soberly dressed young man seated beside Lord Thorpe responded dampeningly. "You could have been robbed, or kidnapped, or worse."

"Worse, Mr. Rutherford?" Lucy said tauntingly. "You mean I could have been *ravished,* for instance?" She watched with some amusement as a deep flush appeared in Mr. Parker Rutherford's sallow cheeks. "Why, Mr. Rutherford, I do believe you have a dirty mind."

"Leave off, brat," Thorpe muttered desultorily. "Much as it pains me to say it, my cousin Parker is not up to your weight. Now stop trying to shock us all with your exploits and your wayward tongue or I shall ship you back to ride with your aunt."

Lucy squirmed uncomfortably in her seat. "I was only twelve at the time," she remarked sulkily, by way of excuse.

"And are still acting it a decade later," the earl observed tightly, his light gray eyes warning her to hold her tongue.

The occupants of the coach lapsed into silence then, each thinking his own thoughts, and Lucy was free to give Parker Rutherford a further inspection than the quick, dismissing survey she had given him upon first entering the coach in Portman Square. No more than a year or two older than Dexter, he had all the starch of a Cambridge dean, and only half the personality. Dex had told her earlier that he considered his distant cousin to be a dull dog, too prosy by half, and Lucy had no reason to doubt that assessment.

Look at him sitting there, she thought to herself—acting like he's been appointed my chaperon or something. It's not as if I'm unescorted, even if Aunt Rachel is riding in our own coach with Deirdre.

Deirdre. Lucy chuckled a bit to herself as she remembered what her maid—actually shared between her and her aunt—

had said when that volatile Irish lass had first spied out
Dexter on his hot-blooded stallion earlier that morning.
"He'll come to a stick end, that one," Deirdre had com-
mented, giving her carroty curls a flip.

"Dexter?" Lucy had questioned, looking at the man and
seeing a smaller, paler, but still attractive replica of her beloved Julian. "I think he's very handsome.

"Hummph," the maid had sniffed. "Handsome is as handsome does, I say, and that one looks prime for trouble."

Lucy, who had great faith in Deirdre's "feelings," now
wondered if her maid could be right. Although, as his immediate heir, Dexter was a prime suspect in any plot to discredit
and imprison the earl, Lucy found it hard to believe Dexter
capable of such deceit. Nevertheless, he would have to be
watched, and she must be careful not to confide overmuch in
him.

That left Parker, whom Dexter did not dislike for any reason more reasonable than the fact that the man was a dead
bore. Lucy already knew from Lord Thorpe that he felt his
cousin to be an exemplary employee: loyal, honest, end-
lessly supportive, and uncomplaining. Lucy, who was used
to complete love and loyalty from all her servants, who were
also her friends, could see no reason for applause in that
statement. Of course the man was loyal—Lord Thorpe was
his cousin, wasn't he?

Two suspects. Two, because—other than to think that
Lord Thorpe had incriminated himself—there were only two
people even in the running for the dubious honor of being
Julian Rutherford's adversary. Well, she thought resignedly,
this line of thought will just have to wait until we get to
Hillcrest and can examine any clues or evidence that may be
waiting for us there. It is pointless to waste time looking for
a bogeyman masquerading as either a witless heir or a lack-
luster personal secretary.

It was just that it was so important that she be able to help Lord Thorpe—and the good Lord knew the man needed help. Just look at him, she told herself, sitting over there like a child whose candy has been taken away. Power and position have been his all, and he does not know how to behave now that he has been brought down to the level of his fellow mortals. How dare he insinuate that I behave like a child— why, I wouldn't be surprised to see him putting his thumb in his mouth, just like a disappointed toddler. If Lady Cynthia could see him now she'd jilt him all over again.

"Lord Thorpe," she said, breaking the silence, "you mustn't look so downpin. Anyone would think you don't believe we will soon have this whole scheme exposed and your good name restored."

His lordship's upper lip curled into a sneer. "Why, Miss Gladwin, whatever do you mean? Do you really think I have no confidence in your ability to sleuth out the person or persons who have perpetrated this malicious bit of gossip? Oh, Miss Faint Heart, how could you imagine any such thing?"

"There's no reason to be nasty," Lucy said, bristling.

"Certainly not!" Thorpe agreed. "My good name has been dragged through the mire; I am, according to your theory, about to be clapped in irons and tried for murder; my mother— once she gets wind of this—shall probably disown me; and my only supporters comprise an overly imaginative minx and my brainless twit of a cousin. Why ever should I be nasty?"

"I am prepared to support you with all the fiber of my being," Parker Rutherford said earnestly, if a bit stuffily.

Julian looked at his cousin for a long moment before replying, "You have a most charming way of expressing yourself, Parker. It nearly unmans me to hear of such loyalty. Of course, the fact that you should be out of a job if I were to swing on the gibbet does not enter into your decision even a little bit, does it?"

"Lord Thorpe!" Lucy cautioned, thinking it unnecessarily brutal to say such a thing aloud—even though she privately agreed with him.

"What? Have I said something that is not true?" he returned, feigning ignorance. "After all, I can't see our friend Dexter retaining my secretary, can you? I rather think Parker has little choice but to be loyal."

Parker broke in before Lucy could say anything else in his defense. "Please do not concern yourself on my account, Miss Gladwin. Lord Thorpe is quite right. I do rely on him for my daily bread. But that is not my only reason for believing in his innocence. If you'll recall, my lord," he said, turning to face his employer, "I was with you at Hillcrest this past winter season. I know you were not involved with any female while we were there."

"Ah, that is more like it, Parker," his lordship said with maddening calm. "Blind loyalty would have been nice, but I find it easier to believe deductive reasoning. I was not openly involved with this Anscom woman while at Hillcrest; ergo, I am blameless in her death. Tell me, my loyal secretary—did you really think that if I were so desperate for a bit of dalliance that I would go about seducing some poor impoverished gentlewoman, I should *advertise* that fact? Disabuse yourself of the notion that you know my every movement."

"And he said *I* was digging his grave for him," Lucy muttered under her breath, watching the questioning look steal into Parker's watery blue eyes. More loudly she trilled, "Oh, look! I believe we could stop for some refreshments? I vow I'm famished!"

Just then, as if Lucy had conjured him up to aid her in her determination to find another topic of conversation, Dexter rode up to the coach window and called, "My belly thinks m'throat's been cut, coz. What say we stop for a bird and a bottle?"

Lucy closeted herself with her aunt and maid during the time they stopped for luncheon at a small country inn, then chose to ride out the rest of that day's leg of the journey with the women. Lord Thorpe needed time to become accustomed to his new situation in life, and she had decided to let him alone a bit to do his adjusting. After all, she wouldn't put it past him to change his mind and send them all back to town at the next posting inn if they gave him any more reason to doubt his decision of allowing them to help clear his name.

"Dexter has decided to ride inside the coach this afternoon, Aunt," she told Rachel as she settled in beside her on the padded seat, "and once that idiot starts in teasing Mr. Rutherford, I would not care to be within earshot of Lord Thorpe's biting tongue. Dex seems to have such a talent for rubbing up his cousin the wrong way."

Just one hour after that statement the entire train drew to a halt to allow the earl to leave the comfort of his well-sprung coach in order to seek a little fresh air—and a bit of peace—atop the mount he had brought along. Before the coachmen restarted the horses, Thorpe rode up to the open window and congratulated Lucy for having the good sense to absent herself from the company of his cousins. "If one of them ends up floating in the village pond, Miss Gladwin, please don't bother trying to defend me. I confess in advance!"

AFTER BREAKING THEIR journey for the night at an inn Thorpe had frequented in the past—and having been treated most coldly by the innkeeper—they were once more on the road, hoping to reach Hillcrest in time for an early supper. Lucy had exited from the inn in riding dress, having cajoled and pleaded with Dexter until that young man (who was at the moment nursing a sore posterior) agreed to give up the thrill of riding his new stallion in favor of allowing Lucy the pleasure of sitting atop such a splendid animal.

Her sidesaddle having been dutifully produced by Deirdre, who had packed everything except the drawing-room clock, Lucy talked soothingly to Dexter's horse for some minutes before mounting with ease and riding off ahead of the coaches. Lord Thorpe, who knew he must do the right thing and ride beside her, gritted his teeth to better endure the splitting head that was the result of another bout of drowning his sorrows, and followed her.

"Isn't it a beautiful morning, my lord?" Lucy chirped merrily once she had succeeded in slowing her fresh mount down to a more manageable pace.

"I would liefer it were raining," Thorpe said, wishing himself and his pounding head inside his comfortable coach.

Lucy pulled a face at him, blighting him with her youth and beauty. "Oh, don't be such a sourpuss," she prodded, unwilling to succumb to his poor mood. After all, she was young, she was in love, and she had finally succeeded in getting the earl off all to herself.

"I am *never* a sourpuss," Thorpe contradicted, raising his eyebrows at her. "I would not stoop so low. I am merely above such transports as waxing poetic merely because our thin English sun has condescended to shine. Besides, it will probably cloud over soon."

"Most assuredly, my lord," Lucy concurred, tongue in cheek. "It may even snow."

"Don't be flippant," he warned, refusing to be shifted from his determined bad mood. "Do you know that our host of last evening demanded to be paid before he would show us our rooms? I have been favoring his establishment these twenty years past, and the man had the *effrontery* to demand his payment in advance! If your aunt had not been so weary I should have pushed on to another inn. How dare he—*how dare he*—treat a Rutherford that way!"

Lucy looked at her companion, easily reading the pain and

confusion that warred so with his anger. "You should have given the idiot a good bash in the noggin. Aunt Rachel and I would have understood."

"Oh, and is that your answer then? To go around bashing noggins every time I am slighted because of this dratted gossip? Considering that it would seem that everyone from the Regent to the rat catcher has heard of my supposed disgrace, I do believe defending my honor could become a full-time occupation."

"Of course I'm not saying that," Lucy said fiercely. "Not that delivering at last one good smash to somebody's bulbous nose wouldn't do you a world of good, for I'm sure it would. No, what we need to do is what we have set out to do—discover who has launched this dastardly plot and clear your good name."

"If wishes were horses, beggars might ride," the earl said acidly. "The closer we get to Hillcrest—not to mention the more I am forced into close company with my bloodless secretary and bacon-brained heir—the more I despair of ever being able to show my face in town again. And when I look at my remaining ally—a silly chit who can delight in a bit of sun when the world is crumbling down atop my head—I begin to know the true meaning of the word 'despair.' Oh God, my head hurts," he ended self-pityingly, lowering his chin onto his chest.

Of course Lord Thorpe did not mention the defection of his fiancée among the trials just now besetting him, but Lucy knew his poor heart must be near to breaking over losing his fair Lady Cynthia. Well, she thought, prodding her horse into a canter, that was one thing she could do something about! Just as she had always felt Lord Thorpe had been resisting his attraction to her, she likewise believed that he was never as committed to Lady Cynthia as the world believed him to be. Once she, Lucy, had succeeded in insinuating herself into the earl's heart, banishing forever the insipid, fickle Lady Cynthia, she would have come a long way toward bringing the man back to his former mental strength.

For she did not like to see him brought so low. It was one thing to picture herself as his savior, but it was another to feel that, to triumph in her mission, she would have to keep taking two steps forward and then going back to drag him along with her for one. Yes, she had seen bouts of righteous anger light his features and stir him into some semblance of action, but these moments were still too few and far apart. He was somehow going to have to be made to take a more active part in his own defense.

"Here," she said, drawing her mount up beside his and handing him her lace-trimmed handkerchief. "As long as you're going to turn into a watering pot on me, you might as well have something with which to wipe your tears away. Really, Julian," she said, daringly addressing him by name, "anyone would think your backbone has turned to jelly."

His blond head snapped erect and cold shards of gray ice glittered in his narrowed eyes. "You go too far, brat," he hissed menacingly. "But then, what else can I expect from someone who has such a long history of impertinence?"

"What else indeed, my lord?" Lucy answered artlessly. "But at least no one could accuse me of being fainthearted, daring to bait the dangerous Lord Thorpe so openly."

Julian looked at her for a long time, thankfully not able to see past her impish expression and into her fluttering heart, then finally shook his head. "This is a serious business, brat," he tried to warn most severely, although his twitching lips betrayed him more than a little.

"It most certainly is, Julian," Lucy agreed, winking. "But then, I find being serious such a terrible bore—don't you?"

The earl cocked his head to one side as if to consider her question. As he looked about him, noticing the wildflowers that grew along the edges of the road and hearing the birds that were singing overhead, his slight smile widened and eventually spread to crinkle the skin beside his eyes. Reaching out his hand, he lifted Lucy's gloved fingers and placed a light kiss on her bare wrist. "Far be it from me to bore a lady, Miss Gladwin." Releasing her hand, he waved his arm, indicating the scenery. "Isn't it a beautiful morning, Lucy?" he asked, borrowing her words.

Blinking rapidly to keep her tears at bay, Lucy responded breathlessly, "Oh, yes indeed, Julian. It is a most beautiful, *beautiful* morning!"

THE SUN WAS HIGH in the sky when the two riders, now very much in harmony with one another, crested a hill to look down into a small valley where a traveling circus and menagerie had set up its brightly colored tents.

"Oh, look, Julian!" Lucy cried, clearly delighted. "Please say we can stop there for awhile. We can have a picnic under the trees."

Julian looked at his companion, seeing her childish excitement, and knew he could only be considered the meanest of men if he denied her this little treat. "I guess it would be easier than having to suffer the cold shoulder from some other bumpkin innkeeper," he temporized, turning his horse to inform his coachman of their change in plans. "Don't ride off without me, however, as one never knows what sort of low-life frequents places such as this."

"Snob!" Lucy called after him playfully, urging her mount forward. "I'll meet you under the big trees beside the first wagon."

By the time Thorpe had assisted Rachel to the ground, and the rest of his small party had stretched a bit to alleviate the stiffness felt after four hours of riding in the coaches, he had lost Lucy's small figure in the crush of people standing around a rather rickety-looking cage containing an ancient, moth-eaten lion.

"I told her she shouldn't go on without me," he complained to Rachel, standing on tiptoe to try to spy out his errant charge.

"A word of advice, my lord," Rachel said, unperturbed. "*Never* say 'cannot' to my niece. Besides serving to encourage her to mutiny, it is, I have found, a sad waste of breath. Never mind me now, Deirdre will stand me company. Just go and find Lucy before she decides to try her hand at bareback riding or some such ridiculousness. I spied out a pieman and will content myself with feeding my face while you young ones play."

As Rachel was only about a dozen years his senior, Julian was surprised to be dismissed as a contemporary of Lucy's, but he was not about to debate his maturity with the woman. He hadn't needed her warnings to know that the younger Miss Gladwin, once set loose in a place such as this, was liable to get up to all sorts of mischief.

"Yes, go ahead, coz," Dexter seconded, running his eyes appreciatively over Deidre's slender form. "I'll do the pretty here."

"Well, I never did!" Deirdre gasped, blushing to the roots of her fiery red hair. "Away with you now, sir. It's a good girl I am, don't you know."

"And just how good would that be, hmm?" Dex said silkily, taking the maid's arm and leading her toward the pieman's table. "Not *too* good, I hope? No—" he smiled, seeing Deirdre's saucy smile "—I didn't think so."

That left Parker Rutherford still engaged in brushing down his drab brown suit, to partner Rachel, who stood placidly waiting for him to notice her. Her short acquaintance with the man had not left any lasting impression other than that of an offhand comment to Lucy that the man "seemed rather

Methodist in his manners," but she was willing to spend an hour in his company if it would mean Lucy could continue her interlude with Lord Thorpe undisturbed.

"Mr. Rutherford!" Rachel prompted now, holding out her arm to the secretary. "Isn't your mouth fairly watering for one of those lovely pies over there?"

Parker looked over at the pieman, seeing the flies that seemed to hang in a cloud above the man's head. "I don't believe my constitution allows such indulgence, madam," he said, shuddering dramatically. "But if you insist..."

Rachel smiled sweetly and slipped her hand around his elbow. "Ah, Mr. Rutherford. But I *do* insist."

"Then that's all settled," the earl said quickly, bowing slightly before turning on his heel and bounding off to the spot where he had last seen Lucy. "Lord Thorpe cavorting at a circus," he muttered under his breath. "The mind boggles!"

# CHAPTER SIX

"DID YOU KNOW that one of these traveling circus lions broke loose not too long ago?" Lord Thorpe asked, whispering into Lucy's ear as he walked up behind her.

Lucy, who had somehow pushed her way to the front of the crowd that was busy either pulling faces or poking sticks at the woebegone king of the jungle, turned to him eagerly. "Really? What happened?"

Thorpe shrugged negligently. "I heard the thing ate up one of the guards on the Exeter coach. It could all be a hum, though."

"Indeed," Lucy agreed, eyeing the caged animal once more. "Unless, of course, the lion *gummed* the man to death. But come away with me now," she pleaded, grinning up at him, "for that lad over there told me this circus also sports a rhinoceros and a pair of alligators. I had half-hoped for a unicorn, but they lost theirs last month—to colic, I believe the lad said."

"Either that or a lack of ready virgins with laps for resting his head," Julian suggested, feeling Lucy's hand slip into his and deciding that he would leave it there. "The rest of our party is sampling some meat pies. Aren't you hungry after our ride?"

Lucy wrinkled her pert little nose. "Piffle! We can always

eat later. First I want to see everything that's here. Do you think they have a rope dancer? I'm particularly fond of rope dancers."

Happily or unhappily for Lord Thorpe's stomach, depending on just how well his aristocratic constitution reacted to greasy meat pies, there was a rope dancer. There were also a gigantic fat lady, a dancing bear, a trio of performing dogs, and several peep shows, games of chance, and an every-hour-on-the-hour performance by a daring man who walked the high wire.

Lucy wanted to see them all, and see them she did—with the earl tagging along beside her, supplying her with coins as she needed them and holding her winnings tucked under his arm. It wasn't until they came at last to the faded red-and-green striped tent at the back of the circus that he balked.

"I refuse to lay down good money for a fortune-teller," he declared, shaking his head as Lucy held out her hand for sixpence. "Only fools believe in such nonsense."

"Of course it's nonsense, Julian," Lucy concurred readily. "That doesn't mean it isn't the grandest good fun. Please, Julian? Maybe the old Gypsy woman will tell me a prince is coming to carry me off to his castle. Oh, please, don't be stuffy."

Julian was insulted. Stuffy? How could she call him stuffy? He, who was standing in the middle of a soggy field holding a belled jester on a stick and a stuffed animal that was supposed to be a dog but looked (and smelled) more like a hedgehog. Certainly he didn't believe he deserved her censure—although he might privately think the events of the last few days had unhinged his mind just a trifle, else why would he be here at all?

"All right, you silly child," he relented, handing her the ready. "Go along inside and cross the old crone's palm with gold. But don't say I didn't warn you."

Once Lucy had disappeared beneath the tent flap, Lord Thorpe stood alone in the sunshine, trying not to feel ridiculous as the belled jester doll waved in the breeze from the string tied at the end of its stick. He felt as conspicuous as a harlot in a roomful of holy sisters, and was determined to call a halt to the whole proceedings the minute Lucy returned. A little bit of cutting loose had served him well, but he still did not feel comfortable enough in this new role to indulge in it for any great length of time.

Already the smell of the place, only mildly off-putting at first, was beginning to oppress him, as were the crush of sweating bodies and general air of abandon that prevailed. But at least here nobody snubbed him or questioned his power to pay. Just imagine, he could loosen his cravat, unbutton his coat, or even slouch a bit, without every eye watching and every tongue wagging. Why is it, he wondered idly, absently twirling the stick in his hand, that it is only now that I have relaxed a bit that I mind the strictures and confinements of my accepted way of life?

But he did not have time to ponder this question overlong, as Lucy fairly blasted from the tent, her cheeks as pale as parchment. "I'm ready to leave, my lord," she told him, grabbing his arm at the elbow and fairly dragging him away from the tent. "I believe you mentioned something about some pies?"

But Julian dug in his heels and refused to move. "Hold hard a minute, Miss Gladwin. Something's amiss here."

"That's very astute of you, my lord," Lucy bit back sharply, "but as I have only myself to blame, I suggest we just push on and join the others. It's just as you said—fortune-tellers are nonsense."

Lucy may have been putting a brave face on things, but Julian could tell she was only holding back the tears with a great deal of effort. Something the fortune-teller had said had hurt her badly, and suddenly the Earl of Thorpe discovered himself to be angry—very angry indeed!

"There's Dexter lazying about over there by himself," he said, pointing at the young exquisite, who was idly watching a dwarf balancing atop a huge ball. "Dexter! Come escort Miss Gladwin back to her aunt," he ordered as that young man skipped over to them. "I will join you shortly."

"But I—" Lucy began, angry with herself for allowing her distress to be so obvious.

"Do not contradict me," the earl ordered starchily, and Dexter, who had heard that tone of voice in the past, pulled Lucy away, leaving his cousin to bend himself nearly in half in order to enter the fortune-teller's tent.

It took a moment or two for his eyes to adjust to the dimness before he saw the pile of colorful rags that slowly reorganized itself into a small crone of a toothless Gypsy. "What did you say to that young woman who was just in here?" he demanded without preamble.

The Gypsy ran her gaze from Thorpe's head to his toes and then hastily made the sign against the evil eye. "It's *you!*" she accused in her gravelly voice. "The blond god of eternal slumber."

A pained expression crossed his lordship's handsome face. "That's me, all right, old woman. So tell me what you told the young lady or be prepared to suffer the consequences." Julian could have been more tactful, but he had always found the direct approach to be the easiest in the long run.

The old crone had a belated attack of scruples. "It's the young lady's fortune. It be her secret." But then, weighing her ethics against the gold guinea piece the "blond god" had produced, she changed her tune. "I saw you in my crystal ball. Then I saw the young miss asleep—*dead* asleep."

"And from that you deduced…" the earl said, feeling much like a Drury Lane prompter.

The Gypsy shrugged inside her rags. "You're going to be the death of that young lady, and so I told her."

"You stupid old bitch!" Thorpe exploded, turning to follow after Lucy and shake some sense into the impressionable chit.

"I could read your palm, m'lord," the Gypsy called after him. "Everyone wants to know his future."

"Not me, you meddling besom. I'm having more than enough trouble with my *present*," he snorted, pushing his way out into the warm sunshine, which did little to ease the chill that had enveloped him while inside the damp tent.

LUCY FELT SIMPLY WRETCHED. How could she have been so silly as to allow the Gypsy's ridiculous prophecy to upset her so? And even worse, how could she have been so transparent as to allow Lord Thorpe to see her agitation?

Of course she didn't *believe* what the Gypsy had said— only a complete ninnyhammer would swallow such drivel whole. It was just that she had described Lord Thorpe so accurately—right down to his arrogance. Why hadn't she immediately realized that the woman must have seen him as they approached the tent?

But, a niggling little voice taunted, why had the woman chosen such a terrible fortune for her? Gypsies were supposed to say that romance was about to come into the persons's life—not foretell of disaster. Lucy couldn't decide which was worse—being told she was to die, or hearing that her beloved was to be the instrument of her death.

"Want to go back to the coach now, Lucy?" Dexter asked, breaking into her thoughts and making her realize that she had been standing lost in thought, totally ignoring her companion. "I should certainly like to conk out a little while before we arrive at Hillcrest. Didn't sleep a wink last night in that dratted inn. The sheets were damp, you know."

"Deirdre always packs our own linen when we travel," Lucy supplied, lacking anything brighter to say. "Very thorough is our Deirdre. I can't imagine what we'd do without her."

"I know what I'd like to do *with* her," Dexter murmured under his breath, looking across to where Rachel Gladwin and her maid were reclining at their ease upon a blanket spread beneath a handy shade tree. Lucy, lost in her own thoughts, did not hear him, which may have been a good thing for Dexter, who was known far and wide for his indiscriminate amorous advances.

Lord Thorpe, too far away to hear his cousin's words, but certainly close enough to see the leer on Dexter's face, immediately jumped to the conclusion that the younger Rutherford was taking dead aim at Lucy as his next flirt. Tumbling smack on top of this thought was the stunning realization that this possibility did not suit him even a little bit.

Wasn't it bad enough that the girl had embroiled herself in his affairs—opening herself up to the scandal of being associated with such a social outcast as himself—and then been frightened out of her wits by some charlatan fortune-teller who warned that the man she had championed was about to murder her? Adding an amorous cousin set on seduction was piling entirely too much on the child's plate.

There wasn't much he could do about either the fortune-teller or Dexter now, he decided as he joined the two of them and urged them to begin thinking about reentering the coaches for the longish last leg of their journey. But Lucy, who knew she still needed a little time by herself before facing her aunt—who was so tiresomely astute when it came to ferreting out anything Lucy didn't wish to tell her—said that she was curious to see what had caused such a crowd to be gathered in front of a nearby wagon.

Taking off before anyone could gainsay her, Lucy led the

way over to the wagon, the two gentlemen lagging behind, sour expressions on their faces. As Dexter was bemoaning the fact that he must linger in this boring spot and Julian was damping down an urge to give the young Romeo a poke in the chops to warn him off his latest prey, it took some time before either of them realized that Lucy was engaged in a deep conversation with a wizened old organ grinder whose monkey had decided to hide himself amid the folds of her riding dress.

Lucy seemed to be listening intently to what the old man had to say, nodding excitedly a time or two, and then looking most sympathetic when the man seemed to be about to burst into tears.

"Come over here," she called to the two gentlemen once the old Gypsy had finished his tale of woe. "It's just the most exciting thing," she declared, smiling at Julian almost as if she hadn't taken a severe shock to her system not ten minutes earlier. "Oh, not that it isn't a sad thing—which to all events it is, for poor Mr. Romano here—but it is exciting nevertheless, for me."

"Perhaps if you could begin at the beginning, Lucille," Lord Thorpe prodded, trying hard not to concentrate on the delightful picture Lucy made when she was enthusiastic about something.

"Oh, of course," she agreed, smiling apologetically. "This is Mr. Romano," she said, indicating the old man, who doffed his cap and bobbed up and down several times. "And this," she continued, pulling on the lead that led to the small brown monkey's red leather collar so that the animal could better be admired by his audience, "*this* is Bartholomew!"

"I make you my compliments," Lord Thorpe intoned solemnly, exaggeratingly bowing to each of them in turn.

"*Yecch!*" Dexter added, never caring very much for such

creatures. His opinion of old Gypsy men who smelled curiously like pressed garlic was not much higher.

But Lucy was not to be sidetracked by either his lordship's sarcasm or his cousin's expression of distaste. "Mr. Romano has just told me the most terrible story. It seems he is quite too ill to continue working and must find a new home for Bartholomew."

"There being a war on, they cannot retire together to the south of France," Dex whispered to his cousin *sotto voce,* getting himself somewhat back in Julian's good books.

"How much money do you want this time?" Thorpe asked, not very severely. After all, it would be a small price to pay if it served to take Lucy's mind off the fortune-teller's words.

"Oh no, Julian, that's not it at all," she corrected, leaning down to chuck the little monkey under his hairy chin. "I said that Mr. Romano cannot keep Bartholomew anymore. I had thought to offer him some money, but it wouldn't really do the thing properly at all. It's a new home that the poor animal needs. Mr. Romano says he's never seen Bartholomew take to anyone the way he has to me. He wishes to make me a gift of him. Isn't that above anything marvelous?" she ended, smiling up at Thorpe, her big blue eyes bright with excitement.

"Absolutely not!" Dexter decreed emphatically before his cousin had a chance to open his mouth. "The damned thing probably has fleas."

At Dexter's words, Mr. Romano's lined, weathered face crumpled itself up like a piece of knotted wood and a huge tear squeezed out of the corner of one eye. "Oh, look what you have done, you horrid boy!" Lucy exclaimed, pointing a finger at the old Gypsy. "That is just too bad of you Julian," she pleaded, rounding on Lord Thorpe, "surely you cannot be so hardhearted? Just think of the pitiable fate of this poor creature if we do not agree to help."

Julian, wondering silently which of the poor creatures she meant, suggested smoothly, "Monkey stew?"

"Oh, fie on you both!" Lucy exclaimed, putting an arm around Mr. Romano's heaving shoulders. "Not only are you refusing to give aid to one of God's creatures, but Mr. Romano here says Bartholomew is very talented. Mr. Romano, have Bartholomew show us one of his tricks."

The old Gypsy may have been too overcome to put his pet through his party tricks, but Bartholomew was not without some little initiative of his own. The little brown monkey, who had been looking up at the people standing about him and measuring them with his brown-bean monkey eyes, made an independent decision. He scampered over to where Dexter stood looking belligerent and bit the man firmly on the shinbone.

"*Ouch!* Get that mangy beast away from me! Lucy, this is all your fault. I'll probably go mad and die—the creature is rabid!"

But Lucy was already cradling the monkey to her protectively, since the astute Bartholomew had, once he released Dexter's leg, immediately clambered up her skirts and clung to her as if his life were in danger—which, looking at Dexter's expression, it quite possibly was.

It was then, after looking at Lucy's angry face, and likewise taking in Dexter's obvious disenchantment with her, that Lord Thorpe decided that adopting Bartholomew might be just the thing to add a little bit of cachet to his small house party.

"Oh, thank you, Julian!" Lucy cried when he gave voice to his opinion. "He won't be any trouble; no trouble at all. I'll keep him with me at all times, and he can entertain us with his little tricks, can't he, Mr. Romano?"

Mr. Romano, already biting down on one of the gold pieces Julian had produced from his purse, vigorously nodded his head in agreement, not bothering to mention that, besides tipping his hat politely at a given signal, Bartholomew's major talent had been taught to him by his last owner, a petty thief who was just now a guest in Newgate prison.

Dexter wasn't the only one to express displeasure over the addition of Bartholomew to their little group. Rachel limited herself to a quiet "tsk, tsk," which Deirdre commented was a mild-enough censure, considering the elder Miss Gladwin wasn't the one who would most probably be assigned the chore of cleaning up after what were bound to be Bartholomew's primitive toilet habits.

"Oh," Dexter drawled artlessly, always happy to stick a needle where it was most likely to prick a sore spot, "I would have thought such *duties* would fall to his lordship's secretary. Parker, my good fellow, you're so good at tidying up after things. Surely you will volunteer your expertise?"

The secretary's pale eyes narrowed for a moment, then reassumed their blank expression. "I serve the earl as he requires, Dexter. But the monkey is not his, not that I haven't been sweeping up after one of his lordship's more trying hangers-on for years," he ended, taking no little satisfaction at the sight of his young cousin's suddenly mottled complexion.

"That will be enough," Lord Thorpe put in dangerously as Dexter's mouth opened to retort to Parker's clear insult. "Miss Gladwin, your arm if you please?" he prodded, turning to Rachel, instinctively seeking out the only person he felt he could rely upon to understand that he wished all of them shed of the place immediately.

As Lucy watched Julian and Rachel making their way back to the coaches, laughing and talking most companionably, she felt a niggling stab of jealousy. Rachel was at least fifteen years Julian's senior. Surely he couldn't be looking at her in a romantic way. Could he?

Poking out her tongue at Dexter, she allowed Parker to escort her to her aunt's coach, leaving Deirdre to fend off Dexter's ridiculous spate of flattery as best she could.

Lord Thorpe's coachman, watching the entire scene with the interest of a longtime servant of the family, could only wonder what else could happen. A bloomin' monkey at Hillcrest? Wait till the old lady hears about this one—there'll be the devil to pay, and no mistake!

# CHAPTER SEVEN

Dearest Jennie and Kit,

As you can see, Lord Thorpe has franked this letter for me at Hillcrest, not more than twenty miles from Bourne Manor! Before Kit drags out his dueling pistols and sets off to save my reputation, I will explain that Aunt Rachel is here with me, as are Julian's cousins Dexter and Parker.

As I told you in my first, hasty letter, Julian (yes, pets, I call him Julian now—see how we progress!) is neck-deep in scandal, but I won't waste paper on the exact circumstances, because unless you two are still so besotted with each other that you are deaf with love, you cannot help but know How Low He Has Sunk.

Of course it is all a hum—Julian couldn't hurt a fly—but beneath the scandal lies, I am quite sure, a Dastardly Plot to rob Julian of his title by having him Hanged for Murder.

We have been in Derbyshire only a scant twenty-four hours, but I can tell you, the air in Hillcrest is Most Oppressive. The servants tippytoe around, forever looking over their shoulders as if someone were about to plant a knife between their shoulder blades, and the villagers—according to Dex, who scouted out the locals to look for clues—are positively terrified! I should be too, if I thought Julian's fine management might be replaced by Dex's selfish style of living. Oh no, the locals do not wish evil on Julian—but it is depressing to see that they have no real affection for him. They only are looking out for themselves.

Tomorrow, our second full day here, we are all going to ride out to reconnoiter. Someone must know something they are not telling, and I Shall Not Rest until I have cleared Julian's name. Poor darling, he has put a brave face on it so far (well, he has had one or two lapses, but that is to be expected in such a proud man), and I know he must be torn between needing our help and wishing us all at the other side of the world so that he can give vent to his frustration without fear of any of us seeing.

I shall try to come to see you, for I wish to see Christopher before much more time has passed, but I shall not be leaving Hillcrest until the Mystery Is Solved!

Julian will be Ever So Grateful—don't you think?

Your most devoted,

Lucy

P.S. Julian has allowed me to keep the most adorable monkey we stumbled upon as we toured a traveling circus on our way to Hillcrest. Isn't he a dear?

WHEN JENNIE FINISHED reading, she looked over to where her husband sat, smiling in bemusement as he shook his head. "Who's a 'dear' do you think, love—Thorpe or the monkey!"

But Jennie wasn't laughing. "This is serious, Kit. You read the stories in the newspapers. Lucy's reputation will be completely destroyed, if it hasn't been already. We have to get her away from him—today if possible!"

"I don't think Wellington can spare a regiment, kitten, and that's what it would take to prize her loose. Relax, Rachel is with her." Kit could see one of Jennie's attacks of protectiveness coming on, and he wished to avoid it at all costs.

"But Lucy says something about murder," Jennie protested, rereading part of the letter. "Do you think she may be right?"

The Earl of Bourne drew his wife down onto his knees and kissed away the worry lines that creased her pale brow. "Lucy has never got the straight of anything in her life," he stated with gentle conviction. "Besides, like she says, Lord Thorpe is 'such a dear.' Surely she can't be in any danger. Now, give me a kiss, kitten—your wriggling about has quite taken my mind off any other subject."

"What? Here in the morning room where anyone might discover us!" Jennie teased, nibbling his earlobe.

Kit leaned her back so that he could leer good-naturedly into her smiling face. "Did you think Lord Thorpe was the only one capable of stirring up a bit of scandal? Ah, woman, how little you know me."

Lucy's letter slipped from Jennie's lap, to float unnoticed to the floor.

LUCY WAS TOTALLY enthralled by Hillcrest. Expecting an ancient, moldering pile dating from the thirteenth century and added onto willy-nilly over the years until it sprawled inelegantly in all directions, she was mightily surprised to find that the residence was no more than twenty years old and, if not modest in size, comfortably large without being intimidating.

Raleigh, Julian's majordomo, had told her that the old residence, situated a scant mile away on the other side of the park, had succumbed to fire, with only some carefully landscaped stone ruins remaining to mark the spot. The new

Hillcrest, built by Julian's father, had been planned to sit closer to the large pond that lay to the left of it, the late earl having thought it prudent to be closer to an ample supply of water if ever fire dared to strike again.

The fire had destroyed more than the ancestral Rutherford home; it had taken generations of badly painted portraits of past earls and their families, as well as nearly every stick of furniture that had been amassed over the years.

This, Lucy reflected happily as she stood in the bright, airy morning room, could only be deemed a blessing, as she had little love of the heavy Tudor pieces, dusty tapestries, and stained suits of armor an ancient domicile would be apt to hold.

The late-Georgian furnishings went well with the decorative ivory stuccoed walls, and the muted greens, blues, and rose pinks of the upholstery and Aubusson carpets found throughout the public rooms were just the sort she would have chosen if she had been given a hand in the decorating.

Yet there was something, some indefinable something, missing. Nibbling on the tip of one finger, she inspected the room once more, finally realizing what was wrong. This room, just like all the others, were perfect. *Too* perfect. The flowers, standing tall in their vases as if they knew they would be banished posthaste if they dared to droop the teeniest little bit, were arranged just a tad too perfectly. The beautiful furniture looked as if a mathematician had placed each piece precisely, making up visual squares, right angles, and perfect triangles staked out on the floor.

Lucy longed to tilt the rose satin heart-backed chair so that it sat more cozily near the matching sofa, while her fingers itched to gather up the carefully displayed embroidered pillows adorning that same sofa and scatter them about more invitingly. And the flowers—why, all they needed was a bit of—

"Good morning, Lucy," came a voice from the doorway.

"Oh!" she exclaimed, whirling about to see the earl entering the room, his well-formed body clad to perfection in "a-gentleman-at-his-ease-in-the-country" buckskins and hacking jacket. "Julian, you startled me for a moment."

He bowed slightly, a smile touching his lips as he took in her flustered look. "Forgive me, please. Next time I shall have Raleigh announce my arrival with a fanfare of trumpets."

Lucy was taken aback for a moment, but then burst into delighted laughter. "Oh, Julian, how wonderful! You have made a joke."

A shattered look came into his eyes. "Is that so surprising?"

Lucy realized at once and mentally kicked herself for drawing the earl's attention to what she had seen as his gradual "thawing" ever since they left London. "Of course I'm not surprised," she improvised hastily. "You have ever been known for your wit." That the renowned Rutherford wit was reputed to be sarcastic rather than rollicking, she declined to think about just then, quickly changing the subject. "I see you are dressed to ride out. I hope you don't mind, but I've asked Raleigh to arrange for a mount for me as well."

"As to that, Lucy," Julian said, smoothly announcing a conclusion that had been reached only after spending a sleepless night of rare inspection of his own motives, "I have decided that you should not take any active part in this… er…investigation. If it is all a hum, you will be needlessly exposing yourself to gossip, whereas, if it is indeed as you believe, a plot against my name and life, I cannot find it in myself to expose you to danger. Therefore, I have concluded that yours is to be a minor part—for the most part already played. Escorting you and your aunt to Hillcrest for a house party did make me feel less like I was skulking away from London with my tail between my legs like some guilty cur."

"But you can't mean that!" Lucy implored hastily. "I mean, I guess you do mean it, but you can't have thought…I mean, you can't have been thinking clearly…I mean… Oh, drat it all Julian, don't fob me off like this. Please, I want to help."

Looking down at the hand Lucy had impulsively pressed on his forearm, Julian—with no little effort on his part—moved to gently disengage himself from her imploring grasp. "I mean every word, Lucy," he said in purposely frigid tones, feeling like he had just torn the wings from a beautiful butterfly. "Besides, I fail to see how I should be in need of petticoat protection—or interference. Dexter, damned loose fish that he may be, has volunteered his services. If he doesn't shoot himself in the foot with that gun I saw him playing with last night, I believe we shall manage to muddle through this tolerably well."

Lucy's blue eyes were bright with unshed tears as she searched his face for some hint of softness and found none. He had climbed back within his shell, she knew, her heart sinking, and there seemed to be no reaching him. Well, if he thought she was just going to sit around the house tending to her knitting, or whatever it was women did in the country, he had another thought or two coming! "You'll make a sad hash of it, Julian," she warned him tightly.

"Your assumptions do not interest me, Miss Gladwin," Julian said dismissively, making a show of lifting a bit of lint from his sleeve.

Miss Gladwin! Lucy repeated in her head, grimacing. How low I have sunk! If I didn't adore the man so entirely I'd go over to him and box his ruddy ears! Aloud, she taunted, "You placed considerable credence in my assumptions when your so-called friends cut you adrift in London. You listened to me then."

"I was temporarily overset," he reminded her, refraining from adding that he had also been three-parts drunk. "This is not open for debate in any case. You may stay or go as you choose—I understand your cousin, Lady Bourne, resides close by—but I cannot countenance your direct involvement in my predicament past the point which you are now. It just wouldn't be proper."

"*Proper!* He dares to speak to me of propriety," she informed the flowers, which were her only other audience. "He, who invaded my home not three days past, dirty, unshaven, and the worse for liquor, begging—yes, *groveling*—as he searched for a single kind word. Oh," she intoned heavily, eyeing the earl disdainfully through slitted eyes, "how soon he forgets. Well, let's just see how well he goes on with the villagers using the high-and-mighty Thorpe manner. Go on, Julian, mount your stallion and ride out to have converse with the lowly peasants. See if they will talk to you, you with your oh-so-open, oh-so-easy air of friendliness. But I warn you, Lord Thorpe—guard your back!" she ended dramatically before flouncing out of the room, stopping only long enough to cock the rose heart-backed chair at an angle.

Julian watched her go, admiring her pluck even as he longed to turn her over his knee and give her a good spanking. Why couldn't she see things his way? He knew he had come to his senses too late to undo the damage done her reputation by publicly championing him at the Selbridges' ball, but no one would know she was with him at Hillcrest if he could just unstick her from the place before news of her residence became common knowledge.

He almost wished he had taken her advice and put a notice in the columns that he was giving a small house party and including a list of guests, but as befuddled as his mind had been at the time, he at least had not been paper-skulled enough to follow that particular suggestion.

Why hadn't Rachel Gladwin used more sense? he questioned, ready to blame that poor lady for his lapse. She had seemed a woman of some intelligence. He walked over to the rose heart-backed chair and replaced it to its former position. "Why are you so willing to place the blame everywhere but where it should be—squarely on your own shoulders?" he asked himself aloud, sitting down heavily. "You wanted her here, and you know it."

A small smile stole about the corners of his mouth as he thought back to the hours he and Lucy had spent in happy companionship riding together along the road on their way to Hillcrest. She was a great gun, as Dexter would have termed her, and no mistake. A little wild in her actions, he temporized, remembering Lucy as she cradled Bartholomew to her breast and calmly introduced the monkey to the rest of their little traveling party as if it were something she did every day, but hadn't he always known that about her? Hadn't her very unconventionality been what had always attracted and repelled him in the past? And was it possible, he thought, sitting up suddenly, that it was her very attraction that had so repelled him?

He shook his head to clear it of these unwanted thoughts. He was an engaged man, he told himself, and had been before Lucy had first barreled into his line of vision three years ago and first set his blood to boiling. She had been an impossible female, always about when he was trying so hard to avoid her, always underfoot, flaunting her small but enticing figure, smiling her "come-hither" smile, eating him with her eyes, teasing him with her—

He jerked to his feet as a sudden thought hit him. He *wasn't* an engaged man! He hadn't been since Cynthia, bless her avaricious heart, had dumped him so royally at that same Selbridge ball!

Julian fairly trotted from the morning room, his haste causing his hip to catch on the rose heart-backed chair and nudge it slightly sideways. "Lucy!" he called up the stairway leading to the bedrooms. "Care to ride out with a bloody fool?"

DEXTER DID NOT SEEM TO BE best pleased to be relegated to the rear of the small riding party, with only a dour-faced groom as his companion, as Lucy and Julian rode side by side, the former exclaiming delightedly over the bits of scenery the latter was taking great pains to point out. "Thought we were ferreting out clues, coz," he called to the earl testily, "not going on a bloody tour of the flora and fauna. Where are we bound, anyway?"

Julian waited until the roadway opened up a bit and then motioned for Dexter to join them. "I had thought we'd ride over to the Anscom farm and have a chat with Miss Anscom's father. I understand he is a widower, and this Susan woman his only offspring."

"Oh, how terrible," Lucy put in, noticing the tightness around Julian's mouth. "You must find the person who preyed on this innocent girl and her poor father and bring him to justice."

"Yes," Julian agreed, comforted by the knowledge that Lucy understood his feelings in the matter. "Once Raleigh informed me of the magnitude of Mr. Anscom's loss, I realized that my problems pale considerably in comparison. Someone must hate me very much, to go to such heartless lengths in order to punish me. Besides being nearly the only female in this area wellborn enough to suit his purpose, Miss Anscom was without motherly influence to guide her away from giving her heart to a man who had not asked for her hand."

"You seem sure there was a man involved," Lucy said, clearly hoping he would enlarge on his theory.

"It only stands to reason, Lucy," Dexter put in airily. "Deuced hard to make babies without 'em."

"Dexter," the earl suggested coldly, "I believe the road narrows just ahead. Please drop back where you belong."

"Put my foot in it, didn't I?" Dexter asked, taking in Lucy's heightened color.

"Why should today be any different?" Julian agreed quietly, wishing his next of kin on the moon of some suitably faraway place.

"He meant no harm," Lucy told him once Dexter had turned his horse and dropped back to wait for the groom.

Julian looked at her piercingly. "Are you suggesting then that he is harmless—for if you are, I agree totally. I would find myself hard pressed to believe Dex capable of the hideous act we are assuming someone has committed."

"Exactly what are we assuming?" she asked, suddenly not so sure of her interpretation of the gossip that had started the entire affair.

Julian adjusted himself in the saddle and explained, "As I see it, we have several theories. One: the whole story is a hum, made up out of whole cloth for scandal's sake by some idiot bent on embarrassing me or, perish the thought, driving Cynthia to breaking our engagement so he can clear the way for himself."

Lucy shook her head. "No, it can't be that—at least the first part of your theory. For Miss Anscom *is* dead." The second part, the one concerning Lady Cynthia, she did not choose to dwell on, as she was sure that subject would cause Julian pain.

"Yes, she certainly is," the earl agreed. "But someone could have used her death for his own purposes—*after* the fact. We have no proof that anyone actually caused her death. After all, anyone could have written those letters."

Lucy considered that theory for a moment, acknowledging that it had some merit, but not willing to believe it. "What are your other ideas? You said you had more."

"I have entertained dozens, my dear, but a few do stand out as being the most feasible. All right, theory two: Miss

Anscom, for reasons of her own, decided to take her life, and not wanting her father to know the real reason, named me as the father of her child."

"You mean, she was protecting someone?"

"Precisely."

Lucy looked over at the earl, amused by his formal speech as he wrestled with speaking to her about so distasteful a subject. "Then it is possible that you are to be the scapegoat for some hot-blooded farmer's son? Oh, Julian, how the mighty have toppled."

Thorpe made a face. "I don't pretend to like it, brat, but as it is only a theory, I imagine I shall learn to live with it."

"But you have another theory?" she pursued, feeling like she was forced to draw every word out of him.

"Yes, I do, and it is the one I am regretfully forced to believe is correct. Someone went to a lot of trouble to impersonate me, seduce Miss Anscom, and then desert her once his mission was accomplished."

Two Lord Thorpes? But didn't everyone know who he was, what he looked like? "How could that be possible?" she asked aloud.

Julian shrugged. "Quite easily, I imagine. I do not make a habit out of residing at Hillcrest. I doubt that my face is that well known, especially this far afield."

"Even if that's so, how could the schemer be sure Miss Anscom would commit suicide—or write letters to all the papers before jumping into the pond? No, Julian," she denied, shaking her head, "I don't believe that theory. Unless…"

"Unless what?" he asked as Lucy hesitated.

Lucy didn't like what she was thinking. It was so horribly cold-blooded, so very *evil*. "Unless," she told him, her voice barely above a whisper, "Miss Anscom was a party to the whole thing, only to be betrayed in the end by her fellow schemer."

"You mean, she wrote her suicide notes with no plan of killing herself—just stirring up trouble?" Julian asked, trying to understand.

She nodded her head furiously. "She wrote her own suicide note and then her lover drowned her. Oh, what a terrible thing!"

"Oh! What a great piece of nonsense!" Dexter quipped, having ridden up closely behind the pair, who were so engrossed with each other that they hadn't noticed his approach. "Where could you hope to find two such people—one so deplorably evil and another so deplorably stupid? You'll not get me to believe such a scatterbrained tale, and neither would anyone else. Hoo! And they say you're so clever, coz. Well, you'd never prove it by me."

"Well then, Mr. Smartypants, what do you think?" Lucy challenged, trying hard not to stick out her tongue at the infuriating young dandy.

"I don't have a theory. Don't have to, as I see it. I'm a suspect, remember? All I have to do is stick around so that no one can say I haven't done my duty by my cousin and watch the fun. Tell me, coz," he asked, clearly full of himself, "don't it make you feel all warm and cozy inside to know that your blood kin is here, watching over you, so to speak, in your time of trouble, ready to either take bows if you're found innocent or step into your shoes if you're found guilty? I feel rather like Georgie Porgie, ready to pull out a plum."

"You're despicable!" Lucy cried, believing Dexter guilty of heaping yet another load of woe on his cousin's weary head.

"On the contrary, my dear," Julian corrected her, giving his cousin a knowing look, "I find my mind to be greatly relieved. I now know that Dexter definitely isn't guilty—if your theory is the correct one."

"How do you know that?" she asked, totally confused to see a smile touching his lordship's lips.

Julian just shook his head and replied with maddening arrogance: "Because nobody, not even a country miss, could ever be brought to believe that this ridiculous ninny could possibly be the Earl of Thorpe. If I am unknown, I assure you my reputation is not. Dexter would have much better luck impersonating my groom back there. Their intellect is about equal, although I must say the groom is a better horseman."

"I think I've been insulted, stap me if I haven't," Dexter said, chuckling. "Does this mean I'm no longer a suspect, coz?"

"You never were," the earl informed him, to Lucy's chagrin. "Neither you nor Parker ever was. As I've said before—you are Rutherfords, and above such low deceit."

"I think I'm going to be sick," Lucy muttered, realizing that she had a long way to go in convincing Julian that "Rutherford" was not a synonym for "perfect." Prodding her mount with her boot heel, she moved ahead of the cousins, calling back over her shoulder, "I don't know which of you I pity more—as it is so hard to choose between arrogance and idiocy. Come! On to face Farmer Anscom and see if he recognizes either of you."

# CHAPTER EIGHT

FOLLOWING DIRECTIONS Dexter had received from the innkeeper in Alsop-en-le-Dale, the small party drew up their horses at the crest of the third hill to the north of the town and looked down into the small valley where the Anscom farm was situated. Julian eyed the unkempt fields with the distaste only a good land manager could know, while Lucy clucked her tongue at the neglected state of the small manor house and outbuildings.

"I thought you said this Anscom fellow was a gentleman farmer," Dexter said, breaking the small silence. "No wonder the chit grabbed at you, coz. She must have been desperate to improve her lot."

Lucy was becoming very weary of Dexter's frequent allusions to the possibility of Julian's guilt. "She did not 'grab' for anything his lordship offered, you thick dolt, for *he* didn't offer anything."

"Of course he didn't," Dexter assured her hastily. "It's just that it gets so confusing trying to separate Julian from the real criminal. In my mind I know he is innocent; it is only my mouth that confuses the issue."

"Then I suggest, my dear cousin, that you keep your mouth shut," the earl put in before Lucy could let loose with what he was sure was bound to be a scathing lecture. "The last thing I need now is another gravedigger—I've already got one person shoveling away at my reputation quite handily as it is."

Dexter again believed himself to have been insulted. "Far be it from me to cast aspersions, coz," he said huffily, "but have you never thought that if you had taken the time to be a bit more *human* in your dealings, you might not have this lamentable tendency of yours to attract people who wish you harm? I mean, you must have done something…"

Lucy winced, realizing that there was a grain of truth hidden somewhere in Dexter's muddled defense. Julian wasn't the easiest person to like, what with his strict code of behavior and somewhat cruel habit of ignoring those he felt beneath him either socially or intellectually. It was possible, even probable, that he had offended more than a few persons either unwittingly or purposely, yet she could not recall ever hearing a single person speak out against him publicly.

She stole a look at the earl, just now sitting stiffly in the saddle, glaring at his cousin, and felt a small shiver climb up her spine. It would take a strong man to stand up to Julian and thus expose himself to the man's rapier tongue as well as the sure censure of his powerful circle of friends. A covert revenge might be the only way open to someone bent on satisfying some real or imagined offense.

"Despite his rather crude way of expressing himself, Dexter may have a point," Lucy said slowly, praying Julian wouldn't take her words the wrong way. "We have never compiled a list of enemies from which to choose possible suspects."

Lucy could feel the chill descending about her shoulders as Thorpe turned his icy gaze on her. "A gentleman doesn't have enemies. He has acquaintances, and if he's fortunate, a few good friends. It is impossible for anyone to wish me ill. I pride myself on being a fair man, an equitable man. The entire notion is ridiculous."

"And he says I'm digging his grave," Dexter muttered under his breath, "when he condemns himself out of his own mouth, unless he wants us to believe this plot was hatched by his 'friends.'" More loudly he said, "What about that fellow you blackballed for having a grandfather in trade, coz? Or the divorcée you snubbed so royally at Almack's? Then there's old Crosley, who left town in disgrace when you refused to sup at his table because you said he smelled of the stable. Oh, yes, and do you remember…?"

Thorpe's expression clouded as Lucy's gaze slid away from his to concentrate on a patch of wildflowers at the edge of the road. It all sounded so petty and priggish when Dexter said it. "Enough!" he commanded, suddenly unwilling to hear more. Was he really as snobbish and unyieldingly arrogant as he sounded, as Lucy's hastily concealed agreement with his cousin made him feel?

His own recent brush with the pain inflicted by society's treatment of those they felt beneath them made him acutely aware of the pain he himself had dealt out from his lofty mountaintop of self-assurance. Telling himself that he hadn't been acting any differently than any of his peers was small comfort to him now. "I begin to wonder," he said at last, "why either of you put up with me."

Dexter was quick to respond, saying kindly, "Oh, you're not such a bad sort, coz. Just hold yourself a trifle high, that's all. I lay it at your mama's feet, personally, filling your head full of her notion that the Rutherfords are just one step short of divine."

The horses were getting restless, dancing about a bit at this lengthy delay. "Do you think we could continue this soul-searching some other time?" Lucy asked as her mount side-stepped impatiently. "Once we're back at Hillcrest you can examine your conscience and compile a list of your bad habits. Personally, I agree with Dexter, Julian. You're not a bad

sort." At Julian's raised eyebrows she added, dimpling prettily, "Why else do you think I've been making a cake of myself over you these three years past?"

Julian watched Lucy as she set her horse off down the hill,
a small one-sided smile lighting his previously somber features. "The chit's dotty over you," Dexter told him, giving
him a hearty clap on the shoulder. "And to think you might
have been saddled with that block Cynthia. When you find
your enemy, coz, I suggest you give him a smacking kiss on
the cheek!"

As Dexter followed Lucy down the hill, the earl steadied
his mount as the small smile on his face spread into a wide
grin. He had been guilty of the sins of pride and social prejudice in the past—rather like that Darcy fellow Lucy had
likened him to not so long ago—but perhaps, just perhaps,
it wasn't too late for him to change. He certainly had been
liking himself better the last few days. With Lucy's help, he
thought hopefully, he just might become the Julian
Rutherford she believed him capable of being.

It was only as he started on down the hill to the Anscom
farm that he remembered that unless he discovered the person behind the plot to ruin him, he might just learn his first
lesson in humility the hard way—from behind prison bars.

"WELL THAT WAS a wasted journey," Dexter said as he lowered himself gingerly into a chair in the drawing room.
"Damn me if that nag of mine didn't have a razorback pig
for a sire. Leave me out of any more gallivanting about the
countryside, coz, unless we do it up behind your team. If man
had been meant to ride horses, we would have been born with
leather bottoms, I say."

Julian ignored his cousin as he poured himself a generous drink before the ladies joined them. He didn't know
which had left the worst taste in his mouth—the truths

about his character Dex and Lucy had brought home to him so clearly or his confrontation with George Anscom. Even with his newfound generosity of spirit, the earl found it impossible to find one thing to praise in the person of Susan Anscom's father. "Wine, Dex?" he asked, hefting the decanter invitingly before pouring himself another portion.

"I'll have a small sherry, if you please," Lucy said, entering the room and taking up the chair Dexter hastened to offer before holding her breath with special care this evening, and knew that the deep rose gown she had chosen would look its best in the complimentary color scheme of the drawing room. "I do hope dinner will be served shortly, as our long ride today has made me quite ravenous."

Thorpe turned to smile at her, a delicate crystal goblet of sherry in his hand, and stopped in his tracks. She had done it again, the wily minx—knocked him off balance with the devastating impact her vibrant good looks tended to have on his traitorous body. Her midnight-dark hair, with its tendency to curl lovingly against her neck, was just untidy enough to invite his fingers to bury themselves in its soft warmth. Her silken white skin, especially the curving expanse visible above her low-cut gown, drew his gaze like a beacon, while his mouth longed to sip at the moist pink pout that she was just then nervously touching with the tip of her tongue. And the rest of his body—ah, the rest of his most traitorous body—was already light-years ahead of his mind in conjuring up the delights it too could discover.

Damn her, he thought automatically, as he had been accustomed to thinking each time Lucy's mere appearance had this effect on him. No gentleman should feel this way about a lady of quality. It was indecent, that's what it was. But then he brought himself up short, remembering that his opinion of what a gentleman should and should not do—or feel—had already been proved faulty. He did not seriously believe that this physical attraction to Lucy was wrong, did he?

It was wrong when he had been an engaged man, surely. But he was now free to court Lucy with a clear conscience. Certainly the girl was not unwilling, he told himself, fighting down the faint feeling that no well-bred young lady should be so frank with her feelings. Where would he be now if Lucy were just another simpering miss? Still standing in the middle of the Selbridges' ballroom like some stuffed owl, he told himself ruefully, that's where.

Lucy watched entranced as Julian's suddenly tense features relaxed and a new warmth crept into his eyes, while Dexter, believing himself to be a man of the world and up to all the rigs, found himself feeling suddenly protective of little Miss Gladwin's virtue. Seeing the assessing look in his cousin's eyes, and knowing his cousin's determination once he had set a course of action, Dexter knew he was going to have a front-row seat for the courting of Lucy. He took a long drink of wine, wondering if he would be shirking his duty if he failed to quickly cast himself in the role of gooseberry.

While Lucy and Julian stared at each other, ridiculous smiles lighting their faces, Parker, who had been busy since their arrival checking on the estate books, entered the drawing room and asked if the earl had met with any success that afternoon.

"That would depend upon your definition of success, Parker, old fellow," Dexter told him glumly, "and whether or not you wish to work under Julian or me. So far, all we seem to be doing is finding more damning evidence. It seems now that our only hope is that we are the only ones to think there is a plot to frame Julian for doing away with Miss Anscom. A mere scandal will blow over in time, but not a charge of murder."

Parker looked at his cousin, his dislike easily read in his

eyes. "You cannot ever say anything without trying to make some sort of jest, can you, Dexter? Cousin Julian is in dire need of our assistance right now, so I suggest you desist from these ridiculous suggestions that you are soon to be the next earl. I find it distasteful in the extreme."

"Oh, really?" Dexter shot back savagely. "How does the thought of me bloodying your lip suit you—that is, if I can find one on your fish face?"

For a moment it looked as if the two cousins were about to come to cuffs there and then, but Thorpe stepped between them, warning: "Have you both forgotten there's a lady present?"

"Two, actually," corrected Rachel smoothly as she entered the room. "Good evening, everyone. May I hope for a report of today's findings? Lucy was so busy preening since her return that I dared not disturb her."

"Aunt," Lucy hissed, coloring prettily.

"We can only thank Lucy for allowing us to enjoy the beautiful results," Julian said, turning Lucy's flush of embarrassment to one of joy. "As to our news, Rachel, I'm afraid it is not all that good. George Anscom was not very forthcoming."

Raleigh chose that moment to call them to table, and as they didn't wish to be heard discussing such a delicate subject in front of the servants, it wasn't until the gentlemen rejoined the ladies in the drawing room that the subject was again broached.

"You didn't linger very long over your brandy and cigars," Rachel remarked, looking mostly at Dexter, who was smiling like a child with his mouth full of candy treats.

"I became weary of the exchange of insults between my cousins and called a halt before one of them stabbed the other with the cheese knife," Julian drawled, scarcely hiding his amusement. "Each was outdoing the other with declarations of their loyalty to me while trying to get in swipes of each other at the same time. I'm still trying to decide if I should be flattered or simply put gloves on them and enjoy the spectacle of having them go at each other on the south lawn. What do you think, Rachel?"

While Julian and her aunt laughed companionably, Lucy felt another unfamiliar pang of jealousy directed toward Rachel. This wasn't the first time she had thought the earl and her aunt got along a little too well. Surely she hadn't been mistaken in thinking Thorpe was beginning to see her in a new light—even admiring her a little? Or did he see her as a child, amusing, soft on the eyes, and flattering in her open infatuation with him, but not to be taken seriously? She gnawed on her bottom lip a bit, thinking furiously. How could she make him realize that she was a woman grown—a woman ready to love and be loved?

"Lucy?" her aunt prompted, clearly calling her to attention. "Julian was just telling me that he believes the newspaper report calling Mr. Anscom a gentleman was in error. Why don't you tell him that story your father is so fond of?"

Remembering the slovenly appearance and crude manners of George Anscom, Lucy smiled as she realized that her father would have enjoyed meeting the man—a man who proved his point so well. For Sir Hale had a fine contempt for the so-called "gentleman's code" that was used to separate Englishmen into classes. Lucy believed this contempt to be one of the driving forces behind her father's eccentric behavior—he kept trying the bounds of propriety just to show the extent to which society would accept ridiculousness from someone they had deemed a gentleman.

Seeing that she had everyone's interest, Lucy sat up straight and prefaced her story by explaining gentlemen in general. "As Papa has told me, gentlemen consider themselves a race apart. A gentleman must have the correct attitude of mind, you know, that puts him above the run of ordinary mortals. Indeed, being a gentleman is a full-time occupation."

Julian found himself shifting uncomfortably in his chair. Lucy made what he had been taught all seem so trivial, so unimportant—rather like a gentleman was all trimming, and no substance. He caught himself up short. What had she said that day in London—that he was so worried about his outside that he was not developing his inside?

Realizing that Lucy was still talking, he called himself back to attention. "...and so, as just one more way of proving his point, Papa used to carry a clipping from *The Observer* that was published in 1806. I believe I have it by heart." She closed her eyes to concentrate for a second, then quoted: "Singular Conviction: A curate of a village near town and one of the overseers of the parish, a gentleman farmer, had a dispute respecting some private business, and the farmer d—d the clergyman's eyes. For this offense he was brought before the magistrates of Marlborough Street, and convicted in the penalty of five shillings. The farmer contended that he was *not* a gentleman, and that he ought pay no more than one shilling. This objection was overruled, as it appeared that he kept sporting dogs and took wine after dinner."

Dexter exploded into laughter. "That's so bloody perfect!" he exclaimed, delighting in the stony expression that had appeared on Parker's thin face. "The man can damn a curate's eyes and still be a gentleman because he slops wine after downing his mutton. Oh, Lucy, you have exposed us in all our ridiculousness. My hat's off to you!"

"One example like that can't disprove the rule," Parker decreed repressively. "Look at Cousin Julian if you wish to see a genuine example of the English gentleman."

A glimmer of rueful amusement entered the earl's gray

eyes. "Yes, indeed, people, look at me. I stand before you accused of driving some poor innocent maid into drowning herself, yet because I have the trappings of a gentleman, I remain
a member of—what was that you called it, Lucy?—oh yes,
a race apart. Well, if George Anscom, using the rules of society, is to be termed a gentleman, then I'd just as soon resign from society."

"Was he really that dreadful?" Rachel asked, reaching for
the silver teapot Raleigh had just brought in and placed before her, clearly singling her out as hostess, a designation
Lucy did not miss.

"He was slovenly, boorish, totally unfeeling about his
daughter's death other than to berate the girl for going off
and leaving him without a handy live-in servant, and nervy
enough to ask if Julian was there to offer him some sort of
monetary settlement to make up for seducing his 'angel,'"
Dexter told her disgustedly. "Other than that, he was very
helpful."

Rachel concentrated on Dexter's last statement. "In what
way? Could he identify Miss Anscom's real lover—if one
does exist?" Clearly Rachel had been entertaining theories
of her own, and come up with much the same muddle of motives and means as the rest of them.

"He gave us Susan's personal journal," Lucy informed her,
blushing as she remembered the passage she had read before
Julian pulled the book from her hands. "It seems she re-
corded every meeting she supposedly had with Julian—and
in some detail."

"Oh, my," Rachel breathed.

"Yes, indeed," the earl agreed. "Oh my!"

"Shame the gel didn't send the journal to the papers, coz,"
Dexter slid in facetiously. "They'd have raised a statue to you
and you'd be battling off the females with a stick."

"That's disgusting!" Parker sneered.

"It's all in the way you look at it, coz," Dexter jeered, wiggling his eyebrows suggestively. "It's all in the way you look at it."

"And we all know your perverted way of looking at things," the secretary said waspishly. "You're a disgrace to your name, do you know that?"

Dexter bowed from the waist. "Thank you, Parker. If I have succeeded in offending you, I can feel that my life is not wasted."

"Oh, stop it, both of you," Lucy interrupted, throwing a quelling look at Lord Thorpe, who was, unbelievably, sitting in his chair doubled up with laughter. "The journal exists, no matter how lurid its contents. And it records everything right down to dates and times—which coincide with the time Julian spent here some months ago."

"How do you know it's genuine?" Rachel asked shrewdly. "Anyone could have written the thing, and then planted it in Miss Anscom's room after the fact."

Julian stood and walked over to lean against the mantelpiece. "That same thought had occurred to me, especially when I read the journal more closely. Either that girl had a fervent imagination or she had some help. Even the Minerva Press would blush to read some of her purple prose."

"Did you read the bit about the tryst you and she had under the moonlight near the spinney?" Dexter asked, leering at his cousin.

"There you go again, Dexter!" Lucy snapped. "Julian never even met the girl. You didn't, did you?" she turned to ask the earl, suddenly remembering the lurid passage she had been reading before he had stripped the journal from her hands.

All traces of humor were stripped from Julian's handsome face. *"Et tu, Brute?"* he asked, making Lucy feel like she had just kicked an orphan puppy.

"No!" she exploded, shaking her head. "It's just…it's just that I was thinking about what I read and, um, I was… Dexter Rutherford, stop grinning like an ape. It's not funny!"

Parker looked at Lucy, who was struggling to regain her composure, and at Julian, who surprised him by looking more than a little pleased at the girl's near-admission of jealousy. "I don't understand," he said in obvious confusion.

"*You* don't have to," Dexter reminded him. "Why don't you go count the silver or something, Parker? I for one won't miss you."

"But…but I think I can be of service," Parker protested, looking at his employer. "Miss Gladwin suggested that the journal might be a forgery. Well, I happen to have in my possession one of the letters Miss Anscom sent to the papers."

Suddenly everyone was interested in what Parker had to say. Looking about the room at the people who were eyeing him either incredulously or suspiciously, he went on, "I visited the newspaper office before we left London, realizing that the letter might be construed to be a clue. Shall I go to my room and get it?"

At Julian's nod of assent, Parker bowed and withdrew, leaving Dexter to comment, "He's a rare bird, ain't he? Who would have thought old Parker would be so resourceful? Not that I like him, understand," he went on hurriedly, just in case someone took it into his head to think he was softening a bit toward his prudish cousin.

# CHAPTER NINE

IT WAS QUIET in the drawing room except for the ticking of the mantel clock, and the candles had burned down low in their holders as Lucy tiptoed into the room to see Julian sitting sprawled in his chair, staring into the cold fireplace.

Two hours had passed since Parker had brought the letter into the room and they had all gathered round to compare the two handwriting samples. There could be no doubt about it—both the documents had been penned by the same hand, an obviously feminine hand. "Right down to the atrocious spelling," Dexter had pointed out sadly.

It could mean everything, or it could mean nothing, depending on who was reviewing the evidence. To Lucy and the rest of the party it just showed that Susan Anscom had indeed been a willing participant in the hoax—right up until the time her co-conspirator had pushed her nose beneath the surface of the pond, as Dexter had so succinctly put it. To a court however—and therein lay the rub—it was just another nail in Lord Thorpe's coffin, for who would believe Miss Anscom could have been so gullible?

Rachel had retired within minutes of their latest discovery, knowing full well that the gentlemen should be left to discuss the matter without the restraints placed on them by having a female within earshot, and had dragged a reluctant Lucy along with her.

Parker, wringing his hands and bemoaning the fact that he had unwittingly strengthened the case against the earl, also retired, leaving Dexter to buck up his cousin's spirits as best he could. This he did in the only way he knew—he poured Julian a generous snifter of brandy and told him to drink up, and then poured him another. And another. And yet another, until, having downed drink for drink just to be sociable, he was forced to retire to his chamber before he disgraced himself by casting up his accounts all over his cousin's carpet.

The clock chimed the hour, halting Lucy in her tracks. "Impossible," she heard Julian say as he sat looking at his watch, his back to her. "My watch couldn't have stopped. My man winds it faithfully before he puts it on me in the morning."

Lucy stifled a giggle. When it came to unbending, Julian had come a long way, but it was obvious he still had a long way to go. She could envision him standing stiffly in his dressing room, allowing "his man" to wind his watch for him and then attach it to his waistcoat. She wondered if he even knew *how* to wind his own timepiece, then dismissed the thought as she heard the earl give out with a long, mournful sigh. Poor man, she commiserated, her tender heart wrung. He must be feeling the whole world is closing in on him.

Not stopping to think about what she was about to do, Lucy sped to Julian's side, dropping to the floor at his knees. "Julian, don't despair," she pleaded, looking up at him with her wide blue eyes. "Everything will be all right. I just know it."

Thorpe looked down at her with brandy-clouded eyes and thought he had conjured up an angel. Clad in a white dressing gown from which peeked the neckline of a soft blue nightgown of finest lace-edged silk, the vision before him blurred a bit and then cleared sufficiently to tell him he had not been imagining the whole thing. "Lucy," he breathed, taking the small hand she held out to him. "You shouldn't be here. It's not proper."

"Of course it's not," she answered, smiling impishly. "Would it be any fun otherwise?"

This was wrong, totally, utterly wrong. He should scold her and send her off to her bed posthaste. He really should. The Julian Rutherford of a scant week ago would have done so without a blink—if not without a secret pang or two.

But this wasn't a week ago. This was now, when his fortunes seemed to be at such a low ebb, when his resistance was weak, when his need for comfort was so very, very strong. Not that he would take advantage of the situation—of being alone in the dark with what even his drink-dimmed mind told him was a willing female he had coveted this age—but what real harm could it do to let her stay awhile and talk to him? None, said the brandy—and he decided not to ask any more questions.

Stroking the palm of her hand with his thumb, and sending tingles of ecstasy up her arm if he only knew it, Julian leaned slightly toward her, the better to see her in the dim half-light. "Thank you for believing in me, brat. I cannot tell you how sorely I am in need of hearing you tell me you think me innocent. As I read that journal, even I began to doubt it myself. It seems so complete, so highly credible."

"Too complete, my lord, and too credible," Lucy protested, squeezing his hand. "I have been sitting upstairs thinking this whole thing through. I believe it was a lucky thing that Parker was quick enough to see the importance of that letter. It is another piece of the puzzle. I think we can be assured now that Susan Anscom didn't act alone. Our only task now is to identify her accomplice. Have you given any more thought to a possible enemy?"

Julian sniffed disdainfully. "It would be easier to give you a list of my friends. Dexter was right—I haven't been the nicest person, you know. But I can't believe anyone in my past could have been so insulted by my actions as to hatch such an elaborate scheme. I mean, this man has already killed one person—just to get back at me? I believe we are dealing with a madman."

Lucy nodded her agreement, and the light from the candelabrum behind her set off golden sparkles in her dark curls, duly noted by the earl. "I think so too. Now we must decide whether the man responsible is either rich enough to have bought Miss Anscom's compliance or handsome enough to have wooed her into going along with the charade."

Fighting back his mounting desire as Lucy dropped her chin onto his knee in a purely innocent gesture, Julian ventured, "I would say the latter, Lucy. After all, the girl was with child. God!" he exploded, his anger at the coldheartedness of the crime coming to the fore. "How could anyone be so despicable?"

"Not how, Julian, but *why*. I believe that we have already covered the fact that men are not always what they seem, never as good or upstanding as we would like. It is the reason behind the crime that will lead us to the murderer."

She was right, Thorpe knew. It was ghoulish to be sitting in a lavish drawing room discussing the terrible crime that had been committed, but they had to face the facts squarely. He looked down at Lucy's bent head and realized that she was shivering, either with cold or as a result of their topic of conversation. "Here now, my dear, enough of this," he said, pulling her to her feet as he stood up. "You'll take a chill. It's time you return to your chamber. I promise not to sulk any longer, and we shall all have a fresh start on our problem in the morning." He put his hand at the back of her waist so that he could help her toward the doorway.

"But, Julian," she protested, tilting her head back to look

into his face. "I don't think I shall be able to get a wink of sleep. I feel wide-awake."

Thorpe looked down at her, acutely aware that her cheek was scant inches from his chest. "Shall I...shall I ring for someone to bring some warmed milk to your chamber?" he asked tightly, damning his heart for pounding so loudly that she was sure to hear it and now he was struggling against his more natural inclinations.

"Do you think warmed milk will help?" Lucy breathed, nervously moistening her lips with her tongue. He was so close, filling her senses with his sight, his smell, the warmth of his hand on her spine.

He brought her round completely so that his hands rested on her shoulders. "I'm sure it would," he whispered, his eyes never leaving her softly parted lips. Without realizing what he was doing, his head lowered, and time stood still as slowly, oh so very slowly, their mouths came together in a light, tentative kiss.

The fireworks at Vauxhall had never burst as brilliantly against the dark London sky as did the skyrockets now blazing into a rainbow of brilliant colors behind his lordship's tightly closed eyelids. The warm body nestled so closely against his felt softer than his comfortable mattress, but definitely did not inspire him to rest. The taste of her young mouth yielding so sweetly beneath his caused such a thunderbolt of shock to race through his system that he was amazed that he could still keep to his feet.

This was not a cool, antiseptic kiss such as the pecks Cynthia occasionally allowed; nor was it the practiced performance of a woman who earned her living by means of well-orchestrated passion. What he held in his arms was one totally honest, totally giving, totally real woman, and the realization shook him right down to his toes.

Julian's arms tightened about her as he sighed his surrender into her mouth. She had been right all along; he had been concentrating on the outward trappings of life and not paying enough attention to what went on inside his head—inside his rapidly thawing heart. The fleeting thought that he might have lost her if not for the Anscom scandal sent a fresh wave of panic through his veins and his embrace hardened as he drew her slim form against his body as if he would never let her go. He felt whole, he felt alive, he felt *real*—possibly for the first time in his life.

Lucy was lost. Lost in a whole new world of sensation she had only dreamt of before this magic moment in time. She had known Julian was the man for her, been sure of her love for him. But no one had prepared her for the bliss that she felt within the circle of his arms. She was his, completely his, and every feathery-light brush of her fingers against his neck, every soft sound mewling deep inside her throat, every frantic heartbeat fluttering against his broad chest told him of her love. She was his, his for the taking; not totally aware of how much she was offering, but more than eager to learn.

"Really, coz, I never expected this of you," said an amused voice, causing the two lovers to spring apart and stare in horror at Dexter, who was just then leaning against the doorframe, an impish grin on his face. "I expect it of *me*—everyone expects it of me—but I must tell you I can scarce believe the truth my eyes are telling me. Getting a bit randy in the dull country, are we, or have the banns been announced?"

"Dexter!" Both of them spoke at once, one in surprise, the other in anger and exasperation not unmixed with thanks—thanks that he had been stopped before his control snapped completely and he carried Lucy off to his rooms without benefit of clergy.

"That's me, all right, Cousin Dexter. But who have we here—Darby and Joan, Romeo and Juliet? No. Can it be the

sweet, innocent Lucy Gladwin and the upstanding Lord
Thorpe?" He shook his head. "Couldn't be the earl. He'd
never stoop to seducing innocent young girls of quality. Now
why, I must ask myself, does that have a ring of familiarity,
do you suppose?"

Julian's hands bunched into fists as he took a step toward
his cousin. "How dare you compare Lucy to that Anscom
woman?" he growled, not giving a tinker's damn that his cousin had likewise once again questioned his innocence. "Name
your seconds, you cur!"

It had taken Lucy a few seconds to recover her equilibrium
after Julian released her so abruptly, but like a lioness springing into defense of her cub, she rallied to place her small form
between the two cousins before irreparable damage was
done. "Stop this nonsense at once, do you hear me!" she
commanded, holding a hand against each of their chests. "I
won't have it!"

Dexter, who had already begun cursing himself for his
loose mouth, realizing that his twisted sense of humor had
allowed it to take a healthy bite out of the hand that fed it,
was more than willing to call it a day. "The girl's right, coz,"
he interposed hastily, stepping back out of range. "I was just
making a joke, honestly. I didn't mean any harm, really I
didn't."

"You never mean any harm," the earl bit out, still longing
to hit something. "That's no excuse. I want you to apologize
to Miss Gladwin and then I want your promise that you'll
forget everything you just saw. Do you understand?" he
ended in a voice that left little doubt of the consequences if
Dexter refused.

His apology made, Dexter could not help but remark on
how fetching Lucy looked, bringing everyone's attention to
the state of her near-undress, and she colored very prettily
before bolting from the room with a hand to her mouth. That

this caused another thundering lecture to be brought down on the young man's head did little to erase the smile from his face, considering the fact that his cousin seemed preoccupied with another problem more pressing than Dexter's penchant for the ladies.

"It is imperative that you understand the reason why none of what you saw this evening can be made public knowledge," Julian told him once they were both seated and holding brandy snifters in their hands. "We have already ascertained that there is a man, possibly a madman, trying his level best to destroy me. If he were to discover that Lucy and I are betrothed, he might decide to get at me through her."

"You're betrothed?" Dexter asked, zeroing in on the one fact he thought truly important. "When you break loose, cousin, you certainly don't do it by half-measures, do you? Congratulations. May you have half a dozen babies—half of them boys. I never did hanker to walk in your shoes, you know, just as long as you don't take it into your head to cut off my allowance to buy nappies."

"Will you be serious?" Julian pleaded, trying hard to remain angry with his cousin and, as usual, failing. "I know you're innocent of the plot against me—it is you who seem to have lapses in faith where I'm concerned. Just let me hear that you understand that Lucy is to be kept safely detached from me until we have unmasked the culprit. I can't lose her now."

Dexter agreed, and after toasting the couple's health, asked, "Was that what you were doing when I so rudely interrupted, coz? Sealing the betrothal?"

Julian smiled then, taking years off his features. "Lucy was saying yes, Dexter, but I never did get around to informing her as to the nature of the question." He leaned back in his chair, looking up at the decorative ceiling as if it contained a vision of heaven. "Just think, Dex, my dear cousin, I'm three-and-thirty years of age and yet I've just been born. Amazing , ain't it?"

LUCY CLOSED HER CHAMBER door behind her and leaned against it, struggling for breath. He had kissed her! Really kissed her! And then, when that dratted Dexter had shown such poor timing as to interrupt them, he had offered to fight a duel over her! If she were any more full of happiness, she believed she would surely burst.

She wanted to dance! She wanted to go to the window and throw back the sash to sing her joy out into the night. She wanted to wake her aunt and hug her with happiness! She looked up at the ceiling and breathed, "Thank you, God. *Oh, thank you!*"

Just then a sound coming from her bed distracted her and she looked over to see Bartholomew sitting smack in the middle of her turned-down spread. She would hug Bartholomew! She had to hug somebody or she would simply expire on the spot.

"Come here to me, you adorable creature," she crooned, skipping over to the bed. But what she saw spread out around the monkey stopped her. There was her Aunt Rachel's garnet necklace. And beside it lay Parker's penknife, Dexter's snuffbox, Julian's quizzing glass, and other small objects whose owners must be wondering where they had disappeared to so completely. A silver lobster fork, a small silver salt cellar, a scattering of coins, even a small, roundish lump of metal she believed to be a bit of shot for a fowling piece.

"Oh, what have you done, you naughty thing?" she asked, scooping up the necklace.

Bartholomew, who had been sitting there beaming proudly at his new mistress, cocked his head to one side at the condemning tone in her voice, clearly puzzled. Why didn't she praise him, pat his capped head, and tell him what a good boy he was? And his treat—where was the treat he always got for bringing pretty, shiny things? He rolled onto his side and looked up at her imploringly, hoping that at the least she would deign to scratch his hairy belly.

"Why, you think you've done something wonderful, don't you?" Lucy said, the truth of the matter slowly dawning on her. "Mr. Romano told me you did tricks. Why, that horrid old man! He's trained you as a thief. Oh, Bartholomew, you poor baby!" She sat down on the bed and gathered the monkey into her arms, wrapping his long arms around her neck. "Forgive me for scolding you, pet, it isn't your fault."

Bartholomew chattered delightedly in monkey language, nibbling at her ear and causing her to giggle. "But we mustn't let the earl catch wind of your little talent, must we, for I don't think he'll find it in the least amusing."

Talking about the earl led instantly to thinking about the man, and Lucy made short work of gathering Bartholomew's ill-gotten booty into a drawer and crawling into bed in order to spend the next few moments dreaming of the bliss she had discovered in his arms. Then she fell into a deep, untroubled sleep, a small smile remaining on her features for the remainder of the short night.

"WILL YOU SIT STILL!" Deirdre snapped, trying without much success to clasp the single strand of pearls around her mistress's neck. "You've been fidgeting around like you've got a burr in your britches all day long. Now, I've put it before me to fix this here necklace, and that's just what I'm goin' to do."

Lucy subsided meekly on the chair placed before her dressing table. "Yes, Deirdre," she said meekly, scarcely hiding her amusement at the sight reflected in the mirror—which depicted the young maid struggling for all her might to focus her eyes on the small gold clasp. "Far be it from me to be the cause of striking you cross-eyed. Dexter Rutherford might stop chasing after you, and it would all be my fault, wouldn't it?"

Deirdre sniffed. "Him! Such a pest of a man. He's like my father said—only a dog, and will go a part of the road with everyone. Don't think he'll be chasing after my heels, for I'm wise to the likes of him. A mouth full of blarney and enough brass to shame a field full of tinkers."

"Then you're not flattered by his attentions?" Lucy asked, watching her maid's reflection closely.

"Soft words butter no parsnips, Miss Lucy, and stolen kisses only lead to trouble with the likes of him. I'll not let my head be turned. Not like some I could mention," she ended, finally managing to close the necklace and then standing back to admire her work. "There, all right and tight."

Lucy studied herself in the mirror and liked what she saw. Her hair seemed to curl more becomingly, her eyes to shine more brightly, and her skin seemed to have taken on a new glow. "You're wrong, you know," she said, rising to her feet and dropping a kiss on her maid's rosy cheek. "Julian is nothing like his cousin. We're in love," she sighed breathlessly, earning herself another sniff.

"Show me the notice in the papers—then talk to me of love," Deirdre said saucily, never one to believe anything unless she could see it for herself. "Your aunt will read it to me if I ask her. I might believe it then, but not before."

"I don't know why I put up with you, Deirdre," Lucy sighed wearily, moving to the long mirror to check her hem.

"I put up with you, don't I?" the maid quipped, lowering a gossamer-thin shawl around her mistress's shoulders. Her hands lingered, giving Lucy a quick hug. "I'll keep your secret, Miss Lucy, but you'll have to hide your face away from Miss Rachel if you mean to keep it from her. If that shrewd one catches a hint of what you were about last night, she'll have you packed and on your way to your cousin Jennie before you have time to take a breath, and no mistake. Now, be gone with you, the gong rang for you long since and m'dinner's getting cold in the servants' hall."

"Deirdre," Lucy called back over her shoulder as she stopped at the door bordering on the hallway. "Have I ever told you that I consider you to be my best, my very best friend?"

Her Irish brogue curling around her suddenly shy tongue, Deirdre gave up the fight. "Go to him now, and may God's fresh blessings be about you." She was thrilled for her mistress, happy to see her so happy, but she could not fight the feeling that Lucy's long struggle to win his lordship's heart was not to be judged settled on the strength of one stolen kiss in the moonlight. And there was still the little matter of his being accused of that terrible thing with that local girl.

No, Deirdre wasn't entirely easy in her conscience about keeping this latest development from Rachel Gladwin. All she could do was hope that the woman would see what was so plainly before her eyes and trust that resourceful lady to keep a cool head. And Deirdre did like the earl. He seemed a good sort, even if he was such a mass of grandeur. Miss Lucy loved him, so he couldn't really be a bad man.

So why, she thought, straightening her carroty locks before the mirror, why did she feel as if she had just sent off a goose to dine in the fox's den?

## CHAPTER TEN

KEEPING DEIRDRE'S WARNING in mind, Lucy tried her best
not to let her eyes linger too long on Lord Thorpe through
dinner, so she was very surprised when, after leaving the gentlemen to their port, Rachel took her to task the moment they
were alone together in the drawing room.

"You've been avoiding me all day," she began just as they
sat down. "I know Julian and Dexter rode out without you
to question the villagers and look for clues, but that was no
reason for you to spend the entire day mooning in the garden. Not that you rose until noon," she added, reaching for
her embroidery hoop.

"I was thinking about Julian's problems," Lucy improvised, knowing that she was being at least halfway honest.
She had been thinking about Julian—about the life they
would have, the children they would share, the love they
would cherish.

Rachel decided she was too weary to play verbal games
with her niece. She had known all day that Lucy was
avoiding her for some reason, and after seeing Julian's
eyes light up like beacons when her niece entered the
room before dinner, she knew she had found an answer.
"Just what did you do, Lucy, hide in his chamber last night
and catch him unawares?"

"I did no such thing!" Lucy cried hotly. "You and Deirdre should form a club, Aunt; one dedicated to believing everything bad about me that could possibly be imagined. Really, if Papa could hear how you think of me, he would be after you with a stick."

Rachel looked at her shrewdly, her hope of shocking Lucy into blurting out the truth having failed, and turned her concentration onto another vexing subject. "Your papa," she said disgustedly. "That's another bone to chew on entirely. I asked for his help in this matter, but did he so much as answer my letter? No, he did not. How he could abandon his only daughter this way is totally beyond my comprehension. Lucy," she ended, sighing, "I think it is time we returned to London. Lord Thorpe has regained his equilibrium. He doesn't need us anymore."

Lucy blanched, and her hands began to shake. Her Aunt Rachel didn't put her foot down often, but when she did she was nearly immovable. "But we can't!" she said, aghast. "Not now, not just as Julian has begun to care!"

"Has he really?" Rachel drawled, and Lucy hopped to her feet indignantly, knowing her aunt had bested her yet again.

"You are wasted bear-leading me, dearest," she told Rachel, pointing a finger at her. "You could spy for Wellington and tie Napoleon up in little knots like those you're making in that frame."

Rachel just smiled. "Sit down, pet," she said placidly. "You know I wouldn't purposely do anything to hurt you. But don't shut me out, please, for I am too old for guessing games. Now, tell me everything, for I could see Julian fairly drooling over you ever since you came down, and I'm dying to know how you finally managed it."

Lucy took pity on the older woman, acknowledging that since she had been such a helpful ally during the past three years of the chase, she deserved to hear all about the glory of the capture. "Not that he has declared himself or anything, you understand," Lucy ended, leaning back against the cushions and sighing happily, "but if he challenged Dexter to a duel I cannot believe he is merely trifling with my affections, can you?"

Rachel closed her eyes, trying to picture Julian Rutherford squaring off to shoot a hole in his cousin, and shook her head. "He must have felt he had been pushed to the limits. Lucy, you are right—we cannot leave now. But do try to keep some distance from his lordship until this madman is found. Julian shall need all his wits about him until then, and from the dreamy-eyed looks he was directing your way earlier, it's clear to see he won't be worth a bent copper if you insist on occupying all his attentions."

A slight noise at the doorway announced the arrival of the three gentlemen. Looking up at the earl as he led the way into the room, Lucy whispered, "Isn't he adorable, Aunt Rachel?"—a description that had the older woman biting her lip as she tried to restrain her mirth.

"Ladies," Julian said, bowing, "I hope we may have some good news for you this evening, Parker, this will be news to you also."

The secretary hastened to a chair and turned his attention to his cousin-employer. "You have discovered a clue?" he asked eagerly.

Dexter eyed his cousin with disdain. "Oh, stop slobbering, Parker. This nauseating show of loyalty is beginning to wear a bit thin. Relax, nobody believes you to be guilty."

"Why not?" Parker asked, clearly affronted. "I'm innocent, of course, but I fail to see why I should be dismissed by the likes of you. And who put you in charge anyway?"

"The nursery brats are at it again," Lucy remarked to her aunt under her breath. "And look at Julian—why, I rather think he enjoys all this squabbling."

"If I might continue?" the earl broke in, walking over to his favorite spot in front of the fireplace. "As you undoubtedly know, Dexter and I rode out today—"

"I would have gone, if only you had asked me," Parker broke in peevishly, thrusting out his thin bottom lip.

"Of course you would have, Mr. Rutherford," Rachel agreed placatingly. "But then, we all know how invaluable you are to us here, don't we?"

"I think I'm going to be sick." Dexter sneered, lifting a glass of port to his lips.

"Dexter!" Julian said icily.

"Yes, coz?"

"Stow it."

Dexter tipped his cousin an imaginary hat. "Your wish is my command, my lord."

"If I believed that, I might be a happier man," the earl observed idly, before getting back to the subject at hand. "As I was saying before that little outburst, Dexter and I rode out today—"

"We took his curricle," his cousin broke in breezily. "I knew I'd never last out the day in the saddle. You should see Julian's new pair. Bang up to the mark, let me tell you. Gray, they are, and—"

*"Dexter!"*

The young dandy broke off immediately and looked at Rachel. "Yes, ma'am?" he asked meekly, recognizing command when he heard it.

"You will sit down and speak only when you are spoken to. Is that clear?" Rachel ordered imperatively, and then waited until Dexter had meekly complied before smiling up at Thorpe and saying with deceptive compliance, "You may continue, Julian."

Lucy, who had been biting down hard on her knuckles to keep from laughing aloud, looked at Julian and saw that he too was holding in his amusement with great difficulty. It was wonderful to share this lighthearted moment with him, and when he lowered one long eyelid in a wink she nearly expired with happiness, only barely controlling the urge to spring up and run into his arms after seeing the startled look on Parker's pale face. He was such a prude, was Parker, but she wouldn't want to injure his delicate sensibilities, so she contented herself by giving Julian a little wink of her own.

"Something in your eye, Cousin Julian?" Parker asked solicitously, a question so ripe for comment that Dexter, who had great respect for any woman who could sound so very much like his mama, was forced to jump up and dash from the room before he was tempted to comment.

Finally, with Lucy still having recourse to her handkerchief to dab at the tears of laughter in the corners of her eyes, Julian was allowed to continue without interruption. He told them of his foray into the village and how they had spoken to many locals who swore they had seen Susan Anscom abroad late at night, seemingly on her way home from some secret assignation.

"We visited the deserted cottage where these clandestine meetings were believed to have taken place, but could turn up nothing of any moment. But I don't think we've merely reached another dead end. If Miss Anscom was seen, it is possible the murderer was as well. I've let it be known that I will reward handsomely anyone who can give me a description of her companion."

"Oh, that's wonderful news!" Lucy exclaimed, clapping her hands. "But you should try going into the village at night, when the men usually go to the inns to have their drinks. If anyone had seen Miss Anscom and her accomplice together, it would be one of these men, don't you think?"

A visit to a common taproom was not high on the earl's list of favored pastimes, and this was evident in his slight

shudder of distaste. "I'm sure the reward will bring someone to us," was his hopeful alternative to rubbing shoulders
with a league of bosky farmers on a spree.

Lucy tried to hide her disappointment. Julian was making great strides, but she would have to remember that nothing really lasting happened in a hurry. She would speak to
Dexter; surely he wouldn't be all that averse to a night on
the town—or village.

Conversation became general once Julian's news had been
discussed for a few more minutes, and Rachel was just about
to propose a game of whist when Raleigh came into the
room, cleared his throat, and announced: "Lord Tristan Rule,
m'lord."

"Cousin Tristan!" Lucy squealed, jumping to her feet and
running toward the doorway, her arms outflung, and
launched herself high into the hearty embrace of the man
who strode purposefully into the room. "Oh, Tristan, how
very good it is to see you!"

"I don't believe it," Rachel muttered incredulously. "Hale
wouldn't do this to me."

Julian watched the scene through narrowed eyes. Tristan
Rule, he mused, struggling to remember where he had heard
that name before. He looked at the man again, still whirling
his Lucy about in a circle like some Viking about to carry off
his captive. Baron Tristan Rule, of course! What did they call
him? Ruthless Rule—that was it. He was Lucy's cousin?
This unnaturally tall, black-haired, black-eyed devil was related to his sweet, warmhearted Lucy? His teeth clenched together tightly. How closely were they related? It had better
be damned close, he told himself silently, or Tristan Rule
would soon be Lucy's *late* cousin!

Lucy finally scrambled out of Tristan's embrace, standing back to have a good look at him. It had been over a year,
a span of time Tristan had spent doing whatever it was he did

for some branch of the government. Lucy had always secretly thought that he was a spy, what with his penchant for black clothing and his noncommittal answers to her many probing questions about his life. "Oh, Tris, it's wonderful to have you here. Did you hear about Jennie's marriage? She lives not more than twenty miles from here. Have you been to visit her? Is that how you knew where to find me? Oh, Tris, do come and sit down. Aunt Rachel is with me—I know she'll wish to say hello."

"Imp," the man named Tristan said in his low, husky voice, "if you will but give me a moment to breathe, I will introduce myself to your host." Walking over to Julian, he extended one hard, tanned hand. "My lord Thorpe," he said formally and with a hint of steel in his voice. "Allow me to introduce myself. I am Tristan Rule, Lucy's cousin. Sir Hale Gladwin has asked me to represent him here and assure him that Lucy is not in any danger. I have made certain inquiries in London, sir, and I have disregarded everything, knowing that Lucy does not place her trust lightly. Please consider me entirely at your service."

"But…but I don't know you," Julian stammered, unable to believe that this stranger would trust him when his acquaintances had not.

"You're refusing my help?" Rule asked, arching one finely sculptured black brow.

Julian shook his head and smiled at the younger man. "Sir, I may be many things, but I have never thought myself to be stupid. I accept your help with thanks."

Lucy released a breath she didn't know she had been holding. Going over to link a hand through each of their arms, she smiled at her aunt. "Now I know everything will be just fine. Wasn't Papa resourceful to have thought of Tristan, Aunt Rachel? How glad I am that you took it upon yourself to write to him."

Rachel Gladwin smiled weakly and wished it were humanly possible for a person to deliver a firm kick to her own backside.

DEXTER WAS OVER THE MOON with excitement. Tristan Rule! Ruthless Rule! At Hillcrest! Within moments of hearing the news, Dexter had burst into the drawing room, eager to see his idol in the flesh. Everyone knew about the baron, and whispered of his exploits, but seeing him in the flesh—or, he amended eagerly, in his famous black and white that was all he ever wore—was heady stuff indeed. It was said the man had no heart; that if you pinked him, he would not bleed. He was a paid assassin, recruited by the War Office, Dexter had heard, and his single-minded determination was legendary.

To hear that he had come to clear Julian raised his cousin's standing a notch or two in Dexter's eyes. Julian must be innocent if Ruthless Rule had taken his part. And he, Dexter Rutherford, was to have a front-row seat to watch the man in action. Oh, how he hoped there would be swordplay, for his friend Bertie Sandover had said that Rule was wicked with a blade.

Parker was not quite so impressed. To him, Rule looked to be a bit too complete to be believed. His dark good looks were too perfect, his perfectly cut black clothing covered a too-well-put-together body. Parker studied the man for more than half an hour and decided that rumors about the man's achievements had been greatly exaggerated. Besides, no one was ever going to solve the puzzle of who was framing his cousin. The plot had been built too well for any amount of amateur sleuthing to topple it. All that was going on now was that a bunch of strangers were making themselves comfortable in his lordship's house, eating his food, drinking his wine, and generally making nuisances of themselves. And that dratted monkey—why, just today he had been forced to call someone to carry the beast from his room, only to find that it had stolen his stickpin with the small diamond set in its center.

Yet, stranger things had happened. Suppose one of these idiots stumbled onto a real clue? Julian seemed to think they were onto something, and Parker didn't lump the earl into the same pot as he did the others. And then there was Lucy Gladwin. She and Julian had been acting very strangely— almost as if they were in love or something. Parker didn't like that thought any more than he had liked anything that had happened ever since the scandal first broke.

Getting quietly to his feet, Parker quit the drawing room unnoticed. If clues were to be found, perhaps it was time he took a hand in things. It didn't do to appear completely worthless—not at a time like this.

LUCY HAD ARISEN to find that another bright sunny day had dawned, and made short work out of dressing to go down to breakfast, hopeful that she would have a moment of private conversation with Lord Thorpe. He had been polite, if a bit distant, the night before, but the wink he had tossed her made her believe he was not regretting their kiss of two nights ago.

The breakfast room was deserted by the time she got there, so that she ate in solitude, but following the direction in which Raleigh's head had jerked slightly when she had asked a footman if he had seen his lordship, she had blown the majordomo a kiss and hotfooted it out to the garden. She ran Thorpe to earth in the rose arbor, sitting on a stone bench staring into the middle distance.

"Lucy!" he breathed happily when he saw her approaching. "How did you know I was sitting here wishing you would appear?" Reaching out his hands to grasp hers, he pulled her down beside him on the bench. "Lucy, I—"

"Julian, I—" she said at the same time, and they both halted, sheepish smiles on their faces.

"I want to apologize for taking advantage of you the other night," he began, only to trail off as Lucy's little face screwed up into a scowl. "What is it, my dear?" he asked as she tried to withdraw her hands from his grip.

"Julian, you're either a fool or a liar," she said feelingly, "and I am not quite sure at the moment which is worse."

Julian looked at her for a long moment, trying to read her expression. Didn't she know he was expected to apologize for what he had done? Lord, he had all but ravished her, and might have if not for Dexter's timely intervention. He would relax his strict code to some extent, but that did not mean he was willing to toss all his ideals over the windmill. "I had no right—" he began, trying to explain.

"Pish, tosh," Lucy said with a toss of her dark curls. "Either you enjoyed it or you didn't, Julian. Rights don't enter into it when a girl clad in only a thin dressing gown throws herself at your feet."

Thorpe's gray eyes blinked once, twice, and then began to twinkle. "You were a shameless little baggage, weren't you?" he teased, running his fingers down her cheek.

"Haven't I always been, where you're concerned?" she answered, unabashed.

How could one man be so lucky? he questioned silently, giving over the last of his doubts as to the rightness of what he felt toward this beautiful young girl. She was outrageous, outspoken, outgoing, and definitely out of the ordinary. And she was, he told himself as the knot in his chest slowly unfolded, leaving him feeling young and free and very much alive, his own true love.

"Marry me," he said urgently, suddenly unable to form anything near the formal proposal he had recited by rote to Cynthia three weeks earlier. "Marry me or I'll sling you over my shoulder and carry you off anyway."

She had dreamed of this moment, agonized over it, prayed

for it. Now that it had come, she was amazed that she found herself able to joke about it. "What?" she quipped, moving into his arms. "Julian, think of the scandal!"

"Brat!" he groaned, before crushing her in his strong embrace. "Willful, outrageous, adorable brat. How I love you."

"Take your hands off her!"

Julian and Lucy flew apart from each other as Tristan Rule planted himself firmly in front of them, arms akimbo. Looking up into the man's night-dark eyes, Julian remembered more of what he had heard about this man. He was a hothead, prone to go off on a tangent with single-minded dedication.

"I am here in my uncle's place, sir," Rule pointed out in heavy accents. "If you have some declaration to make—make it. Otherwise, I suggest you name your seconds."

"Oh, cut line, you looby," came the exasperated voice of Rachel Gladwin. "Must you ever be tilting at windmills, Tristan? Lord Thorpe has already asked my permission to wed Lucy."

Lucy looked around her dazedly. It seemed Raleigh's head had been pointing out Julian's direction to all and sundry. Soon there would be so many of them a servant would show up to serve tea. But wait—had she heard what she thought she had? Had Julian really approached Aunt Rachel? "Julian?" Lucy questioned, hoping her aunt had not just said it to soothe Tristan.

"It's true, my love," Thorpe told her, reclaiming her hands. "But we all must agree to keep it silent until the murderer is caught. I dislike the thought of having you as a target."

Cocking her head to one side, Lucy looked up at him and smiled. "But, my lord, you have not even *really* asked me yet—or heard my answer."

"Really?" Julian retorted, his voice a soft drawl. "I apologize. I thought you had already given your answer the other night." At Lucy's delighted giggle, Thorpe rose and extended his hand to accept Tristan's fervent congratulations. "Forgive my slapdash approach, Lord Rule, if you will. It's just that where Lucy is concerned, I scarce know anymore whether I'm on my head or on my heels."

Tristan looked at his bubbly, clearly-in-love cousin, and nodded his agreement.

Rachel knew that Tristan would have stood there talking, playing the gooseberry in his uncle's stead, until Lucy and Julian began to believe a flight to Gretna to be the only way they would ever get some privacy. Slipping her arm through the baron's, she suggested he accompany her on a tour of the gardens, a suggestion so alien to that young gentleman's inclinations that the resultant look of astonishment that crossed his handsome features had Julian controlling his amusement with some difficulty.

But just as Tristan was about to open his mouth to protest—and earn himself a heartfelt sigh of resignation from his aunt—Raleigh appeared in their midst, a paper-wrapped rock in his hand. "This…er…came through the parlor window, m'lord."

Julian looked at the rock with foreboding while Tristan, Rachel couldn't help noticing, bristled all over with excitement. And therein lay the difference in the two men—Tristan was still a boy, hot for adventure, while Julian was a man, longing for a more peaceful, hopefully shared, life.

But, being a man and therefore sensible of his responsibilities, Julian did not hesitate to relieve Raleigh of his burden. Untying the scrap of paper from the rock, he tossed the rock into the bushes and unfolded the creased single page. After quickly scanning its contents, he handed the note to Tristan. "Someone's kidnapped Parker. They demand a ransom to get him back."

## CHAPTER ELEVEN

TWO HOURS HAD PASSED since Raleigh had brought Julian the ransom note, and in that time they had all learned many things.

Dexter, sent to check out Parker's room, had learned that his cousin's bed had not been slept in, and his questioning of a servant uncovered the fact that the night before, the secretary had left Hillcrest alone while the others were still in the drawing room.

Tristan had learned that although he might not appear to be the forceful sort, Julian had assumed command of the situation, and was not to be swayed from his decision to pay the ransom as soon as possible so that no harm would come to Parker.

Lucy had found out, much to her chagrin, that her beloved had absolutely *no* sense of adventure, and she was still smarting a bit after being told, in quite unromantic tones, to sit down and button her lip before she was sent to her room.

Julian, aware of his position of authority, had nonetheless been forced to acknowledge that, much as he loved his outrageous little Lucy, she did have a tendency to come up with the most harebrained schemes imaginable.

And Rachel, sitting in a corner of the library where they had all closeted themselves to consider their alternatives, had relearned a lesson life had taught her long ago. Given the right set of circumstances, it is possible for anyone to make a complete mull of things.

Dexter, with his glib assessment of Parker as a "bungling jackass," which earned him a blistering lecture from his cousin; Tristan, as usual, immediately going off the deep end and inciting Lucy with his talk of pursuit and punishment; Lucy, whose impulsive "if-ever-I-heard-a-faint-heart!" response to Julian's suggestion that they call in the law; and Julian's exasperated "God give me patience!" had all combined to cause their supposed meeting of the minds to descend rapidly into a near-brawl.

It was, Rachel knew, time she took a hand in the situation, for Julian was just then giving Lucy a very unloving look, which her niece was returning twofold. "If I might interrupt this little comedy with a bit of reality," she broke in, just as Dexter was agreeing with Lucy that they should be out scouring the countryside for clues. "Dexter, I *do* wish you would refrain from inciting her. Julian, what makes you so confident that paying the ransom will ensure Parker's return?"

Dexter snorted. "Who'd want to keep him?" he chortled derisively. "I still fail to see why anybody wanted him in the first place. Dead bore is our Parker, and it's not like he's worth a groat."

Julian silenced his young cousin with a look, then bowed to Rachel. "Answering Dexter's remarks first, I would say that Parker was abducted when he went into the village to talk to the men at the inns. If you recall, we were talking about doing just such a thing ourselves before the baron arrived."

Dexter shook his head. "Impossible. He doesn't have it in him."

"Precisely!" Lucy was quick to agree. "Parker is too timid to go out on his own that way. He must have been grabbed as he was taking the night air before retiring. I'm sure he's being held prisoner in order to get you out in the open, Julian. Why else would the kidnapper demand that you be the one to bring the ransom? It's a trap to shoot at you from ambush, just like I've been trying to tell you. Since the scandal has yet to make anyone realize that you could be charged with murder, the man has become desperate enough to do you in by himself. Oh, please, Julian, listen to Tristan and stop being so all-fired stubborn!"

"If you are quite done?" Julian said coldly. "No matter what the reason, I owe it to Parker to follow my directions to the letter. To do anything less puts him in jeopardy."

Lucy's lips curled and she gritted: "How very noble, my lord. And what of me—am I to be a widow before I am even a wife?"

"You may be spanked before you're put to bed without your supper, if you don't desist from your childish outbursts," the earl informed her, deciding that, love her as he did, it was time she knew just who was in charge. "I'm not so stupid as to set myself up as either a martyr or some madman's target practice. I know enough to be careful."

Dexter sidled over to where Rachel was sitting, smiling happily as she decided that Lucy would be in good hands married to Julian Rutherford. "I say, ma'am," Dexter opined, watching Lucy and Julian as they glared at each other, "I do believe there is a spot of trouble in Paradise."

A commotion at the door brought all their heads around, and a worse-for-wear Parker staggered into the room to drop to his knees dramatically at Thorpe's feet. "I…I got away!" he rasped, before crumbling to the floor, breathing heavily.

Pandemonium prevailed for some minutes as Parker was half-carried to a chair and some restorative spirits poured down his throat. He looked as if he had been dealt a mighty thrashing, for his nose was red and it was obvious that he would soon be showing off one blackened eye. Even Dexter, who would have sworn he didn't give a fig about the timid secretary, felt an incredible need to find whoever had done this terrible thing and beat him into a pulp.

Parker's story, spoken as it was around a swollen mouth and a few loose teeth, was much as Julian had imagined it. Feeling he had been of little help so far in clearing the earl's name, Parker had decided to go to the village and ask a few questions of his own. After finding nothing new at the local inn, he had reluctantly headed home, only to be attacked from behind and dragged off to some run-down cottage.

"The cottage where Miss Anscom went to meet her lover!" Lucy interrupted, feeling that they were getting somewhere at last. "Then the murderer is still in the area. We should be out there right now, hunting the blackguard down before he makes good his escape."

"No," his lordship told her decisively.

Lucy was beside herself. How could he refuse her help like this? Didn't he understand how impossible it was for her to sit back and do nothing at a time like this? "Oh," she exploded, with more emotion than good sense, "if you had any gumption at all you'd do it!"

"Lucille," Julian bit out from between clenched teeth, "I have had all I can stand from you and your maggoty ideas. Please leave us."

Lucy looked from Julian to Tristan to her aunt and then back again to her infuriating beloved. *"Oooohh!"* she erupted, stamping her foot, and then lifted her skirts defiantly and flounced out of the room.

"That's the ticket, coz," Dexter applauded approvingly. "Break her to halter now or she'll lead you a merry chase."

"If I might continue?" Parker whined, looking up from his makeshift bed of pain.

"Sorry, Parker," Dexter apologized, shaking his head yet

again as he took in his cousin's battered appearance. "I have to tell you, though, I never thought you had it in you. Escaped, did you? Now, I would have thought sure you would have bungled it, if I had ever believed you'd try such a thing in the first place. Please go on, I really do want to hear about your adventure."

The secretary made short work of the rest of his tale, relating how he had been carried unconscious to the cottage but awoke before it was full dawn. He had had one foot already out the cottage window when the kidnapper had realized what he was about, and in the ensuing struggle Parker had sustained the injuries that were so apparent to his audience. "But I broke clear at last and stumbled into the trees behind the cottage. I must have run for miles before exhaustion overtook me and I lay down to rest. I would have been back sooner, else. I hope I haven't caused you too much bother."

"No, of course not," Dexter assured him lightly. "Cousin Julian may have lost another fiancée, that's all."

"Fiancée?" Parker questioned, gingerly examining his puffy lower lip. "Miss Gladwin?"

"Well, it ain't me, you fool," Dexter retorted, back in his old form. "Sorry," he added hastily as Julian shot him a warning with his eyes, "it's just that I'm so used to doing it. Parker here has always been such an easy target. Guess I'll have to rethink the thing. Now that he's a hero, you know."

Rachel reentered the room then, dragging Deirdre in tow. "Raleigh has sent for the doctor, but I thought Deirdre could have a look at him for now."

Parker shrank back against the cushions. "I'll wait for the doctor," he said, eyeing the young red-headed woman warily.

"Is that so?" the maid sniffed, insulted. "And didn't you know that a wise woman is better than a foolish doctor, which is all you'd be getting out here in the middle of nowhere. Give over, sir, and let me have a look at you."

There being nothing much more to do, and seeing that Deirdre would be unavailable for pestering for some time, Dexter took himself off to the billiard room and some much-needed practice while Julian and Tristan, who had been very quiet throughout the whole interlude, adjourned to the garden for a council of war.

With everyone occupied elsewhere, it was an easy matter for Lucy, now dressed in her blue riding habit, to sneak off toward the stables.

IT WAS SO CONFUSING. Lucy knew Julian loved her—there wasn't a single doubt left in her mind. And she loved him—had been loving him for what seemed like forever. So why had he yelled at her and looked at her as if he wanted nothing more than to turn her over his knee? And why did she feel like grabbing him by the shoulders and shaking him senseless? This was love? How could you love someone and still be so angry with him that you shouted at him?

As her horse ate up the miles between Hillcrest and the cottage, Lucy struggled with the confusion in her mind. It wasn't as if Julian had entered into their relationship believing she was some simpering miss—he'd had three long years to learn about her. As for herself, she thought, shrugging, she knew Julian tended to be a mite stuffy. It was a part of his charm.

She believed that their love was strong enough to surmount these little obstacles. Besides, Julian looked so adorable when he lost his temper. Much as she aimed to please him, she would have to remember to ruffle his feathers once in a while, just to keep things interesting. She smiled and patted the horse's head, wondering if he really would spank her.

The cottage was just ahead, and she dismounted in order

to keep her approach as quiet as possible. She was sure the place was unoccupied; no murderer, no matter how mad, would be foolish enough to linger when Parker was bound to have told everyone where he had been hidden. Looking around her carefully, she tiptoed up to a window and peered inside.

The cottage was deserted. Circling around to the front door, which hung by only two of its hinges, she stepped inside and began her inspection. The few sticks of furniture were old and broken, and only a pile of rags in the corner that looked as if someone had been lying on them showed any sign of recent habitation. All in all, it seemed like she had wasted a trip.

So much for solving the puzzle and saving the day, she grimaced, knowing full well the scolding she would receive upon her return to Hillcrest. Between the lecture she was sure to receive from Aunt Rachel and the blistering set-down Julian was bound to serve her, she felt no need to hurry her return, and decided to ride past the pond where Susan Anscom had met her end.

The village lad who agreed to hold her horse for a penny also supplied the information that led her to the exact spot where Miss Anscom's body had been discovered. It was a deceptively peaceful scene, what with the willow trees trailing down into the water and lush green grass running clear to the edge of the pond.

Breaking off a slender willow branch, Lucy sat down near the gently sloping bank and stared out over the water, trying to imagine what it had been like there the night of the drowning. The lad had said the body hadn't been found until the morning. Strange, she questioned, looking around and realizing how close the surrounding cottages were to the pond.

How had the murderer done his despicable deed without someone either seeing or hearing something? Surely the girl hadn't willingly walked into the pond so that the murderer wouldn't be put to too much bother when it came time to hold her head under the surface.

Perhaps she had been murdered somewhere else and her body dumped in the pond. Lucy would have to go back and read the suicide note more closely to see if the pond had been mentioned. No, she thought, shaking her head; the contents of the letter really didn't mean anything. It was written according to the murderer's direction, not on the girl's whim.

Lucy hung her head, feeling totally defeated. She had so counted on helping Julian, on being the one to save him. Using the broken end of the willow branch, she dug idly in the dirt as she cudgeled her brain for a plausible excuse for her absence all afternoon. She could say she had gone off in a huff and simply been hacking about aimlessly—heaven only knew Aunt Rachel would believe that.

If only she could come up with something, some little glimmer of hope that would… What was that? The stick she had been stabbing into the soft soil hit on something solid. Probably a stone, she thought, trying to keep down her rising excitement as she scrambled to her knees and began digging in earnest.

With trembling fingers she picked up the large flat bone button—the sort to be found on men's jackets—and held it up in front of her. It was a very distinctive button, with a thin gold design drawn on it, and could only have come from a coat cut in London. She had found their first solid clue, she could feel it in her bones.

Clambering to her feet, she ran back to where the boy waited with her horse and headed back to Hillcrest. Wouldn't Julian be surprised to hear what she had done! She had solved the case! All they had to do was match the button to the coat it belonged to and they would have their man.

It was only when she was more than halfway to Hillcrest

that she realized that there was no way to go about London looking for that one particular coat. It was ludicrous—they had no starting point, no clue as to a likely suspect. Tears of frustration clouded her vision as she rode on, which perhaps accounted for the fact that she did not see the dog that came bounding out onto the roadway and anticipated her frightened mount's reaction.

A scant second later she was lying unconscious in the dirt, the button still clutched in her hand.

"TAKE A DRINK OF THIS for me, Lucy," a male voice crooned, supporting her back with his hand as he held a glass to her lips.

She struggled to open her eyes, but could see little in the dusk-darkened room. "Julian?" she ventured, blinking hard to banish the mist that floated in front of her eyes. "Where am I?"

"You're in your bed at Hillcrest. You had a spill from your horse. Drink this."

She was all right, although her head ached abominably. Julian was with her. She was fine. But she wasn't thirsty. "Don't want any," she slurred, trying to turn her head away.

"You'll sleep better," he urged, pressing the rim to her lips. "It will help your head. It hurts, doesn't it?"

A small smile touched her lips. Dear Julian. He was trying to help her. "Sleep," she said almost eagerly. "Just want to sleep."

"That's right, Lucy," he encouraged, watching her as she tried to drink. "Be careful, you're slopping it onto your nightgown."

"It tastes vile," she protested, trying to squirm from his hold. "Don't want any more. Have to tell you what I found. Sleep later."

"Do as I say," he ordered, his harsh voice setting off a new onslaught of pain in her abused head.

Choking and gasping, she tried not to swallow the brackish-tasting liquid Julian kept forcing into her mouth. "Stop," she spluttered. "Hate you, hate you for this. Don't want to sleep."

After he had satisfied himself that he had gotten enough of the potion into her, he let her fall back against the pillows. "You'll sleep now," he said almost gently as he left the room. "You'll sleep forever."

An alarm bell went off in Lucy's tortured brain. "Eternal sleep," the old Gypsy had told her. She didn't want to sleep forever. She... *Oh God!*

Lucy struggled to sit up, and the room spun around her. She had to get help; Julian was trying to kill her! She opened her mouth to call for Deirdre, but no sound came out. She was so tired; every small movement became a herculean effort.

Poisoned, she decided, and felt her heart pounding painfully in her breast. Julian has poisoned me! Dragging herself over so that her head hung from the side of the bed, she stuck her finger down her throat and tried to empty her stomach. The top of her head was coming off; she had never known such pain. As the retching ended, so did the last of her strength, and she collapsed against the sheets, Julian's name a question on her lips.

JULIAN WAS PACING the library like a caged lion. From the moment Lucy's mount had come into the stableyard alone, he had been fighting a rising panic that had nothing to do with the façade of calm he usually presented to the world.

He and Tristan had ridden out immediately, finding Lucy's unconscious body less than a mile from the estate, and Rule had wisely refrained from coming near him as Thorpe lifted Lucy carefully into his arms and gently carried her back to Hillcrest.

The doctor had been and gone, pronouncing her fit enough except for the concussed head, and had advised them to let her sleep until she awakened naturally. Before leaving, he handed Julian the button he had found clenched in Lucy's hand.

Rachel and Deirdre had announced that they would take turns sitting with their patient, banishing Julian over his protests that he be allowed to watch over her while she slept. But as the day slipped slowly away, Lucy had shown no signs of stirring, and Julian was fast running out of patience.

Lucy had looked so pale, so defenseless, lying there in the road like a child's carelessly discarded doll. It wasn't that he didn't believe the doctor, or Rachel, who had just moments ago at the dinner table told him that Lucy would be just fine by morning.

He had to see her for himself. He *would* see her for himself! His mind made up, he left the library and headed for the stairs, overtaking Rachel, who was just about to return to Lucy's room.

"Deirdre went down to her dinner a little while ago," she told the earl. "Tristan detained me with his latest theory— just as bloodthirsty as all his others—or else I would have been with Lucy by now." Cocking her head to one side, she took in his lordship's strained features. "I don't suppose it would hurt anything to let you peek in on her for a moment."

"I am not by nature a violent man, Rachel," Julian returned amicably, "but may I suggest that it might be decidedly hurtful for you if you believed you could keep me away any longer."

"You really do love her, don't you?" she said, her heart reaching out to him.

"Yes, I really do," he admitted solemnly. "So much so that I am sending the both of you away from here as soon as Lucy is fit to travel. I'm still not sure Lucy's fall was an accident."

They had reached Lucy's bedchamber, and the first thing they noticed when Rachel opened the door was the sour smell that was overlaid with another, cloyingly sweet scent. "Laudanum?" Thorpe ventured, sniffing. "And something else?"

Rachel moved to light some candles. "It can't be laudanum," she told him. "The doctor specifically told me not to give her any—not with the injury being to her head." She looked toward the bed, noticing that the covers had been dragged all to one side. "She must be stirring; the blankets are all tossed about. If you'll just give me a moment to tidy her up a bit, you can… *Oh, dear Lord, Lucy!*"

Julian was at the bedside like a shot, taking in the sight of the soiled carpet and the unnatural stillness of Lucy's body. "She's not…?"

Rachel put her fingers to her niece's neck. "She's all right," she reassured him, leaning over to stroke the damp curls back from Lucy's forehead. "She must have been sick after Deirdre left."

But Julian couldn't believe it was that simple. Looking about him, he discovered Lucy's tooth glass on the table beside the bed. Picking it up, he sniffed at it. "Laudanum," he said, and his handsome features hardened into a tight mask. "Somebody's given her laudanum. Thank God she didn't keep it down!"

"But why?" Rachel asked, one hand to her mouth. "The doctor said—"

"Who was there when he told you?" Julian interrupted, already stripping off his coat.

"Why, nearly everyone, I suppose," Rachel told him, trying hard to think. "Except you. You were upstairs here fighting with Deirdre because she wouldn't let you in to see Lucy. Do you honestly think one of us…?" She let her question dangle, swallowing hard. "Of course you do." She gasped as

Julian threw back the covers and began unbuttoning Lucy's gown. "What are you doing?"

"Get me a clean nightgown, will you?" he asked, already stripping Lucy to the buff. "Come now, woman, this is no time to go prudish on me. It's going to be a long night as it is."

"But you said Lucy had rid herself of the laudanum."

"I don't know if she got rid of all of it, just some of it. We have to wake her, and keep her awake, until the effects wear off." Julian was having great difficulty in inserting Lucy's seemingly boneless arms into the white lawn nightgown Rachel handed him.

"And what are you about?" Deirdre's squawk of protest fell on deaf ears as Thorpe brought the gown down over Lucy's hips.

Rachel filled in the maid on what had transpired before that indignant young woman could launch a physical assault on the earl, which it appeared she was fully capable of doing. "It's right he is, ma'am," Deirdre then said, all business. "We have to wake her. Are you going to walk her around a bit, my lord?" she asked Thorpe, springing to help him lift Lucy from the bed.

"I'll walk her to hell and back if I have to," Julian swore fiercely. "And when I'm sure she's all right, I'm going to assemble everyone in this household and kill somebody!"

# CHAPTER TWELVE

ONE OF LUCY'S ARMS wrapped around each of their shoulders, Julian and Deirdre half-dragged, half-carried Lucy up and down the length of the room, talking to her loudly and occasionally lightly slapping her cheeks.

It seemed like a lifetime had passed before Lucy started showing signs of coming around, and then it was as if she was reluctant to rejoin the land of the living. "No, Julian, no," she would protest feebly. "Don't want to, don't want to."

But her feet had begun to move on their own, and the ungainly trio was forced into an erratic gait as Lucy alternately lurched ahead and then dragged her toes along on the carpet. "Come on, darling," Julian urged her over and over again. "Do it for me. Please, do it for me."

"The Gypsy saw it," Lucy muttered sorrowfully, a tear running down her cheek. "Oh yes, the Gypsy knew."

Julian jerked to a stop, his eyes widening in his head. Rachel and Deirdre thought Lucy to be rambling, but he knew better. His blood ran cold as he realized that Lucy had known someone had tried to kill her. She hadn't merely been sick—she had been using her last strength to try to save her life. "The gypsy was wrong, Lucy, do you hear me?" he declared in a loud voice. "Listen to me, dearest. The Gypsy was wrong!"

Her head lifted slowly and she looked at him with unfocused eyes. "No," she whispered, shaking her head in denial. "She saw you. I saw you. Why, Julian? Why did you do it?"

"What's she talking about?" Rachel asked, as she relieved Deirdre and fell into step with Thorpe. "What's this business about a Gypsy?"

Tersely Julian told her about the Gypsy fortune-teller Lucy had visited at the traveling circus they had stopped at on their journey to Hillcrest. "I was angry at the time, but then I forgot all about it. But Lucy must believe it was I who poisoned her."

"Oh, no, Julian, surely you must be mistaken. Lucy could never believe such a thing. She loves you."

"Hate you, Julian. Hate you, hate you, hate you."

"Of course you do, darling," Julian soothed, although Rachel could hear the agony in his voice. "Just walk for me, Lucy. Come on now, that's a good girl, you can do it."

"She doesn't know what she's saying, Julian," Rachel assured him as she took in the firm set of his jaw.

"I don't want anyone to know what's going on in this room," he suddenly ordered. "As far as the rest of the household is concerned, Lucy is still unconscious due to her fall. Somewhere in this house is the person responsible for this, and I wouldn't want to deny him the joy of believing he has succeeded in his plans. Do I make myself clear, ladies?"

"Ain't Dexter," Deirdre sniffed. "He's a sorry-looking shrimp, but he's harmless. Gormless, almost." Although the Irish maid was too smart to succumb entirely to Dexter's blandishments, she had evidently developed a bit of a soft spot in her heart for the young dandy.

"*Everyone's* a suspect now until I say differently," Thorpe told her harshly, cradling Lucy's head as it lolled helplessly against his shoulder.

"I wouldn't tell Tristan that," Rachel interposed with a bit of a smile. "I do believe he might take exception."

"That only leaves Parker," Julian mused, then shook his head dismissively. "Can't be him. God, the man nearly got himself killed trying to help me. It has to be someone else."

"Yes, but who?" Rachel asked, rubbing her arm once Lucy's weight was gone, Julian having lifted her into his arms and deposited her on his lap as he sat down on the bed.

"Love you, Julian," Lucy whispered, lifting a hand to stroke his cheek. "Always loved you. Why did you do it? It wasn't nice."

His eyes closing on the unspeakable pain he was feeling, Julian answered Rachel's question: "I don't know who yet. But I'll find out. I'll bloody well find out! Now, leave us, please. I believe she's out of the woods."

Deirdre looked to Rachel for guidance and that lady nodded her head. No more harm would come to Lucy that night, not with Julian there to protect her. Motioning to the maid to follow her, Rachel slipped from the room.

Lucy was beginning to come around, and her soft sighs and small squirmings were having a decidedly bracing effect on his lordship's physical condition. "Sit still, love," he warned her softly. "It's been a long night, but I'm not so fatigued that I'm not aware of the thinness of your nightgown. Or forgetful of the treasures I've seen hidden beneath it," he added under his breath.

"Love Julian," Lucy crooned, a silly smile hovering about the corners of her lips. "Lucy loves Julian—*so much!*"

"Yes, darling," he answered, disengaging her arms, which had somehow woven themselves about his neck. "Just let me tuck you in bed now that Deirdre has put fresh linen on for you. Lucy, sweetest," he repeated, as she showed a disinclination to release him, "you have to let me go now."

Lucy pouted, her full lower lip jutting out petulantly. "Don't want to. Lucy loves Julian." She leaned her head back, nearly unbalancing the pair of them. "Does Julian love Lucy?"

"Julian loves Lucy," Thorpe sighed, taking in the bareness of her long, slim throat as she lolled bonelessly in his arms.

"Then give Lucy a kiss," she teased, trying with all her might to pull his face down to her pouting lips.

Julian looked helplessly about the room, half-praying for reinforcements, half-fearing someone would show up and take this willing female off to some safe place, away from his rapidly disintegrating moral judgment. "Lucy, have pity," he begged, just before she shifted her weight one more time, causing the two of them to fall back against the mattress.

Lucy's eyes were still shut tightly, perhaps because of the lingering pain in her head, and her tongue slipped out to moisten her parched lips. "Julian doesn't love Lucy," she intoned sadly, turning her face to one side and giving a deep sigh.

The last remnants of the wall Julian had built around his emotions crumbled into dust as he slid his arms around Lucy's prone body and laid his head on her breast. "Julian loves Lucy more than life itself," he groaned huskily, very aware of just how close he had come to losing her. "I'll always love you."

Lucy's arms lifted up to wrap around his back, cradling him to her, and he turned his head slightly to nuzzle at her throat. This was madness. She had fallen from her horse just that afternoon. She had been drugged—nearly to death. And here he was, like a randy goat, lusting after her body.

But it was more than that. Like humans all through the history of mankind, he was reacting to the fear of loss by wanting nothing more than to celebrate the continuation of life. This was why man was urged to procreate, this was why woman wished above all things to feel a new life growing within her.

Knowing none of this, reasoning very little as to why he was acting this way, Julian succumbed to his heart. Sliding a hand under Lucy's head, he lifted her face to his and allowed nature to take its course.

She was all response, all fire and fluid, giving everything while taking all, and he was totally lost. Her mouth burned beneath his, her body molded to his as if fashioned for just that purpose, her hands branded his face, his neck, his back.

"Lucy, my dearest, darling Lucy," he breathed, his hands shaking as he fumbled with the opening of her gown. "Always and forever, my darling Lucy."

Lucy was floating. Her head, which had been pounding so fiercely just minutes earlier, was now numb to everything but the sensations sent to it from her gloriously alive body. Julian was here; Julian was holding her, touching her, kissing her. Julian was her love. Julian was…

"Julian," she whispered into the ear she was just then nibbling. "Why did you hurt me?"

His hands stilled on the third button from the top of her gown. She still thought that he had been the one who had tried to kill her. His blood ran cold, succeeding in immediately cooling his ardor, though not his fierce love of this girl who could still love him, believing him guilty of trying to murder her.

"Lucy," he begged, stroking her head as he willed his words to penetrate the hazy world of sensation Lucy still inhabited, "I didn't do it. I'd never hurt you. I swear to you, with God as my judge, that I would never harm a single hair on your adorable head."

The fact that he had come perilously close to deflowering his "love" while she was in a near-senseless state caused him to grimace as if he were in deepest pain, but he knew he would have to reserve his guilty feelings to be dealt with later. Right now it was imperative that Lucy be brought to understand that he loved her—would never harm her. "Lucy, you must believe me!" he said, shaking her slightly for emphasis. "My God, please!"

But Lucy was at last slipping into a healing, restful sleep. The last thing she did before her tightly closed eyelids relaxed into a more normal expression was to lift her hand to Julian's cheek and sigh. "It's all right, Julian. All right. Still love you."

He caught her hand as it began to slip away and pressed his lips into her palm. Then, realizing that further attempts to rouse her much before midday would be fruitless, he shifted her body to the middle of the bed and drew up the covers.

He stood beside the bed for a long time, watching over her as she slept. It was nearly dawn before he spoke again, so softly that Rachel, who had peeked in to check on her niece, could barely hear his words. "I'll kill the bloody bastard!" he rasped, his hands clenched into tight fists at his sides. "I swear to God I'll kill him!"

THE SUN WAS FAIRLY HIGH before Julian stirred from his chair in front of the cold fireplace in his, the master bedchamber. Calling for his man, he took advantage of a refreshing bath and allowed himself to be dressed in the casual country elegance that took all of his valet's efforts to create, and then dismissed the servant.

He had already missed the breakfast buffet and it still lacked two hours to luncheon, although he couldn't have forced a single forkful of food past his firmly compressed lips. His whole mind, his entire being, was concentrating on discovering some way to ferret out the murderer and then slowly, carefully, take the bastard apart bit by satisfying bit.

But how was he to succeed now when to date they had all been failing so miserably? There were no new clues, only a new crime; a crime that cast into the shade the plot to discredit his name. If he had been told a fortnight ago that there was a single thing on the earth that mattered more than his reputation, he would have laughed at the absurdity of anything taking precedence over his pride in his lineage.

But now he had learned, through bitter experience, the folly of his previous values. If he could trade all his good name and blue-blooded ancestors for Lucy's safety, he would do so without a blink. All that mattered to him, all that gave him reason to draw breath, was wrapped up in the slim young girl lying injured and vulnerable in her chamber down the hallway.

He had thought over his options as dawn broke over the countryside, and he had decided, not without regret, that the only person, besides Rachel and Deirdre, that he could trust to stand his ally was Tristan Rule—not because he was about to accept the man on blind faith, but because he had been out of the country during the time the scandal broke.

Tristan had a reputation for his intelligence, his loyalty to his friends and his country, his dogged determination. That these attributes could, according to what he had learned from Rachel, also lead Rule to pigheadedness, single-minded pursuit of his own peculiar interpretation of justice, and his well-earned nickname of "Ruthless Rule" was not something he had the luxury of refining on at the moment.

Thorpe was just about to ring for a servant, sending him off with the request that Lord Rule join him in his chambers, when a slight scratching at his chamber door caught his attention. Crossing to the door as quietly as possible, he flung it open in order to surprise whoever was eavesdropping outside.

No one was there. He leaned his head out the door to check the hallway, which was empty of servants or guests, and then his attention was brought closer to the ground. Sitting on his haunches at his lordship's feet was a small brown furry creature, a jaunty red cap pushed down over his ears.

"Bartholomew!" Julian chuckled. "What mischief are you up to this time?" Leaning down to scoop the smiling, chattering monkey into his arms, Thorpe stepped back into his chamber and closed the door.

It would have surprised all who might have been witness to Thorpe's warm reception of the monkey—all but the earl's long-suffering valet, that is, who had spent many an hour brushing stubborn monkey hairs from his master's dressing gown—to know that Bartholomew was a frequent guest in his lordship's private chamber.

Bartholomew was loyal to his new mistress, but perhaps because the creature was accustomed to a male master, he had made it a point to seek Thorpe out. Julian, striving with all his might to become a more open, generous sort of soul, had begun his association with Bartholomew as a gesture of his good intentions, and then pursued the acquaintance when the little monkey, who was quite an affectionate monster, slowly wormed his way into the earl's heart.

It followed most naturally that Julian, rather than Lucy, became the recipient of the items gleaned from Bartholomew's latest foraging expeditions. Lucy, who had not told Julian of Bartholomew's little trick for fear the creature would be punished or even expelled from Hillcrest, had only silently rejoiced when the monkey stopped bringing her thimbles, diamond earrings, and golden guineas.

For his part, Julian saw no reason to inform Lucy of her new pet's larcenous tendencies. All in all, for Bartholomew at least, it made for a satisfying resolution. For the rest of the household, it mattered little either way, for Julian had made it a practice to leave anything of value out in the open where its owners could find it, thinking the item had been merely mislaid, and he still could fill a hatbox with the other miscellaneous booty, so that Bartholomew could play with his treasures during his daily visits.

"What have you pilfered today, O bold highwayman?" Thorpe asked the monkey, setting the creature down on his bed. He needed a moment's respite from his troubles, and looking through Bartholomew's latest haul should provide a small diversion.

"Aha! And what is this?" he questioned, holding up a silver paperweight as the delighted monkey rolled over on the bed and awaited his reward, a satisfying scratching of his tight belly. "Pleased with yourself, aren't you, you little imp of mischief?"

Bartholomew bared his teeth in a wide monkey smile and reached into the little leather pouch that hung around his neck to pull out yet another treasure for his master's delectation and admiration.

Julian's smile faded as he took the object from Bartholomew's fingers and held it to the light. "Isn't that interesting," he mused, rubbing the shiny object between his fingertips. Looking down at the monkey, he asked quietly, "Do you know where you got this, Bartholomew?" The monkey tipped his head and looked at his master inquiringly. Didn't he like it?

Realizing his error, Thorpe proceeded to make a very great business out of congratulating Bartholomew for bringing such a wonderful gift. "Can you bring me another one like it?" he asked the monkey, making clasping motions against his chest, as if to say "More, more." Did the monkey understand? Julian asked himself, his heart beginning to pound as he felt he was hovering on the brink of discovering something truly important.

Bartholomew scampered down from the high bed and over to the door, chattering happily as he waited for the earl to let him out into the hallway.

Looking about quickly to see that the corridor was still deserted, Julian headed off in Bartholomew's wake, hoping against hope that the monkey was leading him straight to the man who had nearly succeeded in his attempt to murder Lucy.

JULIAN WAS BEGINNING to wish he had kept his own counsel. Not only was he getting a crick in his neck from watching Lord Rule as that man paced back and forth across the library carpet (at twice the pace of any other gentleman, but then Lord Rule seemed to do everything with more intensity than any other gentleman), but listening to the man as he described, in graphic detail, just what he would do with the murderer once he got his hands on him was becoming just the teeniest bit annoying.

"Leave the disposition of the man to me," Julian told Tristan, just as the younger man was in the midst of describing the colors the murderer's face would turn as he, as avenger, wrung the man's scrawny neck.

"Just tell me who he is!" Rule demanded for the hundredth time. "I can tell that you know. If you trust me enough to ask me to guard your back, you can tell me whom to guard it against, damn it all to hell! Why don't you give me his name?"

Thorpe looked at Rule, surprised to see that no fire spewed from his mouth as the young hothead spoke. Shaking his head, Julian thanked his lucky stars that the sight of Rule in a temper had served to bring himself back to reason. He would capture the murderer and see that the man was punished. But vengeance, earlier his only desire, was not the way for a sane man to go. In the end, revenge merely for the sake of the satisfaction he would feel in having the man lying dead at his feet would cut at him as well.

"I'm not going to tell you," he stated firmly now, "because I wish to save you from the gallows. The moment you hear the suspect's name you will go off with murder in your eye—

that's as plain to me as is the nose on your face—a nose, by the by, that seems to be breathing smoke at the moment."

"Don't you care that Lucy was nearly killed?" Tristan asked indignantly, looking at Thorpe through dark, narrowed eyes.

The earl jumped to his feet. "That will be enough!" he exclaimed coldly. "I said I have a suspect, a very good suspect. I can't have you going off slaying suspects like you would dragons, until we rid the forest of anyone who seems the least bit suspicious. And," he ended haughtily, "if you ever again question my love and concern for your cousin, sir, you may prepare yourself for the drubbing of your life. Now, are you with me or not?"

Rule ran a hand through his already disordered hair. "My apologies, Thorpe," he offered sincerely, if not humbly.

"Accepted," Julian agreed, and the two men sat down to plan strategy, only to be interrupted by Raleigh as he announced the arrival of Lord and Lady Bourne.

"Jennie, here?" Tristan exclaimed, jumping up so swiftly that he nearly knocked over the chair.

Julian watched, amused, as yet another man looked askance as Tristan Rule, the handsome devil, whirled yet another young, beautiful woman about him as that young woman clung to him in ecstasy. Walking over to Kit Wilde, Julian extended his hand. "Lord Bourne?" he offered silkily. "Perhaps we should join forces and petition the War Office to send him to the front. He does seem to have a most unsettling way with the ladies, doesn't he?"

Kit took the hand Thorpe offered and returned the greeting, not quite sure that this was the same Lord Thorpe he had so thoroughly disliked during his time in London. "The country air seems to agree with you, Thorpe," he remarked, unable at the moment to say anything more sensible.

Julian smiled ruefully. "Being in love with the most beautiful woman in the world agrees with me, Lord Bourne. If your countess is anything like my Lucy, I'm sure we are both changed men."

Jennie, who had been watching her husband and the earl out of the corners of her eyes, dragged Tristan over to meet Kit, saying smugly, "I knew Lucy could do it, dearest. Now we have only Tristan here to settle, and I will be the happiest of women."

Kit drew Jennie into the crook of his arm as he and Tristan shook hands. "Consider yourself warned, my friend," he said jokingly. "My Jennie is happy only when she is settling other people's lives. Oh, the stories I could tell you—but I'll refrain, for fear I should scare you off. Jennie would never forgive me."

"Where's Lucy?" Jennie interrupted, not at all insulted by her husband's words. "We've been quite worried about her, my lord, which is why we have barged in on you so rudely."

Surprisingly, it was Lord Rule who stepped into the breach, explaining that Lucy had taken a slight spill from her horse the day before, and Jennie watched Thorpe closely, hugely gratified to see the concern so clearly written on his face.

For Jennie had received a letter from a friend in London just the day before, which turned out to be the final, convincing argument that had made Kit agree to their visit to Hillcrest. Lady Cynthia's father had announced his daughter's engagement to Lord Seabrook.

It had been Jennie's intention to warn Lucy of this new development before Thorpe could get wind of it through an announcement in the papers, which, fortunately, took so long to reach the country. And yet, she thought, smiling beautifully as Thorpe talked about Lucy with her husband, she now believed that her errand of mercy had been turned into a congratulatory visit.

Rachel Gladwin's entrance into the room confirmed that suspicion, as Jennie quickly cornered her to ask that already answered question: "How fares the campaign?" Her mind no longer troubled, she was ready to hear all the juicy details!

After a pleasant luncheon, a little delayed by the temper tantrum the chef threw after being informed there were to be two more at table, besides the special invalid gruels he had to prepare for Lucy and the tender-mouthed Parker, the men returned to the library to bring Kit up-to-date on events, while the ladies mounted the stairs to check on Lucy's recovery.

With Parker nursing his wounds in his chamber, Dexter, who was smarting a bit at being left out of things, decided to seek out Deirdre and discover whether or not she would like to spend an edifying half-hour in the deserted nursery wing indulging in a little game he had thought up in his idle hours.

All in all, the afternoon passed swiftly, and the growing house party, to an outsider, seemed quite ordinary. It was only as the dinner hour approached, when Lucy would insist on dressing and sitting at the table, that matters were to come to a head.

# CHAPTER THIRTEEN

LUCY HAD AWAKENED, much refreshed by two of the afternoon, immediately remembering the events of the previous night, although those memories came in spurts, not necessarily in order, and served to confuse her not a little bit.

Julian had come into her room and forced her to drink something vile that was meant to poison her. No, she objected, shaking her head (which still ached a bit), Julian had come to her room to save her! She could remember him walking her up and down the room, urging her to wake up and talk to him. And she had awakened, finding herself to be snuggled cozily in his arms, and they had… Oh dear! They nearly had, hadn't they! She pressed her hands to her flaming cheeks. She remembered now—she had tried to seduce him!

And not without a good deal of success, she recalled, smiling a bit in spite of herself before her nagging brain recalled for her the ending of that particular scene. She had accused Julian of trying to murder her! How utterly ridiculous a thought. It couldn't have been Julian. Julian loved her. It had been dark in the room, she told herself, not realizing that it could just as well have been full daylight, for she had kept her eyes tightly closed the whole time, and she couldn't say for sure just who had forced the poison down her throat.

Thank goodness she had remembered the Gypsy's warning—even if the old woman had not quite got the straight of it. A man had tried to murder her—but that man wasn't Julian Rutherford. Lucy lay in bed gnawing on her knuckle, trying with all her might to remember more about her attacker. Yes, it was a man—but who? As to the *why* of the thing, that she would think about later. At the moment, putting a name to the man was paramount in her mind.

Closing her eyes, she tried to recall the feel of the man's body as he had held her, but her memory failed her. Even the Gypsy, with her description of a "blond god of eternal sleep," was of little use. All three Rutherford men were blonds. If only her mind didn't keep straying from the point to concentrate on the memory of Julian's face as it hovered over hers, the feel of his hands as they roved over her body, the scent of his warm breath as he—

"Lucy! You poor darling creature!"

"Jennie! You, here? How marvelous a surprise!" Lucy struggled to sit up in the midst of her tangled bedcovers and was soon wrapped in her cousin's tight embrace.

What followed was a typical meeting between the two, full of teasing banter, shared secrets, and more than a few silly giggles, but at last they sobered, and Lucy brought Jennie up-to-date on what had transpired since her last letter.

"…and so, thanks to Julian's astute reading of the situation, for it seems to me he acted quite rightly, not to mention my own quick thinking—helped by my remembrance of the murder plot in some novel I read long ago—I am here today, ready to help Julian unmask our murderer. Then," she added, hugging herself happily, "we shall be married. Isn't it just like something out of a storybook?"

Jennie tried to look pleased, but a small frown persisted as she said what she had to say. "I received a letter from

London, pet, telling me of Lady Cynthia's betrothal to Lord Seabrook."

Lucy surprised her cousin by clapping her hands in glee. "Oh, it couldn't possibly be any better!" she exclaimed. "It just goes to show that Deirdre's right in her Irish sayings: 'There never was an old slipper but there was an old stocking to match it.' They are a perfect match—a marriage made in their papas' pocketbooks."

"You compare Lady Cynthia to a *shoe?*" Jennie asked, giggling a bit in spite of herself. "Lucy, how naughty!"

Lucy pretended to pout. "Well, she did give Julian the *boot,* didn't she?" she asked facetiously. "We shall have to send them a present, Julian and I. After all, it is only through their foolish snobbery that Julian and I found each other. Let me see, what shall we send them—perhaps a well-executed miniature of Hillcrest in all its glory? That should serve to put a bend or two in their branch, shouldn't it?"

"Lucy," Jennie interrupted, wishing to tell her the rest of her news as soon as possible, unwelcome as that news must be. "We didn't tell Lord Thorpe, although he must be informed shortly—we'll let Kit handle it—but we've had more news from London. It seems scandal wasn't enough—now the tongues are wagging about his lordship's possible involvement in the *way* Miss Anscom died. According to Amanda Delaney—who is quite incensed, let me tell you— some people are acting as if your Julian has already been found guilty of the crime. Much as it confounds Kit to say so, he believes your ideas about the letters to the papers were correct all along. Someone is out to see Lord Thorpe hanged."

"I knew it!" Lucy exploded, pounding her fists into the mattress on either side of her. "It may have taken a bit longer than I thought—although I remember Julian telling me how it is folly to overestimate the intelligence of the average peer—but it would seem Julian's enemy was not too far-fetched in his plans. Thank goodness we shall soon be un-masking the man."

"You shall?" Jennie urged, already feeling better. "I thought something was up when Lord Thorpe asked Kit and Tristan to come to his library with him." A small frown appeared on her pretty face as she added, "Dexter wasn't invited along, though. Surely you don't mean—"

Lucy, exhaled in a frustrated sigh. "I don't know, Jennie. I've been lying here trying to put a face to the man who tried to murder me, but I just can't do it. I...I thought at the time that it was Julian."

"Dexter looks much like Julian, although he's a much smaller man," Jennie pointed out. "But I met Dexter last year when Kit and I were in town. He was such a likeable nod-cock—I can scarcely believe him capable of such a heinous act."

Lucy pushed back the covers and got to her feet, walking to the window to look out over the grounds. "I certainly don't want to believe it either. But Dexter isn't the only suspect. Julian's secretary, his cousin Parker, is also very like Julian in his coloring—although his sallow complexion does not compliment his hair, and his taste in clothing rather runs to the drab and uninspiring. Then there's his expression—Aunt Rachel says it is rather like he had just swallowed a prune whole."

"Well, then?" Jennie urged. "Parker is our man. I trust your instincts, and if you don't like him, he's bound to be the one."

"I said I didn't like the cut of his clothes, Jennie. It doesn't necessarily follow that the man's a murderer. Besides, he was kidnapped not two nights ago, only to return here badly beaten. Much as I would like to think that Dexter is innocent, I can't imagine Parker being able to administer his own beat-

ing. No—it has to be someone we've overlooked. Somewhere there must be someone with either an ax to grind or
a fortune to be made."

Jennie cudgeled her brain, trying to come up with a likely
suspect. "Lord Seabrook!" she offered after some minutes.
"He's got Lady Cynthia, after all."

Lucy snorted, wrinkling her pert nose. "She's no prize.
Besides, Lord Seabrook would have wed a fat crone with
warts if her fortune were big enough, and heaven knows
we've got enough of that sort littering the ground all over
London."

"Lucy, you're incorrigible!" Jennie scolded, highly
amused.

Her cousin grinned unrepentantly and held up a finger,
pointing out, "Ah, but am I right? Indeed I am." Her face fell
slightly as she said wearily, "Which brings us back to our
starting point, doesn't it? Pity—I would rather it had been
Lord Seabrook myself."

Jennie, who had been sitting with her chin cupped in one
palm, mused almost to herself, "You know, if I didn't know
you better, I'd say you were the one who had the most to gain
through all this."

*"What!"* Lucy squeaked incredulously, rounding on her
cousin, her mouth agape. *"Me?"*

Nodding her head absently, Jennie ticked off her reasons
on her fingertips. "One: you wanted Julian for yourself. After
years of chasing him, your love turned to hate and you sought
revenge. Two: you set up the entire scandal, although believing that you had taken an active hand in the seduction and
murder of Miss Anscom leaves open the thought that you
would have had to employ an accomplice. You made sure you
were the one to rescue Thorpe the night of the Selbridge ball
and then talked him into bringing you to Hillcrest. Three:
once here, you insinuated yourself into his heart, causing him

to propose marriage. Then, once Julian was convicted and executed, you would inherit the fortune he would be sure to leave you, along with the dower house and all the jewels that aren't entailed. My goodness—you would even inherit Dexter, in a manner of speaking."

"Dexter!" Lucy interrupted, listening in spite of herself. "Whatever would I do with Dexter?"

This puzzled Lady Bourne for a moment, but did not defeat her. "Dexter must be your accomplice. You both had so much to gain."

"You know," Lucy pointed out, giving her cousin a hug, "it's a good thing you compromised Kit into marrying you. You need a keeper."

"Well, it did make sense." Jennie blushed, ashamed of herself for getting, as she was so prone to do, a bit carried away. "I'm sorry, pet."

"It certainly did make sense." Lucy agreed kindly. "Right up to the point where I drugged myself. Or was that just the enterprising Dexter double-crossing his accomplice?"

Jennie colored and shifted a bit in her chair. "I already said I was sorry, Lucy. Don't keep at me. Besides," she added, tipping her blond head to one side thoughtfully, "it isn't as if you and Dexter couldn't have had a falling-out—"

"Oh, give over, do," Lucy pleaded, dissolving into giggles at the thought of Dexter ever being able to take the place of Julian in her heart. "You just keep to loving your Kit and raising more beautiful babies like Christopher. I don't think you have it in you to be a very successful Bow Street Runner. Besides, I thought we had already ruled out Dexter as a likely suspect?"

"Did you?" came Rachel's voice from the doorway. "I don't know how you came to that conclusion, although I must say I agree with you. He just doesn't strike me as a murderer. Only one thing bothers me—he refuses to tell me where he spent the winter; says he would be breaching a confidence or some such farrididdle. He could have secreted himself in this area, and that's how he struck up an acquaintance with the late Miss Anscom."

The two younger women turned to give Rachel their full attention. Their aunt was a highly intelligent and intuitive woman—as they both learned to their dismay the day they had hidden themselves in Lucy's father's study to read one of the books he kept on the topmost shelf. If Rachel had a theory, they were anxious to hear it.

"I pointed out to Dexter that his evasive attitude didn't exactly enhance his declarations of innocence, but he merely countered with the fact—one we seem to have disregarded—that Parker was with Julian for the whole of the time he resided at Hillcrest last winter. Having already in my mind dismissed Lady Cynthia, Lord Seabrook, and even Lucy here as being the guilty party, I would have to say that either Parker or Dexter is our man. I have just left Julian, my dear," she finished, looking at Lucy, "and it would seem he and the rest have come to much the same conclusion."

"You thought *I* could be guilty?" Lucy exclaimed, astonished, while Jennie looked at her smugly, as if to say, "I told you so."

Rachel patted her niece's hand. "I was just employing deductive reasoning, dearest. Of course I did not *really* consider you. Although I have to tell you that, if pushed, a court could make a mighty case against you. Why, Jennie, I thought you had left those monkey faces of yours in the nursery. Any moment now you will be sticking out your tongue. For shame."

"Yes, Aunt Rachel," Jennie agreed humbly, although her green eyes sparkled with mischief as she dodged Lucy's jabbing elbow.

"Well, we shall know soon enough," Lucy told them confidently, going over to the table beside her bed, picking up the button she had seen there earlier, and holding it up. "Thank goodness I had the good sense to hold on to this when my horse shied."

"Held on to it?" Rachel sniffed. "We had the devil's own time prying it away from you, the doctor and I. Where did you find it?"

"At the scene of the crime," she said, her voice lowering a full octave. "Find the owner of this button, ladies, and we shall have discovered our murderer. Which," she said, brightening, "is what I shall try to do tonight when we all gather for dinner."

There then ensued a heated argument, with Rachel and Jennie protesting that Lucy was still too weak to go downstairs and Lucy pooh-poohing their concern, saying her place was at Julian's side—and failing to mention that she felt the need to see him as soon as possible so that she could apologize for ever doubting him.

JULIAN WAS STANDING with his back to the doorway as Lucy, who had cajoled and coerced Deirdre into helping her into her best gown before Aunt Rachel could show up and gainsay her, walked into the drawing room a full half-hour early for dinner.

Look at him, she told herself, standing there appearing to be so solemn as he gazes out over his land. Her heart showing a tendency to skip several beats, she lost no time in crossing the room to lay her head against his sleeve. "Julian, please, can you ever forgive me?" she asked, looking up into his face.

"Lucy! What are you doing out of bed?" Thorpe exclaimed, turning to clasp her bare upper arms. "I have already told everyone you were still unconscious. Why did Rachel allow you to dress for dinner?"

"And hello to you too, dearest." Lucy grinned, knowing that concern, not anger, colored his questions. "I'm here for several reasons, actually, the most important being that I can remember my atrocious behavior of last night and want nothing more than to throw myself at your feet and beg forgiveness for my stupidity. You must know I would never have thought to accuse you if I had been in control of my senses. I don't know how I could have been so silly."

"The Gypsy," Thorpe reminded her, sliding his hands down her arms to capture her fingers in his tight grip. "You know, darling, I do believe that old charlatan may have helped to save your life. I might not have been so suspicious otherwise when I saw you. Oh, Lucy," he breathed, drawing her against his chest. "You were such a sight, all bruised and turned in on yourself. I was never so frightened in my life. Promise me you'll never do anything like that again."

Lucy closed her eyes as she rubbed her face against his waistcoat. "I promise never to let anyone drug me ever again," she told him solemnly, then raised her face to grin at him. "Besides needlessly upsetting you, my dearest, the stuff tasted quite vile, you know. Although, if my memory serves me correctly, I do believe last night held a few pleasant moments, hmm?"

Julian lowered his head until his forehead touched hers. "You remember?" he asked huskily. "It was unforgiveable of me, taking advantage of you when you were powerless to fend me off."

"Yes," she agreed, wrapping her arms around his waist beneath his jacket. "Your behavior was utterly reprehensible. Julian," she asked, dimpling, "do you promise to be reprehensible again just as soon as you are able? Perhaps later this evening, when I am more awake? My memories are quite pleasant, but regrettably vague."

"You cheeky wench!" Julian said, delighted all over again

by her unabashed openness when it came to expressing her feelings. "However did I exist without you?"

"I can't imagine," she answered airily, pulling his mouth down to within an inch of hers. "But I do believe I can now foretell your fortune, if you'd care to be enlightened. Ah, my blond god of happiness, your days will be filled with love and laughter forevermore, and your nights, ah, yes, those lovely nights, will be spent like this."

Their lips came together in a long kiss that swiftly brought back the powerful feelings that had sprung up between them in the dark hours of the early morning. As they strained together, heedless of their surroundings, all thoughts of murderers and deceitful plots flew out of their minds, and for those too-brief moments in time they were as lovers have always been, totally enmeshed in each other.

But they were not to be left alone for long, as the sound of approaching footsteps brought Thorpe, cursing under his breath, back to his senses. "Stand here beside me," he told Lucy seriously as he turned them toward the open doorway.

"Hmmm," Lucy agreed happily, smiling inanely as Rachel entered the room ready to scold her errant charge. But one look at Lucy's dreamy expression, and Rachel, who had not spent her entire life squiring her niece about, could only sigh resignedly and shake her head. Clearly her days as chaperon were coming to an end. Thank goodness. Tristan didn't require her services—it was more than time she set up an establishment of her own. Besides, she thought, smiling inwardly, Tristan and I would kill each other within a sennight if we were forced to deal with each other too closely.

Julian had just had time to pour each of the ladies glasses of sherry before the rest of their party arrived—Jennie looking delightfully radiant as she walked in beside Kit, and Dexter looking very out of place in his role of supporting prop to his still-swollen-faced cousin Parker. Tristan was the last to arrive, and he merely nodded at Thorpe before positioning himself near the doorway, his shoulder propped against the wall.

The actors were all in place, Julian observed, lifting his glass to his lips as his cold gray eyes surveyed the room and its occupants. It was time for the play to begin.

"YOU'RE LOOKING FIGHTING fit," Dexter told Lucy as he sat down after helping Parker into a chair. "According to Julian, you were at death's door, but I see he has exaggerated the thing out of all proportion. Julian, dear fellow," he said, looking up at his cousin, "you're like an old hen with one chick. When I told poor Parker here what you said about Lucy's condition, the man nearly expired with shock. I'd be careful if I were you—it just might be you have a rival vying for Lucy's affections."

Leave it to Dexter to get straight to the heart of things, Julian thought sardonically, even if he doesn't have the slightest idea of the importance of what he has just said. Exchanging a knowing look with Tristan, who had straightened his posture at Dexter's words, Thorpe walked over to stand in front of Parker. "So you were worried about Lucy, were you, cousin?"

Parker touched a shaking hand to his discolored eye. "Yes…yes, of course," he agreed shakily. "I'm aware of your high regard for Miss Gladwin, and the thought of anything happening to cause you any more pain was very distressing to me."

"Yes." The earl smiled his agreement. "I must remember how very loyal you are to me, Parker. Lucy would be wise to look to you for comfort if I am to soon be clapped into jail for the murder of Miss Anscom. As my countess, which she will be before the week is out, she must needs lean heavily on your knowledge of my affairs."

"Then you do intend to marry her?"

"Ah, cousin," Julian gibed, shaking his head, "surely you have already figured that out for yourself. Isn't that why you went to her room last night and poured laudanum down her throat—so that you wouldn't have rid yourself of me just to be left with an inconvenient countess to share the wealth?"

"What?" Dexter, the only member of the party who had not been privy to any of the events of the previous evening, leapt to his feet, his eyes on Lucy. "You were drugged? By *Parker?* Why in blue blazes hasn't anyone told me?"

Lucy shrugged apologetically. "Because you were our other suspect, Dex, I'm sorry to say. But do wait awhile before flying up into the boughs, for I want to hear the rest of what Julian has to say. There is more, isn't there?" she asked her fiancé.

Parker huddled in his chair, speechless, as Julian expanded on his theme. "There certainly is more, quite a bit more, but we shall require Parker's assistance in order to fill in a few gaps. To begin with the beginning, I suggest we go back to this past winter, and my residence at Hillcrest. It was during this time that you first met Susan Anscom, wasn't it, Parker?"

"I don't know what you're talking about!" the secretary denied hotly. "I never even met Sue Anscom!"

*"Sue?"* Rachel put in pointedly. "Methinks he dost protest too much, don't you?"

"Aunt Rachel, *sshh,*" Jennie whispered, quite caught up in things.

"You met Susan Anscom, seduced her, then talked her into going along with your dirty little scheme," Thorpe persisted, his voice still deadly calm. "Tell me, was murdering Miss Anscom always a part of your plot, or were you initially only out to destroy my good name?"

Parker looked around the room, knowing himself to be the center of attention, and his formerly fearful expression faded, to be replaced by a smile of utmost satisfaction. After years of blending in with the woodwork, being overlooked, dismissed, and discounted, he was suddenly the most important person amid a roomful of some of England's most respected peers. "It was my idea from start to finish." He sneered, sitting up proudly. "Sue thought I was helping her into compromising you into marriage, but I only told her that to keep her in line. I wrote the suicide notes, copying her handwriting from her journal. Stupid cow—as if I was going to all that trouble so that she could end up a countess."

"And then you killed her," Lucy put in, fascinated in spite of herself. "Tell me, Parker, was it your child she carried?"

He threw back his head and laughed aloud. "Child?" he mocked. "There was no child. That was a last-minute inspiration of mine—rather like the finishing icing atop a cake. Her seduction alone wasn't enough, just like disgracing Julian was no longer enough. I always believed I would be a much better earl than he—society might turn a blind eye to Sue's suicide, but it wouldn't overlook a man who had murdered his own unborn child." His smile faded and then he looked down at the hands he had clasped tightly in his lap. "But it took too long for those fools to act—couldn't they see Sue had been murdered?" He glared at Julian. "You should have been arrested by now. And then *she* began to meddle," he complained, jerking his head in Lucy's direction. "I had to be rid of her."

"Naughty puss," Kit Wilde observed mildly. "I always said you were a bit too much of an independent thinker. Jennie would have been content to let me do the sleuthing. I can see why friend Parker here was so put out with you."

Lucy bristled, but then remembered the button she had found and smiled ruefully. "I begin to see Parker's point, much as it pains me. If we were to inspect his jackets, I believe we might just find the one to which this button belongs."

She held up the bone button so that all could see. "I stumbled upon it beside the pool. Miss Anscom must not have agreed with all of Parker's plans and put up a bit of a struggle. You know," she said thoughtfully, "I'm rather distressed that Julian has beat me to it, but I still don't totally understand how he figured it out. Julian?"

"Not yet," Dexter contradicted, clearly quite angry. "I want to hear why he thought I was a suspect, drat it all anyway. I'm highly insulted, coz, and I don't mind saying so."

Julian bowed deeply in his cousin's direction, as Tristan slipped silently behind Parker. "My deepest apologies, Dex. But as my heir, you had to be a suspect."

"And that's another thing," Dexter said, scratching his head. "I *am* the heir. Even if Parker had succeeded in having you hanged, he wouldn't have inherited the title. I stood in his way."

Lord Rule's deep voice made Parker jump slightly in his chair. "Somehow I don't believe that trifling incidental would have deterred our man Parker for very long."

"Why, you…" Dexter swore, lunging toward the secretary, only to halt in his tracks as Parker jumped to his feet, a small silver pistol in his hand.

"Stay away from me, all of you," he warned, moving the pistol about nervously.

"Give it up, Parker," Julian advised smoothly, holding out his hand to show him the bullets Bartholomew had discovered in his room. "And on the off chance you had more of these things hidden elsewhere, I also took the liberty of removing the firing pin. You have often remarked on your dislike of firearms of any sort, and it occurred to me that you would have a pistol only if you felt in need of protection. A guilty man would feel that way, wouldn't he?"

Parker seemed to crumble where he stood. "All for nothing," he mumbled self-pityingly. "All for nothing."

"Yes," Julian agreed, removing the pistol from Parker's slack grip. "I only wish you hadn't gone to the trouble of hiring some local to rearrange your face in order to prove your loyalty. Lord Rule ran the man to earth this afternoon in the village, so there's no sense denying it. Yes, it's a pity. It would have afforded me the greatest pleasure to have smashed you into a pulp."

"I'll take him to the constable," Tristan offered, grabbing Parker none too gently by the elbow and leading the man away. "Kit," he asked, "care to ride along? If we're lucky, the worm will try to make a break for it."

"Trifling incidental?" Dexter repeated dully, looking at Rachel for comfort. "Am I really a trifling incidental?"

"Of course you're not," Rachel soothed, slipping an arm about the young dandy's slim shoulders. "Jennie, let us adjourn to the morning room, where we can ask Raleigh to bring Dexter here a bracing cup of tea, as dinner will certainly be late. Poor Dexter," she clucked as the two ladies led the disillusioned young man from the room.

"It's over," Julian breathed, once he and Lucy were alone in the room. "At long last it's over."

Lucy shook her head, hiding her eyes from him. "Note quite, Julian. I would not be fair if I did not point out that you are now free to marry Lady Cynthia. She's engaged to Lord Seabrook now, but I can't believe she wouldn't take you back once she learns your name has been cleared of scandal."

Julian assumed a thoughtful expression. "I see," he said consideringly. "But what about you, Lucy? I have compromised you a half-dozen times at least. Wouldn't you object?"

Lucy looked up at him with much the lively expression she had shown when successfully handling her hobbyhorse in the park. "Object, Julian? Goodness no. Not me. Why, I should simply resume my pursuit of you with renewed fervor until I had won you back again. What do you think of my secreting myself in your bedchamber and draping my scantily clad body across the bottom of your bed?"

Sweeping her up high into his arms, Julian threw back his head as Lucy dropped butterfly kisses all over his face. "Sounds promising, pet," he growled deep in his throat. "Tell me more."

# EPILOGUE

"OH, POOR DEXTER," Lucy wailed, bringing her hobbyhorse to a halt beside the stylishly clad young exquisite who was just then sprawling inelegantly on the grass in the middle of the park, his fallen hobbyhorse at his side. "I told you not to try that hill until you had a bit more experience."

"Drat it all, Lucy, I was doing just fine till that show-off husband of yours cut me off. Whose idea was this expedition anyway?"

Julian, having already dismounted from his vehicle, strolled over to give Dexter a hand in getting to his feet. "After more than a year of marriage to Lucy, I'm afraid I have been totally corrupted. Forgive me, Dex, but this excursion was my idea."

"You don't do things by half-measures, do you, coz?" Dexter gibed, brushing himself down and then sighing over the grass stain on his left knee. "And to think you used to look down your nose at my exploits. There are times, Julian, when you make me feel like a very old man. Why don't you be a good fellow and go set up your nursery awhile—it may mature you, settle you down a tad."

Winking broadly at his wife, who just as broadly winked back at him, Thorpe refrained from comment. There was time and enough for children next year, he and Lucy had decided. For now they were content to explore all the joys in life that he had previously overlooked—and his Lucy made an excellent teacher.

"Have a slight accident?" asked Lord Rule, who had ridden up atop his pitch-black stallion. "Have a care, Rutherford, else you'll break that leg again."

"How did you know—?" Dexter was startled into saying before he stopped and amended, "Me? I never heard such foolishness. I never broke anything in my life—except a few bottles after dinner, of course."

"That's not what I heard from the lady," Tristan quipped, raising one dark brow. "Nursed you all winter a year ago right here in her rooms above the milliner's shop over past Piccadilly."

"So that's where you were!" Lucy leered, giving Dexter a playful poke in the ribs. "Does this lady have a name?"

"I slipped on the stairs as I was leaving late one night," Dexter explained into his cravat. "Julian," he then pleaded, raising his head, "call her off, please!"

*"Hmm?"* Julian questioned blankly, for his mind had been on other things. He had tried not to think overmuch about the events of the previous year, but Tristan's mentioning of the subject, even vaguely, had recalled it all to his mind. He repressed a slight shudder as he remembered the last time he had visited his cousin in Ringmoor, the well-run asylum he had placed Parker in after the man had broken down completely on the way to jail. "Oh, look," he improvised, trying to change the subject. "There's Sir Henry and his ward, Mary. Pet, didn't you say Rachel was presenting her for Sir Henry?"

"Yes, indeed," Lucy agreed, happy to see that the slight cloud that had passed across her husband's features was now gone. "Aunt Rachel's doing it as a special favor to Sir Henry. Isn't Miss Lawrence a pretty thing?" she added, looking at the young lady in question as the open carriage moved off down a side path. "Aunt Rachel must still be writing that book of hers, and declined to ride along. Isn't it famous that we have a budding Jane Austen in our midst!"

Tristan's dark eyes were following the progress of the carriage, his expression thoughtful. "What?" he asked, scarcely believing what he had heard. "Rachel is penning a novel? My God, I sincerely hope she isn't using any of us in her book."

Lucy cocked her head to one side and considered her cousin as he sat so proudly in the saddle. "Oh, I don't know, Tristan. I think you would make a marvelous hero—tall, dark, handsome, and oh so mysterious."

"What about me?" Dexter pouted. "Wouldn't I make a good hero? Rachel has my permission to use me in her book."

Julian draped a companionable arm around his cousin's shoulder. "If she has a part in there for a village idiot, I'll be sure to suggest your name, coz," he teased affectionately, causing Lucy and Tristan to break into laughter.

"Look at them," Lady Seabrook sniffed, pointing one kid-encased finger at the small but noisy party of people standing on the grass. "They're making spectacles of themselves as usual. I should never think to so demean myself."

Lord Seabrook, who had been eyeing the group with something akin to envy, replied flatly, "Yes, my dear, I know."

Lady Seabrook was about to ask her husband just exactly what he meant by his statement when Julian, uncaring of any audience, leaned down to place a firm kiss smack on his wife's lips. "Well!" Lady Seabrook exclaimed, drawing herself up stiffly. "I never!"

Lord Seabrook flicked the reins and urged his matched pair into movement, never taking his eyes off the clearly happy couple. "No, Cynthia," he sighed with the resigned air of a man who knew what he had as well as what he had missed, "that much is true. You never—never have, and never will. Pity…"

As Dexter remounted his hobbyhorse, he chanced to see Lord and Lady Seabrook as they passed in the promenade. "Hoo! If it isn't Lord and Lady Seaweed. They don't seem to be enjoying themselves, do they? I hear he sold off half his stable at Tatt's last week. Do you think he's retrenching?"

"Gambling," Tristan supplied knowingly, for there was little that went on in London that Tristan did not know of one way or another, although Lucy found it impossible to learn much of anything about his life, no matter how she prodded. Tipping his hat, Tristan then bid them all a fine day and turned his horse in the direction Sir Henry's carriage had taken, although Lucy and the others were not to know that. Mary Lawrence was an enigma; he couldn't seem to get a handle on her and her relationship to Sir Henry. And Tristan didn't like loose ends.

As they watched Rule ride off, Lucy tapped her fingernail against her teeth as she leaned back into Julian's embrace. "If only Tristan would settle down, get married. He seems so restless."

"Here now," Julian protested. "Kit tells me Jennie believes herself in charge of settling everyone she knows into comfortable little niches. Don't tell me you are about to go poaching on her private territory?"

"Jennie's efforts have met with precious little success so far, love," Lucy pointed out, now gnawing on her knuckle as she tilted her head and thought some more. "Perhaps it is time I exerted myself a bit on Tristan's behalf. A man isn't truly happy, truly fulfilled, until he is married."

"Perhaps Tristan is the exception, pet?" Julian suggested, resting his chin on her hair.

"No," she denied such ridiculousness out of hand. "It's

simply that he hasn't yet found the right woman." Just then an idea struck her and she whirled about abruptly to throw her arms around her husband's neck. "Oh, you most wonderful, intelligent man!" she exclaimed, giving him a smacking kiss on the cheek. "The exception! That's who we shall find for Tristan—the Exception to the Rule!"

Dexter slipped away quietly, his sympathies with Tristan, but inwardly thankful that no one considered his flighty self to be good husband material. Married—him? "Then I'd really be the village idiot!" he muttered under his breath, and pushed off down the hill.

Lord and Lady Thorpe, just then gazing contentedly into each other's eyes, never even noticed that he was gone.

MILLS & BOON

*Super*
*Historical*

## On sale 7th August 2009

### *SCANDALOUS DECEPTION*
*by Rosemary Rogers*

**From the glittering ballrooms of London to the shimmering palaces of czarist Russia, *New York Times* bestselling sensation Rosemary Rogers returns with a sweeping tale of dangerous love and divided loyalties.**

Desperate to escape her lecherous stepfather, flame-haired Brianna Quinn seeks refuge with the Duke of Huntley, a childhood friend. But her hopes crumble when she discovers that Edmond, the duke's hot-blooded twin, is masquerading as the duke to thwart an assassination scheme…

With nowhere to turn, Brianna plays into the intrigue as Edmond's fiancée – and soon their forced proximity ignites into a burning desire. But when Edmond's enemies threaten Brianna, he must choose between his countrymen and the woman he loves more than life itself…

# She came to take his company… but would she lose her heart instead?

New York Times bestselling author

## DIANA PALMER

*True Colours*

As a pregnant teenager, Cy Harden's family had driven her out of town. Now Meredith Ashe runs a multi-national corporation – and she's back to take over Harden Properties.

Meredith plans to let Cy think she's the same naive girl he abandoned years ago. But when Meredith falls for Cy again, even her carefully made plans can't protect her.

**Available 7th August 2009**

www.millsandboon.co.uk